The GUERNSEY Diplomat

SANDY L. C. BEZANSON

◆ FriesenPress

One Printers Way
Altona, MB R0G 0B0
Canada

www.friesenpress.com

Copyright © 2023 by Sandy L.C. Bezanson
First Edition — 2023

Photograpy: Monique de St. Croix @uppimage

All rights reserved.

No part of this publication may be reproduced in any form, or by any means, electronic or mechanical, including photocopying, recording, or any information browsing, storage, or retrieval system, without permission in writing from FriesenPress.

ISBN
978-1-5255-5964-8 (Hardcover)
978-1-5255-5965-5 (Paperback)
978-1-5255-5966-2 (eBook)

1. FICTION, ROMANCE, REGENCY

Distributed to the trade by The Ingram Book Company

It is with the sweetness of remembrance and love
that I dedicate this book to my dear parents,
both now gone from this world. They too were
enchanted with the picturesque island of Guernsey,
its history and people.

THE BRI

The Howe
Hanoys
Pshe Mayue
Syr Dawne ville
S. Sampson
Casteau de Mary
S. Peters de Boys
S. Mary of Castell
The Roete
Plymmouth
Tortevills
S. Savour
S. Peters
S. Andrew
The Towne
Trinity
S. Martyn
Corby
Pety Bow
Plymouth
Firmy
Long
Sherebrok
S. Martyns
S. Martyns Bay

| 1 | 2 | 3 | 4 | 5 | 6 |

A SCALE OF ENGLISH MILES

TISH

The Brayntes
The Hummet

The Hayes

Harme

howndt

Gythow

Great Sarck

Brehoe

Little Sarke

SEA

IARSEY PART

CHAPTER ONE

The quay at St. Malo, on the Brittany coast of France, in the spring of 1827.

"You cannot go."

This was spoken in heavily accented English, yet Miss Isobel Radford understood. The meaning was clear, a simple statement, but it was not the answer she wanted. The answer she needed. Perhaps her French was too poor and the clerk had misunderstood. She would ask again.

"*Monsieur, s'il vous plaît, un billet pour aujourd'hui.*" There, she had enunciated precisely; her tutor, Emma, would be pleased. Why was the glum Frenchman behind the counter still staring at her?

Isobel drew the fur collar of her pelisse up firmly around her neck against the early morning dampness. "A ticket for today," she repeated, softly, stupidly, in English. But with the change of language the clerk's glower deepened, as did his Gallic shrug of indifference.

There was movement from behind her. A large man leaned toward the counter and lifted his curly brimmed beaver hat in deference. "Pardon me, miss, may I be of any assistance?"

These words, spoken in a deep voice, were decidedly not from a native son of France. Had his accent not warned her, one glance at the fine wool of the man's overcoat identified him as a fellow countryman. One of her set. This was not good news. The English always congregated together when travelling abroad. They were incestuous, forever wanting to know where you came from and whom you knew. Worse still, men of his class tended to be inquisitive about women travelling alone. Even now, six hundred years after the Crusades, they continued to think of themselves as heroic knights. She was not a woman who needed help, and no longer one who wanted it.

Isobel did not wish to draw attention to herself. She thought of ignoring the tall figure. After all, he had breached protocol in speaking to a lady with whom he was unacquainted. The man's bearing was impressive. His shoulders were thrown back so that the bulk of his strength seemed to be held in check. Yet for all of his size he was graceful, sure of himself, with the poise natural to one of his class. She looked at his face and the penetrating brown eyes swept across her without apology. Isobel knew what that type of appraisal meant from such a man. When he spoke, he was used to being attended to. To avoid a scene she decided to respond.

"Sir, do you know why passengers have not been called to board for Guernsey?"

"Yes. The ship you were asking about is delayed, apparently by this foul weather." The man gazed quickly around the ticket office. "Are your travelling companions nearby? Surely you are not making the crossing alone?"

She sought to still her impatience. The impertinence of the personal questions was another matter. That could not be borne.

"Well, thank you for your trouble." She attempted to step around the man.

He took a half step towards her. In a low voice that extended an offer of intimacy he said, "It was no trouble, miss." Then, with a broad smile, he continued, "No trouble at all."

The arrogance of the man was unbelievable, but it mattered little compared to the consequences of the delay. She had counted on a quick departure. Her recent headlong flight across England and France had gone without a hitch, but this postponement might unravel her plans. If she could not travel immediately she would have to find a quiet place to stay until she could leave.

The spring sea was unpredictable and capable of thwarting anyone's plans. No matter. Time and luck had been on her side so far. She had only to trust in herself, to remind herself that her choice had been as inescapable as it was now irrevocable.

※

Later that afternoon at L'Hotel Anglais, Isobel poured herself a second cup of tea. It had taken her most of the day to find this genteel but rather worn accommodation, and to have her belongings transferred. She had been too frustrated with the delay to bother taking luncheon and was now grateful for the hotel's refreshment. The parlour, dim in the watery light of late afternoon, was almost deserted. The brisk entrance of a large figure into the room made her glance towards the doorway.

Goodness, that nuisance of a man must be staying at the same inn! True, there were few establishments open this time of year, and even fewer of the calibre required, but really, were the fates toying with her? With a tingle of unease she contemplated the alternative: that the man's presence was not a coincidence.

Isobel unwittingly clanked the teaspoon against the side of her cup, cringing at the ungraceful noise it produced. He looked over, and if she hadn't immediately glanced downwards, she would have been staring straight into the same dark eyes that had been curious about her earlier today. Now, at teatime, she wished to be left alone. Her jangled nerves were desperate for the restorative brew of her homeland, and she wanted to enjoy it undisturbed. Such was not to be the case, for the gentleman was approaching.

Isobel hated to be the one to speak first, but the man was standing in front of her table as though he was waiting for her to acknowledge his presence. She felt a blush start to warm her cheeks. Very slowly so that it could have been mistaken for a natural movement she glanced upwards and again marvelled at the intensity of the man. He was composed and yet seemed poised for action. This demeanour was not manifest in restlessness of the body, but was reflected in his intelligent eyes, which seemed to detect the world at large with heightened cautiousness.

Her mind went frighteningly blank and she made herself blink to break the strange moment. She was, as ever, unsure of herself around strangers, particularly in the company of men. The necessity of having to squeeze her personality into a small corner and make an unremarkable package out of herself was second nature to her. The dynamic of conversing with someone new had thrown her momentarily off kilter. She would have to get much better at this. At last, deeply ingrained courtesies and a vestige of her natural amicability surfaced.

"Good afternoon. Are you staying here as well?" This was all she could manage at the moment.

He nodded. "There is little else to be had." The man remained silent for a beat or two of her heart. "The situation is unusual, but permit me to introduce myself. Leonard Fostborough, at your service, miss."

The formal greeting was inevitable. As this was the second time they had spoken it was understood that they had to identify themselves before they could enter into another, even cursory, dialogue. Travelling abroad allowed for a slight relaxing of the rules, so his self-introduction was permitted. Civility would prompt her now to return the courtesy. She was ready for the moment, had practiced it to be comfortable long before she knew whom her interlocutor would be.

She tapped one finger slowly where it lay hidden by the large linen napkin because there was something about that name. Oh dear, Fostborough! Her luck wasn't holding after all.

"I am sorry, you did say Fostborough, Leonard Fostborough? As in, I mean, forgive me, are you then the Earl of Chetton?"

He smiled tightly. "Ah, yes, the very same. As I said, Miss, the circumstances when meeting abroad are often rather awkward."

Although they did not socialize in the same circles, Isobel's perusal of Debrett's famous book on the peerage of England had allowed her to make the connection between the family name of Fostborough and the earldom.

"My Lord." She bowed her head slightly. "Actually, it is Mrs. That is, I am Mrs. Isobel Barnestowe." She spoke in a low voice while slowly spreading her fingers from under the napkin to display her wedding rings.

She could not prevent a slight pursing of her lips as the thought struck her that now there really would be no turning back.

The Englishman tipped his head and looked at her more closely. She had surprised him, no doubt. Earlier she had been wearing gloves and a loose-fitting pelisse. Her age was young enough that she could still be single. Obviously, he had assumed she was by addressing her as miss.

"My husband was a captain." She took a deep breath before continuing. "He was at the harbour battle with General Campbell in Burma."

Lord Chetton paused and looked at her keenly. "My condolences, madame. You have my sympathy, and your husband my respect. That was a sad business indeed."

She bowed her head a fraction to accept the commiseration. British losses while taking the harbour at Rangoon had been well documented. That her husband, the captain, had died three years ago explained why she was no longer dressed in mourning.

She noted Lord Chetton's reaction to news of her married and then widowed state. She did not wish to be drawn into further conversation, particularly as he was watching her so closely. She despaired that he was one of those curious types who thought it their obligation to assist unattached females. At the ticket office she had been preoccupied, almost flustered. For all of her attempted open countenance now, she knew she lacked the confidence that most women of her class showed to the world. Portraying herself as a widow was a double-edged sword. Widowhood afforded her a degree of latitude in decision-making that was unavailable to single women. But with it came a perceived dependency that someone with this man's *noblesse oblige* could not ignore, the more so, as she was an officer's widow.

The clock on the mantle chimed, proclaiming the hour as five.

"You are awaiting a departure for Guernsey. Will you remain in St. Peter Port, madame, or is your destination elsewhere on the island?"

Isobel made a motion to pick up her teacup, then withdrew her hand.

Ah, and here begin the questions, which, she reminded herself, she did not have to endure. Isobel delivered a few well-practiced sneezes, and as she stood to leave, murmured an apology into her handkerchief. This was not a glamorous exit, but plausible enough, and perhaps the only benefit to be had from the damp, starkly chilling weather. No need to explain oneself or beg an indulgence to leave.

❧

Lord Chetton kept the pert figure of the English pepper pot in sight as she left the parlour. He could tell from the erratic swish of her skirts that she was annoyed. Such contained fury in the slim body. He knew all too well the volatile emotions of spoilt upper-class women. Earlier he had been about to offer assistance in procuring suitable lodgings for her, no mean feat in this town during the off season, but was not given the opportunity.

He had spotted her the moment he entered the room, and was rather amused at her little charade of not recognizing him at first. On an impulse he had headed over to her table and waited, curious to see what she would do. But the dictates of courtesy within their class had soon prevailed. No, she was not unaware of him.

Still, she was not his concern and he did not have time for diversions, even pleasant ones. The success of his mission depended on being discreet and keeping a low profile, something he was certain that pampered little lady was not used to doing. Pity though; he rather liked her spark.

An hour later Lord Chetton, dressed now in the serviceable middle class outfit a clerk or country solicitor might wear, settled himself into a relatively quiet alcove of Le Chat d'Or tavern. His immediate concern was to connect with his long-time friend, Jean, who was to introduce him to a man who had the potential to supply important information about the current priorities of the French government. As a diplomat, he was put into the position of using the services of a variety of individuals.

The hectic supper hour would provide enough cover and yet avoid the brawling mess that the evening crowd eventually wound itself into at this modest tavern. First meetings always balanced on a knife blade. Trust was ephemeral, as elusive as a sprite, and as valuable. One could not manage the business of diplomacy without it, yet its complete measure was seldom known until too late.

He spotted Jean entering the tavern and raised a hand to beckon him. Jean Tissier was an enigmatic character. Little was known of his early days on the French island of Martinique, but from the age of fourteen he had been aboard a series of ill-fated French naval ships. Jean had two strikes against him that accelerated the depth and degree of his isolation without recourse to reasoned thought or fairness. He had flamboyant red hair, which itself was enough to deny him comfortable fraternity with his shipmates. A lazy left eye easily transmuted into every sailor's superstition, the evil eye. Thus, Jean's fate as an outcast had been sealed. It left him with an abiding hatred towards the French in general, and the French navy in particular.

Lord Chetton watched his friend lavish attention on the shapely barmaid. Jean eventually ordered drinks and then headed over to him, offering his calloused hand in a firm grip.

"Good evening, Jean. I see you are still up to your old tricks."

Jean flashed a grin. "*Bonsoir* to you, my cold English friend. And what are pretty girls for if not to warm up a chilly day, or possibly the night?"

It was an old joke between them. Jean was a confirmed bachelor and they shared an appreciation of the ladies. Although it still surprised him that Jean's unusual eye proved more of an attraction than a detriment when it came to securing a willing bed partner, it really shouldn't have. He had learned firsthand about the capricious nature of women.

Jean remained standing and glanced around the room. "Here comes Drapeau. The man in the brown cape."

Lord Chetton stood as the man approached and they shook hands while Jean made the introductions.

"And so, *Comte*, without meaning to put too fine a point on the matter, do you understand the nature of what it is I am in the position of being able to provide?"

To diffuse Drapeau's momentum and regain control of the situation, Lord Chetton sat and gestured for the others to follow suit. He paused a moment further before answering.

"I understand that you work for the French Ministry of Trade, Monsieur Drapeau, so I assume you are privy to detailed information about sensitive matters of commerce."

Drapeau shrugged and flashed a self-satisfied grin. "Yes, yes of course, but my sphere of influence goes far beyond that."

Jean nodded, and Chetton caught the glint of humour in his friend's expressive eyes.

"But Monsieur Drapeau is attempting to be modest. He is, in fact, the fastest rising star among the civil service. France is indeed fortunate to have men of his calibre." Jean could not resist adding a touch of comedy to a situation, even if his life should depend upon it.

Lord Chetton watched the man's eagerness unfold as he accepted Jean's blatant flattery, and paused to take out his pocket watch rather than pander to Drapeau's obvious self-esteem. "Why don't you tell me, sir, what you can offer that would be useful to my concerns?" he said as he closed the watch, put it away, and took time to adjust the position of the fob. "Do you have information, for example, about the new restrictions on the press?"

"No, I know nothing further about that situation."

That was a shame. He had heard that the liberal newspaper outcry against reinstating the right of primogeniture had started to create some political unrest in France and he would love to know the full extent of it.

Drapeau took a great breath and sat up taller. "However, you may be interested to know that certain liberal French factions have been hardening their position against reviving the practice of The Royal Touch."

Jean shook his head. "Do you mean that medieval old belief of *Le Roy te touché et Dieu te Guerit?*"

"The King touches you, God cures you," said Chetton with a

shrug. "Well, that is a convenient way to seek legitimacy for your reign, reverting back to the Divine Right of Kings, I suppose. But it doesn't give much comfort to those who treasure the civil liberties granted after the revolution by the Charter of 1814."

"*Exactement, Comte!*" said Drapeau.

Chetton shifted his position on the hard wooden bench. Good Lord, it was true, then. The bloody French were harbouring complaints against their new king on a number of different fronts. "Has Charles taken any notice of this unrest? Goodness, it is hardly two years since his coronation."

Drapeau produced a simpering smile.

"Although we have restored the monarchy, Charles walks a narrow path of acceptance. The wealth of the *haute bourgeoisie* gives them power. Commerce is truly their king, not the Bourbon who sits on the throne."

"And he won't sit on it for long if he continues in his ultra royalist ways," said Jean in an aside.

A half litre of the local watery ale was in front of Lord Chetton. He bit back an oath and took a delusive sip from it, more to promote the illusion of camaraderie than from thirst. He turned to look the rapacious politician straight in the eye so that there could be no misunderstanding. "Find out who the main players are in this conflict on both the liberal and royalist sides. Please believe that your efforts to pass on any developments as the situation unfolds will be *generously* appreciated, Monsieur."

Drapeau smiled and nodded. He drained his portion of ale and then slapped the empty tankard down on the battered tabletop.

Jean, squinting his mismatched eyes to suppress his ever-ready grin, motioned to the attentive barmaid for a refill. Over time they had learned that alcohol helped to ease the conscience of traitors. After their initial recruitment money smoothed the way admirably.

They soon concluded their immediate business. Drapeau left with a swirl of his brown cape and his promise to pass on the undertones of French government life as they came to him. He would receive the sum required to keep him in his extravagant lifestyle for another few months, but the cost to the British Crown would be well worth it if it secured insights into the royal court of its perennial enemy.

Despite the quantity of ale he had downed, it seemed Jean's perceptions remained keen as he turned to watch a new crowd of people enter the tavern. Chetton recognized the characteristics of a fellow survivor.

"So, what do you think of this Drapeau, Jean? Do you trust him?"

Jean rubbed his sleeve across his chin to catch an unruly trickle of ale. "He's a vicious bastard from the stories I've heard. *Mais,* he seems to be adept at delivering what he promises. His greed and ambition should help us to control him, *non*?"

Chetton thought about his reply for a moment before answering his friend. Jean did not seek to profit financially from passing on his contacts. He offered the information for free but only after carefully establishing the bona fides of those with whom he was dealing. A practice, Chetton acknowledged, which had kept them both out of danger on more than one occasion. "Agreed, but has he provided you with any information which has proved valuable?"

Jean shrugged. "Yes, some tax revenue accounts of rival trading companies that were interesting to me. And he was well rewarded for his trouble."

"Fair enough. We shall see what other benefits our investment in the man will bring. And, tell me, how is your legitimate business going these days, Jean?"

"The import-export trade is prospering well enough to get me into the usual trouble, *mon ami.*" Jean smiled and took a moment to watch the barmaid as she made a show of serving a round of drinks. He then moved his chair in closer to their table.

"Lord Chetton, there is another reason I wanted this meeting, besides introducing the *magnifique* Monsieur Drapeau. There's something I need to tell you."

Jean never adhered to the formalities of address, and for him to do so boded ill.

"You may well look concerned. I've had word come my way that your old enemy, Viscount Touché, is plotting his revenge. I told you at the time it wasn't wise to antagonize him."

"Damn it, Jean, that was years ago and you know his wife threw herself at me. I was not pursuing the little coquette."

"*Non*? Well, then you shouldn't have been so adept at catching her, perhaps, my handsome friend. In any case, Touché wants to discredit you and is planning something. All I know is that he has someone in his employ set on watching you."

He rubbed his forehead. "Watching me, Jean? What the devil does that mean?"

"It's vague, I know, but that is all the information I 'ave right now."

"Marvellous. All I need is someone lurking about when I am trying to keep this new situation with Drapeau quiet and behind the scene."

"Ahh, you need to be more positive! Knowing your weakness for the fairer sex, he might even have sent you a *chere-amie*. And no doubt she is pretty in that vivacious way you seem to appreciate."

Chetton frowned and took another sip of ale. "Fine, Jean. Thank you for the warning, if not the sarcasm."

CHAPTER TWO

Isobel awoke slowly, as she preferred to do. This was in stark contrast to the regime of strict early risings that had been forced on her until recently, and she luxuriated in the opportunity to break gently into the new day on her terms. She pulled the quilt firmly over her shoulders to keep away the morning chill, and glanced around the room. The tapestry work on the back of the chair by the fireplace was quite fine, she thought, and strangely better than she had seen in the common rooms of the hotel. It must have been a labour of love. Her friend Emma would have appreciated it.

Last evening she had spent a fretful hour going over her finances at the little escritoire. It was too early, her plans not far enough advanced to pen a few lines to Emma, though she dearly wished to. It was not yet prudent to communicate or even hint at her whereabouts. The chance that her correspondence could be intercepted and she made to return to England, all that such a disgraceful retreat would entail, fizzled through her blood and made her shudder despite the comfort of her generous bedding.

Emma would understand the needed delay in writing to her. The rapport they had shared over the years was one of the foundations of Isobel's life. Emma Le Fournier, officially her governess, was also a surrogate mother, older sister, and trusted friend, returning Isobel's love in full measure. Isobel had persuaded Emma to stay on as her companion long after she was required in any formal capacity. It was to Emma's old cottage in Guernsey that she was now headed.

Isobel heard the sleet patter against the window casement and groaned to think of the possibility of more delay due to inclement weather. This was the third day of waiting. She thought about visiting the ticket office on the quay. There was little point in the excursion except as a way to break the monotony. A continued encampment in the seaside inn would hold no surprises, she was sure. The breakfast room and parlour had been all but deserted on her past visits to them. Of her fellow countryman she had seen nothing. This suited her perfectly as she had no desire for entanglements, conversational or otherwise, with anyone at present. Her new persona shied away from even genteel encounters.

With the aid of one of the hotel maids, Isobel was dressed and attended to an hour later. She chose to breakfast quietly in her room but the indulgence of a second buttery croissant generously spread with tart cherry preserves prompted her to make an effort to get out for a short walk. Having donned her Mackintosh and new galoshes she ventured outside. Her first step into the windy morning air took her breath away. The second step saw her umbrella strain to withhold its shape. She had not been aware of anything except the immediate demands of the weather, but now found herself standing next to the Earl of Chetton. His long arm efficiently grabbed the offending object before it was inverted in the gale. Well, so much for her earlier plans of keeping to herself.

"These make dangerous projectiles if they launch, Mrs. Barnestowe. But being English, I am sure you are aware of this."

His grip relaxed on the umbrella. As he slid his hand down the handle to relinquish it back to her care, his fingers brushed her palm. Isobel, though gloved, felt his heat nonetheless.

"Yes."

The sensation of warmth spread throughout her body as Lord

Chetton leaned closer to deflect the worst of the wind. Isobel became aware of his scent, masculine, with a hint of sandalwood and lime. His breath held a trace of the strong local coffee, and from some pocket the sweet smell of fresh snuff escaped. She took a small step backwards.

"I mean, thank you. For your help."

"Will that deter your excursion?" He nodded in the direction of the door.

She took a breath of the cool fresh air. "No, I don't believe it will. I feel as if I need at least one turn around the square before the rain comes back in earnest."

"Are you unattended by your abigail?"

But Isobel was prepared for this. "Yes, unfortunately she is indisposed."

Lord Chetton looked down the street and hesitated a moment. "May I accompany you?"

"No, I shan't impose on you."

"It would be my pleasure."

Lord Chetton tucked her arm securely in his. He commandeered control of the umbrella, and ushered her towards the town square. Not knowing how this had happened so quickly, nor quite what to say, Isobel concentrated on missing the largest of the puddles. They turned at the corner and the wind abated momentarily. She straightened the angle of her bonnet.

✥

Lord Chetton glanced down at Mrs. Barnestowe. She was looking straight ahead, and her profile was one of youthful beauty, with wind-pinkened cheeks and a delicate curve to her mouth. He felt a tremor along his arm where they were joined, but hardly knew if it came from her or if it was his own reaction to her proximity.

She leaned gently, almost instinctively, towards him. It could be the effect of the wind on her posture. He hoped that was not all it was.

She was a widow. From the ill-concealed quiver in her voice when she had mentioned it, her husband's death must still weigh heavily on her. Perhaps this explained the delicate nature she presented. His friend, Collin, an adjutant to Lord Cochrane in the Admiralty Office, told him ten thousand British and Indian troops had been engaged in the Rangoon Harbour affair three years ago. The Anglo-Burmese War had ended with a treaty signed just last year. But the brief war had cost many British lives, most from the ravages of tropical diseases.

Although the name Barnestowe was not immediately recognizable, General Archibald Campbell certainly was. There were not so many captains as to be untraceable, especially ones who had left behind such a charming young wife. He had been involved with several widows over the years, although they were admittedly older and more sophisticated than this woman appeared to be. Widows tended to create far less drama than married women but could still provide delights that were mutually beneficial.

He smiled to himself.

The whistling wind made conversation awkward, but walking so had a charm all its own. The companionable silence allowed him to surreptitiously watch the lady while seeming to be interested only in the offerings of the little square, meagre as they were. A chandler, a bakery, the town hall, St. Michel's church completed half the perimeter. A chemist, a millinery shop, a tavern, the offices of a trading company and a *chocolaterie* completed the grid. It was in front of this last shop that they finally stopped to look, their pace having slowed as they neared their starting point.

"Do you indulge, Mrs. Barnestowe?"

"No," came the rapid reply. Then, as if she realized she might have been peremptory, she amended her answer to, "At least, not often."

This amused him; the lady was so frugal with her words.

"Would today be one of the days you may transgress?" The smile he had been hoping for appeared briefly.

"Possibly."

"Ah. And what factors most affect your decision in this matter, if I may inquire?"

"The weather. My appetite." A slight pause. "The weight of coin in my purse." A further pause. "The company I am with."

"So this is not always a solitary pleasure then. And, I take it, perhaps not too infrequent a one?"

"I shan't answer for fear of incriminating myself."

"Come, come, Mrs. Barnestowe, have you not heard? Confession is good for the soul."

They were standing side by side perusing the confectioner's selection of sweets. She turned in his direction. He felt, almost viscerally, her gaze pass over him and return to his face. He could not have said what his own expression was, but hers was more dubious yet. Her multi-hued eyes, grey with flecks of green, put him in mind of the storm-tossed sea. Deep and luminous they were, but now with all trace of silly banter disappeared, he felt they held a touch of irritation.

Then, just as quickly, her expression cleared.

"It might be good for your soul, my lord. I suspect you might have a great deal to confess."

She smiled broadly now, the intense look of only a moment ago completely gone, as if he had imagined it.

He spent a few seconds enjoying her open smile.

"Madame, you wound me."

Large dollops of rain had again started to fall and were becoming harder to ignore. He felt the young woman shiver when a drop fell from the edge of her bonnet onto her cheek. Lord Chetton gently positioned the back of his hand to sweep it away. He was taken aback when she jerked her face to the side and quickly wiped her cheek with her gloved hand.

"It is time to return to the inn, Lord Chetton."

Mrs. Barnestowe's movement had been brisk, almost defensive, as had her statement. He could not quite give credit to the idea that he repelled her. Was it possible that she was afraid of him? How odd. He did not usually inspire fear in women, quite the opposite, in fact. It was men who grew nervous when they detected the combative look in his eyes.

Lord Chetton agreed with a curt nod. He was faintly insulted at the idea she would think him capable of anything but delicacy when dealing with the fairer sex.

CHAPTER THREE

La Rocquette, Lord Chetton's Estate in Guernsey.

Norris, Lord Chetton's longest serving retainer, met him at the door of La Rocquette, his expression no different than if he had served his master breakfast that morning. The fact was that Norris had not done so for several weeks, but the phlegmatic older man would never let his surprise show. Lord Chetton held great affection for all of the loyal staff that kept La Rocquette in such good order. Norris, who had first set him astride a horse on his fourth birthday, had also seen him through several scrapes he was happy to have kept from his parents' knowledge when he had attended Elizabeth College, the ancient boys' school in St. Peter Port.

This estate was much smaller than any of his three properties in England. For all its perceived grandeur on the island, La Rocquette was little more than a large manor, but it had the feel of being a home more than any place he had lived. The ancient holding had come to him through his mother's side from an island lineage that dated back, family lore said, almost to the time Robert, Duke of Normandy, had taken shelter on Guernsey, well before his son William the Conqueror became famous. It also offered him a respite from his diplomatic missions and London's many social obligations. Most of the staff, like Norris, held several positions within the household, a feat that would have been impossible in the rigid hierarchy of his larger estates. In truth, here he felt less the Earl and more a simple country squire, and secretly relished the difference for short periods of time.

"Good day, m'lord. Will you be a'wantin' to ride out on Duke this afternoon?" Casting eyes that were exceptional for their weather-reading ability towards the coast, Norris added, "It'll be wet before dusk."

"Hello, Norris. No, I will not require Duke today, as far as I know. How is the old warrior faring?"

"No better, no worse than when you last come to us. Mrs. McClure has fresh pies in t'oven and will be happy enough to see you," he volunteered, taking Lord Chetton's gloves and hat.

Mrs. McClure was the fulltime housekeeper and sometimes cook that managed La Rocquette in his absence. She hailed from Scotland and ran the estate with all the dogged perseverance for which her countrymen were famous. Norris, born and bred in nearby Torteval, had never seen the point in travelling away from his island home. He challenged Mrs. McClure's every directive, more to show her the mettle of Guernseymen, who also had a reputation for being stubborn, than from any real antagonism.

Lord Chetton entered the library and seated himself behind the desk. There were several letters to write but he could not find the energy to tackle them. He poured two fingers of brandy into a snifter and settled back into the worn wing chair, noting with pity that there was no fire set. He had, of late, lost some of his taste for intrigue. The conspiracies and political machinations, which had so thrilled him as a younger man, now more often than not seemed merely ridiculous. He allowed that he was becoming jaded. He wanted peace for his country but knew there could never be peace for himself.

The despondency, which he fought to keep at bay, deepened. His thoughts turned to the irresponsible behaviour that had harmed precious lives in his care. After all the ensuing years the pain sometimes still threatened to undo him. The irony of his situation was galling, so different from what he had once expected from life. While growing up, his parents and grandparents had presented him with clear examples of happy, fulfilled lives.

A discordant movement of the brocade drapery caught his attention. What the devil was this? No one should be in his private study. He stiffened, then opened the left drawer and took out a pistol stored in the false bottom and slipped it quickly into his large pocket. He stretched his senses to locate anything else that was not quite right in the room, cursing the fact he had let down his guard.

He heard a faint noise of movement from the direction of the offending window covering and immediately stood. He pantomimed a stretch and shrugged his shoulders, then slowly walked towards the window, for all the world just like a tired man who needed a breath of fresh air. As he approached the pleated drapery he heard the noise again, but this time it sounded familiar and nonthreatening.

Lord Chetton struggled not to smile as he slid his hand into his jacket. He tucked the weapon further down into the lower pocket and pulled out a small twist of horehound candy from the upper. Just as he was about to unwrap the twist of paper from around the sweet, he dropped it. A second later a small freckled hand darted out from under the drape and snatched the candy from the floor.

"Ah, I have you!" he said as he pulled the material aside. A thin young boy looked up at him in surprise.

"Give that back, you thief. Mrs. McClure would be horrified if she thought you were snitching things off of the floor."

Teddy, his eight-year-old godson, laughed in delight. He was the second son of his good friend Collin, and had always been of delicate health. As a baby Teddy had sickened easily and did not take well to the spirited houseful of children that Collin and his wife had produced. Teddy was trying a term as a day student at Elizabeth College. Chetton had helped to arrange the boy's accommodation with Mr. and Mrs. Hudson, a retired school master and his wife who were thrilled to have a young boy in their lives again. The elderly couple doted on him and the smaller school population and slow-paced island life appeared to suit his constitution. As a bonus, he could visit La Rocquette with ease. Lord Chetton was fond of the boy, but sometimes chafed under the hero worship that shone so openly out of him. It reminded him too much of lost possibilities and the echo of another child's voice no longer to be heard.

"How did you know I was there, sir? I was ever so quiet. I saw you ride in and ran here to surprise you. Did I?"

"Yes, yes. You quite astounded me and I would never have known you were there at all until you got greedy."

He punctuated this speech with a few more gentle shakes and then handed the lad the small sack of sweets. "These are for you. Only two a day and do not tell Mrs. McClure or we will both be in trouble."

"Do not tell Mrs. McClure what, my dear boy?"

He swung around to catch the quizzical look on his mother's face. The Dowager Countess was beautiful still, and looked younger with the hint of humour in her eyes. His mother walked to him energetically for all that she was approaching her sixth decade, and offered her cheek for the obligatory kiss.

"Hello, Chetton. We thought we would surprise you, Teddy and I. Norris picked us up from town yesterday." She ran her hand through the young boy's curly hair. Then, when she spotted the bag of candy clutched in his fist, she winked at him. "You had best put that away now, and no more before your supper. Off you go."

Teddy flashed her a smile and scooted out the door. Chetton couldn't help but roll his eyes, amused at his mother's lax attitude to the child.

"Really, Mama. I cannot believe you winked at that little urchin. I am sure you never winked at Chris and me when we were young."

"Ridiculous! And in any case, when you were a boy I was raising the future Earl of Chetton and had to be strict. You and your brother were terrors, as I recall, and could run circles around your nannies and tutors. You did not need any extra encouragement. Poor Teddy is another case entirely."

His mother smiled with a faraway look that meant she was remembering some aspect of his childhood. He sat back at his desk and let her enjoy her reminiscences in peace. He knew there was a time, now seemingly long past, when she had believed there was nothing he would not be able to achieve.

The continued silence roused him and he saw that his mother was regarding him with quiet determination.

"Do you know it always takes you awhile to come back to yourself when you first see Teddy. I have noticed over the years you hold yourself aloof, as if you do not deserve the child's love, as if . . ."

"For heaven's sake, madame, do not start along that avenue." He rose to leave.

"Yes, well, it is just an observation. Although I had hoped that by now you would have found some happiness in your life, someone for whom you had affection."

He was going to antagonize his mother on purpose and regretted it, but he could not discuss this again, not now when he was both tired and restless. And so, he said the very thing that he knew would silence her.

"I have found someone, Mama, you know that. I have great affection for Lady Durling. In her husband's absence we have grown quite close."

As predicted, the Dowager rose, straightened her regal shoulders, and marched out of the room. When she passed through the door he heard her Parthian shot.

"Enough of these charades, Chetton, enough."

CHAPTER FOUR

Isobel found that L'Ancresse Cottage lived up to Emma's pretty description of it. Made out of the grey blue granite for which Guernsey was famous, flowerbeds of sweet smelling lilies graced each side of the low centre doorway. Though called a cottage, as were many of the modest houses on the island, L'Ancresse had a comfortable front parlour, a small dining room, and several generous bedrooms that offered a view of the common grazing land from which the cottage got its name. A cosy space doubled as a breakfast nook in the morning and a sitting room the rest of the time. The area boasted its own fireplace and was referred to, in the local way, as the "snug." As Emma had predicted, it was Isobel's favourite spot.

Helene, the maid, was a cheery soul ever ready to do her bidding. Victor, the gardener-come-handyman, was taciturn but reliable.

Signs of spring had firmly taken hold since her arrival over a month ago. Isobel, anxious to be outside, was ready for a walk to the nearest farm to bargain for milk, butter, and cheese to be sent to L'Ancresse on a regular basis. Perhaps she would ask for some of the island's style of thick clotted cream to be added to the order. This domestic task was new to Isobel and according to Helene would not be seen as an unusual occurrence within the small island community.

"Don't be offering Farmer LeBlanc those smiles of yours so freely, miss, or he's sure to think you an easy mark."

Casting Isobel an uncommonly stern look, Helene continued her warning.

"He's a good farmer, but known to be greedy. Here, take some of my raspberry preserves to Becky, his wife. That will soften her. She's a new young bride and what pleases her pleases the farmer, if you catch my meaning." Helene handed her a basket with the carefully wrapped jars arranged inside.

Closing the Dutch door to the kitchen, Isobel set out to walk the scant mile to the LeBlanc farm. She was getting used to the distances here; everything was on such a small scale compared to England. The day was fine with only a light sea breeze to ruffle the heads of the hardy yellow and purple crocuses and a few other early wildflowers that were brazen enough to tempt the season. Isobel liked to amble across the fields. The stiles over the high granite fences were a challenge to climb and one pasture looked the same as another to her, though, the locals assured her, she would soon be able to get her bearings.

Her household negotiations went well and she was asked to share a hearty fish pie for lunch. Farmer LeBlanc was insistent that she accompany him to inspect his prize cow, since now she was to have the animal's products on her table every day. Late in the afternoon he left her at the edge of the verge and with a wave set off back to his barn.

The light was fading and the growing fog made Isobel slow her stride, though soon she thought she should begin to see light from L'Ancresse. Victor always left an ancient lantern on the porch by the door. Another quarter hour put her no closer to her destination and quelling a wave of annoyance, Isobel feared she was lost. She tied her wrap firmly around her shoulders to keep it in place and continued walking until a throaty bellowing startled her. She looked in the direction that the sound had come from and saw its source—a large bull. Isobel had been raised in the country and though she was fond of the placid golden dairy cows Guernsey was noted for, the prospect of meeting a bull in the gloaming was another matter altogether. As the threatening noise came again Isobel made a quick decision to scramble up and over the nearest stile. She refrained with ladylike dignity to give voice to the nasty words that threatened to escape her mouth when the hem of her skirt caught on an exposed nail. Really, it was too much!

Just as she wrenched herself free and sought to steady her footing, Isobel heard the noise of hooves approaching. She had a fleeting idea that she would flag down the rider and ask for directions. The thought of Victor and Helene trudging across hill and dale to find her was too humiliating, but she knew they would soon start out if she failed to return. The damp sea air muted the sounds and Isobel realized with rising concern that she had miscalculated the animal's speed as she found herself directly in the path of a large galloping horse.

The rider shouted something unintelligible and veered quickly to the right as she jumped to the left and landed none too softly on her knees on the ground. The basket she had been carrying flew off of her arm, its contents scattering in all directions. From the inflection of his deep voice, the rider was not particularly sympathetic to her plight.

"Blazes," was all she heard in the confusion. She watched in complete disorder as the man used his massive shoulders and thickly muscled legs to contain the power of the horse, turning the animal around in a tight circle. He then looked towards her as she struggled to stand.

"Where the devil did you come from? Have you lost your senses, jumping out of nowhere in the dark in front of a horse?"

Isobel was sufficiently alarmed to have temporarily lost her power of speech. She knew that she was in the wrong and could have caused herself, the rider, and the horse considerable damage. Unfortunately, she had an aversion to being yelled at. For too long she had been the recipient of the loud and harsh voices of her father and then her guardian uncle. Where she normally would have apologized, she found her own ire rising.

"Stupid man, you were riding like you belong in a circus fair."

The man jumped off of his horse and took long strides towards her. The front of his face was in shadow but she could tell from the tense angle of his jaw that he was annoyed. A trickle of fear passed through her. The dismounted rider yanked her to her feet and yelled louder still.

"Like *I* belong in a circus?" He grabbed her shoulders as if to shake her. "You, madame, are a threat to public safety, and your own."

The feeling of being trapped by the power of those strong hands carried Isobel back to another evening. She had worked to suppress those memories for nearly two years and found that now, as before, she could not move to save herself.

All of a sudden the man loosened his grip on her shoulders but did not let go completely. "Good Lord, Mrs. Barnestowe," said the Earl of Chetton. "I could have killed you. Whatever are you doing roaming about in the dark? You are not hurt, are you? Good God, to think of what might have happened!" He continued to stare at her with far too much familiarity. "Are you sure you are not harmed in any way? You took quite a tumble."

Relief that she recognized the rider swept through her. She attempted to regulate her breathing. "No, no. I am quite all right. I have just dropped my basket." When he did not release her, she repeated, "Please, I assure you I am fine."

She stepped back from his warm tweed-clad body but he moved with her as if they were coupled in some bizarre dance. "Would you let me go, sir?"

"Hold on there, you are a little skittish."

"Skittish?" She could not fathom the cheek of the man. "You mean like that great beast you cannot control?"

"My mount? Old Duke?" He let out a hearty laugh. "Oh no. I assure you we understand each other perfectly."

The man was not even clever enough to know when he had been insulted. His conceit rankled her. The supreme confidence she rather admired.

Finally free of him, she leaned over and began throwing her scattered items into the basket. "As I have said, repeatedly, I am fine. I will continue on my way, if you would be so good as to secure your mount. I have people waiting."

Lord Chetton retrieved the reigns of his horse.

"Where are you headed? I will take you. It is too dark to be walking around without a light. You might inadvertently step in front of a horse and rider."

Isobel glanced quickly at his face. The tone had been neutral but she would swear she saw a hint of amusement lurking in those dark eyes.

"I am staying at L'Ancresse Cottage, if you must know. But I can manage on my own, thank you." She scanned the ground for the rest of her items and then straightened her skirt.

"You are a newcomer, madame. That is not how we do things on the island." Allowing her no time to remonstrate, Lord Chetton lifted her and positioned her side-saddle on his now docile horse. He immediately mounted behind her and moved closer to secure his arms lightly around her waist as he held the reigns. Isobel felt the brawn of his thighs as they flexed to expertly guide the horse.

"L'Ancresse Cottage, is it? You were headed entirely in the wrong direction, my dear woman. No matter, it should not take us long to get there."

There was nothing to do but accept the ride. In truth, Isobel had not wanted to continue alone, unsure as she was about the way home.

The forced intimacy was distressing. She had seldom been in such a close physical situation with a man. He tightened the pressure of his hold slightly as the pace increased and she could not suppress a wiggle to try and lean away from him. She thought she heard a low chuckle. Lord Chetton's light touch of hand on the reins slowed down Duke's gait to a trot. She was just about to demand what he found amusing about the circumstances, when he spoke.

"May I inquire what in the world were you doing out on your own in the countryside at the change of day, Mrs. Barnestowe?"

She waited to regain her composure before attempting a response, but could not avoid a sigh of exasperation. "Well, although I am unsure why it could possibly be of any concern to you, my lord, if you must know, I was visiting Farmer LeBlanc."

"LeBlanc, you say?"

"Yes. I was arranging for supplies, not that it would interest you."

"He should be horse-whipped for letting you ramble off on your own. I have half a mind to speak to him on the matter."

Provoked by his temerity, she turned abruptly to face him but the movement put her off balance. She instinctively leaned into him just as he tightened his arm around her. It put their faces very close together.

"Pray, do not do any such thing. It was certainly not the farmer's fault. And, in any case, I am completely capable of taking care of myself."

As if to belie her statement, at that moment an owl hooted loudly nearby, and, startled, she moved closer into his arms. There was no mistaking the chuckle this time. She chose not to dignify this with a remark, although the man deserved a curt set down.

"As you prefer, madame. Did you know, by the way, that you were half a mile into my property? It is somewhat odd, wouldn't you say, how we keep meeting each other. First in France, and now so close to La Rocquette."

She swivelled her head away from him.

"I had not given it any thought, I assure you."

"Still, it is rather fortuitous that I ran into you tonight. Or, perhaps I should amend that to 'nearly ran into you.'"

She shook her head at this bit of folly and took a firmer grip on the handle of the basket.

"Ah, here we are. L'Ancresse is just over this rise."

They arrived much to the surprise of Helene and Victor, who had indeed been about to set off in search of her. Victor appeared a little put out, lest he be seen in Lord Chetton's eyes as having not taken proper care of her. Helene was obviously impressed with the gallantry. She had confided not long after starting work that she thought the young master of La Rocquette to be handsome and did not credit half of the scandalous tales whispered about him to be true.

As they walked into the cosy drawing room together, Lord Chetton said, "Ah, good there is already a fire set. Helene, would you please draw a bath for Mrs. Barnestowe? I am afraid she might catch a chill, not being used to our damp island climate."

"Yes, sir, and I will right away." Helene gave a hasty curtsey.

Lord Chetton watched as the maid scurried off to fulfill his request.

"I have known the family for years. She is a good girl, is she not, Mrs. Barnestowe?"

"The woman is hardly a girl; she is probably older than you. In any case, I can order my own baths as I require them, thank you very much." She had never discussed her bathing habits with a man before. Had he no delicacy?

As if he had not heard her reprimand, the man smiled at her. "Shall I pour you a sherry? Perhaps it would help to calm you a little."

Despite his condescension, Isobel was nonplussed that she had neglected to offer some refreshment to Lord Chetton before he had brought it up. Emma would be ashamed at her lack of manners.

"No, I shall have a pot of tea sent up, thank you. May I get you some?"

She reached for the decanter at the same moment that Lord Chetton's hand found the neck of the container. His fingers closed around hers and held there for a moment. He looked into her eyes, smiled briefly, and then removed his hand.

"Yes, a small one and then I must be off."

The glass wobbled as she concentrated on not spilling the sherry.

"Duke needs feeding and a good rub down. Rescuing damsels in distress is hard work."

She was about to say that she had hardly been in distress when she caught the curl at the corners of his mouth and knew he spoke in jest. Trying to be clever, she quipped, "Are you certain you do not need the same for yourself?"

Isobel could feel the heat spread across her cheeks. Why was she trying to exchange banter with a worldly man like Lord Chetton? The inappropriateness of the remark blistered across her mind. She tried to swallow in a mouth suddenly gone dry. When she was with this odious man she swore her mouth disengaged from her brain and the most ridiculous things came slithering out. He was so provoking.

She saw him flick his gaze towards her after that preposterous retort. The heat in her cheeks burned and she averted her face. She was determined not to look at him. He seemed to take pity on her and, setting the sherry glass down, bid her good night and, thankfully, made his departure.

CHAPTER FIVE

Helene had asked for a day off of service to go to St. Peter Port. Her mother lived there and was feeling poorly. Isobel immediately granted the request. After thinking about it she suggested that they go together in the gig as Isobel was interested in spending some time in Guernsey's main city herself. She had been several times to St. Sampson, which was closer to L'Ancresse Cottage. St. Peter Port she had not revisited since her arrival there in the harbour many weeks ago.

The next morning Isobel and Helene set off early enough to ensure they had a full day in the capital city. Isobel was happy to manoeuvre the light carriage through the winding lanes and byways since Helene was there to give direction. St. Peter Port was south of St. Sampson, about half way along the east coast of the island, and boasted a picturesque harbour that had been in use since Roman times. Some manifestation of Castle Cornet had stood guard over the town for at least seven hundred years and, like Lihou Island, was cut off by the tide for part of the time.

Much of the town of St. Peter Port rose dramatically up from the harbour. This had necessitated the building of steep laneways over the centuries, many of which were too narrow for carriages to negotiate. Parts of the old town, in fact, were only accessible by trudging up daunting sets of stone stairways. This geographical situation had stirred Jerseymen to bestow the nickname of Donkeys on the people of Guernsey as donkeys were widely used to move goods up from the harbour. In retaliation, Jersey residents were called Toads as they could easily access the flat land of St. Hellier, that island's primary town. Neither designation was meant to be in any way complimentary.

It was fortunate that Helene's mother lived but a short distance from the High Street and it would take just a few minutes of walking to arrive there, Isobel was informed. Helene had pointed out the Old Quarter and the Marketplace to Isobel when they left the carriage with the ostler. The women had agreed to meet several hours later by St. Peters church. Isobel went first to the bank to procure some funds and next to a millinery shop which had been recommended to her by Emma. Then, after a happy half hour browsing around the bookshop, she treated herself to crumpets and jam piled high with rich Guernsey clotted cream at the nearby teashop.

Isobel decided to stroll along the High Street and soon stopped to view the display in the window of a jewellery shop. After a few moments a man walked up and stood beside her, leaving much less room than was customary between them. Surely she was safe on this bustling street, but she took a firmer hold on her reticule nonetheless as she felt herself being appraised. She took several steps to the left to create more distance and the impudent fellow followed her. When she turned to upbraid his manners she was met with an open and engaging smile and twinkling blue eyes. He was a young man, a boy really, from his hairless cheeks, but with a tall and sturdy frame. "You are Miss Isobel, ain't you, ma'am? I saw you before with Helene."

This did nothing to relax Isobel, but her curiosity got the better of her and she said, "And who would you be, my young man?"

"Well, I am Michael Le Fourniere," said the youth as he removed his cap with a flourish, "and Emma is my auntie." He dug something out of his vest pocket and thrust it into her hand. "She wrote my mum and said I was to find you and give you this letter when you were alone. I rode over to L'Ancresse and Victor said you had gone into town so I figured I had a good chance of meeting you somewhere today along the High Street and didn't I just." He ended his tale with another charming smile and a nod of his head.

Isobel immediately put the envelope in her reticule and drew the purse closed. "There is nothing amiss with her I take it, um, Michael, is there?"

"Oh no, miss, not as we have heard. She only wanted to have her letter given to you, not go through the post." He took a quick look up and down the street. "Now my mum says as Emma ever did things in a strange way and that is why she took herself off to England without a backward glance those many years ago." He dropped his voice. "My mum is not much pleased with England but I hope to go up to Oxford when I finish at Elizabeth College next year. I can't wait to visit London, but you can't tell that to anyone here without a lecture on all the evils waiting to lure young men in." He ended with a disgusted look.

Isobel schooled her features not to betray the bubble of humour she felt at that youthful diatribe; she wouldn't for the world hurt his feelings. "You seem to have an adventurous spirit, Michael, very much like dear Emma. I remember now her speaking of you and, my goodness, your six other siblings, isn't it?"

He straightened his vest and stood a little taller. "I am the eldest, Miss Isobel, and beside Beverly, they are all still in the schoolroom at home."

"Well thank you for so cleverly arranging to deliver Emma's letter." She handed him a few deniers, the French coins which were still legal tender on Guernsey.

"You are welcome, Miss Isobel. Oh, I shouldn't take the money, miss, I am sure," he said, looking at the copper coins longingly.

Isobel slipped them into his vest pocket and said, "Well, I am quite sure that you should for all of your trouble to locate me. I am certain you will find some use for it at the tuck shop, will you not?"

Michael grinned and patted his pocket. "Much obliged! I might just catch the shop open if I hurry. Good day, miss."

Isobel hardly had the time to say goodbye before the energetic lad turned and hurried away. She repositioned her packages and decided to wait and read Emma's letter when she returned to L'Ancresse.

With only an hour to go before her rendezvous time with Helene, Isobel thought she should make a push to visit the ancient castle, as the causeway was open. Scattered military men, tradesman, and sightseers were making their way across in one direction or the other. The guidebook she had glanced at earlier told of a small museum open to the public that regaled one with highlights from the history of the ancient fortification.

As she paused to admire the pretty view of the castle surrounded by sparkling blue water, Isobel caught sight of the Earl of Chetton walking along the harbour's edge in conversation with a finely dressed older woman. She hesitated about whether or not she should greet them when Lord Chetton looked in her direction and nodded with obvious recognition. It took but a few moments for the three to approach each other, but Isobel was thankful to have even that short length of time to prepare for the chance meeting. Watching the elegant pair move toward her, she wished she had not been caught wearing her serviceable but outmoded navy dress. She appreciated how the lady's light blue spencer over matching day dress trimmed in periwinkle was cut and sewn to perfection. Isobel straighten her wind-tilted bonnet.

Lord Chetton stopped and executed a small bow. "We meet again, Mrs. Barnestowe, and in the safety of full daylight this time."

With this unusual greeting, Isobel could do no more than raise her eyebrows.

The lady with Lord Chetton looked at him expectantly. From the generous smile the lady gave him Isobel could see that their kinship connection was as strong in emotion as it was in genealogy. This woman could be none other than Lord Chetton's mother.

"Mother, may I present Mrs. Isobel Barnestowe. Mrs. Barnestowe, the Dowager Countess of Chetton."

The Countess was not beautiful in the classical sense, though she was indeed a handsome woman. Her eyes held cleverness and compassion mixed with humour and more than a hint of stubbornness.

Isobel gave a demi curtsey and said, "A pleasure to meet you, Lady Chetton."

Lady Chetton responded with a gentle smile. "The same, Mrs. Barnestowe, the same."

"I thought it was you I saw earlier, Mrs. Barnestowe, at the top end of the High Street in conversation with a fellow," said Lord Chetton.

Isobel was nonplussed that she had been observed receiving a letter in such an unconventional way. She gave a noncommittal shrug. "I doubt it was me as I only went as far as the bank, this being my first real visit to the city."

Lord Chetton tilted his head as he looked at her. "Ah, I must be mistaken then."

"I understand that you are quite new to Guernsey, Mrs. Barnestowe," said the Dowager.

Isobel was not certain from whom the lady understood she was lately arrived to the island. She could not believe that Lord Chetton had mentioned their infamous meeting the other evening when she nearly unseated him from his terrifying horse. Still less did she think he would have mentioned the brief and awkward exchanges they had had in St. Malo. She must not refine too much on the statement; it was surely just a polite expression, yet after Lord Chetton's remark about observing her earlier it rattled her nerves.

It required a reply however, and after a pause Isobel said, "I have been on the island almost two months already, my calendar tells me, though my pleasure here has made the time scamper along."

Lady Chetton glanced out to the emerald waters of the sea. "Guernsey is at all times a wonderful place to be, and shows particularly well at this time of year. The onset of spring being several weeks earlier than in England, I am always loath to leave it and return to rain and chill."

Lord Chetton smiled at his mother and then turned to face Isobel. "The Dowager can trace her family connections back almost to the origin of the Bailiwick of Guernsey in 933 and I am sure there was not one person in all those generations who failed to tout Guernsey's vast superiority over England. You are shamelessly biased, Mother, you must admit."

Lady Chetton raised her eyebrows and tut tutted her son, but the affection in her eyes as she turned to Isobel told the real story. "The current Earl of Chetton is of an officious and impertinent nature, more is the pity, my dear Mrs. Barnestowe. Thank goodness my younger son is more congenial and better understands the obligations of filial respect."

Lord Chetton bowed to his parent to graciously acknowledge she had won the point. Isobel was amazed and more than a little enchanted by this exchange between parent and offspring, as she had never experienced any friendly banter between her family members. Her uneasiness was overshadowed by the delight in meeting the engaging woman.

"Since we are now acquainted, I should like to invite you to tea next week," said Lady Chetton.

The polite smile on Isobel's face started to fade at this non sequitur, but before she could decline, Lady Chetton continued.

"It is our annual Spring Tea. My late grandmother started the tradition. She liked to organize several spring activities before the 'summer only' set arrive. With Chetton in residence we are sure to have a fine turnout. I should be most happy to introduce you to society here, and it would be a grand opportunity to meet some of your neighbours."

Etiquette demanded that she acknowledge this favour and since Isobel had formed no opinion on whether she would attend, she said only, "That is very kind of you."

She had spoken so low that Lord Chetton was forced to lean in to catch her words.

※

So busy had the rest of Isobel's day been that she was forced to take Emma's letter to bed with her to read that night. Isobel was greatly moved to see the familiar handwriting and Emma's use of her childhood nickname. The directness of the correspondence was characteristic of her friend's approach to life.

Shall I speak plainly, Izzy? From the tone of your first letter, I perceive a change in your demeanour. Some of that is to be expected simply from the fact that you are again living in the busy outside world. To what extent other things have changed, you will have to apprise me.

It seems that you need to recognize what is possible to change in yourself, and what is not. It is fine to say that past grief should not mar the future, but I have occasion to understand the limits of such a noble sentiment. Even well intentioned people can be so glib. But I do believe that one should strive to live life with an unfettered spirit. The power of a strong will can animate an injured heart. And that you have, Isobel, though you are loath to admit it.

Try to accept the limitations of an imperfect past and not constrain yourself unduly because of them. You should give yourself leave to enjoy life despite your history. You have a big soul. Drink in the luxuries of life a little. Remember, you are alive and there is a peculiar completeness in that alone.

Yes, that's the catch, isn't it, Isobel thought, to have both heart and mind in agreement. I have become so diminished by my past it is difficult to see myself in a new light.

You were ever the dreamer and not without good cause considering your harsh childhood, but now of course, you are a woman and things have changed. Do not derail your chances before they have begun. All things are still possible for you, my dear.

And there are things that I want desperately, mused Isobel as she put away the letter and settled herself under the covers. It is just not that easy to recalibrate the compass of my life. I am changed. Isobel's thoughts turned to Lord Chetton and his formidable mother and she wished she had handled the situation differently when asked about being seen on the High Street. She longed for a space of normalcy in her life so that casual comments would not distress her into having to tell ridiculous falsehoods. If she were not more careful she would surely give herself away by such rash actions.

CHAPTER SIX

"Look what's come for you, mistress," said Helene the next day at lunch. Her cheeks were flushed and she was waving a small buff envelope in her hand. "I hoped you'd get one."

Helene handed Isobel the letter with reverence.

Isobel admired the elegant handwriting before opening the envelope. She paused to read the enclosed card. "Ahh, it's an invitation for Spring Tea at La Rocquette next Tuesday."

"I knew it! You'll get to meet all the best people. Will you accept, madame?"

Isobel had been contemplating the offer since Lady Chetton made it to her. At first she was a little reluctant, as she had often attended large social events with Emma and missed her company sorely. Yet she was determined to follow the mission she had set herself and this was a step in that direction. It was time to pluck up her courage and send an acceptance.

"Yes. I think I shall. Will you help me pick out what to wear?"

꙳

The appointed day and time arrived. Isobel tried not to fuss with the lavender ribbon she had added to highlight the neck of her mauve dress. She had wanted the confidence of wearing a new outfit today but there hadn't been time to have one made up. At least the mauve taffeta had a slightly dropped waist and would not look as outmoded as some of her older empire waist dresses. The ribbon and a new feather for her bonnet were all of the wardrobe updates that must see her through the day. Her position as the new young widow on the island would put her under a degree of scrutiny. Emma had warned her that things changed slowly on the island and it took time before new people were accepted. She had tried to prepare herself, but the last glance she had taken in the mirror before leaving exposed her pallid cheeks. Courage, she chided herself as she entered the gates of the La Rocquette estate. This is your choice, do try to make the most of it.

A liveried footman handed Isobel out of her gig. She followed behind a group of people who were entering the hall. Guests were seating themselves in a pretty yellow salon that overlooked the garden, as there was to be a short music recital to begin the afternoon. Isobel selected a seat near the back of the room. She wanted a moment to get her bearings and observe people to whom she might soon be speaking. As the music began, a little frisson of dread scurried up Isobel's back. What if she couldn't pull this off? What if someone asked a question which she wouldn't be able to answer? It was too early for this charade. Didn't her misstep in St. Peter Port show her that she needed more time to be able to be convincing? Why had she ever agreed to come today?

She rose and exited the room. As she turned into the closest corridor the Earl of Chetton appeared and without hesitation took her arm and guided her a few steps along the way before stopping to speak. "Are you leaving so soon, Mrs. Barnestowe? Surely you have just arrived?"

"No. I mean, yes. I just needed a breath of air." It wasn't really a lie, she told herself.

"Well, that is good to hear. I was afraid someone might have scared you off. We can be a touch hard on newcomers sometimes."

When she didn't respond immediately, Isobel noted a slight frown appear on Lord Chetton's face. "Pray, if you will permit me, madame, I should like to show you the conservatory." He walked with her along the hall and down some steps. "It will give you some time to collect yourself before meeting the other guests."

She was surprised at him accurately divining the delicate nature of her feelings. As she walked slowly along, Isobel could not help but take note of the fine workmanship of the old building. There were few paintings along the walls, but the wooden panels above the doors were painstakingly carved with nautical scenes. She paused to admire the details of a particularly vivid panorama. Lord Chetton glanced back at her.

"That is my study and the closest thing La Rocquette has to a library. Do you wish to look at the books? There are some old volumes, several in French."

"No, no. I was looking at the friezes. They are beautiful."

"Thank you. Most were added during the first renovation about a hundred and fifty years ago. My mother has recently seen to their restoration. The craftsmen she found did a fine job."

"I wanted to thank your mother for the invitation."

"You will, of course, have the opportunity to speak with her later. I am certain she will be delighted you came."

Lord Chetton opened a glass door that led into the conservatory and motioned for Isobel to precede him inside. She took a deep breath of the moist fragrant air created by the wealth of flowers and fruit trees growing around several small pools and a centre fountain. "Well, this is truly beautiful. What a pretty retreat it must make in inclement weather. But won't your guests miss you, Lord Chetton?"

"I do not expect so, at least not until the tea is served, and then only if there are not enough cakes to their liking."

Isobel looked at him more closely. He was clad in a navy coat and fawn trousers that showed off his muscular figure. His cravat and waistcoat were of a subdued blue and gold stripe that managed to be fashionable without being showy. His naturally wavy dark hair served to highlight the accents in his deep brown eyes. Isobel found herself staring into them for a moment longer than was seemly.

"You don't take many things seriously do you, Lord Chetton?"

"On the contrary, I take the fact that you won't use my name very seriously. Please call me Chetton and dispense with the title. And may I in return call you Isobel? After all, we are such old friends, having met on the continent and all."

His light touch of mockery was appealing. Yet it was the vibrancy that shone out from those deep brown eyes that encouraged Isobel to nod her head slightly to accept the civil offer of informality. Emma had forewarned her that this degree of familiarity was another of the subtleties of life on the close-knit island.

Lord Chetton held her in his gaze as he walked slowly around her and she was forced to turn to keep him in sight.

"You look lovely, Isobel. That colour suits you well."

She was flustered under his forthright scrutiny.

"Thank you. I like it too." Well, that should win for the most inane response of the day. The trouble was she was standing too close to him. His potent masculinity enveloped her senses. Such strength. His body had such strength. And in that lay power, the kind of power that could protect or destroy.

"Did you know our early spring gives us an advantage over growers on the mainland?"

He handed her a potted chrysanthemum. She took the flowerpot and looked at the yellow blooms. Emma loved mums. She said their hardiness was like motherlove, tenacious and resourceful.

"Do be careful of the dirt. I want you presentable when I introduce you to my acquaintances later, Isobel."

Isobel glanced down at her dress and smoothed the mauve ribbon into place several times. "But I am not, you see. Very presentable, I mean. I am not sure I should be here."

Lord Chetton looked at her and smiled. "Tut, tut, lady. Calm yourself."

"We must get back before someone misses us and comes searching."

"There is not the least need to concern yourself with that. I have very discreet servants."

She gave him a withering look. "I am sure you do. How very comforting it is for you to point that out to me."

Isobel started to walk away. Lord Chetton touched her shoulder to brush off a small leaf she had not noticed.

"Very well, then. Come with me, I will take you to my mother. They will be serving tea now in the salon."

He led her into the appointed room, through a throng of people, several of whom he stopped beside for a moment to introduce her to. They eventually reached Lady Chetton, who looked stunning in a beautiful green watered silk afternoon gown.

"Lovely to see you again, my dear." Lady Chetton linked arms with her and took a few steps away from her son and the woman she had been conversing with.

"You are at L'Ancresse, I understand. Charming cottage. Do not look so shocked, child. I knew the property had been vacant for some time. Chetton mentioned you were setting up there when I enquired about where to direct your invitation."

Isobel wasn't sure how much to divulge about her situation. She opted for discretion. "Yes. The accommodation, though smaller than what I am used to, suits my needs admirably right now."

"And you met my son on the crossing, did you not?"

"Not quite. We met by chance when delayed in St. Malo, but crossed separately."

"Ah, yes, well, travel interruptions are a trial to us all."

Isobel was relieved that Lady Chetton had the good breeding

not to ask personal questions. Her privacy meant a great deal to her. Just then a rather harried looking servant approached.

"Begging your pardon, m'lady. May I have a word?"

"Certainly, Norris." The countess gave a quick pat to Isobel's hand. "Excuse me, Mrs. Barnestowe. Apparently I have a matter to attend to, but I should love to continue our conversation at another time."

With that she left Isobel adrift in a sea of unfamiliar faces. Lord Chetton was ensconced across the room on a settee between two mature women engaged in a lively looking conversation. Although Isobel had been briefly introduced to several people earlier, by now she felt her resolve to approach them weakening. Perhaps she might leave further conversations for another day. She took a last longing glance at the sweet delicacies on offer at the tea table then pasted a noncommittal smile on her face and headed for the nearest door. Hearing voices from the left she turned in that direction. She passed the yellow salon where the music had been playing. Several people were still in the room and turned to look at her as she paused in the doorway.

Not wishing to engage in conversation she continued down the corridor. It ended in a T-junction. They had gone left, she thought, when Lord Chetton had escorted her to the conservatory, but that was at the back of the house and she needed to find her way out through the front, so she turned right. After a few minutes she found herself outside of a door she vaguely recognized and paused in confusion. Was this Lord Chetton's study? After a quick look to make sure no one was around she tapped at the door. It moved slightly and was clearly unlatched, so she pushed it open a little wider to peer inside. Her guess was correct; it was the study. Then she took a step back and looked above the door at the carved nautical scene she had earlier admired. Goodness, she should have recognized that.

She must have made a mistake somewhere and would have to retrace her steps and start again. She shook her head in annoyance. Then, hearing someone approach from behind, she hurried back down the way she had come, clutching her reticule. She did not want the awkwardness of being found in the private area of the old manor unescorted.

It was not glamorous to run, but she felt unaccountably that she should upon hearing the heavy tread of a man behind her. Mercifully, she caught sight of the rounded edge of the central staircase and knew the front hall and door were just beyond.

CHAPTER SEVEN

The many boats to and from Guernsey and the French coast provided Lord Chetton with the necessary anonymity he needed to slip in and out of France without being detected. A few days after the Spring Tea, he sailed on a packet ship and again met Jean in St. Malo. Since the city was home to another of Jean's numerous warehouse concerns, it was convenient for both men. For security they met in a different tavern across town from Le Chat d'Or.

Their rendezvous had an unexpected aspect for Chetton. On his own initiative, Monsieur Drapeau had procured a Great Seal of France, as well as several copies of correspondence sent between two prominent politicians. Forgery of authentic looking documents, which the seal would help to create, had been used in the past to stir political turmoil. But it was now considered to be a heavy handed, if not dangerous, method of diplomatic intervention. If something were to go wrong, the reputation of the entire British Empire would suffer. Chetton took the seal from Jean with some apprehension.

"I am sorry, *mon ami*, if I have put you in an awkward position, but Drapeau had the seal delivered at night to one of my warehouses and it was a fait accompli before I could intervene."

"Yes, I understand that, Jean. I had better take it with me than leave it here with you. The Great Seal does not interest me half so much as these letters and the information about rising tensions on the political front."

"Do you mean the 'ints about King Charles's plans?"

"Yes, as amazing as it sounds, he seems to have quiet intentions afoot to reimburse former landowners for the abolition of feudalism."

Jean shook his head. "*Mon Dieu*! That flies in the face of everything France has done since *la revolution*. Napoleon must be turning over in 'is grave!"

"Well, surely you don't expect an Englishman to be sentimental about old Boney, do you, Jean?"

Jean let out a guffaw and nearly spilled his ale.

Chetton continued, "Anyway, what also merits attention is proof about those compromised officials. Verification of that type of illegal activity may become quite useful. There is no saying to what advantage I may be able to put such leverage should the necessity arise."

It was possible that the idea of restitution to landowners was just a rumour, but in case it proved to be true, it would be well to ensure that back doors of information were open. Drapeau's papers supplied damning evidence of the habits of two influential French ministers to dip into the public treasury. With this kind of political ammunition, he might be able to apply pressure to persuade the offending ministers to do his bidding. Still, it was a dangerous game he played trying to manipulate such powerful men and their allies. He needed to constantly be on his guard for trickery and double-dealing.

※

It was several days before Lord Chetton was able to return to Guernsey. When he arrived back at La Rocquette in the evening he noticed that Doctor Hoskins's pony cart was pulled up by the stables. A burst of alarm caught at his stomach when, a few moments later, Norris came rushing to meet him as he entered the front hall. The solid old man never hurried about anything.

"What is it, Norris? What is wrong?" He did not like the high colour in the man's face.

"It's wee Teddy, m'lord. They sent him home from school. He's had a bad fall."

He stopped in his tracks and stared at his old retainer. "And what? My God, never tell me he is . . .?"

"No, no, m'lord. Not that, thank God, but he's in a bad way, the poor little chap."

Both men hurried over to the curved staircase that led to the upstairs suites of rooms. Norris stopped at the bottom. Lord Chetton took the stairs three at a time, the mumblings of Norris's hasty prayer in his ears.

He could tell from the flurry of activity outside the door that Teddy had been put into a different room, and was not in the old nursery wing. Mrs. McClure was giving directions to a maid who had an armful of soiled linens when he caught her eye. Dismissing the woman abruptly, she crossed the hallway to speak with him.

"Thank goodness you're back, my lord."

"Yes. Norris told me. How is the boy?"

"Both better and worse than he was, and hopefully not as good as he will be."

Lord Chetton closed his eyes briefly. This was not the time for a bout of old Scottish wisdom. He wanted information and the fact that his unflappable housekeeper was starting out so vaguely concerned him.

"Mrs. McClure, the details, please."

"Yes, my lord. All we know is that Teddy fell out of a tree five days ago in the school ground. He had been here at La Rocquette for the spring fair and Norris took him back to school hale and hearty. Then we got word from Mr. Hudson that he had fallen, but the first message didn't sound so bad. They thought he had a broken arm, no more. I was planning to go to see him at the Hudson's, when we got another urgent note that his condition was much worse. Mr. Hudson and his wife weren't quite up to the task of nursing, and no wonder at their stage of life. They felt he should be here so he could receive proper care."

"A broken arm? That does not sound too serious."

"But, that's not all, you see. The wound went sour right quick and it put the poor wee lamb into a fever, and he was having the fits and, and . . ." Mrs. McClure sniffed loudly into her handkerchief.

"I see. Is Dr. Hoskins with him now?"

"Ach, you've only just missed him, my lord. He's gone down the back stairs just a wee few minutes ago. Mrs. Barnestowe is sitting with the boy."

"Mrs. Barnestowe is here?"

"Yes. That woman is a dear, an angel, really. She met young Teddy at the fair last week. They were teamed up in a race, I think. She came right over as soon as she heard Teddy was hurt and hasn't left his bedside. She's a healer's touch, I'm sure."

"I will just go into his room for a moment, to see how things are."

He walked over to the boy's door, took a calming breath, and entered. The room was darkened as he had expected it to be, but the thick stale air usually found in a sickroom was not present. Instead, there was a light floral, almost spicy scent, coming, he imagined, from a pan sitting on a tiny brazier. The small form of the child was in the middle of the bed, the damaged arm wrapped and sitting on top of the covers. The labouring of Teddy's shallow chest as he breathed was too weak to disturb the bedding.

Isobel was close by, nestled in the depths of an ancient armchair. Her head had fallen back against the chair and her eyes were closed. Lord Chetton moved further into the room. He peered down at the boy, observing his pale colour. He did not know what was stronger, the urge to drop to his knees in supplication or run from the room in black despair. A great weariness hit him and he was unable to stifle a deep sigh.

Isobel's calm voice broke his brief reverie. "You are come home, Chetton. Your ma'ma will be relieved."

He turned to glance at her. "I have just arrived. I hope I did not wake you."

"No, I had only just closed my eyes. Dr. Hoskins was here until a few minutes ago. Did you see him?"

Chetton shook his head in the negative.

"Well, Teddy is much quieter now. But it was a long night for him, poor thing."

"I imagine it was a long night for everyone. Thank you for helping, Isobel, although I am surprised to find you here."

"Are you really, now? Did you think I only eat chocolates and attend tea parties?" She smiled and then continued more seriously. "Teddy's arm is not the real problem. The fever has weakened his lungs. It must break soon. Well, we must bring his fever down, that is all there is to it."

"Do you need anything, is there anything I can do?"

೧೮

Isobel stood, wanting to stretch her cramped muscles. She was wobbly on her feet from lack of sleep. Without making a sound Lord Chetton was beside her, holding her arm to steady her. Isobel was prepared to protest but the feel of his strong warm hand on her was comforting. She had craved that kind of comfort all her life.

"When did you last eat, Isobel?"

"Um, sometime last night, I think."

"What is this I hear? Mrs. McClure has not looked after you

since then? She has some explaining to do."

"You leave dear Mrs. McClure alone. She has been run off of her feet and is so worried about Teddy. And anyway, she sent several lovely trays up, I have just not been hungry, that is all."

He took a step back as she reached to put her palm against the boy's cheek. "She said you met Teddy at the fair."

"Yes. We made a grand team in the egg and spoon race and took second prize. And then suffered together from eating too many strawberry tarts in celebration."

"That sounds like Teddy. How is he really, do you think?"

"According to Dr. Hoskins, he is slowly improving. They splinted his broken arm at the school infirmary but apparently they were not careful enough about the scrapes and wound on his skin and that is why it festered. The Hudsons, I believe, were boarding him?"

Chetton nodded.

"Yes, well, they were most upset over Teddy's decline, but I am sure he is better here under the care of Dr. Hoskins. Although, the poor little fellow cried so when the doctor had to lance the infection and cleanse it." Isobel stoked the child's cheek with a gentle touch. "As long as the fever does not spike again he should be on the mend. When he arrived here he was burning up, his breath very shallow, and then he went into spasms. Dr. Hoskins said it happens sometimes when a body gets too hot. It troubled everyone to see him so."

Chetton picked up Teddy's good hand in his and rubbed the little fingers with his thumb. "I can imagine," he said and then cleared his throat. "Under the circumstances will you come away from the room and rest properly for a bit? I am sure Mrs. McClure or one of the maids would be happy to sit with Teddy since Hoskins feels he is in no immediate danger."

Isobel saw the concern on his face. "Thank you, but no. I would much rather stay here for the time being. The doctor suggested

Teddy be bathed with cool water once more and I want to be here when Nurse does so. Could you ask to have some tea sent up by and by, and perhaps a slice of Mrs. McClure's treacle tart? That would be nice."

While Isobel believed that Teddy was slowly improving, the young boy's generally weak constitution meant a relapse was not impossible. She would stay where she felt she was needed a little longer and hope that Lord Chetton's presence at La Rocquette not prove to be a complication. She had promised Lady Chetton to stay and help care for Teddy without facing the possibility that her son would return so soon. Witnessing his deep concern was unsettling. It made her want to comfort him, and this, when she must guard against revealing her true purpose on the island, was troubling indeed.

Lord Chetton left Isobel as she began to pour clean water into the basin. He met one of the maids on the stairs and requested an ample tea tray be sent up in half an hour. He was to be notified immediately of a change with the boy. If Mrs. Barnestowe required anything her request was to be dealt with promptly.

Lord Chetton went into the library and poured himself a glass of port. He had long relied on Jean to keep him supplied with excellent brandy, wine, and port. This old tawny was really rather special. He thought about calling to have some Stilton and biscuits sent in to go with it, then changed his mind. He was not really hungry. He did not know quite what he was, in fact, other than concerned about Teddy. He had seen more than his share of injuries, most of them from fighting, but the suffering of a child was altogether different. The shadow of his former loss hovered around him. He willed it away. It was not decent that the power of his past should touch the innocent child upstairs who was sick and vulnerable.

He would write to Teddy's father, Collin, and give him an update before he retired for the night.

His mind turned again to his brief interaction with Isobel. She had appeared tired but retained that air of quiet vitality unique to her. When he thought of the looks of affection she had bestowed on Teddy he realized that yes, unfortunately, he was of low enough character that he could indeed feel jealous of the sick boy. Disgusted with himself, he poured another port.

There was strength to the woman, Lord Chetton admitted. Yet she often appeared vulnerable in a way that puzzled him and seemed quite apart from mourning the loss of her husband. She never spoke of him, had not offered one detail about the man. There must be something else he was missing. Perhaps there had been a child. That was something he could understand. It was not always possible to share such losses. Before the onslaught of his own past could pay a visit, he refreshed his glass and carried it up to bed.

※

Lord Chetton had not slept well. He had been sensitive to the muted sounds of the comings and goings from Teddy's room. Twice he had almost gone in but then thought better of it as he did not want to interfere, confident that his household staff would have apprised him in the event of an emergency. He wanted to speak to his mother about the situation. As it happened, they met each other at the stairs, she descending and he about to start on his way up. He waited for his mother to make her way down the last few steps. She looked a little pale but otherwise well.

"Mother, I am sorry I missed you at breakfast. I would have waited but thought you most likely had something sent up to your room."

"No matter. I am just glad that you have returned, Chetton. It has been quite a to do around here."

"Yes, that is what I gathered." He gave her a light kiss on the cheek.

His mother reached out her hands to him. "Oh, my dear son, I appreciate how difficult this must have been for you to come home and find the situation, so similar to . . ."

He ignored the well meant gesture. "Mother, shall we go and see how Teddy fared overnight?"

His mother dropped her hands. "Well, I have just spoken to Mrs. Barnestowe, and apparently, he had a more settled time of it than the night before."

"Glad to hear that."

"Yes, although poor Mrs. Barnestowe looked like she needed a breath of fresh air. I suggested she visit the garden for a spell."

"Ah, yes, an excellent place to blow the cobwebs out. I talked to her briefly when I arrived late last night."

"Mrs. Barnestowe really is a delightful creature. She does not suffer from an inflated sense of self consequence that so many young women seem to nowadays. She jumped right in to be of assistance, and indeed, she has been such a comfort. I asked her to stay at La Rocquette for a few days. You know how Dr. Hoskins frightens poor Teddy. She and Teddy have developed quite a rapport. Of course, the nurse does most of the practical matters but Mrs. Barnestowe seems to know how best to soothe and calm him, which I do not mind admitting is a relief to me."

Lord Chetton kept his eyes straight ahead. He understood neither Isobel nor his mother could be expected to be involved closely with the physical realities of nursing a sick child. If his parent believed Isobel to be able to console Teddy more than their dour family doctor and his nurse, he would certainly not take issue with her decision.

CHAPTER EIGHT

Two days later, as Isobel conferred with Lady Chetton outside the sick room door, Lord Chetton joined them.

Isobel smiled at him. "I am pleased to tell you Teddy is coming along nicely. Dr. Hoskins has just confirmed that his fever is almost gone. And I have the doctor's permission to promise him a game of draughts later if he rests quietly for a few hours."

"Oh, that is good news."

"Yes, it is," said Lady Chetton as she squeezed her son's forearm. "He has eaten the last of the dreaded panada the Doctor ordered and is looking forward to a poached egg and toast points for breakfast tomorrow."

"I am glad to hear it. The crisis seems to be over then?" said Chetton as he turned towards Isobel.

"For the most part, yes. Although Doctor Hoskins said he is still weak and will need to stay in bed for some time."

He nodded his head. "Of course. Still, it is a big improvement, one I should be only too glad to write to his parents about. I have already mentioned your care and attention, Isobel. They will want to thank you, I am sure."

"Yes, I have written to them as well," said Lady Chetton. She smiled at Isobel. "Do you know Lieutenant Collin Ashton and his wife Susan?"

Isobel stiffened at hearing the military connection of Teddy's parents. She shrugged her shoulders but did not answer.

Lady Chetton looked at her expectantly. "It would be a wonder if you do not. He is a Royal Marine officer. I am sure they were stationed in Portsmouth for a time a few years ago, were they not, Chetton? Collin and Susan are a gay couple and love to entertain when he is home. Their Staunton Hall is a storied old building."

Isobel's earlier good mood was beginning to dispel rapidly. She felt a headache coming on and was flustered by the conversation. This was the type of situation she abhorred, trying to embroider a non-existent past with the minimum amount of information so that she appeared believable, but did not get herself caught up in some detail where the fantasy was revealed for what it was—a sham.

Lord Chetton must have noticed her distraction. "How are you faring yourself, Isobel? If I may say so, you look all done in."

"Um, yes, I just need a little time in the fresh air to clear my head. A walk is the best tonic I know."

Lady Chetton patted Isobel's hand. "It is a fine day. Chetton, are you free to take Isobel on a little outing? She has hardly seen anything of the island sites yet, have you, dear?"

Lord Chetton made her a small bow. "It would be my pleasure to take you on a little sortie. I know exactly the place to go, that is to say if you are amenable to an outing, Isobel, rather than an outright walk."

She nodded her agreement to the offer.

"I suggest you collect a warm wrap and I will meet you downstairs presently."

Isobel did so and a few minutes later they walked outside and followed the gravelled path around to the stables. The horses were already harnessed to a charming little carriage and as she settled back against the comfortable squabs, Lord Chetton spoke with the groom just beyond her hearing. She saw the man smile and hand something to him, which he immediately stowed in his pocket before climbing to his seat and grabbing the reins.

"What a beautiful carriage this is," said Isobel as they departed.

Chetton cast a glance at Isobel and quickly turned his attention back to manoeuvring the gig through the narrow estate gates. "I am glad you approve. It is a new model; a Tilbury. I had it sent over for my mother. I thought it better to take it this morning due to the questionable path we must take, but I sorely miss the curricle I drive in England."

"I cannot compare the two, never having been allowed to ride in so vaunted a coach. A well sprung Phaeton is the height of luxury for me. Tell me, is it a racing curricle, and do you like to go very fast in it?"

"I have been known to raise a few hairs but I am not as reckless as some of the young bucks you see betting on their times."

Isobel nodded her head. "Yes, I know what you mean."

"So, you are acquainted with the fast set. Was your husband a madcap racer?"

"No. I was just remembering what it was like to have the freedom to choose your own conveyance. My circumstances are somewhat different here at the cottage." Isobel turned away from him and looked out over the landscape, knowing Chetton would take this as a sign to leave the conversation unfinished.

They drove for half an hour, most of the time in companionable silence. Occasionally Isobel would ask a question or Chetton would comment about a particular view. The route took them past several picturesque cottages, an open common scattered with the golden shapes of the island's famous cows, and many verdant fields coloured with the green heads of an early crop. And always the sea cliffs were to the left.

Lord Chetton stopped the gig in a quiet valley unattended by the usual granite walled fences. He tethered the horse loosely to a tree and aided Isobel down.

"Where are we, my lord?"

"Close to the parish of Vale on the northeast side of the island. But what we want is just through here." He led her between a growth of hardy bushes.

Isobel stopped walking and stared.

The bushes opened up to a clearing, which had at its centre a huge mound of earth covered in grass. It was encircled by a wall of stones. Some of the smaller granite slabs were piled horizontally as if they were part of a stone fence. Other larger pieces stood vertically and formed the edges, as such, of a vague form that was not quite a square and not quite a circle. The unruly shape was perhaps twenty feet in diameter and rose to about four feet at the crest of its centre.

Lord Chetton walked back to Isobel, taking her hand to draw her closer to the structure.

"This is called Le Dehus. It is a dolmen, an ancient burial chamber."

It became apparent to Isobel as they walked around the strange circle that it was not a solid pile of earth but a hollow tomb. Huge stones framed the narrow entrance to an underground cavity. She kept hold of Lord Chetton's hand as he encouraged her through the opening in the rocks.

"Duck your head here, and watch where you step. I am afraid you will have to crouch a bit, there is not much clearance. Well done. Now wait a moment, I will just give us a bit more light."

Although the entrance passage allowed a degree of light to penetrate to the depths, Isobel felt better when Lord Chetton lit the candle stub he produced from his pocket.

"This is amazing."

"It is, is it not? Give me your hand again and come over here." Lord Chetton guided her around the area and it was quite apparent even to her unpractised eye that there were several side chambers held up by massive slabs of roughly hewn granite.

"Now, put your head as far back as you can, and look straight up."

Isobel did as she was directed and slanted her head back while trying to maintain her lowered position. It was worth the awkward effort. She was rewarded with the image of a strange face carved in the rock staring down at her. There was a recognizable nose, mouth, and eyes and a formidable brow. As well, she could make out fingers and a bow, and there was some type of crown, it seemed, on the figure's head. She shivered despite herself.

"Meet Le Gardien, the guardian of the tomb."

Isobel thought it a very apt name for the stylized figure.

They spent a few more minutes soaking up the ambience of the quiet place until Isobel's back began to protest the strain. Just then the candle started to sputter. Isobel knew herself still to be inclined towards occasional childish bouts of imagination, and was sure she saw the textured eyes flicker. It was almost as if Le Gardien was trying to tell her something.

Regaining the sunlight and fresh air was a shock after the muted sounds and filtered light of below.

Lord Chetton gave a great sigh of contentment.

"People have come here for hundreds of years, but the place is much older—unknowable really. Some Oxford scholars came a few years ago to study the site and thought it was at least three, and perhaps four, thousand years old."

He walked a few steps away and looked at the open fields beyond.

"There is still a great deal of superstition on the island, you know, Isobel. Some of it surrounds this place, but there are other old burial sites and tombs with ancient markings. We have lots of standing stones and fairy circles on Guernsey. Its history goes back past all memory."

Isobel moved closer to stand beside him and take in the view.

"The tomb would make quite a hide out, I expect."

"A hideout? Well, I suppose it might. I know that even today young boys dare themselves to camp out on stormy nights, sort of a rite of passage to manhood. I have been to all of Guernsey's ancient sites over the years, in good weather and bad. At night, I tell you, Isobel, there is something special, unexplainable about them. Just imagine all of the lives that have come and gone since some distant group chose this place to celebrate their dead. They built these mounds never conceiving, I will wager, that they would remain so far into the mists of time. How could they know? And for millennia they were deserted, never visited by a living soul."

Isobel noticed a gull overhead looking down on them with its cold glassine stare. She was chilled, despite being back in the warmth of the sunlight, and could not imagine willingly choosing to stay near the tomb through the long dark hours of night.

Lord Chetton's countenance was reverential. He had lowered his voice to just above a whisper and she strained to catch the nuance of each word before it was snatched away on the sea winds.

"It was not until much later, long after Guernsey was inhabited by William the Conqueror's lot, that this was rediscovered." He paused and gestured back towards the large mound of earth. "The bodies were long gone before then, of course, and over time some of the stones have been taken and used in other ways. But the ancient places were not systematically desecrated or destroyed here, despite the fact that good Christians have never sanctioned the dolmens."

"I suppose they feel justified in that. It is a quintessentially pagan site, after all."

"Yes, but the island is still rather a fey place, Isobel. Even with Guernsey's strict Methodist views many of the old beliefs and ways survive. Do you know that witchcraft continues to stir our imagination? People build cottages with chimney ledges for witches to sit on so they will be warm there and not be bothered to come inside. You have seen the little stone ledge high up on the chimney at L'Ancresse Cottage, have you not?"

Isobel nodded in agreement. Her thoughts were centered on Lord Chetton's words about the island's long and exotic history. She touched the rough mounded earth and splayed her fingers through the tufts of grass growing there.

"Oh, I know we are stubborn on Guernsey and far from perfect, but it says something about the acceptance of the people that they can live with so many layered views of the world, I think."

He was looking at her now, the full penetration of his deep eyes directed towards her.

"Perhaps." She looked back across the mound just as a ray of sunlight cast it into high relief. Unbidden, her mind's eye painted the picture of the Le Gardien's timeless features. Something in her was drawn to the idea of an ancient sentinel, a benevolent protector.

"Thank you for bringing me here," Isobel said as her gaze wandered across the vista in front of them. Her mind was still filled with the magic of the Le Gardien. Thoughts of the anonymous lives of the people gone before her played across her mind. The cares and duties, hopes and loves of generations had eventually been laid to rest. Life was indeed fleeting. There was only the present and what you could make of an uncertain future. And what about her own life? Had her desire for anonymity convinced Lord Chetton? And how, she wondered, would her other secrets affect the path of her life?

❧

Lord Chetton drove home at a faster pace, in order, Isobel was sure, to be on time for luncheon. Mrs. McClure would never deign to utter a word of complaint against her employer, but could not refrain from clicking her tongue when the house schedule was disrupted. As they crossed the entrance hall, Lord Chetton leafed through the letters that Norris had handed to him upon entry.

"Ah, finally a reply from Collin, I see. Wait, Isobel, I am sure he has some kind words for your solicitous care of his son."

Isobel's steps faltered a little as she headed for the stairs.

"Isobel, what is the matter?"

"It is just that I do not merit any particular attention. I have only been following Dr. Hoskins's instructions. Anyone would have done the same thing."

"I do not agree. And in any case Teddy has affection for you, which can only gladden his parents' hearts to hear."

She managed a tight smile, despite having an apprehension of what was coming next.

Lord Chetton scanned the letter quickly and then gave her a quizzical look.

"It is odd that Collin does not seem to have heard of you or your late husband. He was stationed in Portsmouth, you said? That would have been under Admiral Sir George Martin, correct?"

"You do not understand!"

"No, I do not."

Against her better judgment she allowed Lord Chetton to draw her into the yellow salon. She crossed immediately to the window and kept her back to him. She was aware he would sense her distress by the taut line of her back and the trembling of her cheek, but could control neither movement. He gently turned her around to face him, the pressure of his large hands warm on her shoulders.

"Why is it that you wish I had not made mention of you?"

Isobel stepped away to dislodge Lord Chetton's hands and again turned her back on him. She did not want to be under his watchful eye at the moment. Not when she was this distraught.

"I do not like to be spoken about, especially to people who, however close to you, remain strangers to me." Even the gesture of Chetton's well meaning letter could serve to complicate her situation.

"I am sorry but that makes no sense at all. It was in thanks that I wrote about you."

An old habit, one that Emma had tried for years to rid her of resurfaced, and Isobel stamped her foot angrily on the floor. "I do not need to explain my sensibilities to you, sir!"

The silence that ensued did nothing to calm her nerves.

"No, madame, you certainly do not. I trust you will forgive my undo familiarity. Blame it, if you will, upon the pressures we have all undergone during the last few days. Please excuse me. I have to attend to some matters in my study."

Isobel blanched at the cold politeness that had seeped into Lord Chetton's voice. She recognized in it the austere formality that he, as the Earl, must often present to the public.

○○

Lord Chetton was crossing the hall, letter in hand, when Norris answered the front door. He was annoyed at the blunt reproof that Isobel had just delivered to him and was preoccupied with rereading Collin's letter.

A moment later a brisk slap on the back brought Lord Chetton quickly around to face a pair of deep brown eyes that mirrored his own. The man, slightly younger, was as tall as he, but had not quite the same degree of breadth across the shoulders. It was a face made for easy goodwill and even now the mouth quirked towards a ready smile.

"Hello, Chetton."

"Chris! Good to see you. Welcome."

"I thought I would pop over for a quick visit while Mother's here. She wrote me about little Teddy, and with the Ball approaching as well I decided to come and see what trouble I could make."

"Nothing changes, then."

"Hah! This from you, big brother? Do not forget that you taught me all I know."

Later that evening Chetton sat in the same worn armchair that Isobel had fallen asleep in a few days previously. Chris had been in to check on Teddy, but had retired early after his travels. Chetton watched the resting form of the young boy, his tawny head barely visible above the quilts. Such a little scrap of a thing, he was. Teddy's frail body had been pressed against Chetton in an unapologetic embrace when he had entered the room earlier. That action told of the boy's fondness for him more emphatically than words ever could. Children, and perhaps a few rare adults, had the ability to express feelings so cleanly, so openly, and with such trust that it humbled the soul. He could not remember his own sweet young son's affection without pain and guilt in equal measure.

Yes, he had believed at one time that he had all the answers, and a worthy plan to follow, which would ultimately benefit everyone. He had had the desire and the will to shepherd all those under his care towards a happy and useful future. But everything had gone so terribly wrong. Far beyond his ability to fix.

Almost beyond his ability to endure.

Now he was faced with a new situation. He could no longer ignore his growing interest in Isobel. Yet he couldn't let go of the notion that there was more to this woman than she let on. He did not yet have a full understanding of how and why she was situated in a cottage so close to his estate. The small population of the tiny island allowed for much more fraternization between the classes of people than was thinkable in England. And Guernsey's long and unique Anglo-French history meant families were interwoven in a way not understood or accepted in other more rigidly stratified societies. Family history was important to island residents and people had very long memories on the island. Isobel seemingly fit into none of those patterns.

He was quite certain that it had in fact been Isobel that he had observed in a quick and somewhat furtive exchange in St. Peter Port the other day. Not wanting to make an issue of it in front of his mother he had let her denial pass, but he had seen her profile and the distinctive shawl she wore quite clearly. He had been about to approach Isobel when the man arrived at the jewellery store and stood so close to her. The fellow's back was to him so he had no clue to his identity other than that he presented a strong youthful figure. He had given her some paper and she appeared to have given him some coins in return. This might all be entirely reasonable, except for the way Isobel had denied it so categorically.

And why, he wondered, had she jumped so rapidly to the idea of Le Dehus being used as a possible hideout. Surely that was a very strange direction to take.

Then, too, her reaction to the letter today had been peculiar, to say the least. He had been momentarily stung by the vehemence of her outburst. Idiot! By now he should be inured to the capricious nature of women, especially if they were hiding something. Both professionally and personally, he did not take well to surprises and mysteries.

CHAPTER NINE

Isobel wanted a respite the next morning from the bustle of Dr. Hoskins's recent visit and wandered into one of the side chambers of the hall in search of a quiet moment. The area was referred to as the Little Picture Gallery and it was not long before she stood entranced by the exotic beauty of a young woman's portrait hung beside the mantle. The artist had captured a note of sadness, unexpected in one so young and fair.

Isobel heard someone enter behind her, and turned.

"Ah, good morning, Isobel. Do you like the Countess, then?"

Isobel smiled at Chris. Chetton had introduced them when he visited Teddy last night. "There is much to admire."

"Yes, and she greatly enjoyed such admiration."

"You said 'the Countess'? So, then to whom is she married?"

"Was. She was Chetton's spouse. They were married briefly. Madeline Perrault. Daughter of Viscount Adrian Perrault. She made him a widower several years ago."

Isobel turned abruptly from the portrait to look at Chris. "Oh, my goodness. How very sad for you all. I am sorry I had no idea."

"Yes, it was tragic."

Still shocked, she could only think to ask, "Is it a fair likeness of her?"

Chris turned his back to the picture. "Well, on a good day, perhaps."

"I am sorry, Chris, I am not sure I understand."

"Oh, nothing. She did not spend much time at La Rocquette as she preferred the season in London. But their son adored it here." Chris pointed to the silhouette of a young child in a plain black frame which sat on an occasional table nearby. "When he was allowed to come."

"Their son! Surely you do not mean to say he too is deceased?"

Chris picked up the silhouette of a cherubic little face to show her. "Isobel, since you are becoming so indispensable to us and have seen her portrait I feel you should know about the matter." Chris blew out a long breath. "You see here Chetton's little son, my nephew, Sam."

"Sam?"

"Yes, an odd name for the nobility, but his mother was adamant on the choice and she usually got her way." Chris ran his thumb gently over the likeness of the child. "The cruel fact is that Sammy died shortly after his mother, from the same contagion. It hit Chetton hard, as you would expect. We, his family and friends, *never* talk about it, nor do the servants. I am sure you will respect his wishes in this."

Isobel was stunned by his words and murmured agreement. Chris continued to stare at the child's silhouette and lapsed into silence. Feeling that she was intruding on a private moment, she quietly excused herself and quitted the room.

❧

Later in the day Isobel set herself the task of mending a rent in her second best day dress, which, she surmised, must have occurred at some point when playing with Teddy. The repair was not advancing well. At first the exact shade of navy thread was not to be found in her sewing basket. It had to be borrowed from Mrs. McClure after the busy housekeeper had been located in the store room checking the inventory of newly set preserves. Then her sewing scissors had to be retrieved, with a light reprimand to Teddy. He had not asked for permission to use them when he had been allowed to play with a bit of paper and chalk under the tight strictures of Dr. Hoskins, and the watchful eyes of the youngest housemaid. Next, her luncheon with Lady Chetton lasted well above an hour due to a lively conversation about Chetton and Chris's exploits in their youth.

Finally settled down to her chore in the cosy little parlour adjoining her room, Isobel found her needlework slowing as her mind wandered to Lord Chetton's sad loss of his wife and son. The brief, almost terse way in which Chris had imparted the story to her this morning had not gone unnoticed. It was not to be wondered at that he should feel the loss of his sister-in-law and young nephew as well. As Emma said, life was always precious, often fragile, and sometimes fleeting. Of course the dual bereavement of wife and child was not unheard of, tragic though it was indeed, yet usually it occurred during or after childbirth. She could hardly fathom the added burden of knowing and loving a young child for years before having them ripped away from you.

Isobel winced as the tip of the errant needle grazed her finger and drew a bead of blood. She kissed the crimson drop away, accepting the sting as the price paid for her inattention, and reset herself to her work, aligning the dark material in a way to best camouflage her repair. The pace of her stitches, though neat and evenly spaced, soon dropped off again as she contemplated the desperate hurt Chetton had suffered. She had noticed Chetton's inconsistent reactions to the affection Teddy lavished on him when allowed to do so. There was no one to compare to his godfather for the little boy. Chetton's response to Teddy was mercurial, however. Sometimes the affection was returned and at other times, kindly but firmly, withheld and discouraged. The young boys must have been close in age from her reckoning, and that was salt in the wound indeed.

It was not in her nature to consider disregarding Chris's constraint about speaking of the deaths, but she vowed that going forward she would allow Chetton his odd quirks of temperament without taking umbrage. She had seen nothing in his demeanour to suggest that Chetton would accept, let alone appreciate, any sign of pity from her, or anyone else for that matter. She tied off her thread and determined, when on her knees before bed, to say a prayer for Chetton and the sweet souls of his departed family.

Isobel was disheartened with this unhappy line of thought and chided herself into more energetic action. She decided to accept Mrs. McClure's offer to show her the "poor wee bit" of herbs growing near the kitchen garden. Isobel spent the last precious hour of sunlight that day tending them. The St. John's wort needed to be split and replanted, the mint thinned out, and the whole section would benefit from another light weeding. Most of the heavy work would naturally be done by the gardener. The smell of the rich dark earth as she picked a few herbs reminded her of the countless hours spent with Sister Bernadette in the large garden at Thrushgrange Abbey.

At first she had only been able to lie by the window and catch glimpses of the sisters at work. After a few weeks at the abbey she started to walk among the rows and take note of the condition of the plants. An unexpected cold snap in the weather had the sisters hurrying to collect precious leaves and stems before the bite of frost ruined them. Isobel knelt down to help. She soon became a regular in the garden and keen to glean tips from Sister Mary Katherine, the wise septuagenarian who sat and directed proceedings from the kitchen doorway.

The fragrant garden had not stayed as a refuge for long. After the curt dismissal of her request to return home, it began to feel more and more like a gaol. As her spirit felt imprisoned in the misfortune that had befallen her, so had she been caught in the callous machinations of her encroaching uncle.

Isobel suddenly had not the strength to continue with her gardening. Already in a melancholy mood from earlier, Isobel's own memories and grief took her away on a storm of sadness. She gave way to the tears which she had been battling and let them course freely down her cheeks, almost welcoming their release for the cathartic effect they allowed.

☙

Lord Chetton felt like he had taken a blow to the gut. He had been returning from the stables and chanced to look at the kitchen garden. When he saw Isobel drop her gardening basket in a rush of tears he hurried to her side.

"Whatever is the matter? Have you hurt yourself? Has someone hurt you?" But she did not answer. It was as if his questions had not registered.

He was annoyed to discover how much her distress affected him. Damnation. Seeing her sobbing had shaken him and brought out his protective instincts. She had stopped the heart rendering noises, although the linen handkerchief he had offered her was damp from her tears. God damn it!

He moved to stand very close to her and dropped his voice. "Isobel, you must tell me. What is the matter?"

She tried to walk away from him but he put his hand on her arm lightly to dissuade her movement.

"Isobel."

"Yes, I am just a little overtired." She tried to smile but it was not at all successful. "Really, I am fine now. Oh, heavens, I do hope there is no one about!"

He had ensured that they were alone in the enclosure as he approached her.

"We are quite private for the moment. I insist on accompanying you back inside, however," he said, refusing her offer to return his handkerchief with a gesture.

Isobel lifted her hand to hide her reddened eyes. "You must forgive me for being such a despicable watering pot. I do not usually act so, I promise you."

Since she would not discuss the reason for her distress, he let that comment pass and offered instead, "Let me take the lead, Isobel. You will not want to converse with anyone we might encounter just yet, I imagine."

He left her at the top of the stairs with a curt demand that she call Mrs. McClure should she require anything. As he watched her enter her room down the hall, he could not help but think that she was in conflict about something and a poor liar indeed.

※

Isobel could not relinquish herself to rest that night. It was impossible not to relive the afternoon's events. Her sudden fit of old grief had astounded her, but no more so than the comfort she had felt from Lord Chetton's attention. His gentle care had been so soothing. All the valid reasons that should have prompted her to pull back from his nearness were lost to her. His quiet movements, the way he softly clasped her arm as if she were precious, stole into her heart and halted all thoughts of what was appropriate behaviour.

He had asked her to tell him the cause of her distress. What was there to say? That she had needed to feel connected to someone then, that she was dispirited in a way she could not put into words.

There were only so many reasons she could suggest to account for her behaviour. With Chetton's perceptive eyes on her face, she did not want him to think madness was the best one, and so had plead fatigue.

The man was too clever for that ruse, too deep to believe in such a light deception. Isobel knew she was taking unfair advantage of him. Social custom had demanded he accept her suggestion without further questions.

Her usual ability to retreat into sleep had deserted her. Warm milk, a cosy fire, a ponderous book, none of these in any combination had the expected results. Her last resource was to take a brisk walk around the gardens and hope the cool night air might provide her with the recipe for slumber. Throwing her favourite shawl around her shoulders, she left the room.

She made her way down the wide staircase with the aid of a small oil lamp and passed through the side doors, which faced the formal garden. It was a clear night and the stars shimmered brightly, a rare event on the island. Isobel thought of how much Emma would appreciate such a sight. She and Emma were devoted stargazers and had huddled under blankets many nights to watch and classify patterns in the heavens.

Isobel conjured the image of her dear friend's face in her mind's eye, unexpectedly seeing the look of deep concern Emma wore in only the most alarming situations. Then a shiver ran up Isobel's arms, so violent she almost dropped the lamp. She experienced an uncanny sense that something was amiss, that her closest ally over so many of the years of her life was desperate. That fate, the most faithless of mistresses, was about to deliver an unsuspecting blow to Emma at a time when distance made it impossible to warn or comfort her caused Isobel to tremble anew. So strong was the premonition that she almost took flight back to the comfort of her room.

Only the unexpected beauty of the night sky stayed her retreat. Isobel tried to calm her wild imaginings and wandered towards a sheltered bench to sit. She chastised herself for letting fanciful notions disturb her peace. After a period of time, she calmed down and slowly unbidden thoughts of a different nature entirely visited her. The image of Chetton's rugged profile flashed across her inner eye.

Deeply hidden in her bosom lay a tiny enclave of hope, the merest whisper of possibility. Too precious and fragile was it to openly acknowledge and yet it existed. Not all of the oppression and experiences of her life had the power to quench it. The need to be a whole woman, to desire and be desired in return, was the secret wish of her soul. With Chetton she felt the first fine stirrings of want. They were as yet gossamer, fluid, as insubstantial and beautiful as the wings of a young butterfly.

There was only the flutter of her heart, the skittering along her skin when he was near, and they left more questions than they provided answers.

&

Lord Chetton sat at the desk in his study and thought about the events of the day. He felt keenly Isobel's refusal to explain to him her obvious turmoil. Seeing her tears had shocked and then angered him. Here was yet another mystery about the woman. He sloshed the last of the brandy around in the snifter and then gulped it quickly, slamming the empty crystal down in a rare fit of uncontrolled annoyance.

Or perhaps, and this was a humbling thought, she felt the bleakness of his nature and believed he could not give her the solace she so obviously needed. His hand sought the decanter to refill his glass, then stopped. He needed to clear his head, not befuddle it with more strong spirits. He rose quickly and stepped outside through the French doors.

The night air was refreshing on the exposed skin at his open neck. It was a welcome change to the closeness of his study. Wanting more freedom, he quickly undid the first few confining buttons of his linen shirt. Visions of he and Chris sneaking out for a night swim in the bay as young boys made him smile with affection.

Then the hairs on the back of his neck stood up as he saw an apparition in white float down the steps to the garden. The ephemeral figure glided behind bushes and was lost to sight. As he did not believe in ghosts, he spared not a moment and headed after it.

Turning a corner behind the rose garden, he beheld Isobel reclining on a bench. She was clothed only in a thin muslin night costume and flowered shawl. Starlight glimmered off of her hair and silhouetted her fine young form to perfection. His blood quickened at the tempting vision she presented. On impulse he plucked a rose from the bush in front of him and quietly walked towards her.

Chetton began to gently stroke the petals back and forth along Isobel's wrist. She fluttered her eyes open and then her gaze followed the path of delicate movement as if mesmerized by the sensation. Gradually her regard shifted upwards over his body until she was staring straight into his eyes.

What was this, wondered Chetton. This acceptance of sensuality and the soft inviting sight of Isobel in dishabille sent an explicit message through his anatomy. He strove to camouflage the affect she was having on him. It would not do to let her know how much power she wielded.

"Lady, there is a sheltered glade over there that beckons."

He leaned back to avoid colliding with the sharp turn of her head as she quickly sat up; the outraged expression in her wide eyes gratifying, though predictable.

"Unbelievable! And if I said yes, you would readily oblige me, no doubt?"

He had meant to shock her, and it was oddly satisfying that she was innocent enough to be so incensed. Yet there was something in the delivery of her response that he could not fathom. It was not a challenge exactly. Not a warning, nor was it a retreat. It transgressed no boundaries, but had he detected a suggestion, a hint only perhaps, of capitulation? Or was he guilty of reading too much into Isobel's words? He should know much better than to fall into the trap of hearing what you most wanted to hear. Not to understand the reasons behind why someone asked a question was a pitfall he had learned to avoid early on in his diplomatic career. This woman had muddled his senses to the point he might be making fundamental errors. How terrifying.

"Now that is a loaded question with no good answer," he said while inhaling the floral scent she exuded. "What I should have done is to ask you what you are doing out here. You seemed far away when I first disturbed you. Has it anything to do with what caused your earlier distress?"

"Your concern about me is quite unwarranted." Isobel was not looking at him right now because she had found a loose thread on the hem of her shawl that was, apparently, quite fascinating. "Let me ask you a question. Are you always so forward, or do you just enjoy being contentious? I thought diplomats were supposed to be discreet."

"Tactful, subtle, restrained? Sadly, those are not my strong suits so I just stumble along in my own dimwitted straightforward way. What makes you think I was ever competent at my job anyway?"

Isobel chuckled at this. "I rather think you could not suffer to *not* excel at whatever you do. You positively reek with that kind of confidence."

Chetton picked up Isobel's hand and looked at it, then turned it over and continued the examination. She snatched her hand away. "Whatever are you doing now?"

"Just looking for the velvet glove. You backhand quite well."

"There you go with the humour. You use it as well as you wield your fists, no doubt. But I am not taken in by such an accomplished flirt."

Lord Chetton looked up into the sky for a moment in silence before he let his gaze fall slowly back to Isobel. "But only in defence, lady. Never as a weapon, and never against you. I find you have quite bested me in keeping your distance. Sometimes I do believe it wars with your nature, and yet you prevail."

Isobel took a slow look around the garden. "I had best be making my way back now. It was a great piece of folly for me to have ventured out here at night," she said in a lowered voice. "It is against the bounds of all propriety that we are together like this, as well you know."

Chetton picked up the oil lamp, noting as he did so that she had not chosen to contradict him.

CHAPTER TEN

Isobel awoke late the next morning. She immediately marshalled her thoughts towards the previous night in the garden. Chetton's closeness had only seemed appropriate after the direction her earlier contemplations had taken. He brightened her spirit in a way that the stars, for all their glory, could never boast of doing. She had revelled in the nearness of him, the scent and texture of his skin. Hardly daring to believe in her boldness she had continued her visual exploration, the shape and thickness of muscle, the sculptured chin and neck. The strong male beauty of him.

She knew that her behaviour had not been without fault. There was much wilful weakness in the way she had allowed herself to scrutinize Chetton so openly, particularly in her state of undress, unchaperoned and at night. Emma would deliver her a tremendous scold for such a want of maidenly conduct.

A light knock on the door had her diving under the covers. She didn't know whether to answer, or just feign sleep and try to ignore the intrusion. She had never been in such a situation before and was not comfortable with the vulnerable position she had permitted herself to get into.

"Yes," she croaked. It was an ignoble start to the day.

Mrs. McClure entered and placed a cup of hot chocolate on the bedside table. She proceeded to open the curtains wide and turned to smile at Isobel. "Lord Chetton requests you meet him downstairs at your convenience, ma'am."

Stretching out her dressing routine as long as she could, Isobel finally entered the breakfast room, which was occupied only by Lord Chetton.

"Well, my lady, you have finally surfaced." He handed her a cup of tea from the tray on the sideboard. "I know you do not take coffee in the morning, but it is late enough that this could double for your afternoon tea."

The tea was piping hot so he must have ordered it recently. The delicacy of not having a servant present in the room was appreciated and took some of the sting out of his sarcasm. She deigned to throw a thin smile in his direction before getting serious.

"I do not know what to say, Chetton, about last night."

"Before you get yourself into a fluster, everything has been taken care of. Mrs. McClure was told you were up again with Teddy and asked to let you sleep. No one is the wiser. So all you need do now is relax and eat something. There is toast, kedgeree, and fresh fruit from the conservatory. If you want something more substantial I can have it cooked up. You do not need to say anything further. Hurry along, it is beautiful outside and there is somewhere I want to take you."

Chetton was dressed for riding and the tan breeches put his legs into high definition. The riding jacket smoothed over his broad shoulders in an inviting way. To be wicked, she dawdled over choosing her breakfast items. She could see the muscle in Chetton's strong jaw flex. He was so impatient to be off, she couldn't suppress a chuckle.

He cast her a formidable look and advanced towards her.

"Are you playing with me, madame?"

She laughed outright and put up her hands in defence. It was a feeble effort as she was one-handed, her cup and saucer in the other.

※

She looks like a young girl, he thought, catching the flash of mischief in her eyes. When he remembered her distress from yesterday it saddened and maddened him at the same time. Chetton wanted to cup the side of her face as she looked up at him, to feel her skin, which was so fine as to be almost translucent. He itched to run the pad of his thumb over the lush line of her lips before kissing her. It was only the innocent expression she was shining up at him that prevented him from acting on this desire. That, and the possibility that someone would catch them, for he did not want to compromise Isobel's reputation in any way. What moon madness had he been under the influence of last evening to contemplate starting a liaison under his own roof when both his mother and brother were in residence? And furthermore, with a woman who was administering to the health of his godson, for heaven's sake. His behaviour was unprecedented and it appalled him.

Best to leave that as only a fantasy for the present. He took a measured step backwards.

"Do not dawdle, my lady, if you would be so obliging. I will expect you outside in half an hour," he said as he headed out of the room.

※

"I am only five minutes late," Isobel said hurrying down the front steps to the drive. It was really more like fifteen but he let it pass when he saw the look of contrition spread across her face.

"It is a glorious morning. What have you planned?"

It was only then that Chetton took note of her lavender day dress. "I thought from my riding clothes that you would understand. We are going to take advantage of the fine weather and go for a ride."

"Oh, are we?"

He heard a distinct lack of enthusiasm in Isobel's voice and her steps slowed perceptibly.

"You ride, you must do."

"Why must I?"

He stopped walking and tapped his leather riding crop along his thigh a few times. "Are you telling me that you, the daughter of English landed gentry, cannot sit a horse?"

She waved away his comment. "Oh, do not be ridiculous. Of course, I can sit on a horse. As long as someone helps me mount and holds the reins."

"What?"

Isobel shielded her eyes to gaze away at the horizon. "All right, that may have been an exaggeration. But, if you must know, I do not get on with horses very well. They are entirely too big and beastly."

"Beastly? What kind of a mount were you given, an uncut stallion, a destrier, or an old plough horse?"

"Very amusing." Isobel nonchalantly straightened the angle of her bonnet. "It is just that my father, and later my uncle, thought that they would turn the fact that I do not have a natural seat to good account, and save the expense of a horse for me. Anyway, I like to walk."

"Well, that type of penurious bookkeeping is short sighted and not at all acceptable. You should really learn." Seeing the apprehension this brought to her eyes, he hastened to add, "But not now, of course. We will take the gig, it isn't too far."

Her eyes lit up with the excitement of a surprise. "What isn't too far?"

"You will see, my lady." He left to instruct the groom to hitch up the gig for them.

By tacit agreement neither touched further on the events which had unfolded the previous night. In fact, their drive was not punctuated with any undue conversation and they both enjoyed the fine morning air in near silence. Eventually Lord Chetton slowed down and nimbly jumped down from the gig to secure the horse.

"This is our destination, L'Ancresse Bay. I thought it time you should visit the beach with the same name as your cottage, Isobel. What do you think of it?"

Isobel surveyed the large, gently sloping, circular shoreline with its turquoise waters and large expanse of white sand.

"It is beautiful indeed, quite breathtaking. The sand seems to shine from within."

"I believe I was told at some time that the manner in which granite ages and weathers by the sea gives us the white sand you just admired. If I recall correctly, granite releases grains of pure quartz and this makes it glow in the sun." He offered his arm to her but Isobel declined it and set off down the beach with an energetic stride that soon took her close to the water's edge.

After rounding half way around the long beach she found a comfortable seat on a convenient weathered rock and became engaged in watching a group of children play on the beach. The two older ones were running in and out to challenge the pattern of the waves while the other three were building sand castles. From the fond looks and tender aid they received from the man and woman overseeing them, Isobel surmised the couple must be their parents. Their laughter and cries of excitement expressed the happy carefree time they were enjoying.

Chetton caught up shortly but stood apart from her watching the happy family scene for several minutes in silence. She could not help but be reminded of the loss of his wife and son, and wondered at his thoughts. A particularly robust wave made him retreat a few steps and seemed to shake him out of his reverie. He turned towards her, and asked, almost as an afterthought, she felt, "Do you wish to accompany me to the far point of the bay?"

"No, thank you. I am rather comfortable and am happy to take advantage of the view right here." She pulled her straw bonnet further down to shade her face. "Please continue on without me and enjoy your walk."

Without replying he delivered a curt bow, turned, and walked on.

Content to be left alone, Isobel registered the warmth of the sun across her shoulders as she sat by the incoming waves. A sweet lethargy that is often the precursor to sleep stole over her. Current problems, past and present worries were sublimated as thought lost the battle for supremacy. The music of the water melded with birdsong and a fresh sea breeze. Her seat on the wave-worn rock was comfort itself. All in all, such an indulgence of the senses was a welcomed reprieve from the fluster of the previous night and the closeness of the sickroom over the past days.

Her mind could fix on no specific topic but flowered in the cornucopia of physical delight in which she currently found herself. She thought of such times as little gifts from heaven—slices of life not tethered to the mundane realm of day-to-day cares. To ignore or question them seemed an affront to imagination, to the creativity of a rarely magnanimous universe.

For so long she had pushed all feeling away into a corner of herself, creating emptiness in her mind. It had been a refuge and contained all the meagre solace she was likely to get. This void of memory was necessary for her sanity, for any form of wellbeing her future might provide. Her chance for happiness had been ripped from her and was lost forever. This was the absolute wall against which all of her dreams were extinguished.

Today she enjoyed her flight of fancy for what it was, just fantasy. She had always been a realist. Even when she was ill and weakened, she understood that eventually she would have to face the enormity of the truth of things. She had admired the practical way that the healing sisters at the abbey dealt only in facts, in the reality of the present. The demands of the moment while caring for someone were paramount: the concreteness of action, planned and taken. The catch was being able to deal with the consequences of those decisions and living with them.

So, she would enjoy her lush seat by the water and the break in routine that it offered, knowing with certainty that her past was not unblemished. Neither could her future be. It was not sane to seriously entertain the possibility of happiness. Flirting along the edges of insubstantial dreams could prove disastrous.

ঙ৹

Returning from his excursion, Chetton waved as he approached Isobel. "Are you ready to leave your comfortable perch, my lady?"

Isobel blinked against the light sparkling off of the water, and again adjusted the angle of her bonnet. "Mmm, not really, no, but I suppose I must since I have no parasol."

"That is an oversight on my part for not warning you properly beforehand, I am afraid." He offered her his hand and pulled her gently to her feet. "Isobel, while we have this opportunity to be alone, can you tell me about what was distressing you yesterday?"

She gracefully shook the sand off of her skirt and then looked up at a flock of screeching seagulls as they circled overhead.

Chetton took a step closer to her. "I know I was very forward in questioning you."

"Please, I do not wish to revisit any part of it."

"Naturally you do not, however it might be best to do so."

"Lord Chetton. Will you kindly cease this line of conversation immediately? I don't wish to be reminded of the affair."

She turned to walk away but he took an agile step in front of her to stay her retreat.

"Isobel, I must know what was the matter. What is your situation?"

She stamped her foot briskly but ineffectually in the sand.

"Really, this is preposterous! Do you actually intend to continue in this vulgar manner when I have expressed my wishes so strongly for you to desist?"

She strode towards the gig. When he arrived and saw the mutinous look on her face he relented and they drove back in uncomfortable silence.

After their awkward return from the bay Lord Chetton left Isobel at the front steps of La Rocquette. Before handing her down and returning the gig to the stables he apologized and did his best to convince her to dine downstairs with his family that evening. Isobel would not hear of it. He drove off unsatisfied with his handling of the situation. He had not gained any more information from Isobel of a personal nature, nor had he enough details to excuse her arrival and subsequent activities in Guernsey from suspicion. And, to boot, the woman had called him vulgar!

☙

Besides the impropriety of staying too much in the earl's company, Isobel wanted some time away from his commanding presence. She needed to digest the happenings of the previous night and sort out her feelings. To do this, a quiet dinner in Teddy's room seemed a wise choice. Not a retreat, but a choice, she reminded herself.

The problem was her defences were always at half-mast when she was with Chetton. Surprise at herself for having let him flirt with her last evening turned into shock when she realized how much she had enjoyed it. She blushed to think of the scene she had created yesterday when her black memories had invaded. Chetton had accepted it all in stride, his concern solely for her wellbeing. The man's generosity of spirit overwhelmed her. His strength was a sweet succour, healing and life affirming. She could not do justice to the enormity of it. That power lay beyond her.

The whole humiliating experience had come upon her so rapidly she could hardly credit it. It was diminishing to think that so many strong hidden emotions could surface against her will after such a long time. But the power of the past could not be measured solely in hours and days. Some hurts affected the nature of how time was perceived, just as they changed the core of oneself. Those locked away feelings had come to the surface in an unexpected fashion and shaken her to the quick. She had been lost to herself for a time and could not block the images. Her despair was linked to her own weak, fateful decision. She was not a fit companion for the notable diplomat. Yes. That would be how she would think of him, as the powerful, prideful man of the world that he was. It would make her choices much easier if she would learn to relate to him as the Earl of Chetton, rather than as the dark-eyed, graceful man who unsettled her so deeply.

He had position and wealth beyond her imaginings. She was not an acceptable choice for him and did not merit his attention. Her unfortunate past could not be avoided. She knew her place. It was not with him. It was not to be with anyone. The cold fact of that reality must be accepted. She would settle herself to act accordingly, beginning with her removal back to L'Ancresse tomorrow.

It was past time to set a strong guard on her wayward emotions.

She would not fail in this obligation. It was a matter of honour.

CHAPTER ELEVEN

Hell and damnation! Lord Chetton struggled to contain his wrath a few days later. All the tranquility of his morning ride on Duke had been burnt out of him in the last hour as he searched his study to find the French seal entrusted to him by Monsieur Drapeau. He slammed his fist against the cabinet door, took a measured breath, and began again to methodically look for the small metallic press. Where could the infernal thing be? He had specifically placed it on the second shelf behind the three volumes of Cicero's Quotations, knowing them to be of no interest to anyone but himself.

His mother kept the books with which she was currently occupied in her room. When visiting, if Chris grew tired of the *Gentleman's Quarterly* and ventured into the study to peruse the selection, he invariably looked no further than the slim volumes of verse or the larger tomes on agricultural matters. All of the above were located in the main bookshelves and were far removed from this old cabinet.

Lord Chetton heard a shuffle behind him and straightened his bowed back to see Norris watching him.

"Sorry to disturb you, m'lord. I heard a noise in here and thought I'd take a gander to make sure all's well. Can't be too careful these days. I heard tell Farmer LeBlanc see'd some men lurking about his new barn t'other night, but they run off quick like when he called out."

"Everything is fine, Norris, it is just me muddling around. Tell me, you have not moved anything in the old cabinet here, have you?"

Norris looked affronted. "Nay, m'lord, and I haven't! It's only McClure who might be a tidying in here. She'll trust none of the girls to touch your study."

"Quite so. And there has been no one in to visit since Chris and I shared a glass the other evening, has there?"

Norris scuffed his boot along the carpet and concentrated his gaze on the spot.

"Well, then? Have you seen anyone else in the study lately?"

"Ahem."

"Norris? Speak up immediately! It is vital that I know."

His long time servant cast his eyes heavenward as though in confusion. "Now, I didn't actually see her in the room, so to speak, m'lord."

Lord Chetton took another measured breath and remembered how tight lipped the old man could be if he got his back up. "This is important, Norris. Exactly who and what did you see?"

Norris took out his well-used handkerchief and started to snuffle into it. The wary Guernseyman must have caught the glint of warning Chetton was trying to control because he quickly shoved the offending scrap of material into his pocket.

"It were Mrs. Barnestowe. The afternoon of the tea she were standing at the door and just staring inside. Odd, it did seem. Then again, early on the morning she left, before the housemaids were even up and about, there she were coming out of your study, m'lord. Kind of quick like."

This news gave Lord Chetton pause. He looked away from Norris and concentrated on the view of the garden beyond the window. "I see. And she was hurrying? Anything else of note?"

He could hear that Norris had reverted to lightly rubbing his boot on the floor. The old man coughed and waited a few seconds before continuing. "She had something in her shawl. Kind of wrapped up and tucked under her arm, it was."

Chetton was becoming more and more dismayed with each answer. Here was intrigue indeed. "Do you have any guess as to what it might have been?"

Norris harrumphed at this. "I wasn't spying on the little slip of a thing, m'lord! I heard you say she could borrow a book or two if she wanted while being here for poor Teddy. I thought as she'd had a restless night, is all."

"Very likely, Norris. I am certain that explains it. Thank you, that will be all for now."

Norris nodded, did a quick turn, and left the room. Lord Chetton heard him mumbling as he went down the hallway, "We'll have brigands and highwaymen roaming here if we don't watch out. Or worse, Jerseymen, by God!"

Lord Chetton encountered the high-pitched squeal of childish laughter the next afternoon on entering Teddy's room. Norris had informed him that Isobel was visiting Teddy and he didn't want to miss the opportunity to see her. The lower cadence of Isobel's mirth was also in evidence, and it struck Lord Chetton that it was the first time he had heard the lady laugh in such an uninhibited manner. She certainly did so with the abandon of one who had a clear conscience.

The giddy pair had been caught in the act of loading sling shots with bits of paper in order to hit a hastily painted target pinned to the back of the door. The debris landed at Lord Chetton's feet when he entered the room and he looked from one to the other for an explanation.

"Oh, I am so sorry, we did not, of course, mean to hit you!" It appeared Isobel was trying to regain her composure.

"Yes, we did. We heard footsteps and thought it was you, sir," said the young conspirator.

This brought on another fit of the giggles as the culprits looked at each other in shock.

"Teddy, you little traitor. We were not supposed to let him know our plan." Isobel stooped to clean up the mess of paper projectiles.

"But Miss Isobel," said Teddy in a side whisper, "you always have to tell him the truth."

Looking not the least contrite, Isobel shrugged her shoulders. "Perhaps, but I am convinced we should not have made it so easy for him."

"To think I have a conspiracy brewing right under my nose," Lord Chetton spoke with exaggerated gravity. The irony that this might indeed be the case was not lost on him. "Now that I am aware that the crime was intentional, the penalty will be greater, you know."

Teddy trilled a scream and dove under the covers.

Careful to avoid the injured little arm, Lord Chetton shook the bundle under the quilt. "You, young man, will have to suffer two pieces of Mrs. McClure's apple tart for your tea."

Turning towards Isobel, Lord Chetton was struck with an idea. "And you, madame, for your part will have to endure my company for at least two dances at the upcoming ball."

Isobel stopped collecting the rubbish, and stood to face him. "Oh, dear. I had not planned to attend, not after all the business this last while. I have barely been home in a fortnight."

Lord Chetton turned the full penetration of his gaze upon Isobel. He was no longer smiling. Attending the ball would give him the opportunity to converse with her in public. It had been his experience that trying to elicit information from people often worked better when they least expected questions and could not run or cause a scene.

"I am hoping you will change your mind; in fact, I am depending on it. You deserve an evening of entertainment, and it would be my pleasure to provide it for you."

"But really, I am not certain that I should."

"No, consider it all settled. You cannot decline. My mother has everything arranged, and I know she anticipates your presence. I am sure you would not want to disappoint her." He was warming to the idea and wanted her to agree to attend. He took a step towards her, and said quietly, "Please, Isobel, do come."

Teddy popped his head up from the covers and watched the two adults intently. He knew something serious was being discussed.

Isobel glanced his way and smiled. On impulse she said, "Well, all right then, if you put it that way. I will be delighted to attend."

"And don't forget the dances you owe him," put in Teddy.

"No, madame, you must not forget those!"

The evening of the ball came and Chetton was pleased to be in residence with his mother and brother. It was a rare occurrence that they were all in Guernsey at the same time and not spread across their estates in England or enjoying the end of the season in London. After a day of ceaseless activity with tradesmen's carts pulling up and servants of all manner bustling here and there on errands, La Rocquette shone with beeswax and elbow grease. The scent of freshly cut Guernsey lilies sweetened the air, candelabras were aglow and musicians at the ready. His mother's planning, coupled with Mrs. McClure and her domestic army, had outdone themselves with sumptuous refreshments and all the guests were prepared to have a grand evening. Lord Chetton had the added interest of claiming his dances with Isobel.

When he first saw her she was talking to an ancient vessel of a man, what was his name, Durant or something? Her attention was focused on the chatty fossil and so he could indulge in a moment of inconspicuous staring. The dress suited her both in colour and form. The green silk was several degrees lighter in shade than emerald and subtly complemented her fascinating eyes and fair complexion. Her honey blonde hair was up in one of those complicated styles that defied gravity, and ringlets softly framed her face. What was that old fool going on about, wanting to secure her for the waltz?

Not on his watch! He moved to intercede.

"So good of you to come, Durant. I see that you have met the fair Mrs. Barnestowe. Wonderful, and do remember to ask Norris for the burgundy. I was thinking of you when we brought it up from the cellar, old chap." Without waiting for a reply he manoeuvred his way beside Isobel. "Good evening and welcome to our spring ball. I hope it is only the first of many you attend." Then, for her hearing only, he added, "You look magnificent."

Isobel pursed her lips at the second comment and bid him good evening in return.

"Teddy sends you a message to buck up and pay your dues tonight, madame. He was very brave in taking his apple tart punishment."

"Yes, I am quite prepared to make reparations for my evil ways and will be at your disposal."

He was satisfied with Isobel's ready compliance to fulfill her debt of honour to him. "I can hear the strings tuning up, would you accompany me now and we can take our first dance?"

Chetton took Isobel's elbow and negotiated the maze of people to enter the dance floor just as the music began. He had called in a favour from the commanding officer at Castle Coronet and The Royal Guernsey Militia Band had been engaged for the evening. Isobel fit into his arms entirely too well. Her first few steps were taken tentatively, as if she were unused to the pattern and to him.

She glanced quickly around the room and her cheeks began to tinge with pink.

"Do not worry, Isobel, everyone always watches who I have the first few dances with. After that they attend to their own business."

"I am sure it is something that you have grown used to and take no notice of, but I find it very uncomfortable, to be sure. And being partnered for this particular dance, well, I must attend to my steps lest I put us both to shame."

He happily pulled her just that shade closer, his arm secure at her waist to help her manage the next steps. Their difference in height meant Isobel's head barely reached his shoulder. He thought he caught a shy smile but it was impossible to be sure with the angle of her head canted down and away from him. He moved his hand to more fully join her slender fingers with his.

He had cleverly arranged to dance the one and only waltz of the evening with Isobel. With the repressive view that the large Methodist population on Guernsey held towards dancing generally, it was daring to feature the waltz in the dancing program. Much to his surprise and delight, his mother had suggested they be the first on the island to be so bold. She explained to him that being born at La Rocquette and her genealogy established her credentials of respectability more so than if she was just a temporary leaseholder. And in any case, she added, her dear islanders needed to be shaken up occasionally in their adherence to their restrictive old-fashioned ways. After Chris had kissed his mother's cheek and Chetton had said bravo to her, there was no turning back.

Isobel did not engage in the idle chitchat that so many dance partners thought necessary to the dance ritual. This rather intrigued him, and was in fact a boon on several levels. It afforded him the opportunity to revel in the clean sweet smell of her, marvel at the lustre of her convoluted mass of curls and, most importantly, direct the conversation.

"Do you miss the dashing blue and gold, Isobel?"
"Beg pardon?"
"Of the men."
"The blue and gold of the men?" she repeated.
"Yes."
"I am sorry, but I am afraid that I am not following you. Or do you mean that since the French Revolution men favour sober colours in their evening fashions? Which, if you will permit me, I think allows ladies' apparel to sparkle all the more?"

He thought she must be intimidated indeed not to catch his blatant reference to the vibrant hue that British Naval officers' uniforms usually added to such festivities.

"Well, although I acknowledge your bit of feminine wisdom, Isobel, that is not at all what I meant. I was referring to the fact that even in Portsmouth, I dare say, the officers chanced a dance or two."

Isobel smiled vaguely at him and the bloom deepened across her face in the most charming way.

As a seasoned campaigner with women, he was at a loss to explain the chaos she incited in him. He was used to the subtle exchanges between the sexes that often harboured not so subtle relationships. With Isobel at times he felt as awkward as a raw youth. That thought rankled and he smoothly brought the hand holding hers to rest over his heart. This time he saw her mouth make a little moue of surprise but she registered her disapproval in no other way.

"I take it you have not had the opportunity to dance for some time."

He watched as she unsuccessfully tried to tamp down the fluster she displayed at every mention of her past life. It was one of the many things that confused him about her and gave him pause. It was difficult to believe that she harboured the capacity to be successful at subterfuge. And yet to be found at the door of his study just when the seal went missing seemed hard to explain.

"No, I have not."

"How long have you been out into society after your period of mourning? Only a short while, surely?"

"It has been a little over a year now, I suppose. But please, I do not want to think about that tonight."

Chetton bowed slightly to indicate he would acquiesce to her wishes and they paused to take a breath during the brief intermission before the next dance began. He felt it prudent to tread lightly. Action was best suited to a complete understanding of a situation.

CHAPTER TWELVE

Despite her earlier uncertainty about going to the ball, Isobel had anticipated the evening's entertainment with excitement. She assured herself this had everything to do with the fit of her new gown and nothing at all to do with the prospect of dancing with Lord Chetton.

Although she was a realist at heart, she did indulge in embroidering life with colourful elements of good fortune if they came her way. The trouble was that she appreciated serendipity, that often quirky and surprising aspect that defied explanation. It laid the foundations for flights of fancy and Isobel was ever a ready participant to this type of mental escape. Her entire relationship with Lord Chetton from the first meeting contained the seeds of ungovernable circumstance. Part coincidence, part wilful persistence, he had come to her real and imagined aid several times. It was these seeming happenstances that unnerved her.

She knew not what to think of her feelings for the man. He was unlike anyone she had ever met.

It was difficult to deny he fascinated her. His warm good looks, easy nature and irreverent humour were meant to captivate, and did. He was the very image of civility with his polite manners and fine speech. The cut of his expensive clothes bespoke a high sense of style that enhanced his masculine attributes. His smile, the appreciative glances he bestowed on her, his attentive manner all contributed to his easy grace. And yet, the man was dangerous. She felt the truth of this on a level that defied any ready explanation.

He also reached her on a physical level that she had not contemplated was possible. She was very aware of his potent masculinity as he escorted her to the side of the ballroom after their second dance. But then she ruthlessly reminder herself of the impossibility of developing a *tendre* for the man, despite the exquisite feeling of being whisked around the room in his arms during the "wicked" waltz.

"By the way, I have been meaning to ask you," said Chetton as he stood next to her when the music ended, "did you find a book that entertained you?"

She could not think what he meant. In the enchantment of the moment she had not followed his rapid segue and shook her head.

"The other morning, you were looking for something in my study. One of the books on the history of Guernsey we had spoken about, was it?"

Now the incident came crashing back into her memory. She was so sure no one had witnessed her clandestine visit to Lord Chetton's study. Without doubt no one would guess at the nature of her mission. It was not possible to betray the confidence, so she merely smiled.

"Oh dear, it is rather close in here. Could you excuse me, please? I think I need a few moments in the ladies' parlour."

Lord Chetton stared at her for a moment before agreeing to her request. He could hardly do otherwise. Fortunately they were at the edge of the ballroom floor and he directed her expertly to the door she required.

After a quarter of an hour's rest Isobel returned to the main rooms. She was not at a loss for partners the rest of the evening. It was rather wonderful. And perhaps, she admitted to herself, a little unexpected. She was not used to being fussed over and there were several young men who were pleased to show her attention as the new woman in their small social circle. It had been so long since Isobel had danced that she could measure it in years, much to her chagrin. Her youth, her modest season had been pre-empted, cut permanently, if the truth be told, by her plight.

Isobel had been whirled and twirled to the point that her feet felt pinched in her new dancing slippers and she coveted a moment's respite. Philippe someone or other was to provide her with refreshment on the balcony and she welcomed the cooler air as she looked for a place to discreetly wiggle her toes for a moment while waiting. It was not long before she heard footsteps approach. She had closed her eyes for a few seconds as she rested on the bench. She felt a cup being placed in her hand, and without opening her eyes she said, "Thank you, Philippe."

Unaccountably, the cup was hastily removed. Her eyes flew open and she beheld Lord Chetton's scowling face looking down at her.

"Sorry to disappoint you, but as you see, I am not Philippe."

"Oh, dear. Am I in your bad books again so soon!" She could not suppress a giggle. "If I say that I am desperately sorry, will you give me back my drink?" she said, not feeling in the least contrite.

She noted Chetton's eyes as they roved over her form. They seemed to take in all of the silk and lace and lingered on her shoulders and neck. She sat up straighter.

"I think I will need more than that to convince me."

Isobel ignored his comment and reached for the cup. "Well, I have already danced with you and paid that debt. I cannot think of what else you might require."

He seated himself on the bench. Leaning towards her, he whispered out of the side of his mouth. "I could help you there. I have a few suggestions on the matter."

She froze for a moment as the possibilities of his remark washed over her. Then Lord Chetton broke out in an unrestrained chuckle, his brown eyes beaming, as guileless as a young child. He was very aware that he had shocked her and was very pleased with himself. Really, the man was incorrigible.

She took a sip of the aromatic punch. "Whatever have you done with poor Philippe?"

"Poor Philippe? I am astounded you can remember his name after the hordes you have been dancing with. Have you enjoyed being the reigning belle of the ball tonight?"

"Come now, you exaggerate, my lord, there were not that many, and Philippe is a sweet boy."

"I have known 'poor Philippe' since he was a youth but I am becoming less and less fond of him by the moment. He has been dispatched on an errand for Lady Williams, I believe, but if you continue to go on about him I shall change it to the coal cellar."

Lord Chetton glanced up at the sky and inhaled a deep breath of the evening air. "What were you doing in France when we first met, Isobel?"

She swallowed her sip of punch with some difficulty and took a moment to pat her mouth with the linen napkin "My goodness, that is an odd question. Why do you ask?"

"Oh, no particular reason. It just seems like an unusual time to travel, especially unaccompanied."

Isobel had a practiced answer for this.

"Well, generally speaking, I needed some time to come to terms with the changes in my life. I had not the least reason to stay in England any longer and desired an abrupt change in scenery. My abigail was with me, naturally, but was called home for a death in the family. I knew I would be cared for at L'Ancresse and decided to do the crossing by myself. Unfortunately, I had not anticipated such a delay at St. Malo."

Isobel moved to the edge of the balcony and set the empty cup down on the wide stone balustrade. She turned and saw Chetton had followed closely in her wake. She hated the lies and falsehoods and wished to be beyond the point in her mission where they were necessary.

The crunch of gravel as a carriage was brought around to the entrance below drew her attention. Isobel watched as a gentleman assisted two ladies to enter. Another man standing partly in shadow lit a pipe. From this distance the momentary flare of light cast his face into sinister relief. All these people were complete strangers to her.

It was a vivid reminder that she was the outsider here and had to keep her own council. She must not let down her guard to anyone.

"Lord Chetton, I just wanted to tell you that I have had a lovely evening. It is my first soiree since coming out of mourning. I certainly have had enough excitement for the evening and am ready to retire. Thank you for your attentiveness. I was afraid at first that I would not feel as though I belonged here."

෴

Lord Chetton moved closer. "Do you mean in Guernsey?" He enveloped her hands in a light embrace. "Or here in my home?"

The fact that she did not immediately withdraw pleased him inordinately. It felt so damned good to be close to her but he could not let that delight cloud the bigger issue at hand. Although he was not happy to use her vulnerability against her, he did want to press his advantage. Who knew when he would get another opportunity?

Earlier in the evening, as he watched Isobel twirl around the floor with other guests, he had cursed the dictates of custom that prevented him from sharing only those two dances with her. Whether his actions were for patriotic reasons, or more pleasurable ones, he had not wanted to wager a bet. The only certainty was that any more public attention paid to her would flaunt etiquette and be tantamount to a declaration of interest between the two of them.

For the moment they were alone on the balcony, and he took the opportunity to shift closer to Isobel. Almost immediately she began to resist and push away from him. He felt it as a delayed reaction, as if Isobel's response was the one she thought she should have had, rather than a true representation of her reaction to him. If she had been sent to seduce him she was missing a grand opportunity.

Yet it was now clearly her wish to be let alone and so he released her with a brief shudder of annoyance. He felt like a thirsty man long denied a drink and then forced to contend with being teased about the possibility of having one.

Isobel moved away abruptly. "I am sorry," she said, not looking at him.

Lord Chetton had rarely been so conflicted in his assessment of a person's character. It amazed him that despite needing to solve the question of the missing seal he also wanted to spare Isobel any unnecessary embarrassment, recognizing the rashness was on his part.

"I suppose I should be the one to say that."

He heard Isobel's rapid breathing. No, it was more like she was blowing out little measured puffs of air to calm herself.

"Isobel?"

She put her hands up to her flushed cheeks and closed her eyes briefly. When she opened them to look at Lord Chetton they were still partially hooded, whether from nervousness or another emotion he couldn't name.

"I am out of all patience with you, my lord! You are very forward with the liberties you take. Indeed, I cannot think why this should be the case, for I believe that I have in no way encouraged them." She fiddled with the tiny pearl buttons on her glove for a moment, refusing to look in his direction. "I must pay my respects to your mother. Good night." With this she walked across the balcony and back towards the ballroom.

"Isobel. I do not want you to think this is finished between us.

Not for a moment."

She straightened her shoulders and marched back inside without acknowledging his comment. Her skirts swayed in the same manner they had when he had first met her. Delightful.

He left the balcony but was delayed in following Isobel across the ballroom by the immediate demands of his guests. He found himself ushered into conversation with a brace of young ladies by the expedient of a nearby matron holding onto his elbow. His eyes followed Isobel through the crowd as she exited the room and he twice had to beg the pardon of the ladies to repeat what they were saying to him. Confound the awkwardness of having to play host.

CHAPTER THIRTEEN

It was a quiet time for the Dowager at La Rocquette on the following day, although a busy day of recovery for the help. Lady Chetton preferred to let the capable Mrs. McClure and her staff get on with it and drove over to L'Ancresse to visit Isobel. Isobel and Lady Chetton had a convivial afternoon tea together, and much like Isobel used to do with Emma the night after a ball, shared their impressions of the evening in all of its many intricacies. When Lady Chetton rose to leave the room, she turned to address Isobel again.

"That reminds me, I have been entrusted to give you this from a certain little rascal who thought it more exciting if I delivered it to you personally," said Lady Chetton as she handed her a thick wad of folder paper tied rather crookedly with a pink ribbon. "Teddy eschewed the idea of an envelope, thinking you should much prefer the ribbon embellishment."

"Oh, how sweet. Thank him for me, will you please." Isobel untied the ribbon and opened the small bundle. A squashed and not quite dried lily fell out and Isobel read the wobbly printing.

Dear Miss Isobel,

You are kindly ~~invitd~~ invited to come for a very fun ride out on the bay with me to thank you for making me so jolly when I was sick. Do not worry, my goodfather will do the rowing and sailing part. There will be a picnic lunch. Please come this Thursdee at elevn oh clock.

Master Teddy

Isobel could not disappoint the boy and arrived at La Rocquette as the invitation directed. Teddy was oblivious to the admonitions placed on him by the concerned staff to take care of himself. He had pestered Norris about the weather until the old man retreated to the stables for a moment of respite to smoke his pipe in peace.

Lord Chetton had spent most of his formative summers sailing with his brother around the island's many bays and coves. Nestled all around Guernsey were perilous grey rocks that formed a broken ring of hidden passages and spiky outcroppings. The lives of untold men had been lost in storms or doomed by an unwary crew in these formidable waters.

But today was warm and clear, the sky a bright periwinkle blue. Norris had prophesized that the sea would be docile till sundown, if not beyond, and the tides were aligned for a perfect launch into the bay. The passengers were loaded into the vessel and Chetton rowed them out to deeper water before setting the sail on the small craft.

"Isn't the *Faithful* grand, miss?" said Teddy beaming a smile at her.

Isobel latched onto the side of the boat with the rise and dip of a larger-than-expected wave. "It is as fine a craft as I have ever been on," she agreed.

"Your grandfather had it built for you as a present for your sixteenth birthday. Isn't that right, sir?" asked Teddy from the prow.

"Yes, it is," Lord Chetton said, then winked at Isobel. "Teddy, do you remember what I am called at sea."

"You are the captain, are you?" Isobel intervened.

Teddy cast a worried glance at her. "No, Miss Isobel, he is the admiral."

Isobel pressed her lips together to stop the giggle rising in her throat and thanked the serious boy for the correction. Chetton looked at her and raised his cap.

Isobel was trying, rather unsuccessfully, to quell the effect on her senses of the dashing nautical figure that Chetton presented. The sea breeze ruffled his thick dark hair, which only served to accentuate the masculine lines of his face, as his strong arms manoeuvred the boat through the waves.

"Oh, I am so sorry, I had no knowledge of your elevated rank, Admiral. How remiss of me."

"Thank you, I do not stand on ceremony. But, I must ask, Isobel, are you quite well?"

Isobel nodded in affirmation.

"It is just that you will get cramp if you continue with that death grip for much longer."

Isobel continued her white knuckled hold on the side of the boat. Teddy patted her hand. "It's all right, miss, sometimes I'm not such a good sailor. One time I even upchucked my—"

"Yes, that will be quite enough seafaring tales for now, Teddy. Do not worry, Isobel, we are just going round the point to the next cove. There is a lovely view from the top of the cliff walk and the scramble up is not too difficult with the tide as it is."

Isobel was happy with this information and it proved to be accurate. They ascended to the apex of the cliff by a rough stairway cut into the rock. The first few steps were made awkward by seaweed on the rocks and the spray they continuously received from the stronger waves, but then the going got easier. Teddy dashed ahead of them, calling out directions or information of some kind, but his voice was carried away from them. She could understand nothing except the fact that he was having a wonderful time and had regained some of his childish vigour.

Isobel stopped to catch her breath. She was winded from the climb and this made her wobble on the last uneven step. Lord Chetton reached out his arms to assist her and then she felt herself being lifted in the air and set on her feet beside him. She marvelled at the latent strength in his shoulders and upper body, and the casual use of it for her benefit.

Reaching the top of the stairs afforded them a grand outlook to the neighbouring bays. Lord Chetton pointed out a few stalwart fishing boats bobbing on the blue green water.

"What is that little island so close to us?"

"That is Herm. It is only inhabited by a few hardy souls and then just during the warm months."

"What about the other islands?"

He pointed to the east. "Less than an hour sail from here on a keen wind is Sark. We call it the little sister of Guernsey. Further east is Jersey."

Isobel looked in the direction Lord Chetton indicated.

"Jersey, yes, that makes sense. We stopped there briefly on my trip here."

"Jersey and Guernsey are arch rivals, you understand. Do not, for heaven's sake, broach the subject of Jersey with Norris unless you wish to hear a tirade of stories dealing with their inferior natures."

"Thank you, my lord, I am well warned now."

"Beyond that is the Normandy coast of France. We are almost directly across from St. Malo, where I had the good fortune to meet you."

Isobel smiled at the remembrance.

"Then a little to the north is Alderney. It is rather sparse and barren."

Isobel nodded. "The water around Guernsey is a perfect aquamarine, so different from the dull brown of the Thames and most of the North Sea."

"Yes, it is very different from those bodies of water. And of course, if you head west for a few months, the Atlantic Ocean will take you all the way to North America."

They turned to follow Teddy's path and, in a few minutes, they were seated far enough back from the cliff top to avoid most of the wind. Isobel happily played Mum to the two males as she passed out Mrs. McClure's roast beef sandwiches and thick wedges of Guernsey gâche, the island's version of rich fruit cake. It was not long before Teddy's eyes started to flutter shut as his full belly and the warmth of the sun worked their magic. Isobel drew him up against her and settled his head on her lap with a whispered, "Shush, sleep now, angel."

She noticed Lord Chetton was staring at her in a very fixed way. He seemed remote and unapproachable, as if she and Teddy were complete strangers, and she wondered if she had unwittingly offended him in some way. Then it occurred to her that perhaps it wasn't indifference, but a deep sadness over the loss of his family that caused him to regard her with if not animosity, then at least with seeming disdain. Although it made her uncomfortable and, she could admit, a little hurt, she forgave him utterly for the melancholy.

∽

Lord Chetton's heart took a funny little turn at the endearment and the sweet picture the two of them made. He was tempted to think, *this should have been my life*, but the old familiar darkness was too bitter for him to really believe it. Even the warmth and light of this fine day could not protect him against the remembrance of his savage loss. He rose and looked down on his little craft to ensure it was still safely beached, though this did nothing to dispel his excess energy.

Isobel's puzzlement at his restlessness showed on her face. He attempted a smile to waylay her concern, but he didn't believe the perceptive lady was fooled by his diversion. He was thankful when she began an ordinary conversation.

"I spent some time with your brother at the ball. He was very attentive."

"Yes, that is Chris all over."

"He told me he has a townhouse in London and his own estate in Surrey, but, like you, his heart is in Guernsey. Does he mirror you in other ways?"

Lord Chetton was unsure what Isobel meant by this unusually direct question.

"Well, true, I am also very attached to Guernsey. The island is in our blood, I suppose. But other than that, he is his own man."

"He was not tempted by the diplomatic services though? I was given to understand that your family has a distinguished history there."

"Yes, there is a rather long tradition of service to our country that I am proud to be a part of." He laughed. "But Chris is too clever to follow in my steps. He is much more practical than that, more of a gentleman farmer, and of course this suits nicely with him being the second son."

"A handsome man with such aplomb and address not yet married must be coveted at all the London soirees by both the young ladies and their mamas. Unless there is already a lady who has captured his particular attention, I wonder?"

"No, there is not a particular one at present, I believe." Chetton took a deep breath of the fresh sea air. "Though my mother would gladly have us both attach ourselves to someone. It is a never ending campaign of hers, however I am sure the same could be said of most mothers."

Isobel stroked the straw-coloured hair back from Teddy's forehead. Her gentleness with the boy was very appealing to him. It stood in stark contrast to most of the women he spent time with, who filled their days pursing only their own satisfaction.

"Do you like what you do? Travelling to other countries and meeting with so many different people?"

"It is what I was introduced to a long time ago."

"I was going to say it sounds very exciting, but I suppose that is a naive view." She sighed. "Things are really never as straightforward as they first seem."

"You are correct there. I do gain a degree of satisfaction from what I do, at least some of the time. At other times it all seems rather like a game played by spoiled children and uncertain rules."

Isobel squinted her eyes slightly as if he had surprised her, as well he might have, because he had bloody well surprised himself. He did not divulge his mixed feelings to people and never to a woman he was attracted to, let alone suspicious of. To date, this had been a nonissue, since none of his paramours had been remotely interested in his affairs outside of the bedroom. Jean would think him besotted!

"What are you working on now? Anything that I have read about in the papers, or is what you do always behind closed doors?"

Lord Chetton was used to this kind of a question and felt on firmer ground. Gents that had had too much to drink often asked him this when he was at one of his clubs in London. The younger ones thought about issues mainly in terms of cloak and dagger missions, the more seasoned knew by now not to waste their breath on any serious line of inquiry. He wondered if Isobel was asking about his work for a different reason.

"A great deal of what I do is tedious, reading reports, writing proposals, and that kind of thing. Much too boring to interest a charming young woman such as yourself."

He could see by the pursing of her lips that she was not to be put off by his vague response, although she continued to look down at Teddy. He was fascinated by the way she continued to smooth the curly hair of the sleeping boy and had to listen carefully to catch her words.

"Well, I certainly deserve that patronizing set down for being so inquisitive, do I not, my lord?"

"I beg pardon, Isobel, I did not mean to be so blatantly condescending," he sat back down beside her, "but I would much prefer learning about you. So, you have been on Guernsey for a while now. What do you think about our island?"

"I believe I like it even more than I had hoped I would. It is very picturesque. So pretty in fact that I think as a member of an old island family you must be fishing for a compliment."

He laughed at that. "Tell me, do you not miss your family?"

"I do not have much of a family left to speak of."

"No family?"

"There is only an estranged uncle and cousin. I have not been in touch with them for some time." Isobel started to fold the napkins and collect the plates they had used. She struggled with the clasp on the wicker hamper until it popped open and then returned items to the basket in a hurried manner.

"And from your husband's side, there is no one with whom you associate, no connections that you keep?"

Isobel leaned over the sleeping form of Teddy to retrieve a napkin.

"Could you hand me that plate, please, I do not want to leave anything behind. This is a lovely set, from Fortnum and Mason, is it not? They do put together some fine sets. And their tea puts Twinings' to shame."

Lord Chetton gave her a pointed look. "Now I fear it is my turn to apologize again, Isobel. You never mention your family relations. Tell me, why did you decide to come to Guernsey, if you do not have any particular connections here?"

"Oh, I do not know, really. After the loss of my husband, I was trying to find my new place in the world, I suppose. I closed my eyes and put my finger on the map and Guernsey it was!" She grinned up at him. "I think I will wake Teddy now so we can be on our way. We would not want to compromise the boy by keeping him out too long just as he is on the mend, now would we?"

Lord Chetton reluctantly ceded to her suggestion and they were soon on their way back to the boat. He had failed again to fill in any meaningful history of Isobel's past or ascertain a credible reason for her to be on the island. Her easy response seemed as capricious as the vagaries of a seagull's flight.

CHAPTER FOURTEEN

Chetton sent an urgent message to Jean upon his return home. Directing the activities of the French politicians was proving to be more difficult than anticipated. He needed a meeting with Jean to update the situation. Chetton knew he had been dragging his feet over the issue but it was time to act. He didn't wish to absent himself from Guernsey now, especially as issues with Isobel were not clear, but he had little choice in the matter. He met Jean a few days later at a tavern in Le Havre in Normandy. Usually Jean was pleased to rendezvous in Le Havre, as the large harbour was the location of one of his most profitable import-export warehouses. As such, it was also a crossroads for his vast network of information gatherers up and down the French coast, which provided him with a lucrative second trading commodity.

But this time Jean was furious. It showed in his dishevelment.

His fire red hair, the bane of his existence, usually pulled back neatly and held with a leather thong, was now unkempt. It protruded in spiky thatches all over his head as if he had been pulling at it by the very roots. His jabot was soiled, his jacket buttons misaligned. Most unsettling to Chetton was the fact that he had repeatedly declined the offer of a drink. Just the thought of Jean as a teetotaller made Chetton want to down several large brandies immediately.

Jean leaned his head against his hand and stared at Chetton.

"You remember La Rue?"

"Of course. Michel La Rue. He is the intermediary we have been using between Drapeau and the compromised French politicians."

"I 'ave told you that Drapeau had not been in contact with me for some time, heh?"

"Yes, and that you were worried something was amiss," agreed Chetton. Surprised at Jean's loss of *sang-froid*, Chetton kept his own concerns that La Rue might have disappeared with the bribe money to himself for the moment.

Jean launched off into a volley of French vulgarity that included both the Virgin Mary and the devil, and was accompanied by vehement gesticulations.

"Again, Jean, but calmly this time, what have you heard that is so distressing?"

"I 'ave not heard it, I 'ave seen it! La Rue's dead body, hung and left to rot in his own house."

"What? Who would have done that? Christ! Would La Rue have told anybody about your involvement, Jean?"

"*C'est possible, mais . . .*"

"It's possible, but what?"

Jean lowered his voice. "*Merde, mon ami.* It's more likely that he spoke about you. There are rumours circulating. La Rue told me a few weeks ago that 'e had learned someone is spreading threats against you. 'E was not always strong in his loyalty, perhaps, maybe . . ."

"Maybe what, Jean? What are you thinking?"

Jean threw up his hands. "That 'e gave you up and was of no more use, so they kill him as a warning!"

Chetton digested this information. It was not the first time that people would benefit from his demise. He usually didn't receive a deliberate announcement of their intentions, however. The latest communiqué from England implored him to proceed carefully, but the directive was clear. The Ministry wanted assurances about whether or not the French king was in jeopardy. But it was imperative there be no compromise or duplicity traceable back to him or his activities. His duty was clear, but the path to success was proving to be elusive.

"If the threat is directed at me personally, do you think it means that Touché is involved? This might not have anything to do with politics at all, Jean."

"Well, that would be a 'andy explanation, *mon ami, mais* I am not sure I believe it. I haven't been able to find out the source of the violent threats, but they have one thing in common, and let's just say things don't end well for you either."

Chetton did not like the slide into violence that La Rue's death had started. He was not at all against the use of physical altercation or murder if the need arose, but as a final solution only. The use of extreme force was often clumsy, the end results unsure. It did not produce loyalty and often led to further problems or the desire for revenge. Keeping business firmly in the realm of money, power, and greed was easier to manage; the outcomes more predictable.

"Well, we will leave that aside for now. What do your sources tell you about the mood in Paris?"

"You will 'ave heard about the latest riot? The mob was stirred into a ghoulish frenzy again by the rising cost of food," said Jean, the shadow in his one good eye deepening with reflections of his own.

"That is not unexpected since the money to compensate people for their nationalized lands comes at the expense of the bourgeois who hold those devalued government bonds."

"*Oui*. Yes, I agree, it is a recipe baked perfectly to alienate King Charles."

"Jean, I have more bad news, I was about to write it to you, but it is safer telling you face to face. The bloody French seal Drapeau was so pleased to present to me for future use has gone missing."

"Stolen?"

"I have to concede that it must have been, and right from its hiding place in my study."

Jean frowned at this development. "Nothing else was taken?"

"Not that I know of."

"So someone knew what they were looking for, it wasn't 'ow you say . . . random."

"That is my fear."

"*Merde*! Do you suspect anyone in particular?"

Chetton rubbed his hand across his forehead, and blew out a breath.

Jean banged his fist down on the table with blistering force. "*Oui*, there is someone?"

"Blast it, I don't know, not for certain. There is a woman, a young widow, who was staying at La Rocquette to help look after Teddy in his illness."

"What makes you think it might 'ave been her?"

"I don't necessarily think it was her. It is just that she had full access to the house and was seen coming out of my study early one morning."

Jean started to shake his head.

"Before you jump to conclusions, my mother trusts her and asked her to stay on. I am making inquiries about her deceased husband, and as he was a military man, I doubt his wife is a planted spy. Anyway, she doesn't seem the type. Too timid, too fragile . . ."

"Too beautiful." Jean finished for him.

"Well, she is lovely, but you can't fault her for that."

"*Jesu*, I told you Touché was thought to have sent someone, probably a woman?"

"I remember, Jean, I remember. And may I remind you that it is spring and, as every year, we probably hire half a dozen young women to help with the cleaning and social events. I am just not certain Isobel is the one, and Teddy's injury was a random event. As well, she is very unworldly and naive."

"*Fantastique*! And what do you know of her other than her beauty and supposed innocence?"

Trying to ignore his friend's sarcasm, Lord Chetton continued as patiently as he could. "She is not from Guernsey. It was probably just happenstance, but I met her in France waiting to sail."

Jean muttered something that sounded suspiciously like, "'Appenstance? Another stupid English word."

Chetton took a drink, rather than the verbal bait. "Well, I do not think you can reasonably assume she controls the weather, Jean. It was storming, for God's sake, and she was clearly upset about the delay. I approached her first, she wanted nothing to do with me."

"That you know of."

He cast his friend a dirty look.

"So she has been in France as well! Do you know anything else about her? Her background, family?"

Chetton realized, had realized for some time, in fact, that he had very conflicting feelings about Isobel. He did not entirely trust her, for he gave no woman that power over him, but he also felt unaccountably protective of her. It annoyed him that he could not answer Jean's questions with more equanimity.

"As I have said, she is a widow and has come to the island to recover from her loss. She has no family to speak of, and does not know anyone there."

Jean gave a great shrug of his shoulders. "*Mon Dieu*, this only improves!"

They sat in silence for a few moments. Jean shoved his hand roughly though his unruly hair again. Chetton noted the emotion simmering in his French friend with dismay.

"You had best vent your spleen, Jean. Go ahead and call me a fool."

"*Non, non, mon ami.* I 'ave said all I can on the matter. Just take caution. Keep the woman close and watch her carefully."

"I intend to. Do not doubt my resolve in this. I will be ready to act, and act ruthlessly, if I am wrong and she is playing me for a fool."

Jean nodded. "So, there is not much more I 'ave to say except be on your guard. If I discover who butchered La Rue I will take care of it myself. Keep out of France for a while, *mon ami*; it will be safer for you. And that goes for your brother as well. Adieu, and may God stay with you."

Chetton nodded in farewell but remained seated after Jean took his leave. The death of La Rue weighed on him. It was not that he had particularly liked or admired Michel La Rue, he had not, but the man had, at his bidding, attempted a task that may have led directly to his death. He could live with the fact. La Rue was a mercenary and had been aware of the risks he took for the considerable gain he received. But it meant Chetton's own enemies had taken a step closer to him, and that he was not prepared to accept without retaliation.

Seeing the situation through Jean's eyes had forced an unwanted weight of suspicion on the matter. Despite what he wanted to be true, perhaps Isobel was not an innocent; perhaps she was there to do someone's bidding.

He hoped to God for both their sakes this was not the case.

Yet, he could no longer reasonably give her the benefit of the doubt. She had not given a credible accounting of herself or many of her actions. Christ, all he needed was another woman who wanted to use him, manipulate his emotions. He had thought, had wanted, that part of his life to be over.

Well, by God he would see to it that it was! He was the master strategist and this young beauty, as vulnerable as she seemed, would not deceive him.

The week of Lord Chetton's absence passed slowly for Isobel on Guernsey. The weather had been inclement with heavy rains and wind but this morning had dawned brighter and warmer. Isobel was desperate for an excursion after being forced to stay inside and planned a visit to the ruins on Lihou Island. Benedictine monks from Mont-Saint-Michel, on the Normandy coast, had started St Mary's Priory there in the 1200s. She would share a ride with Victor along the west coast as he had business in Castel and at the end of the day he would return to take her home. This gave Isobel several hours to cross the causeway linking the tiny island to Guernsey and visit the old remains.

Helene had wrapped a fresh meat pastie for Isobel's lunch and placed it in a small basket. Isobel usually liked to walk unencumbered but today the basket suited her plans as she had her sketchbook and pastels, and intended to try her hand at drawing what remained of the ancient site. Victor left her at the side of the path leading down to the beach, reminding her that he would be back by late afternoon to collect her.

Other than by boat, Lihou Island was only accessible at low tide by crossing a ridge of rocks that formed the so-called causeway. Isobel picked her way carefully across the slick natural pathway and, after a short meander, sat down to sketch. Saint Helier, she knew, had brought Christianity to Jersey and the main city on that island bore his name. It was Saint Samson of Dol who had evangelized Guernsey, and he was celebrated by having a town and parish named after him. She thought about the early monks and the difficulties they must have faced to construct even such modest buildings on this tiny bit of land.

The bite of hunger reminded Isobel of the passage of time and of the lunch that awaited her and she hurried to put away her papers. She was feeling rather proud of one likeness in particular that caught the old stones of the priory wall at just the right angle, and so was distressed when a gust of wind sailed by, taking most of her work with it. Isobel dropped the pastie and hurried forward to retrieve the fluttering pages before they took to the air again or were blown into the sea. She managed to collect most of the work but her favourite piece was missing. She caught sight of it snagged between some rocks by the steep shoreline. Trying to be careful she nonetheless moved swiftly toward the waving paper and grabbed it securely with one hand. But she had not counted on the strength of her forward momentum and had to turn abruptly to avoid pitching down into the water. This she managed, but at the cost of wrenching her ankle painfully between two large rocks.

Uttering a rather unladylike word, Isobel sat to assess the damage, shaking her head at the ridiculousness of the situation. She did not want to take her boot off completely lest she not be able to put it on again due to the swelling she could already detect. Well, there was nothing for it but to hobble back to her basket and slowly make her return to the causeway. Victor would be arriving shortly and could assist her to cross it.

Afternoon was fast fading into evening and there was no sign of Victor approaching. The discomfort of her ankle, for it was well and truly sprained, made Isobel all the more impatient to be on her way home. She sat for a moment to contemplate the path she might take across the causeway. It would be better if Victor was here to help her, but as he wasn't, Isobel thought she would try to manage the crossing herself. She stood and gingerly placed weight on the injured ankle to see how she would fare with it on the slippery rocks and was disappointed to discover how much it hurt and what little mobility she could expect from it. Apparently she would have to wait right where she was until Victor arrived and assisted her across to the main island.

Isobel looked in the direction of the causeway. She was sure the path had been wider and more secure when she had crossed it earlier. Of course it had been, she realized, the tide is on its way in now. The unusually strong and high tides of the Channel Islands were well known. Even as these thoughts occurred to Isobel she noted that the green grey waters swirled up to cover more of the exposed rocks closing her only path of escape.

After a quarter of an hour spent glowering at the water several things became apparent to Isobel. If Victor did not arrive quite soon he wouldn't be able to get her across should he even attempt to carry her. Then the much more daunting prospect of having to spend a night alone on the tiny exposed island catapulted itself into Isobel's mind. She shivered as much from the thought as from the spray of the waves that were now splashing her.

Isobel watched in despair. The causeway was covered by a foot of water and was no longer visible. It was time for a decision, time to move. The only thing that seemed to make sense to Isobel was to retreat to the priory. Its broken walls would afford a limited degree of protection from the elements. She must move now before darkness fell completely. Casting a last longing look towards the big island, she slowly retraced her earlier steps back to the ruins.

She tried to comfort herself with the thought that help would arrive, that surely even if Victor was unable to come he would send someone. Huddled into a low corner of the ruined structure, Isobel wondered if God was testing her when she saw the flash of lightning streak across the sky, and heard the answering clap of thunder. A cold rain started moments later.

It wasn't long before she was soaked through and shivering. This did not stop the rain from lashing her and the wind from continuing to rip at her clothes. Her pretty flowered shawl had been torn from her shoulders and disappeared into the darkness. Her ankle hurt dreadfully. And she was hungry, so mad at herself for casually dropping the pastie in favour of her second-rate artwork. But that was looking back a few hours, back to when she seemed to have had a choice in matters; now her opportunities were much more limited.

    Isobel stewed in the bleak reality of her isolation. She had hated the dark as a child. Had not grown accustomed to it in her youth, as prophesized by every grownup she knew. Now a heavy darkness blanked out the stars, the salt air was thick on her tongue. She kept the tears at bay for a while, and then succumbed to them wholeheartedly, almost in relief. After a few moments of self-pity, she chided herself for weakness and resolved to endure the night as best she could.

CHAPTER FIFTEEN

Lord Chetton had returned to La Rocquette earlier in the day and was seated at his desk in the library. Chris had left but an hour ago on his way to a reunion with his latest paramour and the house was already quieter for his departure. Chetton cringed at the thought that his younger brother would imitate his attitude towards women, but Chris seemed very far removed from settling down. Time was a hungry monster and he often felt he had little to show for the years except some modest diplomatic successes and several disposable relationships.

The noise of a horse quickly galloping towards the front doors broke his reverie. He wondered absently if Chris had returned for some reason. The rider dismounted awkwardly, from the sounds of it. It was not his competent athletic brother then. The decisive banging on the front door was shortly followed by a perfunctory rap to the library door. Norris entered muttering loudly in Guernésiais, the old French language peculiar to the island that had been handed down the generations from medieval times. The tidings must not be good; Norris rarely lapsed into the old language.

"M'lord, excuse me but the little lady needs help. Victor from over L'Ancresse way has had trouble. His horse got lamed up and he couldn't get back in time."

The mention of L'Ancresse had gotten his attention and the

'little lady' could only mean one person.

"What's wrong, Norris? Where is Mrs. Barnestowe?"

Norris wasted little time in describing the situation as he had heard it from Victor a moment ago. Victor had been delayed due to a lame horse and could not get back to Lihou Island in time before the tides had closed off the causeway. He had searched frantically up and down the roadway, assuming Isobel had crossed back over to Guernsey, but finding no sign of her there, or back at the cottage, was in great despair.

Chetton's fists clenched instinctively. The tides were monumentally strong around Guernsey, the sea unforgiving. Many people over the years had succumbed to the pull of the tides even when in plain view of the shore; sometimes with boats only a few yards away as others struggled to save them. They were often strong fishermen wise to the ways of the water, not a delicate slip of a girl dressed in long skirts and petticoats. But now was not the time to ponder why the hell she was on that treacherous bit of land.

His mind flew to the necessities, to the fundamentals of what must be done. Lihou Island was too far up the coast to attempt to sail or row there from La Rocquette. And then it came to him, the obvious choice. He would take his sturdy little boat *Faithful* to the Lihou causeway. His men could load it in the back of the hay wagon and hitch Nabby, their patient workhorse, to it. A few wooden planks would allow him to slide the boat into the water and then he would row out from the shore. It was both the fastest and most direct plan. All would be well.

If only he were not too late.

With the supplies hastily piled into the small craft there was no room for Victor and he had persuaded the man to return to L'Ancresse. Less than an hour later Chetton unharnessed Nabby, and secured him under some trees. He had already backed the wagon around in a position to launch *Faithful*.

Chetton soon felt the surge of incoming tide, but it was not a match for his determination. The bulk of his muscles strained under the effort and *Faithful* shot forward and reached the narrow rocky beach of Lihou. He leapt from the prow, then scrambled up the rocky shoreline and with some difficulty pulled the small well-built craft beyond the catch of the waves. He put his hand inside his jacket and touched the wet fabric over his heart. Despair had almost overwhelmed him earlier when he had caught the wet length of material with his oar and worked it free. Her shawl.

He climbed the rough slope to the top of the island and could just make out the shadow of the priory. She must be there, he thought, as he headed in the direction of the only bit of shelter available. "She will be there," he whispered, as he rounded the broken corner of the largest wall. And there she was. Thank God!

Seeing the pitiful little form hunched over and shivering clutched at his insides. Relief swept over him as he made his way towards her. Part of him wanted to move slowly so she wouldn't be terrified and part of him wanted to drag her up to him and shake her for the scare she had caused.

Then he heard the words. Was she praying out loud?

No. She was singing. A child's song, or perhaps a lullaby. Bits of words and fragments of the melody came to him on the wind. He listened, mesmerized by the sweet sound. Then the voice wobbled and stopped. Something broke in his heart and he called her name and bent to her and she was clasped in his arms.

"Chetton." Her voice was hoarse with the damp chill.

"Again with the rescue, my dear."

At which point she balled up her small fist and punched him in the chest. Though he hardly felt the hit, he asked in a shocked voice, "Shall I go and leave you then?"

But she grabbed his arm and put it back around her and he relented, knowing she was close to tears and could handle no such jests.

"Let us get you home, Isobel. The *Faithful* is here and I will row you back to where I left the wagon."

He moved to help Isobel stand. He had expected her to be stiff from the cold and wet but when he saw the flash of pain in her eyes he stopped immediately.

"What is wrong? Are you hurt?"

Already his eyes were travelling up and down the length of her trying to access any injuries.

"It is my ankle, I think it might be sprained. It hurts rather badly."

"Can you walk?"

"I am afraid not, at least not very steadily."

"Well then we must change our plans. Stay here and do not try to move. I will return as quickly as I can."

Isobel stifled a sneeze but she didn't answer.

He smothered a curse and squeezed her hand.

"Isobel, mind now. I will not be long. I have supplies in the boat. Unfortunately, I believe we will have to stay here, depending on the tide, until first light at least. I will not risk carrying you over the rocks in full dark in this nasty weather. It is just too dangerous."

"We have to stay here for the night? Alone? Together? That is impossible!"

"Your logic is faulty, my dear. How can we be alone if we are together?"

Isobel struggled to rise again but Chetton was too quick for her and grasped her shoulders to keep her seated. "I see that it is appalling of me indeed to try and make light of the matter but needs must, my dear. Your reputation shall be keenly guarded by the family, I assure you. On my honour as a gentleman, there is not a jot to worry about on that account."

He smoothed a lock of sodden hair away from her face. "Luckily I have food and blankets; we shall make a picnic out of it."

She managed a lopsided grim. "Pray, do not be over long."

"Or what, you will decide to take a swim while I am gone? Never fear, I will be back momentarily."

Lord Chetton returned with an armful of goods. No one had been sure what to expect and it was the island way to generously over-provide in case of emergencies. He was able to rig a cover over their heads with oiled sailcloth that managed to keep out some of the wind and most of the rain. He built a small but hardy fire with some of the chunks of coal that Norris had tucked into the stern. There was bread, cheese, Guernsey gâche, and a leather-covered flask of brandy. He made Isobel drink several straight swigs of it until her coughing alarmed him and then pressed her to have a healthy shot in some water he had warmed over the fire. When she had eaten and drunk her fill she sat back and looked at him.

"Thank you, once again. I cannot imagine how you came to know I was here."

He explained the chain of events that had set him in motion to find her.

"What in God's name were you doing here?" he asked.

"I read about the priory in the book you lent me. I thought it would be a nice sketching project."

"A sketching project? At this season, with the high tides?"

"Well, Victor had planned to pick me up earlier, naturally. We did look at the tide tables, you know. Then I hurt my ankle and could not get back to the causeway in time."

He supposed it made some kind of sense. "Now that you have had something to sustain you I am going to make a trip back to *Faithful* to replenish the coal and see what else we may require. I suggest you take off your wet garments while I am away and prepare for the night." And so saying, he left Isobel to do his bidding.

A quarter of an hour later he slowly approached their campsite and stopped a short distance away in order he not catch Isobel at a delicate moment. He noted with a fair degree of exasperation that she had not followed his directive and was still fully clothed. Just as he was about to make his presence known Isobel removed something from her pocket and threw it into the fire. He could tell from the way it burned that is was several pages of paper. By the time he reached the shelter the fire had consumed them and Isobel was stirring the ashes as she gazed into the flames.

"What are you doing?" he asked.

Startled, Isobel shook her head. "Oh nothing, just tending the fire a little, waiting for you." She put the stick down and spread her fingers to catch the warm of the fire. "Have you gotten everything we need, then?"

He stood still for a moment and contemplated her profile in the firelight, and was only roused to answer when Isobel turned to look at him. "I believe so, yes. Here are two extra blankets and I really think you should get yourself out of those wet clothes." He manoeuvred a branch closer to the fire. "We will put them here where it is hot enough to dry them."

"But I am not at all sure that is the best plan."

"Isobel, I can see that you shivering," he said with great practicality.

"But I am much better now."

His patience was drawing thin as he beheld Isobel's slight figure draped in the sodden garments. "There are no buts to this. You undress or I shall do it for you."

Looking affronted, she stammered, "Don't be ridiculous. You would not dare to attempt such a thing!"

"If that is the way you wish to proceed, then."

He moved towards her. She started to turn away from him and he really hoped she was not going to make a maidenly fuss because the clothes were coming off of her, one way or another. He was not about to let her take a chill and sicken.

"No," she managed through chattering teeth.

"NO WHAT?" His tolerance was at an end. Isobel was trembling from the cold and he did not like her pallor.

"I cannot, I cannot, do it by myself. The lacings are wet. But . . ."

"What is it now, or are you just stalling?"

"I, well, it is just that, that I do not want you to see me. You must not."

"It is dark, for heaven's sake." He glared at the stubborn and shivering little feminine package.

"Chetton." This time he heard the plea in her voice and remembered her acute distress with intimacy and so he calmed his voice and tried to produce what he hoped was a disinterested smile. Which was really a big lie, because all he could think of was the upcoming agony of having to spend a night lying next to this beautiful woman who was soon to be unclothed.

"Fine. I will just assist you and then turn away to ensure your modesty."

He was going to remark about the problem of undoing feminine attire in such wet circumstances, but by the time she turned and revealed her half bared back to him he realized he did not have a voice.

Isobel was docile in his arms as he angled her to undo the tight lacings at the back of her dress. Even his rather vivid imagination had not prepared him for the feel of her soft skin. The damp night air and the firelight gave it a rosy glow, it felt like satin under his touch, so inviting. He couldn't help but run his fingers over her exposed back when he saw a slight bruise that must have happened when she fell. Thank the Lord she had landed away from the traitorous cliff where it was so easy to slide unimpeded right down into the sea.

When she tried to move away from his touch, a tiny shudder skittered down her spine. He gritted his teeth. Time to cover up all that lovely skin and make sure she didn't catch a chill. Her dress was off and the layers underneath, all but the thin linen of her chemise which she insisted on retaining. He put his coat over her shoulders and then scooted around to the front of her to remove her boots and stockings and to have a closer look at the damaged ankle. Her small feet were like icicles and he rubbed them, taking extreme care with the sore one. His hand slid beneath her ankle and up around the curve of her calf towards the back of her knee. More satin, round, feminine flesh. His fingers were itching to move higher, much higher.

He heard the small sigh and the little giggle that maddened his senses further. He looked to her face but the little minx's eyes were closed as if she half slumbered. He could see the rise and fall of her chest beneath the blankets and imagined kissing a path there.

The erotic spell broke on the harsh reality of their situation and his concern for Isobel when he heard the unmistakable slur of strong drink on her tongue.

"That's not strick'ly my ankle."

Silently cursing himself, her, and the heavens, he folded a blanket for a makeshift pillow and made sure the other blankets covered what most needed to be covered. He settled down a short distance away and prayed for a quick release of his torment with an early dawn. The slight bundle beside him wiggled closer, gave the gentlest of sighs, and then was silent in deep sleep.

It could not be considered his fault that they had been thrown together in this way. There was no alternative but to go searching for Isobel when he heard Victor's tale of woe. Staying on Lihou through the night was also necessary, considering the injury Isobel had sustained. Getting her out of the wet clothes was the only sensible thing to do. Not his fault, not his fault. Not His Fault!

Chetton awoke much later with a start, some nameless sense jabbing him into semi awareness. It took a moment to orient himself in time and place and then he remembered the disaster that was yesterday. Isobel lay quietly beside him with closed eyes. He kissed his fingertips and raised that hand to cup the side of her face. Then he bedded back down.

Chetton smiled to himself as he let sleep reclaim him.

※

There was just enough coal augmented by a few sticks of wood to keep a low fire going until the first rays of sun crept over the eastern horizon. They shared the last of the bread and cheese before the sun took control of the sky. Chetton made a trip back to the boat to stow the extra supplies and secure it against the height of the tide, *Faithful* to be collected later.

Norris and Victor met them at the edge of the causeway full of questions about the night and the state of Isobel, who was held protectively in Lord Chetton's arms. She let him do the talking in his calm measured voice, rich and deep and capable of persuading even one such as the crusty old Norris into believing whatever he said. The diplomat in him, the negotiator, the born raconteur, was in his element and yet wielded his power with such delicacy and finesse that the magic and skill of it were not apparent. His explanations were commonplace, mundane, no cause for worry, nothing to be questioned.

The necessity of them having to remain overnight together, would, Lord Chetton had repeatedly assured Isobel, never become common knowledge. He had a very loyal and trustworthy household and he would extract assurances from all staff concerned.

Lord Chetton noticed that Isobel was quiet in the morning and a little pale, the ordeal and night in the open starting to take their toll. He sensed also a hint of reserve, a slight timidity that he chose to ignore. Might it be that she was shy after their intimacy, or, on a darker thought, was she nervous because of thwarted plans? The isolation of Lihou afforded the opportunity for clandestine meetings, and the origin of the papers that Isobel had burnt had not been firmly established, after all. He had in no way been taken in by her explanation about just tending to the fire.

He wanted Isobel to return with him to La Rocquette. He explained to her it was for the simple expedient that his household could more easily see to the needs of a disabled guest. It was only fair, he continued, since she had taken such good care of Teddy.

His other reason to want her near was to keep her under scrutiny. She seemed capable of getting into the most awful fixes entirely on her own. Perhaps it would be better if she were closer to him for her own sake. He knew it sounded positively gothic, but that did not change the fundamental truth of the matter. He was adamant about his need to protect her, and keep an eye on her activities as well.

God damnit.

However, Isobel very firmly rejected his invitation and requested she be taken back to L'Ancresse cottage, agreeing only with the proviso that Helene would send word if she did not see improvement soon. Chetton countered that an additional servant would be sent to help Helene under strict orders from Mrs. McClure. These difficult negotiations ended only when they passed through the gates of the cottage laneway.

Lord Chetton carefully lifted Isobel down from the wagon and carried her into the cottage with Helene hovering over her all the way. He placed Isobel in the chair he was directed to and stood back to scrutinize her face for undue signs of strain. As he did so, Helene withdrew a letter from her apron pocket and handed it to Isobel, who took one look at it and thrust it under the nearby cushion. She glanced quickly up at him and then away again and thanked him for conveying her home, but plead fatigue when Helene offered to bring in tea for them. He took this as his cue to leave and said good day. As he followed the stone path back to where Victor held the carriage horse for him, he chanced to gaze through the open window of the parlour and saw Isobel fairly lunge at the cushion to retrieve the letter and tear it open.

CHAPTER SIXTEEN

Lady Chetton made an unannounced courtesy visit two days after Isobel returned from her ordeal on Lihou Island. Isobel was resting comfortably on the chaise lounge in the sunny front room and heard the carriage pull up. Not long after Helene rushed into the room to announce the visitor. Isobel was surprised, but pleased, to see Lady Chetton and tried to stand as she entered the sitting room.

"No my dear, you must not get up for me. Chetton warned me particularly that you would in all probability endeavour to do so, and I am under strict orders from him to forgo the niceties and to keep you comfortable." With this Lady Chetton dropped a brief kiss on her forehead as she eased Isobel back onto the chaise lounge. "I just wanted to see for myself that you are well situated here."

Isobel was touched by her motherly concern. "How kind of you to come, please be seated, Lady Chetton. The blue chintz is probably the most comfortable chair for you. Shall I have some tea brought in?"

"Not on my account, I shan't stay above a few minutes. And I believe Helene is unpacking the basket of treats that Mrs. McClure has sent over for you. Tell me, my dear, how you are getting on?"

"I am well on the mend and am able to hobble around with the aid of a cane, though it stretches my vanity to have to do so, I must admit."

The Dowager smiled at that. "And you are managing the discomfort well, then?"

"Yes, thank you. Dr. Hoskins confirmed it was only a bad sprain and left a sleeping draught should I require it. I have not yet been reduced to that measure, despite a restless first night. I blush to own that my biggest concern right now is boredom, for I miss my daily walks dreadfully."

"That is welcome news and a good indication that you are well on the way to mending, my dear, for you recall how fractious Teddy was once he was over the worst of his troubles."

"I do indeed, the little rascal had me racketing my brains to pull out every childhood game that could be played within the bounds of the sick room."

"That reminds me to give you this," said Lady Chetton as she withdrew a paper from her reticule and handed it to Isobel. "It is the directions to make a lavender poultice. I am not clear on the reasoning behind Mrs. McClure sending it to you for a sprained ankle but be assured the practical woman desired Helene to make one up for you by following these instructions *to the letter*, as she adjured me to advise Helene."

Isobel set the missive on the table beside her. "I shall save that treat for later."

Lady Chetton closed the small purse and replaced it on her knee. "I also wanted to speak to you on another matter. Recently I have received some correspondence from Emma Le Fourniere. I can see by your startled expression that this has surprised you, dear. Did you never wonder that I might know Emma, living so close by? Well, there was a time when we were bosom buddies, and despite the fact that our lives took different paths, we still occasionally correspond."

The polite smile faded from Isobel's face and was replaced by a rosy blush.

"Emma spoke of you warmly, said to tell you that she will write again presently. Without going into details, she gave me to understand that you are going through a trying time, which explains, of course, why you are living so quietly."

Lady Chetton glanced around the room and sighed. "Isn't it odd, my dear, how life works itself out? That you should be the one to help poor little Teddy at La Rocquette and then turn out to be so closely connected to an old friend of mine. Ahh, it is these occasional accidents of fate that keep one young at heart!"

Lady Chetton reached over and patted Isobel's knee. "Now do not, I beg of you, let your feathers be ruffled by this, Isobel. Emma exhorted me on our years of friendship to keep a quiet eye on you and offer support in her stead, should you require any, as she is so far away and unable to provide timely assistance. I wrote to her expressing my willingness to do so, but I just wanted to apprise you of the situation and assure you that you have a friend in me. Naturally, my dear, I have not spoken a word of this to Chetton or anyone and do not intend to do so."

Isobel was unsure how to feel about this development but it was necessary to respond politely in some way, especially as Lady Chetton was now regarding her with a marked degree of attention. "Well, I am sure that is kind of Emma to solicit you on my behalf and very amenable of you to agree to her request, although I hope entirely unnecessary on both your parts." Recognizing that this might not show a sufficient amount of appreciation, she hastened to add her gratitude for being enclosed in Lady Chetton's scope of concern in this way.

"I shall never encroach on your privacy, Isobel, that is not my intention, nor in my nature. My conjecture is that this has something to do with your bereavement at such a young age. If you find yourself becoming blue devilled at any point, you must let me know. Perhaps you might pay a visit to me at Foster House in London during the season and I shall endeavour to brighten things up for you there. It would be my pleasure, I assure you."

Isobel was much affected by this kind offer and also relieved by the very little Lady Chetton must understand about her situation to suggest she return to England, even under the protection of the Dowager Countess at their palatial town house.

"You are very generous, indeed, my lady, and I thank you for your offer."

On this note Lady Chetton rose and took her leave with the admonition that Isobel continue to take care with herself. After sitting quietly and listening to La Rocquette's carriage fade away down the lane, Isobel stirred herself to call for Helene. She gave her the poultice instructions and asked if there was any of Mrs. McClure's treacle tart in the gift basket. As the cake and tea were being prepared for her, Isobel reread lines from her most recent letter from Emma.

> *I will tell you something, Izzy, that is hard to understand, and indeed it has taken me most of my life to come to terms with it. There is a beauty in truth. In this life, wholeness includes at least a degree of imperfection. It is a great challenge to embrace the complexity of that, and to be able to adapt it to an understanding of yourself. But as God wills it, our lives are layered and lumpy and emblazoned with detail.*
>
> *I am going to leave you with one more thought, my sweet girl, and it is this: do not think of your unhappiness as an end, try to picture it all as an unwelcome curve in the pattern of your life, a detour on your journey, not the destination itself.*

This seemed like such sensible advice and yet, as tears wallowed up in her eyes, Isobel felt she was not yet at the point where she could put it into practice, despite her desire to do so.

※

Chetton had had a hectic few days since rescuing Isobel from Lihou. On this, the third night after the adventure, he fell into sleep as if he had been drugged. He dreamt not at all during the first several hours of his rest and then fell prey to visions of old demons. Disjointed episodes from his past curled through his night-time mind, and always just below the surface of his consciousness there was something he should be able to grasp onto. An elemental discord of his spirit held sway and he could not wake to clear himself of it, nor wilfully recede into the dream world to chase its meaning. Caught in between sleep and wakefulness, he was a prisoner of the mystic realm where one has no control over destiny, and reality has not the stamp of permanence, nor a soul the solace of God's benevolence.

He was startled awake by an unearthly scream. Filled with apprehension he pulled on his trousers and boots. By then he heard Norris yelling and the shouts of other men in the distance. Racing down the stairs he charged through the door to find the night air filled with flame and smoke. One of the outbuildings was ablaze. Running towards it, he met Norris and a look passed between them that needed no explanation.

"You heard it too?"

"Yes, sir. There be nae animals in the shed, only in the barns and the . . ."

"Stable. I will go there. Send half the men to the barn to see to the animals. You take the others to put the fire out."

He raced to the stable, wrenched the heavy door open ready to plunge in, but then halted stock still in the doorway. The horses were mad with terror and their high-pitched screams and stamping hoofs were deafening. The smoke made them all nervous and he knew they would have to be moved soon before the panic drove them into further frenzy. He slowly advanced into the room wanting to calm the terrified animals.

Chetton traced a path to the stall in the corner. A proud dark head should have been visible over the railings but was not. When he looked into the stall he was appalled at the ruin that met his eyes, the desecration. A huge form was spread out in the stall, motionless, its lifeblood soaking even now into the straw. Duke lay butchered, completely gutted. The stench of blood and offal was thick and made Chetton's eyes stream, although the tears were not due to the stink alone. His mind dull with the shock of the carnage, he cast his eyes around the rest of the stables, horrified to think he might find more victims.

There was something nailed to the wall above the stall and he stretched to pull down the piece of dirty parchment. In poor penmanship a warning was written:

**Stop your dealings with the French officials
or your life will end like this.**

He felt like retching. The bastards had known Duke was his favourite mount and targeted him in particular. There was no point in asking why someone would do such a thing; the answer had been posted on the wall. The who was more difficult to explain but undoubtedly had something to do with the same people who had murdered La Rue. Now the stakes were much higher. He shoved the parchment into his pocket as Norris entered. He moved abruptly to head him off, wanting to spare the older man the shock he had just had.

"It is Duke. He has been slain, he . . ." He coughed to clear his throat but his voice was not right and gave out. He swore silently and tried again. "Someone killed him."

Norris just looked at Chetton for a moment and then put a knurled hand on his shoulder and gave him a strong squeeze. "Oh, laddie!"

Chetton raised a hand to cover his eyes. Norris had not called him that since he had been ten years old.

"The fire, how is it?"

"Nearly out, it wasn't too bad and didn't spread. A lot of smoke but not much real damage, thank t' heavens."

"It must have been a diversionary tactic to keep everybody away from here, so they could . . . Christ." Chetton thudded the wooden stall with his fist.

"Should we make a search for the heathens, do you think?"

"No. No, there is little chance they would still be about now. We had best make sure the fire is out and then have some men come and, and, help me see to Duke."

He spent some time sitting with Duke before relinquishing his remains to the men and returning inside. He found Lady Chetton in the midst of giving the staff directions and held her for a moment of mutual comfort.

By then Chetton desperately needed a stiff drink and went into his study to pour a brandy from his special stock. He would raise a glass to old Duke, the proud mount his father had given him. As he sat stiffly in his chair he noticed a piece of parchment lying on his desk. It was the same grain and colour as the one posted in the stable. He opened up the piece of thick paper with an odd feeling of detachment.

Consider tonight your only warning.

Chetton thought this second note was only to prove that the wretches had access to his home. They had dared to come onto his land and defile it in such an ignominious way! He would go on the offensive. When he discovered those responsible they would be made to understand just how much of a mistake they had made and would pay the price for their temerity.

But who had gone undetected and been able to slip the note into his study?

CHAPTER SEVENTEEN

There are times in your life, thought Isobel, when it really is better to mind your own business. Helene and the young maid sent over from La Rocquette were having a dispute loud enough to be heard in the parlour where Isobel sat with her foot resting upon a stool. It had begun with a normal discussion about who made the lightest, most buttery croissants, and progressed through the merits of crème brûlée and madeleines. A brisk discussion was now continuing about the best apple tart to ever grace a table. Not surprisingly, there had been no point of agreement during the entire gastronomic dialogue. The women's tempers were frayed and conversation was now laced with the icy extreme politeness that thinly masked the opposite intent.

"Marie, surely someone with your, um, experience in the kitchen would know that my mother's tarte a la Normande is the best on the island," said Helene with just enough of a pause to give insult.

The effect was not lost on the clever Marie.

"Well, my friend, I thought someone with your good taste would prefer Mrs. McClure's tarte. She is known for her light hand with pastry."

"Yes, her pastry is superb and she uses a great deal of it. Mother's crust is thinness itself," sniffed Helene.

"It would have to be to support the meagre amount of apples she uses," came the crisp reply.

"What do you mean, my dear? My mother's tarte is generous and full."

And so it went on. Isobel was as nervous as a sitting duck lest the pair descend on her for judgment in the matter. Her ankle, though improved, was not healed to the point where she could make a quick enough getaway if they came in her direction. She was not, she decided, above feigning sleep rather than having to decide who was the best baker.

She was pleased when Victor entered from collecting the post and delivered it to her. He said he was going to the kitchen for coffee and asked if she wanted anything. She shook her head to decline his offer, happy that the pressure no longer rested on her alone.

The familiar handwriting on one of the letters she was shuffling through made her sit up straight. Another letter from Emma so soon was unexpected. She broke the seal and unfolded the missive, dated, she realized, the day following her own disjointed premonition of trouble. She expected word about Lady Chetton or another epistle about life in general and the happenings of their village in particular. Instead the letter was short and very much to the point. What it said drove all other thoughts out of her mind and filled her with a dizzying dread.

She sat rooted to the spot for over an hour trying to piece things together and come up with a response. There was only one option. As unsettling as the idea was, she could see no other way around the problem.

※

Isobel had written Lord Chetton a sympathetic note when appraised of the tragedy with Duke. Three days later he was passing within sight of L'Ancresse cottage on the return leg of a trip to St. Sampson. He decided on the spur of the moment to drop in and see for himself how the lady was faring.

Helene was the one to tell him.

Isobel was not in residence and had not been for several days. Two nights ago she had asked Helene to pack a valise and her portmanteau. Victor had taken her to the quay at St. Peter Port early the next morning. She had not mentioned, even after Victor dropped broad hints, where she was headed or precisely how long she expected to be away.

This news was both unexpected and unwelcome to Lord Chetton. Isobel had slipped out right from under his nose, more fool he. The seal that a great part of his professional reputation depended on was still missing. Now Isobel had mysteriously and abruptly left the island right after La Rocquette had been violated and the sinister warnings of ending his work with French officials had been issued.

Much too much coincidence from his point of view.

If the woman had been playing him! He ground his teeth is fury.

Helene was making a drama out of beating the rug in the back garden. Her swats of the broom against the hanging carpet increased with every word she spoke, as if to punctuate them with added meaning.

"Forgive me for speaking so, m'lord, but the affair has an oddness about it."

Exactly what he thought! He waited until the woman caught her breath from the exertion.

"In what way, Helene?"

Helene leaned on the broom handle, her stance at once defensive and defeated.

"Well, she tried to hide it but she was upset about something. I think it all started when she got that letter. Victor says I'm making it up to fit the story. But that's not true, m'lord, I never would make up a tale about Mrs. Barnestowe. There's not a lovelier mistress to work for and—"

"Yes, Helene, I am sure you are correct. Now, what is all this about a letter? Do you know whom it was from? Was it local?"

"No, m'lord, though I didn't see it directly. Victor collects the post and said there was a letter with a foreign stamp. That must have been the one she was reading when I took in tea, the others were left unopened."

"Think carefully now, Helene, did Mrs. Barnestowe usually receive foreign letters or packages, or send them?"

"Not that I know of, but you should ask Victor, as I said."

Chetton knew he might be saying too much, but he had to chance the next query.

"Have you ever witnessed anything slightly odd or out of the ordinary with Mrs. Barnestowe, Helene? I am sure you heard of the trouble at La Rocquette recently, we can't be too careful."

Helene slowly turned to continue her rug beating.

Knowing that Helene was loyal to her mistress, Chetton sought for just the right tone of understanding and authority before he spoke again. "Helene. It could be important for her safety, please tell me what you know."

She paused in her work but did not turn to face him. "Well, a while ago I was in St. Peter Port to do a shop for my old mum, who was doing poorly. When I got back home I saw Mistress down the end of the garden talking to a man. He had his back to me and I didn't recognize him. He gave her something that she quickly put into her pocket and then Mistress handed him something. The way he glanced at his hand I assumed it was money, like a payment. Then he hurried off and she came back into the cottage and asked me about how my mum was getting on, quite ordinary like. I thought it slightly odd at the time, but of no consequence to me and I carried on with my own business."

"Did she mention the incident to you at all?"

Helen swivelled abruptly and stared up into his face. "No, m'lord, and why would she? I am sure it was her own concern."

Yes, thought Chetton. And that might be just the problem.

He had heard enough to be disturbed. When questioned, Victor, reserved as always, could shed no more light on packages, letters, or his mistress's abrupt departure.

There was entirely too much mystery surrounding the woman. It could but bode ill. Chetton didn't know from whom she had received this last letter. But she had obviously been corresponding clandestinely with someone over time. He had never learned the reason she had decided to all but sequester herself on this particular island. But he would find out this and much more; he took it as his mission to do so.

Lord Chetton galloped to St. Peter Port and went directly to the port authority office. Utilizing his family position on the island, along with the liberal dispersal of coin, he persuaded the harbour master to look up the passenger manifests for departures leaving two days ago. Three vessels were listed, the *Duchess*, on its return to the home port of Southampton, the ferry *Cornelius II* had departed for the Isle of Man, and the *Liberte* set sail for Le Havre on the Normandy coast.

None of the entries contained the name of Isobel Barnestowe.

Lord Chetton was at a momentary loss. Damn her. He needed to calm down and think this thing through. Over the years he had tracked many persons across many countries for many reasons. He had to figure out a starting point and then use his imagination and experience as guides. A woman, particularly a young, beautiful woman of a certain class, always caught someone's attention. The fact that she was travelling alone as she had been when he first met her was also noteworthy.

He did not want to speculate on all of the unsavoury situations that might befall the foolish woman before he could find her. When he did, she would indeed furnish him with all of the information he desired.

And heaven help her if she was playing him.

Two of the ships leaving that morning were destined for England. It would seem plausible that she could have returned to England then, except for the fact that only couples and families were registered aboard those ships. One ship had departed recently for France. He scanned the list for the *Liberte*. A Miss Elizabeth Meadows had apparently travelled to France yesterday. Miss Meadows may not have realized it, but she was in fact the only unaccompanied female listed on the manifest for that sailing to Le Havre. He looked at the name of the ship and smiled. How fortuitous for young "Elizabeth" that liberty had taken her under its wing. But it was a pity for the real life Isobel that as a hunter he had few equals.

Chetton arrived in Le Havre early the next morning. After disembarkation he sent a short note to Jean to inform him of the situation. He was hopeful that one of the sources Jean kept on his payroll in the old port city would come up with tidings of Isobel's whereabouts. It would take a little more patience, a little more time, and probably a lot more money, but he felt he was moving in the right direction.

The following evening Chetton entered the crowded main posting house on the outskirts of the city. He was ready for a drink to ward off his chill and deepening depression. He had not made much headway during the day. Surprisingly, the leads he thought would be invaluable in helping to narrow in on Isobel's whereabouts had not materialized. His only explanation for this was that she must have changed her identity again.

It was not the money he had spent that irritated him, but that his time could have been put to better use. Since he had no specific information about Isobel yet he would have to change tactics and rely on what he knew from experience were the choices and chances that those on the run had to face. He shouldered his way up to the long bar to order a cognac.

The patron to his left was a large middle-aged man who reeked of spirits and wet wool. "Two gin and make them large, barkeep. I need to persuade a little lovely to be mine tonight," he said in a provincial dialect. The man noticed Lord Chetton and gave him a lascivious wink to make sure his remark was understood. Lord Chetton was in no mood to suffer fools and cast the man such a cold stare that the fellow turned on his heel and left without another word. The barman had seen the silent exchange and gave a wearied smile.

"That's Henri, figures himself a bit of a ladies man, he does. What can I get you, sir?"

"Your best cognac, please, a double. You have a good crowd in here tonight, haven't you?" He turned to survey the room.

"Aye, that we do. What with the mail coach broke down and having to return here for repairs and all, we're full up."

Lord Chetton looked to the far corner of the smoky room where a flutter of activity had drawn his attention. His line of sight provided a view of the back of a set of feminine shoulders covered in a rough wool cloak and a slender neck topped by a very out-of-date bonnet.

"What did you say?" he asked vaguely as he took a deep drink of the fragrant spirit.

The woman was leaning as far as possible away from the obnoxious Henri, the same man who had been standing at the bar moments ago. Even from this distance Lord Chetton could tell that the age-old drama of aggressive male pursuing reluctant female was taking place. People sitting near the couple were starting to take notice. Henri looked to be trying to coax the unfortunate woman into accepting a drink from him. When he grabbed the woman's arm and tried to pull her towards him, and no one sitting nearby did anything about it, Lord Chetton decided he would. He was ready for a knock-up with somebody and this obnoxious character had just given him reason enough.

He swallowed the rest of his cognac and strode across the room. From experience he knew his size and fierce look of determination would convince people to make way, and they scattered to do so. The din in the room was increasing as Henri became bolder and although he couldn't yet make out what the woman was saying, Lord Chetton could hear acute distress in the cadence of her speech. Without glancing at the woman, his concentration wholly centered on the despicable predator, Chetton pulled Henri's arm from the woman and deftly wrenched it hard behind his back. This rapidly brought the surprised man to his toes in an effort to relieve some of the deadly pressure on his shoulder and arm. He heard the quick intake of breath, sharp with alarm, from behind him. Turning to calm the fears of the woman, he suddenly realized whose pretty little face was staring up at him from under the horrible hat.

"Isobel, what the bloody hell are you doing in this kind of establishment?"

His attention had switched away from holding Henri and towards grabbing Isobel. Henri took advantage of his broken concentration and in the next second the man's substantial fist connected solidly with Lord Chetton's chin. Taken by surprise, Lord Chetton landed heavily on the floor and was treated to a dreamlike view of the flounces of Isobel's quickly retreating skirts. He jumped up, shaking his head to clear his vision, furious with everything and everybody in sight.

"Isobel, wait," he fairly bellowed. Henri the opportunist obviously thought he had a good chance in taking him after the success of his first punch and drew his arm back to swing. But Chetton was not to be fooled twice and blocked the punch, using a rapid one, two, three combination to drop the man to the floor. He was about to dash after Isobel when he made the connection of just whom Henri had been touching and what he wanted from her. The rage almost blinded him and he pivoted and drop kicked the Frenchman just as he was staggering to regain his feet. Hearing the satisfying crash as Henri landed on the floor again, Lord Chetton barrelled out the door, frantic to catch sight of Isobel, terrified that she would be hiding from him, or worse, on the run somewhere again.

She was standing by the corner of the building not twenty paces from him.

Her hands were clasped and she was looking down at them. Her small foot was tapping out a rhythm on the wooden step.

He walked over to her and stopped within touching distance. Isobel slowly raised her head to look at him. She was pale with anger, trembling with it.

"How dare you follow me!" She enunciated in a clipped voice, her frown deepening with each word uttered.

He couldn't help it, he started to laugh.

"You are not even going to try and deny it, are you? Do you indeed think this is amusing, sir?"

He grabbed her to him and then lifted her high in the air, still laughing. He swung her around and settled her in his arms, her feet kicking and her arms trying to wiggle free, and he continued to laugh. He kept laughing on the way back into the posting house and up the stairs to the suite he had secured for the night. Still shaking with pent up mirth and frustration he deposited her on the bed and turned to secure the door, thinking she might try to bolt right back out.

But the bundle on the bed didn't move and his laughter died away at the unaccustomed quiet surrender from Isobel.

☙

Isobel was nearly comatose from weariness. Her nerves were stretched to the breaking point after so many days of desperate choices and uncertain travel. She had taken chill on the open coach seat early yesterday morning and never warmed up. She was queasy from being too nervous to eat and tired to the bone from having to survive on broken snatches of sleep. Her constant, her only companions, had been loneliness and worry. She was numb and heartsick when the coach broke down and the passengers had to be carted all the way back to Le Havre.

Things had gone from bad to worse when the man from the tavern had tried to force an unwanted drink and his vile attentions on her.

Then, Lord Chetton had arrived, from out of nowhere.

To save her.

Yet again.

And he thought the whole thing was a lark. Something hilarious. He had hijacked her up to his room, carrying her up past all those people just as if he had a right to, like she was a common hussy. He wouldn't get away with it unscathed, she would give him a piece of her mind, she would. In a moment or so. When she got her energy back and the relief was under control. Anger. She meant when her anger was under control. She was sure she would rally soon.

CHAPTER EIGHTEEN

Lord Chetton had spent a restless night in the adjoining room to Isobel's. When he asked the innkeeper's wife to look in on her he was told the lady must have woken and been ravenous because the food he had ordered for her was finished, but she was back to sleep. And apparently she was still asleep now, hours later.

The trouble was, she was stealing his thunder because every minute he waited for her to awaken he became just a little less angry about her possible sins and a little more concerned about her condition. The little witch, it was probably a ploy of hers.

This was ridiculous. He was not a child to be kept waiting. Had he not just traversed across the Channel to find and question her? He would wait no longer. Stamping down the wooden hall in his disdain, he started to open the door to the suite, only to have it pulled inwards so forcefully that it was snatched quite out of his hand. The small figure on the inside was also surprised and halted her brusque exit.

Isobel was fully awake now and from the look on her face was quite ready to settle a few matters with him. So be it. He was equally prepared for the confrontation, but knew he had to tread softly and use his concern to gain Isobel's confidence and thus keep tabs on her. If she distrusted his motives it would prove to be much more difficult to stay close and to ultimately retrieve the missing government seal, if she had indeed stashed it somewhere or passed it on to another. A quick sort through her bag while she slept had proved fruitless. He had to play this carefully and make her believe he was there solely for her benefit.

"Isobel! You look well rested." When she didn't answer his cheerful greeting, he continued with, "You were asleep for hours, you must have needed it."

Chetton advanced into the room, which forced Isobel to walk backwards into it. He sat down in a chair by the fireplace. Isobel continued to retreat and came to a standstill as far away as possible from him with her back to the window. He glanced at her then, only to realize she was staring tight-lipped at him. They held each other's eyes for several moments. When he spoke again he had to work to keep the ring of annoyance out of his voice.

"I can see from your expression that you are not best pleased to see me, Isobel. You may well ask why I am here and I will inquire the same from you. What has happened that sent you running off so quickly from Guernsey?"

༺༻

Lord Chetton had shown extreme diligence in tracking her down, thought Isobel. She could only hope that the others pursuing her had not the same tenacity and cleverness or she would be shortly apprehended. What then would she do? Nothing would prevail against the corrupt malignance that wanted her captured and returned to England as little more than a prisoner. There were so many unknown factors. She spoke precisely and forcefully, wanting distance to seep into her voice.

"That is none of your concern, sir. I would remind you that I am not answerable to you or anyone for that matter."

Lord Chetton passed a hand across his forehead. "No, lady, you are not required to explain yourself to me. I had hoped, however, that as a friend, if you were in need in any way, that you would apply to me."

He paused for a moment and then stood and approached her.

"We are not strangers Isobel. We have shared a part of ourselves with each other and you must know that I cannot be unaffected if something should upset you." He took her hands in his and gently squeezed them. "What has occurred to distress you so? And how, in any way, may I be of assistance to you?"

Lord Chetton's solicitous manner disarmed Isobel somewhat. All she could remember was the understanding and care he had shown her on so many occasions. He had calmed and comforted her and it had not fazed him in the least. To the contrary, he had tended to her on Lihou with such a degree of solicitude that it had touched her soul. And yet, it was hard to trust, to believe in that sentiment at this moment.

Her present situation was calamitous, and she on the brink of despair at the thought of what failure could mean. Beyond that there was the consideration of how her association with Lord Chetton could damage him, and his reputation.

His fine sense of the possibilities of life was precious, rare, in fact. It had afforded her a few brief moments of respite against the dark reality of her past. She had been drawn to his light, greedy for his touch and for the vistas of choice that seemed possible when she was with him. There was a deep part of her that craved more of the same and was mad enough to give thought to a future that was not possible to attain. Such selfishness was dangerous and could, if she let it have free rein, shrivel the life and beauty of his gifts to her.

There was no denying that this Guernsey diplomat had been a friend to her and she could not count upon many friends in recent years. He had introduced his family to her and eased her way into life on Guernsey. He deserved a modicum of explanation regarding her behaviour of late, and she was ready now to share a version of that with him before they parted company.

She sat down abruptly on the nearby chair. "Chetton, oh, there is so much to tell, I cannot imagine what you will think of me when you know the half of it."

With as little detail as possible she recounted her reluctant stay at Thrushgrange Abbey, where she had been sent to recuperate after the death of her husband. She told of how her uncle and cousin had discouraged her return home and indicated they wished her to stay at the abbey indefinitely. Isobel attempted to keep emotion out of the tale, but the humiliation and sting of rejection went deep and crept, unbidden, into her voice.

"Several days ago, I received a short letter from my old governess, Emma, warning me that my uncle Alex Radford had hired men to find me and return me to England. He has applied to a judge there and has papers that . . ." Isobel could not continue and bent her head, covering her eyes.

Lord Chetton gently lifted her chin and looked at her sadly.

"What are the papers about? Do you mean legal documents?"

Isobel nodded her head in agreement and said in a broken voice, "He was my guardian and is my next of kin. He wants me committed permanently to a convent, if the church will permit it, or," she gulped involuntarily, "an insane asylum if not. I am thought not to be in my right mind after, well after, my husband's death, you see."

"Intolerable! No wonder you are at your wit's end, my dear. And tell me, your uncle would stand to gain some benefit, would he not, if you were declared insane? How good of the man to be so meticulous about your welfare, the cad."

"So, you see, there is nothing to be done except continue on the move so they don't find me."

"Under the circumstances, that would be fatal. Isobel, you

must understand, I have extensive experience in this kind of thing. Sooner or later, you will be found out, and France is harsher in its treatment of supposedly wayward women than England. You will find no leniency here from the authorities, especially if a little cash is circulated to ease the way."

She looked at him in horror, but the truth had to be faced, an assessment of her predicament analyzed in full.

"In any case, that is no way to live the rest of your life, always looking over your shoulders to gauge who may be in pursuit."

"What other choice is there? I cannot just sit and wait to be found and I will not submit to being returned to England."

"Did your governess mention anything about plans he may have put in motion?"

"No. Emma did not know the names of the men, but apparently there were several of them. And unfortunately my clever uncle armed them all with a sketched likeness of me for identification." The thought of being shut away, possibly for the rest of her life, drained her energy and she leaned back in the chair for support.

"How did you find me, was it easy? When did you figure it out?"

Isobel watched Lord Chetton closely as he explained the particulars of his search. He began to pack her bag and retrieved the few items she had unpacked earlier. The efficiency of his movements and his confidence to affect change were a part of his very essence. She was drawn to that sureness and competence like a moth to a flame. And therein lay the danger of being too long in his company. She must not let herself come to rely on him, but make her own way and her own decisions.

There was something that Isobel wanted to ask of Lord Chetton but she knew she did not have the courage to actually put it into words. She was sure whatever his answer was to the question of why he had followed her would be problematic in one way or another. It would say too much or too little for her to bear. She did not know which would be worse, to have him declare sentiments that she had no right to expect, or distance himself with talk of duty and responsibility. It was best to keep silent and not tempt fate in such a flagrant manner.

He had found her and could now relieve the worry of Helene and Victor, and, no doubt, his own rampant curiosity. It had been foolish and ill thought out not to have provided them with some innocuous story about her need to travel. She could trust Chetton to make a viable explanation on her behalf. He would leave soon to return with the mystery solved. She would change her destination. When she ventured forth again she would perhaps try to disguise her appearance more comprehensively to throw those in pursuit off the track.

Lord Chetton put her case down by the door and returned to Isobel's side. He put his hand lightly on her shoulder.

"Time to go, my dear. I have a hired carriage and driver waiting. If we leave immediately we can get several hours of travel in before night."

"Whatever do you mean by 'we'?" She was unprepared for this development. "Surely you are not expecting to accompany me?"

Chetton's brow darkened. "And surely you jest, madame, to imagine I would let you continue on your own, particularly after the tale you have just shared with me?"

She opted to ignore the ominous clenching of his jaw and strove for a breezy tone of voice. "This is no time for foolishness. You can inform Victor and Helene that you located me and that I will be travelling indefinitely. There is no need for you to accompany me. Why would you think of such a thing?"

The noise of heavy boots shuffling in the hall interrupted him from responding. It was followed by a loud knock and the officious voice of the local gendarme asking that the door be opened, "*Immediatement, s'il vous plait!*"

Lord Chetton motioned for Isobel to move to the side of the room farthest from the entry and then he opened the door to admit the official. A portly man with a large moustache entered and swept the room with a practiced eye. His glance had obviously taken her in, but he drew himself up to his full height, removed his cap, and addressed himself exclusively to Lord Chetton.

"*Excuzez-moi, monsieur. Je suis Captaine Pictou et—*"

"In the King's English if you please, sir! Not everyone speaks your bloody language you know."

This came out in the plumiest over-the top-British accent that Isobel could imagine. That alone would have flummoxed her, but his impatient request added to her confusion for she knew Chetton to be perfectly bilingual.

The man made no attempt to suppress a frown and then said in passable English, "Pardon me. I am Captain Pictou on official business. I am to intercept this lady and detain her for questioning. Miss, if you will come with me now."

Isobel grabbed on to the back on the nearest chair to steady herself. The worst of her fears had come to pass.

Captain Pictou turned to skewer her with his best look of indomitable French authority.

"The lady is not a miss, she is a married woman," countered Lord Chetton in a deceptively calm, almost bored, voice.

"If you wish, but even as Madame Barnestowe she must accompany me. There are legal matters she must answer to." And so saying, he tossed an official-looking document on the bed and grabbed hold of her upper arm. Lord Chetton bent to retrieve the paper and when he stood up he was aiming a pistol directly at the captain's temple.

"You will take your grimy French hand off of my wife immediately, captain, or I shall happily blow your brains out. I am the Earl of Chetton of the British Counsel, here on a mission of diplomacy. Do you wish to embarrass your government by having to explain why the new bride of a foreign diplomat was treated so abominably? *Well? Do you, sir?*"

The captain hesitated when Lord Chetton began to speak and by the end of the tirade had visibly deflated in front of them. His shoulders sagged, his chin drew in, and the colour drained out of his face. He dropped his hand from her arm like a hot coal and slowly backed towards the door with his hands in a "don't shoot me" posture.

"She is your wife? You are a diplomat? A *conte? Mon Dieu*! I am sorry, sir. I shall find whoever is responsible for this error and they shall not remain unpunished. My apologies, madame. Good day."

CHAPTER NINETEEN

Isobel was rooted to the spot. She could hardly take in what had just happened. The relief from being so close to disaster was overwhelming, followed swiftly by the realization of how Lord Chetton had averted it.

"Your wife? You said I was your wife," she said on a slow exhalation of breath.

She glimpsed the deep tide of sorrow Chetton held so tightly in check. He did not permit it to gain hold, then all was ruthlessly hidden as he refocused. She marvelled at the strength of his will.

"Yes. Well, it seemed the prudent thing to do and it shut the captain up quite smartly, did it not?" Lord Chetton didn't look at her as he replaced the pistol in the oversized pocket of his riding cape.

"You should not have involved yourself in this mess any further."

"Why not, Isobel? And do not tell me it is because you don't need any help, which is a precious bit of whimsy, not to mention a blatant falsehood. Travelling as a couple will throw immediate suspicion off of you, and as my wife I can afford you more protection. Let us not argue about this now. We need to leave before the captain gets his second wind and thinks to come back and ask to see our marriage certificate."

And so saying, he shuffled her out the door, down the stairs, and into the awaiting carriage.

Since Lord Chetton had elected to ride his horse rather than travel in the carriage with her, Isobel was able to stretch out on the seat in comfort. She had never had the luxury of travelling alone in such a conveyance and it was a novelty she was enjoying. It also gave her the opportunity to reflect on her present circumstances in solitude. She had been baffled by Chetton's precipitous declaration to the French captain, but could now see the wisdom of such an arrangement. In theory. How the hour by hour reality would play out was another matter entirely.

She also had to face the fact that the benefit of this fictitious arrangement fell solely to her. The possible risks would accrue to Lord Chetton, not herself. If their ruse was discovered it would be his reputation that would be damaged, hers was beyond repair. His future would be put in jeopardy, and heaven knew her aspirations for a future were insignificant compared to the good that a man of Chetton's courage and foresight could achieve for the nation. She had wrestled with this problem before and thought then that the solution would be to distance herself from the man and the constant temptation he provided. Now fate had intervened and seemed to demand that the very reverse of that decision come to pass. It was her obligation to take the lead in the matter. She must remain resolute about containing her feelings for the good of them both.

It was going to be a monumental task. Just the idea of being in his company again for extended periods of time quickened her breath. The thought of them having to play out even the basics of a marital relationship in public put a blush on her cheeks. She would not permit herself to indulge in imagining any further familiarities.

Lord Chetton was engaged in his own evaluation of the situation from a vastly different perspective. First and foremost was his concern for Isobel's safety and wellbeing. The need to protect her was elemental to him and overshadowed all other considerations. He had not hesitated one moment in returning to France once he determined it was Isobel's probable location. He was pleased to have found her but appalled at the reason for her having to flee from Guernsey.

It chaffed his manhood that she had not applied to him for aid and yet he was not truly surprised at her audacity. Had she not recently left England and travelled across France by herself in order to get to Guernsey? Sadly, she had not gained the measure of safety she required to keep out of the clutches of her conniving relatives.

Duke's chilling death had brought the possibility of danger into sharp relief, but this worried him only in so far as it might bring Isobel into his orbit of violence by association.

But all of that depended upon the questionable fact of whether or not she was really telling the truth.

He would be a fool to accept all of her explanations, meagre as they were, at face value. Where there was smoke there was often fire, he reminded himself. Therefore, he would continue with his official mission and at the same time investigate the truth of Isobel's story. Now that the die was cast he had the perfect excuse to stay on and see to Isobel's safety. And to monitor her movements. Two birds with one sharp stone. Rarely had the French, even inadvertently, aided him so well.

The heavy mist of earlier had percolated itself into a light drizzle and Lord Chetton turned the collar of his riding coat up against the damp. He reckoned they were quite close to the modest inn that he had in mind for tonight's lodgings. Complete dark had fallen and it was best to keep off the roads at such a time if possible. He knew the innkeeper, Gustav, of old and would have no trouble securing accommodation.

When he opened the door to the carriage a few minutes later to assist Isobel out, he found her propped against the squabs fast asleep. When she did not waken to the gentle call of her name he left her where she was to secure their accommodation. Upon returning to the carriage a short time later he gently lifted her into his arms, and with Gustav's directions in mind, carried her to the modest room that would have to suffice for them both for the night. The small establishment was full and Chetton's request for a second room for the comfort of his wife, who was, he said, slightly indisposed, had regretfully been refused. Lord Chetton hesitated about whether to lay his soft burden on the bed or ease her into a chair. He could not believe his indecision. Usually in such a situation the answer was a foregone conclusion in favour of the horizontal. As he stood in the middle of the cramped room Isobel stirred in his arms.

"Where are we? Oh my, you are all wet."

She brushed her hand across his damp face. Just the touch of her fingers on his cheek was enough to enflame his blood. The pressure of her form as he held her added to the delightful torture. She struggled a little to be put down and rocked gently against him as he set her on her feet. He cursed his brilliance for thinking of this solution to their problem. Man and wife in the same room all night. His supposed wife was not just anyone, of course, it was Isobel, and it was not going to be just for tonight either, but for the foreseeable future. Yes, he was a clever chap. Torment was his middle name.

"We will stay here tonight and get an early start in the morning."

He was trying to ignore the scent of her hair as she continued to stand close to him. To distract himself, he asked, "Are you hungry?"

"Yes, I am rather."

His predatory look must have surprised her and she stumbled as she took a quick, involuntary step away. The back of her legs bumped the side of the nearby bed and she sat down abruptly. Then, seeming to notice where she had landed, she quickly stood back up.

"That is, if you are. Hungry."

Sometimes even innocuous words could be dangerous, he thought, striving to gain control after her innocent double entendre. In fact he doubted she would even understand what it was his libidinous mind was picturing as they spoke. Christ, but it was going to be one long, glorious night of temptation. He must try harder to mask his suppressed desire; he was not an untested youth, for God's sake.

Chetton explained that his request for a second room had not been granted. Although it would have been preferable, he noted that there was some merit to them being together on the very unlikely chance that the gendarme had followed them. He promised her that he would respect her privacy and reassured her, on his word as a gentleman, that we should have no worries of him taking advantage of their situation.

Long before his explanations were completed, Isobel's cheeks were tinged with a sweet blush and she would not look at him.

"I understand that this must be extremely awkward for you, Isobel. Society judges women harshly in these matters, but listen to me for a moment, please."

She would not raise her head. Apprehensive now that he had offended her completely, Chetton lifted her chin with his hand, and was appalled to find that her eyes were firmly squeezed shut. Chetton didn't hesitate from that moment. He simply picked her up and settled them both down on the settee.

Chetton was close enough to feel her warmth, but not quite touching. This way he could observe her lovely face and assess the truth of her reactions. He could see she was struggling with herself, with him, in a private way that did not allow him access to her thoughts or deep emotions, because he simply was not a part of her inner dialogue. He was not pleased that she had segregated a part of herself from him, but there was nothing he could do, nothing he could aspire to change right now that would ease her conflict or advance his cause.

No further word was spoken between them until Isobel finally opened her eyes. Then he spoke. "I am the one who precipitated us into this current untoward situation, but I must ask you, Isobel, are you afraid of me?"

She looked surprised at the question. "No. It has just been such a confusing few days."

He digested this answer in silence. But he wanted to be clear, that there be no mistake.

She began to fiddle with the decorative buttons sewn along the wrists of her dress. "Are you having second thoughts about, about our arrangement?" she whispered.

"Not in the least. Can you, Isobel, say the same?"

He put a light, restraining hand over hers to still the movement of her restless, nervous fingers. He needed to understand what exactly was happening here as well.

"Look Isobel, I am not trying to confuse you. If I have learned one thing it is that the past should not overshadow the present. But something seems to be bothering you. Will you tell me what it is?"

She looked right through him until he removed his hand, and then graced him with a crooked, quizzical smile that asked, *whatever could you be driving at*. He was not fooled by the display.

"How do you do it?" she asked in a flat voice.

"Do what?" He absently wound a curl of her hair around his fingers.

"Make it all sound so easy."

"I am not following you." He lifted the lock of her hair to his nose and breathed in the clean scent, fascinated by the soft texture of it.

Isobel frowned at him and impatiently unwound the captured

lock and smoothed it back with the rest of her tresses in a practiced feminine move. Chetton got the message that this was going to be a deeper conversation and so stood up to confront it.

When Isobel spoke again her gaze was cast out towards the middle distance of the room. "You just said the past should not change the present. But how do you live like that? I mean, surely a person's history affects who and what they are."

"Yes, it affects them. I am just saying it should not loom over their future and stunt it."

"But you are a strong man; you have such a decisive will. What about others who are not like you? There are people who cannot escape their demons. Not everyone is able to sidestep their past as nimbly as you."

Chetton noticed the defensive tone she used and wondered at its source. If she was sent to lead him astray, surely she must have an inkling of his earlier life.

He coughed discreetly. "I have not exactly, as you put it, 'sidestepped' my history."

"But you seem to be able to control yourself, to shut the door on things."

She was not going to let up on this, apparently.

"Isobel, if I have said something to insult you, please believe me that it was the farthest thing from my intention."

She stood and started to walk towards the door. "Goodness gracious, I have been a fool. I must get out of here."

"There is really no alternative. I am afraid you must stay."

She turned to him and said with savage sarcasm, "That would be so nice, so easy for you, would it not? To have a woman close by, at your pleasure. So convenient and uncomplicated. For you. The man without a past to bother him."

Chetton was not prepared to have Isobel flee, but neither he did want her to entertain this view of himself. The woman could exasperate him to no end.

"Will you cease that line of thought, Isobel? You know full well this has nothing to do with my convenience, for God's sake. Do not insult me, or yourself, for that matter."

Just the movement of her hips as she walked away from him had the power to increase the speed of his blood. Chetton was rather annoyed at Isobel for her flippant explanation of what he wanted from her. He was more annoyed with himself for not being able to fully comprehend her intentions. And he was spectacularly annoyed that Isobel's unconscious movement across a room could so captivate him despite the intrigue swirling around her. Chetton could not understand her behaviour and so chanced a theory. "Has this anything to do with your husband, Isobel? Did you not get on well?"

CHAPTER TWENTY

Chetton's bold question shocked Isobel. Weary beyond belief, she tried to piece together the pattern of events.

From the moment she had heard Chetton pronounce them as man and wife she had wanted to set some part of herself free. She had been seeking something she did not truly understand and had been caught in a strange state of mind. It was as if she was playing the role of another person in a make-believe life and she was reluctant to let the enchantment go. That person was someone decent and truthful, a woman who was acceptable, was worthy of this man's affections and respect.

Isobel knew that if she chose to get close to Chetton, she would not be able to refrain from delving into her history. Because that was what she really wanted to reconcile. She wished to find a cure for her own particular predicament. She wanted so much, and for so many selfish motives. But it meant using Chetton for her own ends. When this aspect of the truth registered with her, she knew they had to separate from each other.

Yet she had not had the strength to leave him early enough and thus had sown the seeds of her own destruction.

"My dear, what is this all really about?" asked Chetton.

Isobel felt drained of energy and could just manage a slow shake of her head. She really did not want to discuss anything with him of this nature, but he would apparently not be denied some kind of an answer.

"Isobel, there is nowhere to go. Do come and sit back down and tell me what is wrong."

The man was relentless. She knew he expected a response that would explain her continued reluctance to speak about her past. She sighed deeply, crossed the room, and perched herself on the very edge of the settee.

"I have seen people react so after they have had a great tragedy."

From this comment Isobel understood Chetton was contemplating another way to broach the subject. Neither of them spoke for several moments and then Isobel turned towards him.

"If I tell you the truth, Chetton, you will not like me any better than I like myself."

"What does that mean exactly?"

She finally said in a hushed voice, "I have never been in this situation with a man before."

"Are you trying to tell me this is the first time you've ever *been* with a man?" asked Lord Chetton considerably surprised. "Then the captain must have been a poor husband indeed, madam."

Isobel put her hands on her cheeks and attempted to hide her burning face. This would not do. She fixed her mouth into a frown. "That is hardly an appropriate comment, my Lord Chetton."

Obviously her lapse into formality did not bother the determined man. He simply raised his eyebrows and tilted his chin at her. "You never speak of your husband. Is it too painful, too soon?"

She drew in a large breath and let it out slowly. "There is nothing to be done."

"I am sorry. I have no right to pry. You just seem so forlorn sometimes, almost lost."

Isobel rose and walked over to survey her image in the ornate mirror hanging above the fireplace. She attempted to pin up a few strands of her hair, then gave up on the effort and frowned at her reflection.

"I suppose you have been circumstanced like this with a great many women."

Chetton followed and stood close behind her. He answered her only with a patient look in the mirror.

"Forgive me, that was unnecessary, and not to the point. It is just that I am afraid I am out of my depth. You see my past, that is, my husband, we did not . . ."

This was going from bad to worse.

Well, she had better dive in and try and offer some kind of a plausible explanation for her outburst. The situation was abhorrent to her and she was going to be brief, so she prayed Chetton would understand and she would not have to embroider too much.

"Willoughby, my husband, we, well you must understand, he was older than I. He was very much a military man. Quite forbidding in his way. He was used to the company of men. He was not like you, comfortable around women."

She circled the small room once to collect herself, and sat down again on the settee, thankful that Chetton did not follow her. His expression was serious now and he seemed to understand that she needed some space between them.

"We were not married very long, just over a year, and most of that time we were apart. So, you see, we did not have much time together as man and wife. To get to know each other, to . . . to . . ."

Chetton cleared his throat and finished her thought, "To become intimate?"

Oh God, this was intolerable. How to explain?

"Did you never lie together?" he asked quietly.

Her mouth had gone completely dry.

"Do you mean you are a virgin still, Isobel?"

She felt ill at the question, at the use of that very personal and intimate word. The word that insinuated so much.

"No, no. We were together on our wedding night, but it was never," she sighed. "He, he was not careful with me." She could not help herself from getting upset. The tears in the corner of her eyes slipped out despite herself. "I did not, I could not . . . And you are the first since then. There has been no one else."

It was only a second until Chetton's arms were around her and he laid his hand on her cheek. She was glad that he had both common sense and delicacy enough to realize what the admission has cost her.

"Shush, my dear, you need not say anymore."

She cried softly this time, her heart laid open at the thought of such things. Thank God he had understood, for she could not have said or borne anything further. It would have to do.

※

Much later, when he hoped she could endure it, Lord Chetton spoke of practical matters. "I will go downstairs and order us some supper. Fortuitously, the private dining room is free and we shall not have to venture into the public room to dine."

"Yes, thank you, that will be fine. I will just tidy up and be right down."

Neither spoke much during dinner. Even the exchange of common pleasantries was an effort after what had just transpired. Chetton was unsure how to proceed with the prospect of sharing a room for the night before them.

He elected to stay for a second brandy to make sure that Isobel had enough time for privacy and to ensure that his defences were fully under control. Isobel was in bed, covered up to her nose with bedding and pushed far back against the wall when Lord Chetton came in an hour later. He deftly undressed and slipped on his nightshirt, left on his trousers for good measure, and got into the bed.

If Isobel was awake, she gave no sign of it and Chetton eventually relaxed enough to let sleep claim him. It was there in the dream world that he met her. She came to him willingly and they joined in every way he had ever fantasized about and completed him in a way he had never thought possible. They lay together afterwards blissfully sated in each other's arms. Slowly their comfort was eroded by an aura of fear and the anticipation of danger. An unseen menace invaded the cocoon of love they had created and to his horror he was unable to stop it from pulling them apart. The last he saw of Isobel was her tear-stained face as she was forced away and faded from his sight.

He awoke with a fine sheen of sweat covering his body. His discomfort took a surge towards terror as he registered an empty bed beside him. He sat up and saw the small form crouched by the fireplace with her head buried in her arms. No force on earth could have stopped him from going to her although he doubted the wisdom of the move instantly.

He knelt beside Isobel and scooped her up into his arms. Her slim arms wrapped themselves around his neck and he settled himself down with her on his lap. It wasn't a time for words and so he rocked her gently and rubbed her back and waited for a semblance of calm to find her.

"I am so sorry, dreadfully weak behaviour on my part. Not at all the thing! It is just that I am at a loss and rather scared," said Isobel.

That admission nearly wrung the heart out of him. "Why, love? Of what?"

She gave him an ineffectual thump on his chest for his cavalier question.

"Of what? You cannot be serious? Just my vindictive uncle and the henchmen he has sent out after me, not to mention the French authorities. And now, now, you are here and that makes everything so much worse."

He forced a chuckle out. "Well, that is not quite the reception I was hoping for. Please enlighten me as to why it should be worse that I am here? You must know that I will do everything in my power to see that nothing happens to you?"

"You see, that is just the point."

"What is, my dear, you are not making any sense."

He managed to snag the handkerchief out of his jacket and handed it to her.

"Before it was just myself I had to worry about." She dabbed at her eyes with the clean square of linen and her finger traced the stitched monogram of his name. Isobel sighed. "If something untoward happened it would only affect me. But now that you are here, I have put you in danger as well."

She blew delicately into the handkerchief.

"That does not sound as if you have much confidence in my ability. May I remind you, madame, that I do this sort of thing, on the quiet, of course, as part of my job? Why, I was born to be a swashbuckling hero. And any damsels I find in my travels I naturally sweep along with me to safety. You have no need to fear for the future, not one wit."

He was punished for this latest foolishness by another punch and a slight giggle.

"Really, you are incorrigible. Are you not worried?"

"No, Isobel, I am not. I do not believe in worrying generally, I prefer to spend my energy in planning and anticipating different possibilities which might occur."

When he saw Isobel's delicate fingers shake he encircled them with his hand. A moment's inspiration gave him the opening he might need to further convince Isobel that pretending to be married offered more than one-sided advantages.

"Please attend to my reasoning in this matter. I do not want you to think you are the only one to benefit from this ruse we find ourselves in. I have matters of state of a very delicate nature that I have to deal with, and masquerading as a married couple creates a good cover. I am only sorry that we will have to travel under a rather low profile in the meantime to avoid being recognized. Other than that, we should fare very well. So stop worrying that I am here entirely for your assistance. The benefits, as you can now understand, are mutual."

She managed a tentative smile. "So I will not be taking you totally away from your mission then?"

"Not at all. Tomorrow the carriage will go off in one direction and we will head in another on horseback. So it is imperative that you get a good night's rest tonight." With this last statement he stood and settled Isobel back on the bed and, for good measure, positioned himself as far away from her as humanly possible.

As he began to drift into sleep he could hardly credit the story she had told him earlier. Blessed as he had been with a caring and supportive family, he found it hard to imagine the coldness and cruelty Isobel's relatives had subjected her to. She did not even have the memory of a close relationship with her husband to comfort her. Some men were just bastards with women. Of course, that rested on the condition that she was telling the truth. He felt that she was, but was that enough?

Isobel had been wrong in at least one aspect of what she had said. She was totally in error when she mentioned being the only one who would be affected if she should come to any harm.

CHAPTER TWENTY-ONE

The following day was quite warm, and the unseasonable heat made travel tiring for both horse and rider. Isobel had exaggerated when she said she could not ride. It was just that she did it badly. Very badly. Chetton had a natural seat that was honed to perfection by training and experience. He cringed so often during the morning when he saw horse and woman struggle that he thought he would give himself the headache before lunch. Lord Chetton had done his best to find a docile mount for Isobel. He chose character over size and so the grey she rode stood over sixteen hands but took direction very well and had a good head to be relied upon. Isobel was nervous on the big animal. God bless her, he thought, she was not graceful or athletic in the least. She was altogether too rigid and so bounced when she should have glided as one with her horse. But it was not the kind of thing you could teach anyone quickly, and certainly not when they had to be in the saddle all day. In his experience, especially when dealing with women, logic did not have the power to overcome nerves or fear. The last thing he wanted to do was to embarrass or frustrate Isobel any further by giving unsolicited advice, so he watched and waited with all the patience he could muster. And by late afternoon every iota of it was required for him not to simply pluck her off the grey and straddle her across his mount.

He dismounted in a shaded roadside clearing and stretched his shoulders in order that Isobel not think he was calling another halt for her benefit. Taking note of her flushed and dishevelled state, Chetton moved to help her dismount. He could well imagine her discomfort from the day's travel. For anyone unaccustomed to it, a full day in the saddle was hard going. If you were a woman, particularly one who had inadequate skill, the resulting aches and strain would be much worse.

Patting the side of the horse's neck, she said, "Mystic Grey."

"I am sorry," he said.

She cast him a look of uninhibited triumph. "Mystic Grey. It is what I am going to call my horse. Mystic for short. I know I do not deserve her, but she has been very patient today. We have become friends and so I wanted to name her."

He shook his head and the trim little figure walked away and gingerly seated herself in the shade of a tree. His expression did not go unnoticed by Isobel. As she watched him approach, she began to apologize for her slowness all day. Surprised and a little ashamed that she had misconstrued his behaviour, he hurried to explain his actions.

"You have misunderstood my intentions completely. That is not at all what I had in mind, it was something else entirely. I am familiar with this area. Just behind that coppice of trees is a seldom used cottage owned by an acquaintance of mine. I happen to know he is engaged elsewhere for a few weeks. Luckily I have stayed at this little out-of-the-way cottage several times and know where the key is hidden."

Isobel cocked her head at this.

Lord Chetton continued, "Let me assure you we will be quite comfortable there. With the basket of supplies Gustav packed for us we shall be provisioned with the basics. It should only be for a night or two and then we can safely go back to civilization."

The cottage was neat, if a bit dusty, and reminded Isobel of L'Ancresse, though on a more modest scale. After a quick inspection of it, Isobel took off her bonnet and gloves and set to work. It became quickly evident that she was not at all adept at starting fires.

"Do, I beg of you, leave the fire to me, Isobel. Perhaps you would be so good as to begin unpacking the food and organizing what we should prepare for dinner," said Lord Chetton after half a dozen matches went out to no avail.

Isobel stared at the cold fireplace for a moment, and then stood. "I daresay that is a good idea. Simple cooking is an area in which I have some proficiency. At least Emma has always given me to understand so. She often used to mention how skilled I was at preparing broths and custards. I feel it incumbent of me to help in some way toward our common good."

However gratified Lord Chetton was in hearing of Isobel's willingness to pitch in, after a full day on the road he felt that the prospect of broths and custards might not fully satisfy his hunger.

"Marvellous. But before we lose the light entirely, if you do not object, I might just elect to try for a fish in the river. It can supplement our dinner so that Gustav's basket need not be depleted too quickly," said Lord Chetton as he inspected the sturdy fishing rod that was propped up by the door. "Chris is perhaps more proficient at cooking our meal when we venture out together to fish, but I believe I can achieve a palatable enough result to accompany Gustav's offerings."

"It would be shockingly selfish of me to deprive you of a bit of sport, after all you have done for me," said Isobel, then catching Lord Chetton's startled look, quickly added, "and of course fresh fish will be delightful."

Lord Chetton left the fire stoked high and Isobel humming softly as he took the rod and headed towards the nearby river. Ninety minutes and two of the regions delicious wild brown trout later, he retraced his path back to the small cottage. He could hear the rustling and stamping of the grey as he approached. Wondering what had riled the calm beast he went over to take a look and saw several large boot marks in the dirt. Was someone following them? Had she made contact with somebody while he was catching their dinner, by God?

He quickly laid down the catch and moved towards a clump of bushes that would afford him cover while allowing him a view of the cottage. The door was open and he could see inside.

Isobel was seated with her hands and mouth bound. There was a mutinous look on her face but she couldn't hide the fear in her eyes. Lord Chetton's heart quickened to see her obvious distress. A man was routing through his saddlebags. Although the intruder wore no pistols he had a large curved knife tucked in his belt.

Lord Chetton cautiously circled round the bushes to get a better vantage point. He was now behind the unwary man and from this point, his view was unimpeded. He could see a nearly empty bottle of Gustav's good brandy sitting on the table. The man must be a petty criminal. He had no discipline and probably no plan, other than to rob them. However, the situation was unpredictable and could still prove to be dangerous. He would take no chances with Isobel in a vulnerable position. He debated about allowing the robber to take what he wanted and letting him go none the wiser. Everything was replaceable and it would cause less fuss than confronting him.

When the ruffian stood and walked over to Isobel with an unmistakable leer on his face, Lord Chetton changed his mind. Isobel turned her head away from the man and Lord Chetton saw a large welt on the side of her face. It was then that the fate of the intruder was sealed. Chetton felt his hunter instinct rise within him and he gave it free rein. Wasting no more time, he stepped from behind the bushes and before the man had the chance of putting his filthy hand on Isobel again, Lord Chetton rushed through the door and rapped him sharply on the side of the head with the sturdy fishing pole. He dropped like a stone and Isobel screamed into the rag gagging her mouth.

Lord Chetton checked the man to ensure that he would not cause any immediate trouble and then hurried over to Isobel. She was coughing and crying into the rag and could hardly breathe by the time he removed it from her. When her arms were released she scrambled away from him, horror etched across her beautiful face.

"Good Lord, have you killed him?"

"I doubt it, but if not he will certainly feel the crack on his head later." He could see the tremble in Isobel's hands as she tried to tuck in the dishevelled strands of her hair.

"It was the only way to be sure he would not hurt you."

She stared at him, her eyes still wide with fright.

He desperately wanted to get a better look at the bruise on the side of her head and examine the rest of her for other injury, but he could see she was in no mood to be touched just yet.

"I am going to drag him out to the old shed in the back. He should be out for several hours and will no doubt want to leave the area after he wakes up. You sit there and drink this." He drained the last of the brandy into a cup and handed it to her. "I will not be long."

When he returned from that task, Isobel was sitting beside the fire. The livid abrasions on her wrists from being bound so tight made him grate his teeth. As he squatted down beside her she gave him a hasty glance and then took a tentative sip of the brandy. Christ, she wasn't disgusted with him, was she? Not that she didn't have a right to be after what she had just witnessed. Although he felt it had been a necessary and successful conclusion to the incident, he could understand how it would seem to Isobel. And wasn't that a thought to gall him.

His guts were twisted up with the want of her. Seeing her with that man, and imagining what could have happened took his breath away. The need to protect her fused with the call to battle and was still singing through his veins. It took the last of his reservoir of strength not to reach out to touch her.

☙

Isobel was nearly beside herself with agitation. The panic that man had caused her when he grabbed her, combined with the shock of seeing him downed so unexpectedly had not worn off. Almost equal to that, though, was the anxiety she felt for Chetton. Oh, the amount of trouble she had caused this man was incalculable.

She touched the contusion on her head with a shaking hand. "I am so unbelievably sorry for this, Chetton."

He frowned. "Indeed? But to what do you refer? Certainly you can take no blame in this matter."

"I regret that you were forced to . . ." She waved her hand in a vague gesture.

"You regret that I had to intervene with that rogue? Well, I am not in any way of the same opinion. I see that you have a soft heart and care about people, but, well, we differ greatly, Isobel."

She shook her head and started to demur but he interrupted. "No, I speak the truth. That man hurt you, it could have been worse. To me he is disposable and I do not scruple to tell you that I have half a mind to return to the shed and dispatch the cur posthaste." He held out his hand to her and smiled. "Now do come here and let me attend to that head of yours."

Lord Chetton moved towards her to gauge the severity of the wound. While he was gently cleaning it with a cloth dipped in water, he whispered in her ear. "You must tell me, did he harm you in any other way?"

She put a finger against his mouth to stop any more speech.

"I am fine, he just scared me. He said such things, and I was frightened." Isobel glanced at the dust on her skirt from the skirmish and began to methodically brush it off. She continued in a small voice, "That's what I wanted to tell you, what I want you to know. I'm glad you punished him. I hated the brute for how he treated me. I'm just sorry you had to assume the burden of protecting me again."

Isobel had been so terrified by the robber that she could hardly credit her unscathed escape. Chetton had come to her rescue yet again. She had told him she hated the man and this was no lie. But she didn't hate all men. She didn't want to hate all men. She didn't want to hate and fear what men and women did together. It was what men could do to women in hate that she despised. Somehow the near calamity of today had brought it all home to her.

CHAPTER TWENTY-TWO

Considering the vagabond attack, and not wanting to leave themselves open to him returning with friends and bent on revenge, Chetton decided it was best to move on early the next morning. Although Isobel was more competent on Mystic Grey, she still tired easily as the hours accumulated throughout the day. They had spoken very little and Isobel became more withdrawn as the day wore on. By early evening they were more than ready to check into an inn. It should be safe enough to stay in a small town and take advantage of the amenities.

Isobel stayed outside the inn fiddling with her saddlebag while Lord Chetton made the arrangements. They were continuing with his suggestion of not disclosing his title or the privileges due to his consequence, as he had explained it made no sense to do so when travelling on clandestine business. Procuring suitable chambers was not nearly as easy a task as it would otherwise have been, as he had no manservant attending him to ride ahead and secure arrangements. Isobel's lack of an abigail would also draw attention if they attempted to travel more luxuriously. Luckily, he had established connections with several smaller, discreet inns over the years and planned on using their services when he could. This would also make it easier for Jean to forward communication to him as they travelled.

Isobel found she could not stand in front of innkeepers while Lord Chetton made arrangements for them as a married couple. It seemed such an intimate thing. She couldn't fully explain their unconventional situation even to herself. Although it was only a make-believe marriage she felt she was stealing from him somehow. The rights and privileges that would be accorded to his wife were not hers. His very name with all its noble history was not hers. She could only diminish its value and tarnish it, despite her wishes to the opposite.

After a delicious though solemn dinner consisting of asparagus soup, trout amandine, slices of veal, roasted potatoes, and petits pois, finished with chocolate gateau and a cheese plate, Isobel was ready to retire for the evening.

Lord Chetton took his time at the dinner table before he returned upstairs. He carried his glass and a decanter of fine old brandy with him to savour in the room. Isobel was in her nightgown but seated by the fire. She was bundled in a blanket. He was not pleased with this arrangement. It was not even chilly in the room. He feared the barriers were also in her mind. He set the decanter of brandy down on the table with more force than was his custom.

"Will you not take the bed? Or is it that you are afraid that I shall attempt to get in it with you?"

Her colour rose at his directness, but she did not speak.

He felt appalled at the thought of asking the next question. Yet it needed to be done. He sat across from her so he could see Isobel's face when she answered it. If she answered it. He took a sip of the strong flavourful liquor.

"Do you regret last night, Isobel? Do you wish it had not happened?"

He tried to gauge the situation from her perspective, how it might have been for her, and he was not happy with the image. He had held Isobel for a short time to overcome her immediate desperation from the altercation in the cottage. And then she had purposefully moved to the far side of the bed to drift off to sleep. But to achieve his own selfish pleasure, he had resumed his closeness to Isobel while she slept. It must have shocked her to awaken in such a position. He was at a loss as to how his behaviour could have seemed acceptable to him at the time. Isobel was under his protection and honour forbade him to take advantage of the circumstances.

"I apologize for the way I behaved towards you."

"Please," she whispered on an exhalation of breath. "Do not apologize for last evening. You made me feel completely safe and cared for. Do not try to change that now. Please, I couldn't bear it. Unless, that is to say, have you any misgivings?"

His head buzzed from her admission. It was so at odds with her recent behaviour. He could not reconcile the two. "No, not one."

"Well then."

She said this as if it were the end of the conversation, as if some mutual understanding had been reached, but he was still at a loss as to what could be bothering her.

"I want to believe that you have no second thoughts, Isobel, but you have been so sad, so distant today."

She looked away and concentrated her vision on the fire burning in the hearth.

"I know you have a generous heart, Isobel. Be honest with me."

"After the fright from that horrid man, our time together last night was very precious. But it was also something of a revelation to me. It is not a situation that can continue. It would not be fair to you."

"Fair to me? What on earth can you mean?"

The flickering light from the fireplace cast a sombre hue over her grey green eyes, and her lips were semi pursed as if she had been caught in mid-thought about a distasteful matter.

She took a big breath and let it out slowly. "I fear you have the wrong impression of who I am, Chetton, what I am like."

"To the contrary, I think I know you pretty well. You have told me about your unfulfilled marriage. Is that what this is about?"

"No, not that. It is impossible for our contrived marriage to endure for much longer, you must understand that, surely? I cannot expect you to continue to come to my aid in such a manner. It is not at all the thing."

Was she thinking of leaving then, of making other plans, wondered Lord Chetton. "I do not have all the answers either, but one thing is certain, and that is you are not yet out of danger. Your uncle's agents could be just behind us, it has only been a few days."

Isobel did not respond and continued to stare at the fire. He was left with many questions as to her real state of mind.

The sky darkened and they could hear the hotel staff settle into their night time routines but no further conversation passed between the two of them. Chetton was surprised to find how unsettled he was about Isobel's indication that she foresaw an approaching end to their arrangement. Her concern for the troubles she had caused him, as she phrased it, seemed real and he was touched by it. No women of his recent acquaintance would have given any inconvenience to him a second thought. Not one of them had ever worried about the toll it took on him to fulfill his duty and obligations.

A deep yearning to connect to Isobel so that she would understand him better took hold of him. He recognized that even as she kept a part of herself veiled from him, so he did to her. Perhaps it was time to take a chance on the truth, or at least a part of it.

"Isobel, do you know about the loss of my wife and young son?" he asked without preamble.

Isobel's hand drifted to her throat. "Yes, such a tragedy. Chris told me about them."

"Did he give you all the details? No, never mind, he would not have done so. And I am sure you did not hear them from my mother either." He smiled grimly.

"Actually, I only ever overheard a few whispered comments about you from the staff. Most of the things were vague. I attributed it to the fact that your family is held in such kind regard in Guernsey. I am so sorry about your loss." She dabbed at her eyes, "I cannot conceive of the grief which that must have caused you."

Chetton went very still and continued to look at Isobel. "Their names were Madeline and Samuel, you know. Maddie and Sam." But all he could think of was a letter written with malicious intent.

There had been a time in his life when he had been positive about all the things he desired. Chief among these was his love for Maddie Perrault, the darkhaired vixen who had been in his blood since he had first set eyes on her at her coming out ball in London. Then seventeen, Madeleine Perrault was a full-bodied young woman of high spirits who had cast her spell on a whole army of men that season. Three years her senior and believing himself to be worldly, Chetton had just taken a first in politics at Oxford.

He had used all of his considerable charm, and a great deal of his family money, in order to impress the lady, all to no avail. As she approached her eighteenth birthday, Chetton was only one in a long line of suitors and felt he did not hold any particular advantage in the beautiful Miss Perrault's affections. He was becoming desperate and believed she would surely accept another proposal as her marriageable age neared.

During this time he had been approached to accompany a trade mission abroad in the capacity of a junior diplomat. His family had for generations been intimate with those in political power. The opportunity was too good to decline and he left England, torn between what he felt at the time to be a broken heart and a sense of high adventure that he was beginning his adult responsibilities in earnest. It was to be nearly eight months before he returned to London.

Isobel touched his hand, and it brought him back to the present.

"And you loved them very much, you still do. I could see it in your eyes a moment ago."

"Did you? Was that what you think you saw? Well, yes, naturally I loved them." But he could not go on with the lie. Not to her. "Look, Isobel, the truth is, the truth is I loved my son."

"Your *son?*"

"Yes. You see, I, well, I knew he wasn't mine."

"My God, oh, Chetton!"

He stood and made a quick circuit around the room, ending up back at his chair, though he did not sit again. "I have only told that to one other person before, not even my whole family knows. I never said the words out loud. I did not even want to think them, to give them that little power of truth."

Isobel was stunned into silence, as much by his admission, no doubt, as by the dark and vicious appearance he knew he could not hide from his face. His entire body was rigid. Emotion, deep and raw, was radiating from him in waves. It was rage. Unmitigated and unforgiving anger, this was the hard edge of what lingered in his heart. Soul deep it went and simmered now, under the surface of his grief.

"Your wife, she was unfaithful. How awful for you. And yet, to lose them to illness in such a bitter way must have been much worse."

Chetton was struggling to keep some degree of composure. He wanted Isobel in his arms as he had wanted little else in his life, but was equally afraid the touch of her would unman him further. She would see him for the posturing shadow of a man he was and she would loathe him.

"Despite her sins, surely you have had to make peace with your wife. I mean, after her death?"

"Make peace?"

"And your poor little boy, so tragic nothing could have been done to save him either."

Chetton heard the strangled laugh, the horrible mirthless noise he had produced, and it forced him to continue.

"From the moment Sam was born I accepted Maddie's child as my own. I admit that the shock of uncovering her deception on our wedding night was a great blow. But I had a decision to make. There were no voyeurs in our chamber to gainsay my paternity. Apparently the Perrault family did not know of their daughter's impropriety. Maddie repeatedly assured me that the indiscretion had only occurred once and was a mistake from the outset. She neither harboured any feelings for the man, nor wished ever to see him again."

"I do not quite understand."

He looked at the amber liquid in his glass and took a long swallow. "I did not ask, you see, nor did I want to know, the identity of the suitor. Apparently, he had travelled abroad soon after the brief liaison, none the wiser. Her rounding stomach was the reason for our short engagement, the more fool I. With the conceit of youth, I thought she had finally succumbed to my charms, you see."

Isobel sighed and adjusted the fall of her skirts, but did not look his way.

"Well, Isobel, life does not stop for tragedy, does it, but it often forces us to take an alternate route. So, I could have repudiated the marriage and caused untold scandal and humiliation for both families, or I could have chosen to dwell on her duplicity privately, thus setting up a life of continuous discord between us. Instead, I decided to ignore the original deception and seek to heal the breach in trust, to accept the babe. And although I could not love Maddie the same way, still I cared for her."

Chetton rolled the empty brandy glass between his palms then set it down and with a hint of a smile continued. "It feels strange, to tell you this, the first person after so many years. I reveal myself as a type of cuckold. Not a very appealing picture, is it?"

Isobel made some reassuring little noises as she leaned in closer. "If you can speak of it, how did it happen, their deaths?"

He needed to finish, to get everything out in the open.

"I can remember it all with such clarity. It never leaves me. Chris and I had been out to a late dinner with friends. The house was ablaze with light when we returned. This in itself was not an unusual situation, Maddie sometimes went through a nervous spell where she could not bear to be in the dark and the household was kept well lit for her restless nightly wanderings. It did seem out of the ordinary, however, to have a horse and carriage tied up at the front door. We entered and were halfway up the stairs when we realized something was amiss, a woman was softly crying. It was not Maddie, that was certain, she seldom cried."

He looked down at his clenched fists and frowned.

"When excess emotion overwhelmed Maddie she was more likely to yell out her frustration or throw something. More than one housemaid had been reduced to tears after being subjected to one of her tirades. No, it was Mrs. McClure's pain we heard that night, and her fear."

He heard Isobel's sharp intake of breath. "It is extraordinary how I always see this unfold in my mind like a tragic play that cannot be stopped." He shook himself and continued. "We were heading towards the wing where the bedrooms are located and noticed a figure seated on the hallway bench. I felt a jolt of concern when I recognized the man as Dr. Hoskins. He stood as I approached him.

"'Lord Chetton. I am afraid I have bad news for you,' he said gravely. I kept up my pace and continued walking right past the doctor to the door of Maddie's room, and asked, 'What is wrong, is Maddie ill again?'

"I was about to turn the handle of the door when the doctor's hand gripped mine and firmly held it in place. 'You do not want to go in there just yet, son,' he said. Hoskins's uncharacteristic familiarity alarmed me and I attempted to shake off his grip and enter the room, but he grabbed me by the shoulders and turned me so that we were face to face. 'Trust me, you need to wait a moment, hear what I have to say.'"

Chetton sat back down and crossed his legs.

"You know me, Isobel, I was not about to let anyone manhandle me, particularly in my own home, and I told the doctor to remove his hands from me immediately. Chris, God bless him, was really concerned by that time and told me to calm down and hear the doctor out."

Chetton took a breath and tried to steady his voice as he continued.

"'They are gone, son,' the doctor said. 'I am sorry to have to tell you they are dead.' A jolt of blackness swirled around my eyes for a second. 'They? Who are they?' I yelled and then, uncontrolled, I pushed the doctor away from me, grabbed Chris, and rushed into the room. We both halted mid stride. The lamps were low, but I could clearly see the waxy white face of Maddie on the pillow. Her body was preternaturally still and I knew she was dead from where I stood."

Chetton picked up his glass, refilled it, and drank down the contents in one go.

"There was another form, much smaller, lying beside her. I dragged my feet closer to the bed, as if instinct was fighting my every step. When I saw my small son tucked beside my wife, despair warred with my reason. The grief was so intense that for a moment I swear I nearly lost my mind."

Isobel closed her eyes and sighed, "Dear God."

Chetton put his hand on her shoulder lightly. "I do not believe God was anywhere near there that night, more's the pity."

Isobel looked down at the strong hands on her shoulder as he continued.

"Sometime later Dr. Hoskins explained to us that Maddie had taken an overdose of laudanum." He could feel the tendons in his neck tighten but his voice was calm now. "The witch had given the same to Sammy in a cup of apple cider."

Isobel blinked her eyes. He could make out the glint of tears there. "You do not mean? But she could not have, the very thought is appalling, Chetton!" she whispered.

"Yes. Apparently she had remained cloistered in her room since breakfast and then unexpectedly ordered a splendid afternoon tea to be sent up to her room. She wanted her son; they were to make an indoor picnic out of it and were not to be disturbed. It was not until several hours later that Mrs. McClure worked up enough courage to disregard the orders and knock on the door. After several attempts at conversation she called Norris to force it open. The poor old pair, I do not think they have ever forgiven themselves. Hoskins was summoned immediately, but it was hours too late to make any difference."

"No wonder you seem so melancholy when I look at you sometimes, Chetton. It is particularly evident when you are with Teddy, the way you watch him so intently."

"The little boys are alike in many ways, especially at this innocent trusting age, and it is very hard for me to accept Teddy's affection at certain times, though I do try and hide it from him."

"I do not mean to suggest that you are despondent; you have too much natural life force for that. And surely you know that you can do no wrong in Teddy's eyes. I am certain with his naive merry ways, he does not take notice of your occasional subdued mood. Forgive me my directness, but why did you choose to share this with me tonight?"

He picked up the brass fire shovel to bank down the coals for the night. "I have been looking to answer the same question throughout this entire conversation. The best I can come up with is that I wanted you to understand that the so-called trouble you say you have caused me is negligible compared to the real harms I have experienced over the years, Isobel. I would hate for you to make a rash decision based on a perceived imposition to me. I am, you see, made of sterner stuff."

He took an overlong time to reposition the angle of the fire screen, and thought what a coward he was. The explanation he had given to Isobel was of course part of the truth, but how much a part and to what extent he had simply wanted to have her understand him was a mystery even to him. He had now taken the unprecedented step of sharing what tore at his heart so relentlessly. God help him if she tried to use it against him in some way.

CHAPTER TWENTY-THREE

Isobel had not slept well. The intermittent sound of movement from the settee across the room indicated that Chetton had fared no better. An image of the proud face she remembered from Maddie's portrait at La Rocquette haunted her imagination and thoughts of the little boy, so close in age to Teddy, had brought tears to her eyes several times before sunrise ended the long hours of night. Betrayal was something she could understand. Isobel was in no position to judge the woman, she reminded herself, but she sympathized with Chetton about how damaging it was to have a family member deceive you.

It was a pain that dug deep inside of you, the kind of thing that changed who you were and what you felt about your place in the world. It undermined your sense of self. Perhaps even more disturbing, betrayal by an intimate set up an antagonistic barrier. It kept you wary of trusting again wholeheartedly and thus distanced you from the possibility of intimacy, from going to a place where you could be hurt again.

With these sobering thoughts shifting through her mind, Isobel was not at all equal to the task of morning conversation and was relieved that Chetton had already left the room before she pulled back the curtains of the bed to access her much awaited morning cup of hot chocolate.

The morning brought gloomy news to Lord Chetton. As requested, Jean had written to him in care of the hotel where they were staying and a letter had been on Chetton's breakfast tray when it was delivered to his table. The opened correspondence now sat before him beside the remains of his breakfast.

As usual, Jean had spared few words in his missive and went straight to the point. After calling him an imbecile for returning to France so soon he went on to say that the circumstances around La Rue's death were still unclear. He asked Chetton to continue to keep him informed of his movements so that he could forward him Drapeau's information as soon as possible.

Chetton's attention had turned to other matters, particularly his unexpected conversation with Isobel last night. He was trying to grasp onto what exactly had prompted him to have disclosed so much to her after so long a silence with everyone else when Isobel entered the crowded breakfast room.

She had eaten a light meal in the room, as he knew she preferred, and was now dressed for travel. He stood to get her attention and the shy smile that touched her lips when she sighted him helped to diminish his concerns for the moment. As she approached he bristled at the obvious male interest she innocently attracted. They were in France he reminded himself, a place where the sexes more openly played at the game of love.

"Good morning. You were up and away early this morning, my lord."

He gave her an oblique look. "Perhaps it was the best choice for both of us."

She nodded her head absently. "It was indeed a fractious night. Now enlighten me, if you will, where are we headed today?"

With an air of determination, he grasped Isobel's elbow to direct her out of the room.

"I think it best if we set off for Caen. A few days of travel should see us there. The sooner we are in an anonymous larger city the better, for a number of reasons."

The immediate one being, mused Chetton, the practicality of requiring access to funds at a bank. Chetton understood enough about Isobel's character to know that she was sensitive about finances. Several times she had tried to bring up the topic of paying him for her part of their travels. It had taken a good deal of his adroitness and diplomacy to avert outright hostilities between them on this matter. He did not want to tempt fate or the fragile detente between them by even an oblique reference to the subject or his carefully constructed truce might take an uncomfortable and entirely unnecessary wobble. It would be much better to refrain from uttering anything remotely related to financial matters at this point.

He had had cause over the years to rely on the discretion of bankers, and other well placed individuals in France, and despite some English prejudices on the matter had never been disappointed in their efficiency when it came to matters of finance. In his line of work this fact alone made up for a great deal of other deficiencies. Jean was a prime example of this for all of his rough manners.

"And so to Caen. What do you say?"

"If you think it best, I agree. I have always wanted to see William the Conqueror's castle."

"Excellent, then. I am partial to the old city myself. We will need to procure more supplies and hire a coach. I will make the arrangements. Before we leave would you like to spend a few hours along the high street and get what you might need?"

She flashed him a bright smile at the prospect of exploring the local shops.

Lord Chetton escorted her to the first of a series of establishments that dealt in ladies' necessities with the agreement of meeting back at the hotel at one o'clock.

Isobel enjoyed shopping. She had never had a vast amount of money to spend, but at least when her uncle took over the running of the family estate he had provided her with a generous monthly stipend. She was sure the money was not given due to affection but rather from the need to be seen by their social circle to be attending to the needs of his ward. In any case, she had been appreciative of the gesture, and looked forward to the times she and Emma spent looking at *La Belle Assemblée*, their favourite women's magazine known for its stylish fashion plates and patterns. She missed Emma every day and sighed at how simple her life had been at one time.

It was not long before the shopkeeper at a millinery establishment handed Isobel a fine Norwich silk shawl. "Miss, this is the one from the window that you asked about. If I may say so, it looks lovely with your colouring."

Isobel ignored the kind words. Not having received many compliments in her life, she was unsure of their sincerity. The disaster on Lihou Island had ruined her favourite shawl and she was determined to replace it with something fine. As she was asking the clerk to wrap it up for her, a man entered the store. When the cheerful clerk begged his pardon and told him she would be able to help him in a moment and the man didn't respond, Isobel thought it impolite as well as slightly odd.

She thanked the lady and left the shop, not having had a good look at the rude man as he deftly turned away when she passed him. The incident made no other impression on Isobel until an hour later. It was then that she noticed a man of similar build and dress sitting across the teashop from her. He had his head buried behind a newspaper yet Isobel was certain he was furtively watching her. A few minutes later her unease quickly mounted to alarm as the man rose, and when passing her table unobtrusively dropped a folded piece of paper on it. The first impulse she had was to cry out to him and demand an explanation for his insolence. Something in the glimpse she had gotten of his profile stopped her.

There was nothing for it but to read the note and decide just how worried she should be. She held the paper in her hands for a moment and then unfolded it decisively. The handwriting was rather crude, and the message definitely so.

Send the English lord to the north pier at dusk or the authorities will come for you, English runaway.

Isobel was glad she was seated. She feared she would have fainted from reading the hateful note had she not been. She took a large sip of her tea to restore her nerves. She could not imagine who it was that had made a connection between her and Lord Chetton so quickly, and why in the world they would want to see him. It didn't portend anything positive, of that she was sure. Clearly, telling Lord Chetton of the message would only ensure that he go to the meeting to take up the challenge. Since it might be a trap of some kind, that response would serve no good purpose.

She had a little less than an hour before she was supposed to meet Chetton at the hotel. If she hurried she could return there and collect her bag and discreetly head out of town prior to that deadline. It was imperative that she direct this trouble away from Lord Chetton whatever the consequences to her would be. With her mind made up she quit the teashop and turned her steps toward the hotel.

Packing only the bare essentials in her portmanteau, Isobel donned her cape and bonnet and proceeded down the stairs. She struggled a little with the burden of her bag and was looking at her feet lest she trip in her long skirts. She heard someone approach the steps from the bottom. The tread was heavy, though rapid. It stopped abruptly and she caught the echo of a vehement curse from a voice she recognized all too well. Then the footsteps resumed their ascent with a quicker pace and she was terrified to look up at all. The bag was wrenched out of her grasp and a large male hand grabbed her arm. She was pivoted around and marched back up the stairs. It wasn't until they had reached the top that she started to react and shake her arm free. The grip tightened and bit into her arm.

"Do not," was all Lord Chetton uttered, but it was said in a voice she hardly recognized for all the contained fury it held.

⁂

Lord Chetton led Isobel into their room and almost shoved her into a chair. He threw her portmanteau into the corner and crossed the room to look out of the window. He was so incensed with her that he needed to put some distance between the two of them for her own safety or he would surely shake her silly till she explained her behaviour.

"Well?" was all he could choke out.

As her silence continued he grabbed the windowsill and could feel the old wood disintegrate beneath his blistering grip. He prayed the woman would speak to him soon or he would lose what little remained of his control. He turned to look at her and was met with a glare that slowly dissolved to a look of dismay on her pretty face. *Wonderful, she is now terrified of me. That will certainly loosen her tongue.*

He cleared his throat and tried to gentle his voice somewhat.

"I need to know what it is you think you were doing, and I need to know now."

Still there was silence. He felt a splinter of wood jab into his palm and squeezed harder until he felt blood begin to ooze. The pain helped to center him and draw some of his anger away from the quiet woman.

"It is obvious you were running away. Again. And I would know the reason for it, madame."

He viciously ground the splinter a little harder and pain shot through his hand. He felt wetness on his wrist but did not look down. Another curse let loose from his lips. The stubborn woman would be the death of him, he was sure. A drop of blood hit the floor. And it was starting now.

A cry of shock rang out in the room and Isobel bolted from her chair. She grabbed at his hand and cried out when she saw the swollen, torn flesh and the blood.

"What have you done?"

He tried to free his hand but she held on to it.

"Why? Why would you do this to yourself?"

"Why indeed?" he answered with a mirthless laugh.

Her concern over the slight injury softened his attitude a little. He gritted his teeth then whispered in a broken voice, "What happened? Why must you always be leaving me?"

Isobel tried to move his hand into the light so she could see the damage. He impatiently wrenched it free.

"Leave it. Now tell me what this is all about."

He desired, with a surprising degree of yearning, that she tell him the truth. He could tell the exact moment when she saw the impossibility of procrastinating any further.

"I am so sorry. It is just that I have given this much thought and I do not want you to continue your involvement with my situation after all."

He felt the muscles in his neck stiffen at the effort it took to suppress displaying the irritation this caused him. "And how exactly did you come to this conclusion, if I may inquire?"

Isobel spent the next few minutes explaining her line of reasoning to him. She told him that at times today she felt as if she was being followed. But more than that, and this was the important part, she emphasized, she had had an honest change of heart once she had time to think things through on her own. It was not possible for her to entertain the idea that her personal troubles interfere with his mission, which, she surmised, despite his proclamation last night, was of national importance. The little witch made no mention of the note he had seen her receive as he glanced in the window of the teashop earlier, even though he had given her ample opportunity to bring it up. The man was certainly not a gentleman, and the furtive manner in which he had passed her the paper was very irregular and highly suspicious, to say the least.

He thought she looked particularly drawn throughout the whole ridiculous conversation, as if blatant lying was finally taking its toll on her. But he should be careful of attributing the finer feelings of conscience to her, for had she not just proven that she was false?

Isobel was kneeling at his side now in order to attend to the imbedded splinter. She glanced up at him in confusion. "I do not understand why you cannot see that your obligation to me is over."

"To begin with, I thought I had made myself quite clear on this point last night. And to reiterate, despite not being at liberty to go into details, my official business is not at all in jeopardy from you. Furthermore, do you honestly not know me well enough by now? I am supposed to be protecting you, not the other way around."

"Why? Why is that so? Do you think my feelings do not run as deep as yours just because I am a woman? That I do not have any integrity or am capable of sacrifice if it is required?"

He could tell her ire was up and had expected a scathing retort, but was surprised at the direction it came from. Of all the things they had spoken about it was amazing to him that she had taken offence at his last remark.

"No, that is not my meaning at all. I think you are as brave and true as any man I have met." He almost choked on the words, because deep within he wanted them to be true, even if he had just found evidence that they were not. Well, he could play the game as well as she, if not better. Had he not spent the best part of his life ingratiating himself with people he needed to manipulate?

He moved towards her and bent his head so she automatically leaned forward to hear his next words. "It is just that you are a rather diminutive woman." She bristled as he knew she would. "And one I want very much to take care of."

He was so close to her that the words floated along her cheek and her warm breath mingled with his. "In every way. It is important to me that you come to no harm and that you have the opportunity to safely establish yourself somewhere desirable. Life on the run is not sustainable and certainly not what I wish for your future, Isobel."

Isobel remained very near to him, and closed her eyes briefly. He enjoyed the sweetness of their proximity for a few blissful moments and then reluctantly pulled away, leaving them both a touch breathless.

"I would love to continue this discussion in more detail but under the circumstances, my dear lady, I fear we must be off."

"You are still determined to stay with me?" Isobel asked, returning from the drugging pleasantness of their encounter with a visible jolt that he took savage delight in. She would not best him.

"Yes. Yes, I think that has been established. Well, we will need a change of plans it appears. So we will put off going to Caen for a few days to thwart those who may be following you." He absently tapped his chin in deep thought. "Let's see. Ahh, I have an idea that would suit our situation admirably. I am going to have to go and do a little quick bartering. Change into your plainest, sturdiest clothes, Isobel. We will have the luggage sent on separately later."

He grinned at her as he opened the door to leave. "I will be back as soon as I can. Yes, if we hurry, we should have just enough time to make it."

CHAPTER TWENTY-FOUR

Not understanding the reason for Lord Chetton's strange instructions, Isobel nonetheless changed into her oldest dress. It was made of brown serge and was scratchy and dull. But like Chetton, she had sometimes found it necessary to disguise her class and dress down when she was travelling incognito. She hated the garment and would have discarded it a long time ago but it was the only clothing she owned that was serviceable enough for wear and tear situations.

Isobel was taking in the view of the small town that the window afforded when Chetton came back. She turned to make a passing comment on the weather and was shocked when she saw the changed man before her. He was kitted out in a threadbare shirt, leather vest, and patched trousers and, if she could believe her eyes, wore an ancient pair of muddy clogs on his feet.

"Excuse me, the pig pen is out back, and what, pray tell, have you done with the Earl of Chetton?"

"Yes, Claude the watchman definitely got the better side of the trade of clothes, but needs must. And I come bearing gifts for you too, my dear," said Chetton as he handed her a coarse apron and hideously patterned kerchief.

"Don't fret, they have both just come off of the laundry line. That's right, put them on and let me see you, Isobel. You do not look quite right just yet. If I may be so bold."

He advanced on her and before she could protest he had mussed up her hair and painted her serviceable boots with a dollop of mud from his clogs. "There me beauty, yer a fine ol' sight."

"Really, was that necessary? And did you have to enjoy it quite so much, you rogue?"

"Yes, I am afraid that it was, you looked altogether too pristine, and yes, madame, I do not deny taking more than a little pleasure from the task."

He gave her a quick, bright smile as he placed her portmanteau back on the bed. "One additional request, pack only a few essentials in this canvas sack and nothing of value. We cannot take our own luggage with us now. That would be fatal. I have made arrangements for it to be secured and delivered to Caen in a few days' time along with the horses. The rest will do them good."

Isobel reluctantly did as she was bid. Added to this not insubstantial degree of annoyance came the realization that it would not immediately be prudent for her to wear her fetching new shawl.

Lord Chetton grabbed the canvas bags and they hustled down the back stairs and into the alley and then they half trotted a few blocks to the outskirts of the small town. Isobel was surprised to see a group of about a dozen men and women milling about in a disorganized crowd. They were all dressed in a similar fashion to the clothes she and Chetton had on and were clearly workers of some kind. Isobel raised her eyebrows in question.

"This, wife, is the 'or worse' side of the vow. I have hired myself out as a day labourer to work in Farmer DuPont's apple orchard. They say his calvados is the best in the area, and here in the heart of Normandy that means something indeed. Do not worry, that fate is not for you; I have secured you an easier job helping in the dairy. There is no need to make such a face, you will not have to milk the cows or churn butter, but will only have to wrap and help sell the cheese. I boasted that my wife knew her ciphers. The wagon will be here shortly to take us out to DuPont's with these other good folk."

"You cannot be serious."

"Oh, but sadly I am. We will only stay for a few days. We must do a little honest work or people might get suspicious that we just availed ourselves of a ride and find it unusual enough to remember. But no one will remark on a transient country couple moving from job to job. I have used this kind of a ruse before, it is the perfect cover. Do not become too friendly with anyone, and try to mimic the old French type of Guernsey accent that Victor uses when you speak. Everyone will just assume you are a country bumpkin."

"Charming," Isobel muttered as they shuffled forward to climb into a crowded old wagon. "Charming," she repeated as Chetton steadied her from being jostled out of her seat while they bumped along the rutted road. "Perfect," she said at the astonished look on his face as the men were ordered into the barn for the night and the women were safely sequestered in a cottage.

Chetton swore loudly a few days later when, just as he began to climb his ladder, it started to slide sideways along the tree branch. He jumped down to the ground, kicked away the previously unseen rock, and secured the ladder properly. His thoughts were not on the orchard work but centered on the mysterious note Isobel had received. Since the men were sequestered away from the women at night on this old fashioned farm he had not been able to search her belongings for the communication. It grated that he had now, in all probability, lost the opportunity for good since it was unlikely that she would have retained possession of it. What he wouldn't give to know the contents of that communiqué. He was desperate to understand whom the directive was from and what it contained.

If the message had been from or about her uncle, then she would surely have told him. What would there be to gain from hiding such information? That left only sinister reasons for her wilful silence.

Perhaps he had made the wrong decision at the time, and he should have followed the large man who dropped the note so stealthily on her table. But then again, he was sure Isobel would have been gone by the time he had caught the fellow, forced out his answers, and returned to the hotel.

He reclimbed the ladder and reached to prune yet another stunted downward growing branch of the gnarled apple tree. The work was tedious rather than hard but that did not bother him as it afforded him an excellent opportunity to wonder about how Isobel was faring. He had seen her only briefly at the communal meal times and she appeared to be more fatigued with each meeting. This would be their final day of work, he decided, and they would head to the inn where he had arranged to have their belongings sent.

By midmorning he was ready to call it quits. If they left after the midday meal they would have enough travelling time to reach their immediate destination in relative comfort. His annoyance at not being able to find Isobel during the break for lunch turned to unease when one of the women he questioned said Farmer DuPont had come into the dairy and taken her away in his cart several hours ago.

"T'is unusual," she agreed. "I've not see'd him do that a'fore. Course your little wife's a pretty speck of a thing now, ain't she."

Suppressing a volley of curses, he sprinted towards the barns and outbuildings. A quick pass through them found nothing amiss and so he started for the farmhouse. The door was closed and the curtains were all drawn tight over the windows. Odd, he thought grimly, for the middle of a working day. It was fortunate that the front door was not barred shut. Chetton slipped inside and waited for his eyes to adjust to the dim light in the ancient stone structure.

He could hear soft movement from the rear of the building. As he moved towards the back room he picked up the sounds of heavy breathing and recognized the low guttural voice of the farmer.

"Come here and earn your fee, you stubborn woman."

He could detect the rustle of clothing and the unmistakable sounds of a tussle on the wooden floorboards.

A light voice answered, "Leave me alone. I do not want your money and I will not do what you want of me."

"You'll see to my needs before you leave, miss," came the guttural, slightly slurred, response.

With rising dread, and the hint of inevitability, he could distinguish Isobel's dismayed voice answer, "I'll not serve you that way, let me go."

The house was cluttered and unkempt. Chetton looked around for something he could use as a weapon and spotted a heavy earthenware jug with a broken handle. He snuck down the hall and peeked around the corner into what must be the farmer's makeshift office. Farmer DuPont was reclining on a wooden cot. He was without his shirt and was holding onto Isobel by the arm. Without waiting any further Chetton rushed into the room and smacked the farmer in the temple with the solid jug.

Chetton was just about to grab Isobel when she let out a cry and then turned and kicked him solidly in the shins.

"Now see what you've done. Emma was right, so like a man. When most wanted he is least found, and when not wanted he pops up like a mushroom, you may depend upon it!"

She knelt down beside the prostrate farmer and wiped his brow with a wet cloth from the nearby bowl of water. It was only then that he began to understand that Isobel had been in no danger and was attending Dupont in some medical matter.

"What in the world?"

"You should really try talking before fighting, Mr. Diplomat.

What did you suppose you were doing?"

"I thought, that is, I heard a very threatening conversation."

"Thank you for your concern, I am sure, but in this case it was misplaced."

"All right, Miss Snippety, that will do!"

Isobel turned away quickly but was unable to hide a giggle from bursting forth. He still felt hostility towards the farmer, blended with wounded outrage at her hasty behaviour towards himself.

"Farmer DuPont heard me giving some advice to one of the young mothers and guessed I had some experience with healing. Oh, do please stop glaring at me in that odious manner! In any case, he has been suffering for some time with stomach pain and wanted me to bleed him. Apart from the fact that I am not trained in the art, I do not believe in that old method, it has such mixed results. He became a little insistent, as people sometimes do, but it was nothing I could not handle."

She glanced up at him. "What are you doing here, by the way?"

He was still trying to reconcile the whole situation, and absently rubbed his shin.

"I thought it about time we headed off." He heard the farmer groan as he started to regain consciousness. "Now I suppose we shall have to make a hasty departure."

"Yes, well, we need not feel desperate. I steeped some valerian and peppermint that I found at the back of his cupboard and he agreed to try a little, washed down by a generous glass of his strong cider. I imagine he will sleep for a while."

Chetton pointed to several empty bottles of calvados on the table. "I imagine if he reduced sampling his wares his constitution would improve somewhat too."

She frowned as she watched him massaging his leg. "Perhaps it is best we go now."

Lord Chetton walked out of the room with an exaggerated limp.

"I am sorry about that kick."

"Humph."

She grabbed his arm to slow him down and looked up into his face. "It was an accident, you know, sort of a surprised reaction, I suppose."

"I shall remember that. You can be a dangerous and unpredictable woman," he said, but seeing the uncertainty in her eyes, added, "At least you were not wearing great wooden clogs at the time."

Within the hour a passing dairyman happily made room for them in his empty cart and conveyed them to the town where their belongings had been forwarded. Chetton was relieved to find that the rustic inn there had been expecting their arrival and were fully prepared to pamper them.

That night when sleep eluded him yet again, he brooded over the incident with Farmer DuPont. He was surprised at his mild reaction. What the hell was he doing? How pathetic I have become, he thought in disgust. It appears I can no longer even feign anger against the woman. He was, however, viciously aware of the warm curvy little body across the room from him.

As expected he had been unable to locate the note when he had a moment alone. And he raged further at the impotence of his position.

CHAPTER TWENTY-FIVE

They had reached Caen under dull skies two days ago and Isobel was just now feeling rested and ready to explore the city. The elegance of the Grand Hotel de La Place Royale was a wonderful change from their recent accommodations. Caen was the next largest city after Le Havre and Rouen in Normandy and offered many amenities. Chetton had arranged through the hotel manager for a modiste to visit Isobel immediately upon their arrival. The fashionable milliner assured her a day dress could be made up very quickly. The fittings went well and required little alteration and today Isobel was pleased to be able to wear a sky-blue dress overset with navy embroidery at the sleeves, hem, and neckline, suitable for an afternoon promenade. She was to meet Chetton in the lobby and had descended halfway down the grand front staircase of the hotel when she saw him standing near the entrance in conversation with an attractive woman.

The lady looked to be a few years older than Isobel was herself and was dressed a la mode in a daring vermillion ensemble. The way the lady gazed up at Chetton and stood just a shade closer to him than was customary gave Isobel the impression that they knew each other very well. It was odd to think, she realized, that she had so seldom witnessed Chetton among his friends and acquaintances. The unusual circumstances that had often thrown her and Chetton together, the pretence of being married, and their almost continuous travel had deprived them of regular interactions with other members of their class.

The sound of his laughter and flash of brown eyes assured her that Chetton was enjoying himself with the striking woman. This was of course a good thing, Isobel reminded herself. Had she not wanted Chetton to be rid of his responsibility towards her? Had she not expected an end was near to their saga? It was unexceptional that Chetton and such a lady should find each other's company pleasurable. He was, after all, a handsome man with charming manners and if the lowcut nature of the lady's attire was more eye catching than Isobel thought seemly, certainly that was no reason for her to take the woman in instant dislike. They were in all likelihood old acquaintances and on easy terms, for surely there could be no other reason why the alluring female should put her hand on Chetton's arm in such a familiar manner or continue to detain him with her constant chatter.

The thought that the lady was perhaps a family member, even a distant relative, was soon put to rest as the enticing form raised a shoulder in a sensuous shrug and blew a fingertip kiss towards Chetton in response to something he said to her. It was no doubt a practiced move and one that would put any decent woman to the blush. Any decent woman, who I am not, Isobel thought suddenly. The sting of her guilt pricked and she could not quash the belief that continuing in Chetton's company was detrimental to him. As this harsh reminder came to her she realized the awkward position she was in, both socially and physically, the one mirroring the other at present. Having stood now for several moments on the landing in the middle of the staircase, she would be attracting unwanted attention if she did not soon move. Although she was tempted to descend and approach the couple she knew it was impossible to do so.

The matter was soon taken out of her hands. The charismatic woman of a forward disposition captured Chetton's arm in a half embrace and turned him to walk towards the main door. Isobel understood he would be hard pressed to decline such a manoeuvre without creating a scene, although why he should appear to enjoy being commandeered in such a blatant manner she could not fathom. Just as Chetton was about to go out of sight, he turned his head to look behind him and saw her frozen on the stairs. He gave her a curt negative shake of his head and then, without further ado, resumed his detour with the temptress.

For a moment Isobel thought about rushing down the stairs to follow the pair, then laughed at her herself in chagrin. She was not at all that type of woman. Instead she retraced her steps and returned to her room. Determined that her afternoon would not be ruined she decided to treat herself and pulled the bell to order afternoon tea, *for one,* to be sent up. If she happened to study herself in the long oval dressing mirror while she waited and noted her trim figure set off to advantage by her new outfit, surely it was no one's concern but her own.

The ritual of taking afternoon tea, the very act of pouring steaming tea into a cup with milk already added, always produced a calming effect on Isobel's disposition. Sipping the fragrant warm beverage while admiring the pretty flowered bone china tea set soothed her. It was impossible not to feel pampered when tucking into cucumber or smoked salmon finger sandwiches and little iced cakes. The observance seldom failed to lift her spirits and Isobel thought of the many times she and Emma had enjoyed sharing the experience.

Emma would no doubt call her a silly goose for allowing the scene she had witnessed earlier to discomfort her. Isobel finished drinking her tea and thought well of herself for leaving one sandwich and two cakes untouched for the sake of discipline. It was upwards of an hour since Chetton had abandoned her; she was well fortified and now ready to retrieve what remained of the afternoon with a walk through the Botanical Garden, an excursion that thankfully was quite unexceptionable for unaccompanied women. Just as Isobel found the exact jaunty angle to pin her navy hat to frame her face to best advantage, there was a knock at the door. She expected it to be the maid come to remove her tea tray, and said, 'enter' with her back to the door. With both arms above her head in the act of adjusting her curls to fall attractively from beneath the hat, she was a perfect target for two long strong arms to catch her around the shoulders and turn her around.

"Ouch! Fiddle!" Isobel yelped and shook her finger. "Look, you have made me stab myself, you impertinent man."

‿

Chetton took a step back. "I apologise for startling you, Isobel. Although I am not quite sure that a hat pin jab qualifies as a *stab*, more of a poke perhaps?"

Chetton could see by the baleful glare and pursed lips that his attempt at levity was not going to suit Isobel. Not at all. He took another step back. "I expect you want to know what all that was about downstairs a little while ago, do you not?"

Isobel made an adorable act of sucking her injured finger, but as this was not his first go around with such uncomfortable situations, he assumed it was not only the digit of the lady in front of him that was injured.

"Yes, well, the fact is that it was rather awkward there for a few moments."

"Oh, I do pity you for that, I am sure," said Isobel, gracing him with a patently false smile.

"You see, the thing is that . . ."

"Please, Chetton, you need not feel that I am due any explanation of your personal entanglements."

So I must try harder, thought Chetton, struggling to contain a grin. The diplomat in him rose to take the bait. "You are not interested in knowing about the woman I met, then? Well, that simplifies things. I see you are preparing to go for the walk I was to accompany you on. May we proceed to the gardens together now?"

Witnessing the look of irritation that passed over Isobel's pretty face, followed by a flash of vulnerability, lessened his glow of easy victory. She really was a desperately poor actress, he thought. Could she really have been sent to manipulate anyone, let alone a man such as himself whose entire career had been spent reading people's true desires and assessing their foibles?

"Let us not quibble over an absurdity, Isobel. The day is too fine and you look far too fetching in your new outfit for that. Quite simply, the lady you saw me with is Mrs. Durling."

Isobel's insouciant shrug and look of indifference did not fool him.

"I have been acquainted with her and *her husband* for many years."

"Oh, I did not see her husband. Is he accompanying her?"

It was surprising to Chetton how tawdry and tasteless Caroline Durling had seemed this afternoon. He was honest enough to admit that in this she had not so much changed as that his appreciation of her manners and wayward charms had altered.

Isobel continued, "Is that why you left the hotel with her on your arm, to meet up with Mr. Durling, perhaps?"

"Yes, quite so. And it is Lieutenant Durling. Fortunately, they are just passing through on their way to Paris. They leave early in the morning and will not be a concern for us."

Isobel shook her head. "A concern? What you mean is that our make-believe marriage, but I should not call it make-believe, that sounds like a fairy tale. It is our lie, and it would be revealed if they were to meet me. And so you must be denied your friends because of our untenable situation."

Chetton spread his hands. "You are making too much of this chance encounter, Isobel. Our association is not close. I only know of them through Collin and cannot even remember the last time we met. Their absence is of no consequence to me at all and should not be so to you."

Isobel looked back to her reflection in the mirror and gazed at it for a moment. "I acknowledge that this particular situation is perhaps not important. I suppose it is a reminder of the peculiarity of our situation and that, on a broader scale, I have disrupted the social intercourse of your life. Normally you would have been free to spend the evening with your friends, but for me."

"There is no 'but' here." Chetton moved behind Isobel so that he was in her line of slight in the mirror and their eyes met in the polished glass. "Your premise is misguided if you think I would prefer the Durling's company over yours at any time. She is rather ostentatious and he is a pompous old windbag. I hold you in complete charity for saving me from further contact with them."

Isobel shook her head and turned to face him. He could see the sparkle of amusement in her eyes. "And as I said soon after I met you, I believe, you do not take many things seriously, Lord Chetton, do you?"

"Ah, if memory serves that was at the Spring Tea when I had to spirit you off to the conservatory." He shifted his gaze to her person and smiled. "Then, as now, you look very appealing."

"You are an outrageous flirt, sir, and if you think to fob me off with that meagre effort at changing the subject I will tell you, you have failed miserably."

He raised an eyebrow. "Fobbed me off, madame? Such language! You must be keeping very low company, such as with common farmers, to utter that phrase."

Isobel opened her mouth and stared at him in mock outrage. "I will have you know Farmer DuPont was a most uncommon man." She burst into laughter, clearly unable to keep up the ridiculous position.

Gratified to see her mood had lifted, Chetton took Isobel's arm and they exited the room. The afternoon sun and the walk that took them through the garden were equally delightful.

CHAPTER TWENTY-SIX

Ten days later, Chetton, now impeccably dressed, was seated at a fashionable café near the Grand Hotel. He threw down the French broadsheet in disgust, his recent meal threatening to curdle. The paper was a Parisian publication and had taken two days to reach Caen. The French headline shouted something execrable about England's rampant colonialism; the underlying article continuing on about how England's nation building schemes were responsible for France's loss of power on the world scene. Page two was primarily taken up with an account of the history of the cruel treatment of the French nobility during the revolution. Apparently, the long article was aimed at softening up the citizenry to the idea of indemnifying the noble families for confiscating their ancestral lands, and this position was backed by the Catholic church.

Chetton imagined the current political climate in London was not pretty.

He became aware of a light floral scent in the air just as Isobel moved into his line of sight. She sat down across from him and he automatically shifted his long legs to accommodate her at the small café table. He took a moment to admire the jaunty angle of the yellow ribboned bonnet artfully pinned into her curls. The new clothes she had purchased since arriving suited her well.

"Oh, dear, my lord. That is not a face I want to see. Whatever is the matter now?"

His smile had not appeared fast enough to fool her, it seemed.

"There is no sign of the men your uncle sent out to find you, if that is your concern. Shall I order a fresh pot?" He motioned to the coffee service on the table.

She declined and glanced at the headline. "Oh, I see, our national interests and France's are still at dagger draw, are they not? I daresay that begs the question of when you will have to leave."

He would not play games with her. "Tomorrow evening at the latest, earlier if I can manage it."

He drank the last sip of his coffee even though he knew it would be cold and slightly bitter. She was playing with the strings of her handbag, trying to keep her face neutral.

"Look Isobel, I wish things were more settled before I go but there is no more time. Stay here in Caen at the Grand Hotel. Everything is paid for until the end of the month. My accounts are in the hands of the banker we spoke about and he is set to assist you. And pray, let us not get into another brangle over my extending you a little assistance in that way. You have already made it plain that you will reimburse me for the funds, as completely unnecessary as that is. In any case, do not hesitate to approach the banker should anything seem odd to you, anything at all. He has been instructed by me and will know what to do."

She nodded her head in agreement with everything he said, but did she really understand the significance of what he was offering her?

"I will not leave you unprotected."

She continued to fidget with her bag and he leant across the table to still her hands.

"Don't," Isobel said.

"Don't what, Isobel?"

"Don't hold my hands."

She had managed to undo the strings of her reticule and pulled something out of it. She lifted one of his hands and placed a cool object on his palm, closing his fingers over it.

"I bought you something when I was out walking the other day and took a wrong turn on my way back to the hotel. Now, do not, I beg of you, scold me again about my poor sense of direction, Chetton, please."

He unclenched his jaw enough to say, "I should never engage to take you to task on your poor sense of direction, as you have *no* sense of direction at all, my dear lady. However, I feel I have reason to remind you that jaunting off on your own is unadvisable at best and possibly dangerous." He couldn't shake away the whisper of thought about what other reason she may have had to go out alone.

Isobel dismissed his rebuke with a graceful wave of her finely gloved hand. "Moot point, my Lord, as I had the hotel abigail with me, but sadly she is new to the city and so was not much help." She returned her hand to cover his. "In any case, with your leaving now imminent, this seems fitting. Consider it a little parting gift, if you will. Can you guess what it is?"

"Well, let me consider, it is bumpy and irregular." He moved his fingers around and squeezed. "It has a good heft for the size of it and is slightly cool to the touch, so I am guessing it is made of metal. A figure of something, but I do not know what."

"Think hard, Guernseyman." She was staring at him and made a face.

He laughed and squeezed the shape of the small item. "I do not know. Wait a minute. Perhaps I do." He understood the puzzle of it. It was a donkey.

"I found it in a collectable shop. It is only made of brass. Although I cannot vouch for its entire provenance, this is where I purchased it." With a flourish she presented him with a card.

THE GUERNSEY DIPLOMAT

> *Friedrick Felton's Famous & Fantastic Emporium*
> *Featuring Phenomenal Finds from the Curious to the Finest*
> *From Around the World*

Isobel gently traced the shape of the tiny animal as it lay against his palm. "The great, shall I say it, Alliterative Man, was not there. It was said, by one of his fast-talking shop clerks, that he was in deepest Africa, while another insisted that, 'Dunnomany times I have's to tell you, Carl, he's in blasted Brazil anow.'" Isobel laughed, merriment sparkling in her green eyes. "I am sorry, I could not resist the details, rough language and all."

"Isobel." Though not a sentimental man, the carving in his hand and the gesture it represented unexpectedly meant a great deal to him. Chetton saw the smile melt away from Isobel's face. She glanced at where their hands had met on the table a moment ago.

"I know it sounds silly, but you have been my own Guernsey donkey. Stubborn and strong, and full of character. Thank you for all the help you have given me, my dear Guernsey Diplomat. You have been my Guardian from the Isle."

She looked him straight in the eye. "If you cannot come back, I will understand."

※

Chetton met up with Jean two days later in Lisieux, a comfortable town half way between Caen and Le Havre. He was happy to note that Jean had reverted to his usual habits and was motioning for a third bottle of white burgundy to be brought to a table already covered with food.

"Jean, before we discuss the main reason I am here, what progress have you made on the, uh, delicate matter I described to you?"

"It is all unfolding as it should. Don't worry, I expect completion soon. Eat, eat, you are in gastronomic heaven again. None of that plain heavy fare you usually have to put up with. *Mon Dieu*! At least the French know how to enjoy life. Try the delicate *poisson* and see how we do not kill it as you English do when cooking fish."

Jean cut a generous piece of *sole meunière* and placed it on his plate, motioning him to pour some of the luscious sauce on top of it. Chetton went through the ritual and acknowledged it was indeed delicious.

"The butter, parsley, and lemon are married beautifully with the sole, *non*?" Jean grinned as if he had been personally involved in preparing the dish. "So, *mon ami*, you are in France against my advice. I suppose your English sang-froid is to be complimented. Me, I'm not so noble. I want to see old age."

"Yes Jean, we both know your position on my coming here, but things have gone too far and we need a solution." He took a sip of the wine in appreciation. "A dependable solution."

Jean gave the shrug that his countrymen were world famous for. "And this is to be achieved by?"

"By me handing over the proof that Villiers and Mercier bilked the French government out of millions of francs over the last few years."

"And that will?"

"Hopefully that will be enough political leverage to direct Villiers and Mercier to put all of their considerable efforts into quashing the king's plan to have his reactionary ministry pay out all that money to reimburse former landowners. It seems King Charles and his advisors are hell bent on somersaulting themselves right into the middle of another revolution. Has the madman not learned anything from recent history about the volatility of his own peasants? The last thing England, or Europe for that matter, needs is another descent into hell like the last revolution which eventually spawned Napoleon and the havoc he created."

"*Mon ami*, is that not what you call the blackmail?"

He took a large draught of the strong wine and glared at Jean. "You know very well it is. And do stop asking questions you already know the answers to. You agreed about the necessity of the plan weeks ago."

"I agreed to the basic plan, *oui*, but not to you being the one to deliver the documents. That was to be done by Michel La Rue." Jean spooned a great helping of an aromatic dish onto Chetton's plate. "Have some of the *caneton à la rouennaise*, their ducking here is *superbe*." Then he served himself another huge portion.

"Yes, well, needs must, old chap, and all that. La Rue is unfortunately dead and Drapeau of no use to us." Chetton put down his fork and wiped his fingers on the napkin. "Any more news on his possible whereabouts?"

"*Non*. He has, as you English say, flown the *stoop*."

Jean beamed proudly at Chetton, who had to exercise all of his considerable will not to burst out laughing.

"Just so, my man, just so."

※

With all the complaints Jean had made about Lord Chetton being in France, nothing would do in the end, but that he accompany him to Rouen. As the capital city of Normandy, Rouen was an optimal location to meet politicians at the annual Joan of Arc festival held near Rouen castle. The age-old celebration helped with the upkeep of the ancient cathedral and other historical edifices. This year, the Gros Horloge, the fourteenth century astrological clock, was to be a beneficiary and the list of dignitaries scheduled to appear was a formidable one. Lord Chetton and Jean agreed to travel together but separately on the same conveyances, with the pretence of being strangers. This would enable them to spread the threat between them and better keep up surveillance for potentially dangerous situations.

Jean and Lord Chetton met an hour before the departure time for the first segment of their coach ride to Rouen. Chetton had taken a low seat by the window and had to snake his long arm out rapidly to catch the leather folder that Jean tossed his way.

"I would never want to brag, *mais*, I must say, I impressed myself with being able to have this ready for you so soon after your request. Your friend seems to attract unsavoury characters."

Lord Chetton opened the pouch and removed a series of pages that had notes, times, and schedules on them. He looked over at Jean.

"Once again, my wily friend, I am happy to benefit from the vast network of watchful eyes and ready ears that you have in place. It is one of the advantages of having a thriving shipping and import-export business."

Jean gave him a quick salute. "It was not so 'ard to find one of the pairs. They like to live well when they travel about and were not cautious in their questioning of people. You can see from the information they did not do much more than eat, drink, and whore their way around a small section of the country. They 'ave been detained for the time being in a remote location. At your pleasure, shall we say?"

The predatory surge he felt must have shown in Chetton's eyes.

Jean cleared his throat deliberately. "Unfortunately, the other couple 'as not yet been located."

Chetton's hand tightened imperceptibly on the documents.

"*Merci,* Jean. I owe you."

"Well naturally you do, *mon ami,*" said the Frenchman with a grin.

Mail coaches were barbaric modes of transport and forced too much intimacy upon travellers, thought Lord Chetton. He had had occasion to ponder the limits of friendship and much more over the course of his travel. On the one hand, he was inclined to agree that familiarity breeds contempt. For example, he had considered how hard a blow to the solar plexus would have to be to stop Jean's annoying habit of humming to himself. The other side of the matter was that absence makes the heart grow fonder. Of that he had no doubt. He often touched the tiny brass animal that he kept in his coat pocket. Thoughts of Isobel constantly assailed him, many of an erotic nature that had him shifting his position on the hard coach seat. The idea that he was using her for his own benefit had less and less appeal. Yet he could not stop wondering to what use she was putting her time.

The night before the festival he met Jean in a brothel. Jean had rented a dingy back room from the Madame who raised not an eyebrow when Chetton followed him in a few minutes later. The liberal use of coin smoothed over any inconveniences. Any moral objections she might once have harboured about the oddity of two men renting a room had long since been eroded by the practicalities of a hard life.

Jean was perched on the edge of the room's one chair. Lord Chetton deigned not to sit on any of the room's suspect surfaces and stood, his large figure commanding most of the small space.

Jean squinted innocuously into his drink. "You're sure you want to go to the celebration by yourself tomorrow night? As it 'appens I am free and could accompany you."

"What," Lord Chetton said with a gesture that encompassed the room, "and miss out on visiting another such establishment? That would be unlike you, Jean."

Jean gave him a wry smile. "For you I could postpone my gratification for an evening." With a look that bespoke the harsh lessons learned over many years of high adventure, he continued, "You're not infallible, *mon ami*, best you remember that."

Lord Chetton nodded in agreement. He must tread lightly with his present commission.

The original plan, he reflected, had been for La Rue to confront Villiers and Mercier with the irrefutable proof of the flagrant misuse of their offices in order to manipulate their voting power in the Chamber of Deputies and thus block the proposal for the land compensation. This approach was no longer viable. The death of La Rue combined with the speed with which events were taking place called for a change in tactics. A more direct method would now have to be employed. He thought it best that the dossier of incriminating information should be placed directly in the hands of Minister Laurent.

The advantages of this strategy were twofold. Finance Minister Laurent was a confirmed liberal reformer and known to be a political rival of the other men. He had an almost religious zeal for fighting corruption, though often lacked support for his reforms. The ammunition Chetton would provide him with was timely, since Laurent had just undergone a humiliating defeat with his latest proposed budget cuts spearheaded by Villiers and Mercier and their supporters. A covert audience with the finance minister was important so that no official trail would lead to a foreign representative having intervened in the workings of French domestic politics.

The powerful duo of Villiers and Mercier were deeply entrenched in corruption and embezzlement and this meant they had many people openly working for them and an even greater number covertly on their lucrative payroll. Lord Chetton's diplomatic status ensured him an invitation to the state dinner to be held after the private ball at La Couronne, a restaurant founded in 1345 and said to be the oldest in France. But to take advantage of the invitation, he obviously had to don his official persona of a representative of the British government upon arriving in the Normandy capital.

During the years of the French Revolution, the ideals of liberty, brotherhood, and equality had become entrenched in the bureaucracy of government. That the fruits of their toil now went to taxes for the restored monarchy showed that little had changed in the lives of the peasants' meagre existence, as far as Lord Chetton could discern. He was honest enough to admit that he was a royalist at heart and though he didn't believe in the divine right of kings, per se, he and his family had prospered by supporting the British monarchy for many generations, a situation he hoped would not be undone in his lifetime or the foreseeable future. And having a stable France with a restored monarchy was best for England, and peace in the world generally.

Perhaps by French standards the ceremonial ball wasn't an ostentatious show of wealth, but by his sedate British upbringing the pomp and ceremony of the evening's entertainment was rich indeed. The palatial venue was steeped in history. There were enough statues and paintings in elaborate gilded frames to furnish a small museum. The walls and ceilings of the chateau were themselves works of art complete with frescoes and painted panels. Several centuries worth of ornate furniture filled the grand spaces and decorative styles of draperies complemented lush carpets.

The principal rooms were illuminated by hundreds of candles in strategically located sconces, chandeliers, and candelabras, the light shimmering reflectively off of mirrors, crystal, and a myriad of shiny surfaces. The men were splendid in evening attire and the women were beautifully costumed in ballgown finery of colourful brocades, silks, and satins. The air was heavy with the mixed scents of flowers, perfume, bodies, and the remnants of rich food and cigar smoke.

Sporadic conversations, whether animated or subdued, overlaid the best efforts of the orchestra and the resulting cacophony drummed through the senses. The hour was late enough that the evening no longer felt new, but not yet so advanced that it seemed worn out. As was often the case in such diversified and distinguished company, the anticipation of romance was starting to bloom for some, while the continuation of successful liaisons existed for others. Acknowledgement of disappointment could be held off for a while longer, surely until at least the end of the next waltz, and so did not yet weigh on the brow of many.

During the evening, Lord Chetton had paid due diligence to the evening's host, the Marque and his wife, danced with the requisite number of young ladies, moved with ease between several sets of gentlemen in the smoking room, and later chatted briefly with Minister Laurent in a quiet timbered alcove of the famous La Couronne restaurant. Lord Chetton had dangled his idea of a political bombshell in front of Laurent and was rewarded with the promise of a clandestine meeting in two days' time. Pleased that he had accomplished the first part of what he needed to do, he felt he could withdraw from the social engagement without incident. He had arranged an early breakfast meeting with Jean and planned to use the time between now and then to write a note to Isobel to apprise her of a possible early return to Caen.

He passed through the reception room on his way to exit the building. The front doors formed part of the building's medieval façade and led to the street. Place du Vieux-Marche was deserted this time of the evening, the throng of carriages not yet called for. He suspected the grooms would be nearby, probably tasting the local ale and telling tales of their employers. With his thoughts engaged far away he did not notice the shuffle behind him until it was too late. A club to his temple dropped him to the ground. A rag was shoved into his mouth as he started to react but his tardy protest was quelled by another wallop to the head. He was dragged to a waiting wagon and unceremoniously deposited by two burly individuals who disappeared into the night as the conveyance jolted off in the opposite direction.

CHAPTER TWENTY-SEVEN

Isobel had changed into her nightgown and was settling down in bed with a book. After a great sigh she leaned down to open the drawer on the bedside table. She withdrew a pretty filigreed box and sat staring at it for a moment. Then she quickly opened the lid, selected a chocolate from the dwindling selection, and popped it into her mouth. There was no need for her to look at the accompanying note again. She had committed it to memory from the first reading.

> *My dearest Isobel,*
>
> *During our travels I missed the opportunity to treat you to any of these delicacies. Caen seems the perfect place to do so. But this goes beyond sweets for the sweet, Isobel. If you indulge only once a day, there is a good chance I shall be back before the box is empty.*

Isobel smiled to think of how he had signed the card so imperiously as "The Right Honourable, The Earl of Chetton," and then drawn the caricature of a fat little donkey beside it.

Despite her appreciation of the pampering and the entertainment available in the Grand Hotel, Isobel soon tired of being inside. She hatched a very different plan that proved to be challenging to her spirits, body, and humour. In order to extend her sense of independence and confidence, she had engaged the services of a riding master to fill in the equine skills and horsemanship lacking in her upbringing. It seemed quite possible that travelling for extended periods on horseback might very well be in her future, so she wanted to be better prepared.

The instructor was a tall wiry fellow by the name of Monsieur Gagnon and though he had terrorized the imagination of countless schoolgirls with his stern discipline, his manner towards her was thankfully more relaxed. She was happy to learn that Monsieur Gagnon was not fond of females riding side-saddle. He felt it was dangerous to women should they fall and the uneven weight distribution was not good for the horse over time. His approach to controlling an animal encouraged her to delve into the calm spirit of her healing nature and communicate with the animal rather than to try to master it with whip or spurs as her uncle had expected.

Changing her riding style was proving to be hard work. She had strained every area of her body at one time or another, but was making headway in trotting without being unduly jostled and was well satisfied with her first week's endeavour.

The next morning she was resting on a low stool by the stable door at the conclusion of a lesson. A gentleman rode up and called for a stable hand as he dismounted. A surge of excitement passed through her as she heard the man speak and caught sight of his profile. She stood and the movement caught Chris's attention.

"By Jove, I did not expect it would be this easy to find you, Isobel."

He crossed the few steps that separated them to take her hand.

"I would like to say that I am your one-woman welcoming committee, but I did not know you would be coming."

She acknowledged the brief kiss on her fingers with a wide smile, the corners of which slowly turned down as she said, "Chetton is not here anymore, Chris."

The quizzical lift of his expressive eyebrows returned the smile to her lips. "But you were already aware of that. He sent you to me, didn't he?"

"He did indeed, and I have seldom been happier to fulfill a request of his." Chris linked her arm in his and proceeded out of the stables.

Isobel's head was swimming from this unexpected turn of events. She had no frame of reference for what it meant. At no time in her life had she envisioned herself as part of a family that would close ranks and seek to protect her. The brothers' open devotion to each other she had witnessed firsthand, but it had seemed to her to be of a unique nature, existing on a separate plane of existence that was apart from her, and would ever be so. That someone would seek to include her within the strength of a family unit was at the same time wildly exhilarating and rather terrifying.

"He needn't have troubled you. I am situated here at the hotel and they are taking fine care of me."

Chris stopped walking and put his hand on his chest as if wounded.

"Never say I am not required, Isobel. My brother usually sends me on boring errands without the opportunity to spend time with pretty ladies."

Isobel shook her head at such nonsense but was touched by the concern of both brothers. She was pleased to have Chris as company; his easy manner was infectious and helped to keep worries at bay. She soon brought Chris into her confidence regarding her exploits at horsemanship. If he thought it an unusual pursuit at her age he showed no sign of it to her.

Chris was a competent, classically trained rider and took her out to practice her newly honed skills with enthusiasm. They rode out early the next morning to escape the midday heat and stopped to rest under the branches of an old chestnut tree. She was fiddling with the cap of a leather flask of water. Chris took it out of her hand and opened it with one deft twist, handing it back to her without a word.

"You are very like your brother."

"Am I? In what way?"

"You are kind. You take care of people as a matter of course."

"Well, I cannot take much credit in that, it is just the way we were brought up, you know."

The casual way he said this only served to heighten awareness of her emotionally barren early years. The brothers could take for granted family support and generosity because that was what they had been reared on and it had become second nature to them. Her mother had died within a year of giving Isobel life. A distant father clouded her earliest memories, and after his death, she had endured miserly dealings with her uncle. He resented any expenditure for her upbringing. She saw now how his excessively frugal control had been cleverly deployed as a yoke of restraint meant to diminish her spirit. Only when she was of an age for others to notice had he begrudgingly loosened the purse strings for her maintenance.

Her uncle's avarice was of a particular kind. She was sure he took no personal pleasure in having riches for the kind of life they could offer him. He wanted to accumulate wealth in order to be able to exert authority over people and to direct the paths of their lives. Though he pampered his son with all the privileges money could buy, she understood that her cousin was under the thumb of his father without the sense to realize it. Her cousin Maxwell had been raised to expect luxury and live in the moment, without any thought to how it had come about or how it could be sustained. He was a user, a consumer of things whose venal pursuit of pleasure was insatiable. Maxwell was not burdened with a sense of responsibility to plan for the future of his family, his land, or his country. In many ways she could almost feel sorry for the weak, solitary figure who had not the wit nor inclination to examine his life.

Even now she could hardly keep the note of longing out of her voice, such had been her desire for familial affection as a child.

"What was your father like?"

Chris smiled to himself. "He was a capital fellow and quite good to us. My parents were suited to each other, very much in love, and as you are aware, that is not too often the case within our class. My father was, for his station in life, a practical man at heart. He was a bit of a rogue inventor, and loved to tinker with machines and new ways of doing things. He drove my mother demented with his 'improvements' as he called them. One day he nearly set the east wing on fire trying out a new method for the men to clean the chimney." He laughed at the memory.

His eyes softened. "Thank God we still have Mother with us. You know her easy manner. She was smart enough to let my father have his way unless she really opposed something. Mother was quite sporty for a woman, I suppose. She was adept at archery in her youth and is an accomplished horsewoman."

Chris must have noted the look on her face after divulging that last bit of information. He patted her arm. "Never mind that, my mother likes you. She is very clever at reading people, can see inside them."

She did not know how to respond to this. The thought filled her mind with a fantastic kind of chaos at all of the possibilities. She could not formulate one question to ask.

But Chris went on in his friendly, loquacious way.

"She has taken to you because you took such good care of little Teddy and also because she believes Chetton cares for you."

The colour rose with alarming rapidity to heat her face. "I am not sure that is true."

"It is certainly true regarding my mother, she can be quite fierce about her sons." Chris lowered his voice to just above a gravelly whisper. "And I rather think it also true about my brother. He seems more at ease than I can remember seeing him for a long time. His past, the things that he tries so hard to bury, never really leave him in any sort of peace."

"It would be a wonder if it was different." She was still daunted by the disaster that had befallen Chetton.

Chris nodded to acknowledge the shared sentiment.

"To be candid, he has never truly recovered. Friends thought over time that he had healed. He resumed his duties for the crown before the mourning period had really ended. Travel is the mainstay of his profession and a high degree of sociability is expected of him. Our father died when Chetton was twenty-eight. He assumed the mantle of the earldom with all the responsibilities that it entails, and he performs his roles well, but nothing touches him."

He rubbed his forehead and briefly closed his eyes. "To tell you the truth, Isobel, I worry sometimes that deep emotion has been burnt out of him. That one incendiary night, long ago, has permanently scoured off a degree of his humanity, of his connectedness to others."

"Chetton did share with me how you and he came home to find out about the sad situation that evening."

"Did he indeed! Well then, you understand the shadow that hangs over my brother, at least so far as I understand it myself."

"Chris, I am glad to have this opportunity to speak to you so privately." Isobel glanced away from him. She realized that the snug familiarity of the past weeks with Chetton was much harder to hold onto in the greater reality of others being aware of their situation.

"I know of course that Chetton must have written to you about our circumstances. I am sure you must think it odd if not completely disgraceful of me. I wanted to speak of it to you before but could not conceive of how to begin."

"Now, Isobel, there is not the least need to explain further, I assure you."

"Oh, but there is. You must understand that this sham marriage was your brother's solution to an immediate problem with the authorities. I had no wish to encumber him further with my situation but you know how decisive and forceful he can be."

"I do indeed."

"But to represent ourselves as man and wife, to associate in such a manner, you must think me morally reprehensible, and indeed, I have no tolerable excuse with which to defend myself."

"Do not chastise yourself on that account, Isobel. I would not presume to judge you or Chetton in any way. And if I may speak as plainly as you, he gave me to believe that despite the sham marriage, as much propriety as it is possible to achieve is maintained between you."

This was impossible to allude to any further. Isobel lowered her voice and turned to face Chris. "I just want to try and assure you that I have no future expectations regarding your brother. It exceeds my imagination to attempt to, excuse the vulgarity, 'latch on to him' or cause your family any embarrassment."

"My dear lady, please stop. I understand perfectly and really, I assure you, it is not a matter of anxiety to me. No one of any consequence knows of the arrangement and Chetton assures me they shan't. Do not tease yourself with any further disquieting thoughts. Rather, let us enjoy the day, shall we?" He gave her a wink. "Chetton would take much pleasure in murdering me for talking about him so."

Although Isobel could speak no more on the matter at present, she was not at peace with herself, but she succumbed to his wink with a muted smile.

Chris walked over to untether the horses, speaking over his shoulder. "Well, now that I have interfered so blatantly, I am going to take you for a lovely luncheon to try and make up for it, and all we shall talk about will be the most trivial of things. How does that sound?"

The pause before she answered was deliberate. She knew he was a man who truly appreciated his food and loved to suggest unusual dishes from the menu or new things to try. Chetton joked that he was a Frenchman at heart and liked to talk about food as much as eat it. When she spoke, she hoped her agitation was hidden by her frivolous question. "And you will not even comment on what I choose to order?"

Now that the intensity of their conversation had diminished, he smiled at her bravely. He conceded her small victory with a bow. "I shall utter not a word, madame."

CHAPTER TWENTY-EIGHT

Consciousness returned to Chetton as a gust of cool air blew over him. His hearing returned and the darkness cleared, though his mind was still foggy and his head hurt with a blazing pain along his left temple. Finding himself in this predicament was galling. He felt like a new recruit who has been outwitted on his first practice mission. His previous military education kicked in and he remained motionless with his eyes closed. He had been trained by a huge Scot named Macready, who professed he could trace his ancestry straight back to William Wallace, the famous warrior who still warmed Scottish hearts after four hundred years. Whether or not this was true, the man was a hand-to-hand fighting specialist and adept at teaching what he knew.

Chetton remembered how the large man would circulate between he and Chris and deliver a stout kick to their backsides if they stirred more than he liked. His booming voice hushed to the point that one had to strain to hear the soft words. *"Keep quiet, laddies, move not a muscle at first. Keep yer wits about ye and take in all ye can. What do ye smell, and feel and hear? How bad are ye hurt? Don't let the foe ken that yer back in the world 'til it suits ye t' do so."*

The tactical and self-defence instruction that his father had insisted be part of their upbringing had stood them well on many occasions. It was not deemed by polite society to be part of a gentleman's education. Nor was it acceptable in the way Gentleman Jackson's boxing club in London was. But his unconventional and extremely practical father considered personal defence a necessity for the roles his sons would take in the world, even if they were not military men per se. Their mother would agree to anything that might keep her boys safer when they grew to men.

Taking Macready's words to heart Chetton assessed what he could of his surroundings. He was clearly lying on a rough floor somewhere. He could discern patterns of shadow and shade through his closed eyes and guessed that he must be inside some crude shed or cottage. That made sense because the air was otherwise stale; the breath of cooler air that had roused him must have come from a door or window. For the moment he was alone, at least he could not hear any conversation nor the breathing or movement of another individual close by.

He opened his eyes a slit and found his guess of being in a hut was correct. There was little in the one-room shack. A pine sideboard that had seen better days by the slant of its shelves graced the wall opposite the single window. A table and three mismatched chairs sat across from the door and a pallet of sorts was in the corner farthest from him.

Slowly he began to move his extremities and found that his hands and feet were bound. While he ached in a few places from the rough handling he had no real injuries except for the swelling on his head. That would not impede him significantly.

In an effort to make some sense out of his present situation he cast his mind back and tried to recall what had happened to him. He had left La Couronne restaurant through the front doors and walked around the corner towards the staging area for carriages. He remembered now, though it hardly registered at the time, that there was not much activity in the vicinity, but that could have been due to the fact that the music and wine were still flowing generously and guests were not yet ready to relinquish the night's pleasures. Thoughts of Isobel had occupied his mind and he winced inwardly now at his own foolishness for not taking better notice of his surroundings. It was embarrassing to note that he had not exercised the most basic safety precautions and had let himself be caught with only putting up a token resistance.

He had been unforgivably incautious and gotten himself into this mess. Well, now he would have to get himself out of it.

There was no indication of who had taken him or for what reason he had been waylaid. Robbery did not seem likely. Although both his watch and wallet were missing, his gold cufflinks still bound the cuffs of his fine linen shirt. He supposed he should be happy that whoever had snatched him did not seem intent on harming him at present. It was a chilling thought that due to his carelessness he could have just as easily been killed as taken captive.

He vowed there would be no more such mistakes on his part.

It was difficult to tell what the hour might be, but he estimated he had been unconscious for between four and five hours, which would be normal for the location and severity of his head wound, he thought. Also, though he was thirsty he was not desperately so, nor was he particularly hungry. He guessed it to be about seven in the morning then, which again fit with the gust of cool fresh air that had recently brought him around to full consciousness. He had absolutely no idea which direction he had travelled, or indeed how long he had been travelling, but a foggy notion of perceived motion made him believe he had been carried in some type of conveyance at one point.

He heard footsteps approaching the door and quickly stretched his sore muscles before once again closing his eyes and lying prostrate on the floor. The door creaked open and he heard two sets of footfalls cross the pounded earth floor. One approached him and then drew away.

"He's still out, the lazy bugger," said a young male, speaking in midland country English. This was a surprise. As he was in France he had expected Frenchmen to be holding him.

"Makes less fuss for us that way," answered a gruff voiced man, also in midland English.

"How long we got to stay here, again, Shep?"

There was a grunt of annoyance. "Long as we're told to, so don't go gettin' antsy, Jonny. The guv said we'd be here for a bit."

"Aye, but do you think we both need to sit with him all the time? There's a tavern just round the corner, what say I go and get us a few tankards of ale to see us through the day?"

Another piece of information—he was in a town, not the open countryside. This too was good news. If he had a chance to escape there would be people, buildings, and opportunities not readily available in a remote country location.

"There's a plan, ol' son. Bring back some victuals as well. Nothing too French."

He heard the clink of coins and the door open and shut.

That meant he had a few minutes alone with one of his captors, who did not yet know he was alert. From his prone position he envisioned delivering a stout wallop to the knee or groin of the captor from the force of his tied legs. A rapid head butt would follow this to the stomach, or forehead, should he be able to gain his footing quickly enough. It was a chance, if only the remaining man would approach him. He wondered if it would serve his purpose to groan a little to tempt the person to come closer to investigate. He tensed in preparation but the next sound he heard had him stifling a genuine groan of frustration, since it was the unmistakable rhythm of snoring. And they had had the nerve to call him lazy!

The minutes stretched on with increasing tension until he heard footfalls and the door opened once again, ending his chances for the moment. Immediately the aroma of freshly baked bread assailed him. Apparently he was hungrier than he realized, because the food smelled delicious. Chris would laugh at him now, he thought fondly. He was always amazed at how a spot of trouble triggered his appetite while it had the opposite effect on his younger brother. Repeated episodes in their youth had proven this phenomenon to be true, and he had usually been the beneficiary and received a large portion of Chris's unwanted meal.

To distract himself from the demands of his stomach he tried to imagine what Chris might be doing now. He was glad that he had asked him to go to Caen to be with Isobel. They enjoyed each other's company and he felt more secure with Chris near her. His brother might show an amicable disposition to the world but he could fight like the devil and was a good man to have at your side. He wondered if Jean had found out any more information regarding the whereabouts of the second pair of men Isobel's uncle had dispatched to find her. He'd briefed Chris extensively in a very long letter on what to do should that happen. And he had also had the decidedly awkward conversation needed to apprise Chris of the delicate state of affairs currently existing between Isobel and himself.

He turned his resolve against thinking of Isobel. It was not the time to engage in visions of her fair face and the sweet feel of her in his arms. He must concentrate on the present and find a way to escape. His captors must be hungry as well for there had been no conversation since he heard the food being served out into bowls and the accompanying breaking of bread.

After several minutes of overloud mastication and a prolonged belch, the older man spoke.

"Here, Jonny give the fella a poke. We're to see to him, not starve the blighter."

Well, that was welcome news. He tried to stay still and anticipate where the attack might come from and so was quite convincing in his surprise and annoyance at having an unexpected pail of water dumped on him.

"That works as well," said Jonny. What a clever little bastard this Jonny was.

He had sat up automatically when the water came crashing down on him and despite sputtering was now grabbed roughly by the hair. A dark unshaven face was glaring at him. Jonny was a prize indeed.

But it was the other man, Shep, who did the talking.

"Look, mate, this is the way it is. We don't know who you are and we don't care. You're just a job to us, see. Just a few easy quid. So don't make no trouble for us, and we won't give any to you. Savvy?"

"It seems at present you have the advantage of me."

"Good. I'm glad you're a sensible type." Shep slapped Jonny on the shoulder to indicate he could let go of him, which the younger man did, but not before snarling at him.

"Don't mind young Jonny there, he ain't got better to do than act out. You want something to eat? It's not fancy but it'll fill you."

"Yes, please, and some water if you've any to hand."

"I think we can manage that. I'd offer you some ale, but it would hardly seem proper considering." He was becoming fonder of this Shep by the minute. He was clearly no killer, just an aging ne'er do well who had probably stepped on the wrong side of the law a few times.

"Jonny, get a bowl of porridge for our guest, will you?"

Jonny sent an impressive gob of spit flying towards him.

"Serve him yourself if you want, old man, I'll not stoop to do it." Jonny gulped down a mouthful of ale.

"Oh, the folly of youth, eh, mister," said Shep as he went to the table and spooned out a generous helping from the pot. "What's your name anyway, first one only if you don't mind. It keeps things simple."

He decided to follow this advice and also see if his earldom would be acknowledged. "I am Chetton."

Without a shadow of recognition, Shep walked over to him and crouched down.

"Right, now we got ourselves what's known as a quandary here, Chetton. I don't like to see a man eat off the floor like an animal. But we need to keep you here for a while and don't want no funny stuff. So what I'm proposing is that I untie you and then you stand up, walk over to the table there, and just eat your food like the fine civilized man I can see you are. If you was to try anything stupid, well, my young friend here is well armed for trouble and only too happy to find it, if you take my meaning."

"I will behave." Now was not the time to instigate a fight.

"Good man. Come here then."

Shep untied him and helped him to stand. Chetton sat down at the worn table and tucked into the food. Shep put a cup of water in front of him and handed him a slab of the bread he had smelled earlier.

"Christ, Shep, you'd think he was the King of England hisself the way you do go on." In a bid to impress, Jonny made a show of cleaning his fingernails with a large knife and then laid it down in front of him on the table.

"There's no need to treat people bad, Jonny. You got to learn that. Not unless they done something to you. And this gent here ain't done nuffin to me, now has he?"

Jonny muttered a curse under his breath.

"My thanks for the food." He motioned towards the jug of water. "May I?" He refilled his water and sat back in his chair.

"Y'er welcome," said Shep.

I have never met a more polite gaoler, Chetton thought with amusement.

"Now, Chetton, is it? What say you to the idea I let you sit up in the chair a bit. I'll have to retie your hands, for I'm not a fool, but it's better than lying on the ground again, ain't it?"

He smiled at the old man despite himself.

"It is indeed."

He offered up his hands. It was better to have Shep bind them than Jonny, who would no doubt make a much bigger deal of the job.

For a good part of the day he sat at the table watching Shep beat Jonny at backgammon. The younger man was too impatient and had a terrible back game. He complained about not having lady luck with him but the truth was that the dice were only part of the story. It was skill at strategy and foresight of your opponent's possible moves that won the ancient game and not just "the fickle whore" that Jonny ranted about. Still, it passed the time and allowed Chetton a degree of conversation between himself and Shep.

At one point he had asked the old man why he was being kept as a prisoner and under whose authority but an answer was not forthcoming, except to say he didn't think it had anything to do with asking for a ransom. He then asked about Touché, and every other personal enemy he could think of, but the names meant nothing to the old man. Shep was good natured about it all, as if he did this sort of thing all the time and there was no need to worry. Chetton was having a harder time taking it all so patiently, especially since he wasn't sure who was behind the insanity.

CHAPTER TWENTY-NINE

Chris kept his promise about restricting lunchtime conversation to safe and unremarkable topics. He could tell that he had rattled Isobel with his earlier diversion into his brother's affairs by her quieter than usual replies during the meal. He was convinced he had acted in both their best interests but could quite well understand Isobel's desire for some solitary time in order to contemplate her situation.

The prospect of an afternoon of independence in Caen was not a burden to him and he quickly ran down the list of possibilities the opportunity afforded. He opted for a walk down the famous Rue du Petit Mouton to admire the fourteenth century timber framed buildings and possibly a visit to the hotel card room prior to an early dinner.

The ancient street was well populated this time of year. This and the cooperation of the weather ensured a prosperous day's takings for the shop vendors and street merchants in the generally sedate town. He chose a conveniently placed bench as a vantage point to watch the many young ladies as they made their way up and down the street. His attention was drawn to the antics of a young boy racing away from his nanny. The child was impervious to the shouted entreaties of the plump woman to slow down and gained greater distance from her as the seconds passed.

It was the shift in the slats of the seat beside him that alerted him to the presence of someone else on the bench. A raggedy urchin about ten years of age was staring at him with a fixed grin.

"The man standing by the flower stall said you would give me a franc if I told you that he wanted to talk to you. Will you do it, sir?" said the boy rapidly, nodding to a nearby kiosk as he spoke.

Chris flipped the young messenger the agreed upon coin and rose to cross the laneway, intrigued about who it was that had used such tactics.

The man was facing away from him assiduously studying nosegays of fragrant lavender tied together with ribbon. Without turning, he spoke a few quiet words.

Chris's fingers crushed the rose he had picked up, to the consternation of the flower girl. The savage look he threw her silenced any protestations. He hardly felt the sting of the thorn as it pricked his finger. His voice thickened despite his best effort to keep it level as he thanked the burly figure. He wiped the dot of scarlet blood off of his finger as he watched the red haired man with the mismatched eyes walk away.

Tamping down the burst of rage Jean's words had incited, he tossed the flower girl a coin and directed his steps away from the promenade towards a quiet side street and began to marshal his thoughts towards the logistics of immediate departure. As if by rote he entered the offices of Banque Courtois, the oldest bank in France and the one his family had done business with for generations. Ties to Guernsey and frequent travel on the continent meant they kept financial resources readily available in many places. He was immediately taken to the director, who escorted him to the vaults below street level. A few minutes alone with the collection of family items entrusted to the bank ensured he had the papers and financial means to travel extensively and meet any needs that should arise. With those practicalities seen to, he headed back to the hotel.

Isobel's surprise at hearing Chris's voice at the door quickly turned to alarm when he entered without a word and put his hands lightly on her shoulders. Chris gave her a brief squeeze, which she was sure he meant as encouragement, but which had the opposite effect. Her nerves ratcheted a degree higher.

"Isobel, I have some upsetting news. I wanted to tell you right away."

A surge of dread lanced through her. "My uncle's men are here?"

"No. It has nothing to do with that." Chris gave her a comforting smile. "You are safe."

She found it suddenly difficult to breathe and whispered on an indrawn breath, "It's Chetton, then." The tiny moment of time, a heartbeat only, between her words and Chris's answer seemed to stretch out. She read the truth of her guess in his eyes before she heard his reply.

"Yes. He went missing from Rouen several days ago and a mutual friend came to inform me."

She forced herself to think, but could only formulate a single question. "Went missing, what does that mean?"

Chris's firm chin clenched as he swallowed.

"I've just heard myself and don't know many details. There is someone I want you to meet, Isobel." He released her and opened the door to admit a man who must have been waiting outside. "This is an old friend of ours, Jean Tissier."

For perhaps the first time in her life Isobel decided to forgo the conventions of polite conversation and spoke to the newcomer bluntly.

"Where was he taken from and how long ago?"

The man seemed to understand her consternation and answered in passable English.

"He didn't show up to a meeting we had arranged in Rouen four days ago. I waited twenty-four hours for a message and when none came, I set off here to find Chris."

Chris nodded. "That is the same protocol that Chetton set up with me years ago when he first took me into his confidence. I am glad Jean followed it and wasted no time in seeking me. We met surreptitiously so no one knows of our association in case he was followed here."

She was stunned by their casual acceptance of danger in Chetton's life. The situation with her uncle had so occupied her mind that the possibility of Chetton being in jeopardy had not occurred to her. No, that was not completely true. She had played the ostrich and deluded herself. Chetton's strength, competent nature, and will power had overshadowed any such thoughts. The hints were there had she wanted to see them. It was so blessed easy not to be the sole person in charge of her safety that she had unwittingly passed the burden to him, and he had become her guardian. Now the reality of the world reasserted itself, and she was shown to be woefully lacking once more.

But she would not fail him in this.

"What is the plan, Chris? When are we leaving?"

She could see by the shrug of his shoulders that he had anticipated this question and was ready to try and gainsay her accompanying him. She took a step closer to him and spoke as firmly as her nervous state would allow.

"Do not attempt to stop me. I will be going with you, just tell me when to be ready."

"If mademoiselle will permit me to interfere on her behalf, I agree that she should come with us. You will be worried about her, Chris, should she stay alone, and you will need all your concentration directed towards finding your brother."

She was heartened by the Frenchman's support, even though his logic didn't entirely appeal to her. She wanted to be an active participant in the search for Chetton, not just a reduction in liability. Still, his response was to her liking and seemed to shift the balance of indecision with Chris in her favour.

"Be ready in an hour, and dress for riding. We will make better time on horses."

Chris tossed her a grim smile as he opened the door. She watched Jean follow him out and whispered after him, "Merci, monsieur."

He must have heard her as he raised his hand in a small wave, but did not turn. There appeared to be more to the man than his rustic appearance would suggest. She must remember that. To benefit Chetton she would take aid wherever she could find it.

※

Isobel's first impression of Jean held to be true, and as the long days on horseback wound by she was thankful for his attentive nature when they took their brief rests.

"Will you have more bread and cheese, madame? It is a fine Port Salut and will not keep long in the heat."

"No, thank you, but save it for Chris, he might want it."

"Oh, that one, he will probably not want much now." Jean spoke with such good humour that his words sounded more of praise than of condemnation. "At least when he is hungry he savours his food and has some imagination in constructing a meal. The big brother, well, you could feed him anything and as long as the quantity was there, you would not hear a word of complaint." Jean gave a shrug to punctuate his opinion on the sad lacking of his friend.

Knowing this to be only half true, she smiled at his attempt to lighten the mood.

Chris crested the small incline from the nearby stream and raised the canteen to offer a drink.

"Looks like your improved horsemanship is paying off, Isobel, you took that narrow trail well."

"Thank you for saying so, but I must give Monsieur Gagnon his due as well. There are parts of me that are protesting but I feel more in control of my mount." Her mind was suddenly full of the time she had spent with Chetton traversing their way across France. He always saw to her wellbeing and safety. She could not bear the fact that he was missing now and in possible danger. He had protected and comforted her continually during the time she had known him. With a sense of determination she approached her horse to remount.

"I am ready to continue."

"Just as well, we can make a few more miles before nightfall."

Chris gave her a leg up. The sooner they reached Rouen the quicker the search for Chetton could begin.

❧

Despite the dire reason for their travel it was impossible to be immune to the beauty around them as they traversed the rolling countryside. The route was well trodden and did not tax the mounts overly. Isobel was doing well and Chris was pleased after all that she had come. A cool breeze redolent of wildflowers ruffled his loosened cravat and he inhaled deeply. He loved this part of the world. Ownership of the land they were now crossing had been disputed for centuries between the French and the English, the region coming to terms with both influences. Even their beloved Guernsey had historical connections to Normandy.

Today this thought gave him but meagre solace. Jean had not said so, but it seemed obvious to him that his brother's disappearance was outside the bounds of what might have been expected to happen. This could be either a boon or a further impediment to finding him. Only time and perhaps Jean's intricate network of news gatherers would tell.

One more night at a wayside inn should see them to the outskirts of Rouen. He prayed to God that there might be some news they had missed, some clue not yet appreciated. He would vouch for his brother's success in any fair fistfight, and give him better than even odds with a pistol or knife. If it came to outwitting an opponent or convincing someone to switch alliance and aid him, Chetton would have the upper hand. He knew Chetton would not falter under the pressure of isolation or the rough treatment associated with imprisonment. But there were so many unknowns with his silent abduction that were unfathomable. Injury or sickness, drugging or poison, transportation out of the country, and a hundred other things, could not be ruled out.

The path was wider here and he moved up to travel alongside Isobel. She pointed to a large dense woodland in the distance.

"Do you know what that forest is called?"

The name of the landscape feature ahead escaped him. "No, I should though," he confessed. "It featured in a tale Chetton told me last time we passed this way together. There was something about three daughters of a Norman lord and a task he sent them on. No, sorry, it seems that I cannot remember it just now."

He stifled a flood of unease, irritated at his faulty memory. He was not superstitious but it bothered him that he could not recall the details from his brother's tale.

Isobel must have picked up on his disquiet. She smiled at him and shook her head. "It is of no matter. Just something to pass the time other than the bleak imaginings I have been creating."

"I know this is difficult, Isobel. Try not to let your fancy get carried away. Chetton is a strong, capable man and we will find him. After all, it is not likely that anyone would be foolish enough to treat a man of his position and background too badly."

But as he spoke, he knew he was trying to reassure himself as much as Isobel.

※

Chetton shifted his position on the thin pallet. It was difficult to get comfortable, and he acknowledged that he had seldom spent many nights in worse conditions. But that was not what was keeping him from sleep. Nor was it the raspy breathing from Jonny, who had again drunk too much, nor the deeper snores from Shep, annoying as they both were. He was frustrated he had not been able to discern the reason for his detention. The additional days with Jonny had only served to confirm his impression of the weak and surly nature of the man. Old Shep was proving to be wily and held his own counsel, garrulous though he was about other matters.

It was his own fault he couldn't find the path to slumber. He had been weak and allowed himself to fantasize about Isobel, where she was, what she was doing, wearing, eating, thinking, wanting. He created a picture of her in his mind complete from the little black slippers she wore to the blue ribbons in her hair. The tender expression of her green eyes, the texture of her curls, her sweet scent and the feel of her in his arms all haunted his senses till rest was nigh on impossible and sleep out of the question.

The dizzying aura of her conjured nearness gave him a small degree of comfort. She would be sleeping now, her delicate body curled up under the covers to seek the warmth she always craved. Perhaps she would break her fast with Chris. He could see her slender fingers wrapped around a cup of the fragrant tea she so loved and the wild highlights in her eyes as she laughed at some amusing remark Chris made. He clung to the image of her being safe and happy and prayed she would come to no harm through her association with him.

Jean would have known of his disappearance for several days

now and was no doubt launching all of his considerable talent and resources to glean some information. With little to do to help himself at present, he tried once more to coax sweet thoughts of Isobel to blanket his mind. She was his only solace.

CHAPTER THIRTY

Isobel's Uncle Alex was not nearly so far away as she imagined him to be. Buoyed up by his current success, he was quite pleased with what was proving to be his adeptness at subterfuge. He had always believed himself to be a cut above the average in cleverness and manipulation and it was heartwarming to finally give free rein to his Machiavellian machinations. A pair of the men he had sent out had more than earned their fee and helped to finally point him in his wayward niece's direction. That meddlesome Guernsey man had effectively been taken out of the picture and he was now at leisure to continue the pursuit of Isobel. He had a fix on her location and had only to await her arrival in Rouen. He knew the little tramp would follow her lover like a fish to the bait and he would be ready to receive her and deposit the troublesome package in a home for insane females on the bleak Yorkshire coast. They were known for the severity of their discipline. The girl deserved whatever he paid the staff to deliver for daring to defy him and leave the abbey. As the devoted next of kin, her lands and inheritance would continue to be in her safekeeping. And he had plans for every last farthing.

The smell of burnt toast permeated his senses as Lord Chetton awoke abruptly. He half expected the cottage to be ablaze from the careless way Jonny lit the fires, but only Shep was in the room this morning. The old man threw a toothless grin in his direction.

"Y'er awake. Fancy a bit of toast an' cheese?"

Shep transferred a hunk of dripping toast onto a plate. Chetton knew nothing else would be offered until evening so he accepted the greasy fare held out to him.

"So, what are your plans for this fine day, my friend?" he asked. Clearly something was afoot. The hearth had been swept and the empty ale kegs were nowhere to be seen. Shep's shirt was tucked in and it appeared as if a comb had been dragged through his unruly hair. That was a portent indeed.

"We're expecting word from the Guv soon. Might have to be ready to move quickish."

"I take it I would be accompanying you then."

Shep took a large bite out of his portion and wiped his mouth on his shirt sleeve. "Well, you being the guest of honour, an all, old son, we wouldn't be leaving ye here."

"Right." He sniffed his piece of blackened bread and tried not to grimace as the pungent smell assaulted his nose.

"And where might we be headed?"

Shep washed down the last of his meal with a swig of small beer.

"Now that would be telling, wouldn't it, mate?"

It was not a particularly reassuring reply. He had expected some change to occur after a message Jonny brought yesterday. Shep had read the contents with a distinct sense of anticipation and seemed pleased at whatever information it contained. Jonny was absent for what passed for breakfast this morning, so he must be doing something important. It might be worth it to try and convince Shep to make a deal with him again, although the man was disarmingly loyal in his criminal activities.

"I do not suppose you would like to tell me more about who the Guv is? You know I would be able to more than match whatever he is paying you to keep me."

Shep just grinned at him and lifted a battered jug.

"A cup of home brew suit you about now?"

"Why is it you are so set on helping this 'Guv' when you know I could make it profitable for you to let me go? Surely it cannot just be honour among thieves, you are too clever for that."

Shep set the jug on the table. "Well, to tell you the truth, it's personal like."

"Personal? And here you have been telling me just the opposite from the moment I gained back my senses. You have repeatedly indicated that 'I am just a job for the money,' have you not?"

Shep placed another cup on the marred tabletop. He had the good grace to look a little contrite.

"It's not personal like that. I got nuffin against you, mate, I tol' you. But somebody what I know got theirselves into a spot of trouble a ways back and this here will clean the slate, if you know what I mean."

Lord Chetton digested this piece of information, but it only answered part of the puzzle. "You must be very close to this person, having to leave home at your age and come abroad to play gaoler to the likes of me."

"Too right I am. She's a good girl really, she just made a stupid mistake, is all."

"Your wife—no, your daughter, I'll wager! Is that the reason you are here, to help your daughter out of trouble?"

He watched Shep take a steadying breath and almost felt pity for the old man. "Nah, she ain't no relation to me, just a kid what needs help."

"If you say so."

Shep looked relieved as he refilled his beer.

"But if that is true, then Jonny must be the King of England!" It gave Chetton little satisfaction to see the old man spill his beer as he raised the cup to his mouth.

※

On their ride to Rouen, Jean had been unrelenting in heaping abuse on Chris. The older man could not understand Chris's decision to ignore his labyrinthine network of information gatherers. He had tried to explain to the Frenchman that an overabundance of caution about Chetton's position had at first stayed his hand. Now Chris was ready to admit that he was wrong and Jean lost no opportunity to hammer this point home.

"*Zut alors, mon ami*, what were you thinking? But you weren't thinking, unless you were doing it with that large dull thing you sit upon all day, and not your God given brain."

Chris clung to the reasoning upon which his decision had been based.

"Jean, you know the problems it could cause if Chetton's enemies know he is at a disadvantage, not to mention the political ramifications if it was made public. We did not have enough details at the time to justify such a risk. Now that over a week has passed and no new information has surfaced, I have changed my mind, and think we should carefully pursue all of your contacts."

"*Absolument!*" Jean delivered a substantial wallop across Chris's back and then left the modest suite of rooms they had rented, muttering all the while about the stubbornness of Englishmen. Chris looked in on Isobel as she slept upon the narrow bed one of the rooms afforded. He didn't like to see her in such miserable surroundings as the ones they were now in, but they both understood the continued need to keep a low profile. She was exhausted from the overland journey, and had fallen asleep almost immediately despite a desperate attempt to stay awake. He noted how pale and fragile she appeared against the cheap bed throw. As he adjusted the thin spread to cover her more fully he was hit with a moment of affection, laced with a little jealousy, and thought how fortunate Chetton was to find such a woman. His often taciturn brother needed someone as tender-hearted and generous as Isobel to sustain and heal him.

In the early hours of the morning, before the sun had begun to show itself over the many spires of the city, Chris was shaken awake by a meaty hand upon his shoulder and a throaty whisper by his ear.

"Wake up, *mon ami*, and follow me."

Chris noticed the door to Isobel's small room was still closed. He pulled on his jacket and stepped into the hallway with Jean. "You have news."

"*Oui*, yes, I have news, and quickly too my friend, is it not so?"

Chris resisted the urge to wipe the self-satisfied smile off the older man's face. "Well?"

"Chetton is being held on the outskirts of the city in an abandoned house. It seems 'e's been there all along. Whoever took him has not the wit to keep him on the move. My informants know the location; it's just around the corner from the local tavern they go to."

"And who is responsible for this?"

"They know nothing for certain, only that two Englishmen have him."

Chris could hardly suppress his anger at this news, but was relieved to know where his brother was being kept.

"Englishmen, that is very odd. Do they know what condition he is in?"

Jean looked at the floor and didn't answer immediately.

"Jean?"

"They know only that a man is being held because the English are buying supplies from the locals. Little is seen of them."

"And why in bloody hell do they think it is my brother?"

"Because a young Englishman pawned this nearly a week ago."

Jean placed a familiar gold watch into his hands. There was no need to open it to read the inscription he knew would be inside. The Chetton family crest was embossed on the watch cover. He grasped the watch in his hands and swore vehemently in several languages.

A plan was quickly and efficiently put into motion with the help of Jean and his underground network. He had personally sworn to the loyalty of all his men, and had endowed each with a sizable purse of coin for their participation. Jean turned to Chris when the last man left for the rendezvous point. He blessed himself, raised his eyes heavenward, and squeezed his hands together.

There was no credible response Chris could make to that, and so with a sad smile, Jean left him.

※

After the first flush of excitement over the news of Lord Chetton's whereabouts had passed, Isobel became uncharacteristically quiet. Her relief that he had been located was profound. She did not want to complicate the situation to even a small degree by giving in to her desire to accompany the rescue party, though she would dearly love to be among those who would soon go to his aid. Common sense won the battle and she acknowledged she would be of little help in the situation and possibly hinder a successful outcome. She could not for a moment countenance the idea of being a liability and so bent her will to imagining seeing Chetton whole and healthy when he returned. Her knees were stiff from two hours spent in the dim vastness of the magnificent medieval cathedral that afternoon. Such discomfort was slight compared to the deeper pain at the thought that Chetton could be injured or worse.

Jean gave her a fatherly kiss and promised to bring Chetton to her before the next night fell. She smiled at the uneven eyes that could convey such meaning and emotion. Chris held her tightly before he left. The same thoughts were left unsaid, but not unfelt, between them.

Her vigil was solitary. A sense of unease lurked around her that was reminiscent of many of the restless nights she had spent alone at Thrushgrange Abbey. That time now seemed long past. The disquiet of these dark hours was a thing apart. It paled in comparison to the dread of contemplating danger to Chetton. She slid to her knees again in silent supplication, undeterred by the rough wooden planking beneath her.

CHAPTER THIRTY-ONE

They arrived just before dawn and positioned themselves to have a view of the old building where Lord Chetton was supposedly being held. Remnants of river fog in the bowl of land created by the circular sweep of the river Seine swirled around the bushes and held thick along the base of the dilapidated shelter. The men had waited near an hour outside to be certain that no lookout lurked in hiding to betray their presence.

Chris prayed that their meagre information was accurate, that his brother was inside, and that there were only a few people guarding him. His thoughts strayed back to a few of the many scrapes in his life where Chetton had come to his rescue, sometimes by request, at other times arriving unannounced, but always as an ally who didn't question the need. He wanted to provide that kind of help and that kind of uncomplicated loyalty to his brother now.

Jean was in his element, the excitement palpable in his asymmetrical eyes.

"You are enjoying this, you old pirate, aren't you, Jean?"

"I was never a pirate! But, *mon Dieu*, I have used their services many a time." He laughed in his gruff way. "Years ago, when my trading company was still small and fighting for survival, I paid the captains of three rum runners out of Jamaica to harass my rival's ships for a season. My competitor was a ruthless bastard anyway, and 'ad set fire to *Le Loup* while it was up for repairs in port. The Wolf, she was my best ship."

Jean spat to the side and shrugged his shoulders.

"Anyway, it worked well and the pirates kept 'im too busy to plan any other damage to my fleet. But in late spring during a thick fog the Jamaicans got confused and ended up blowing the mast off of my fastest frigate by accident." He laughed quietly, eyes gleaming with mirth. "God, 'e has a sense of humour too, don't you think?"

"Chetton always said you were a man and a half to contend with, Jean." Chris clapped him on the back. "Maybe he underestimated you at that."

"*Merde*, don't get soft on me now, son. Your brother has been a true friend to me these many years and I count few enough among that rank." His look turned vicious. "Let's go free him and string the others up."

"Remember, we're not going to kill anybody unless forced to, they may have answers we want."

"*Certainement*." Jean cast his eyes back to the hut. "In any case, I hope they said their prayers last night, because they won't be having a comfortable day today. I'll see to that myself."

Jean gave a three-note whistle that sounded not unlike the kind Chris had heard aboard ships. Their men began to quietly surround the structure, stealth being important at first, until speed and possibly violence became paramount. It would be his decision when that fine line would be crossed. He took a last calming breath and then followed Jean in a low crouch towards the front door of the old building.

There was no plausible reason to knock on the door this early in the morning so they shattered it open with a makeshift battering ram and entered quickly, hoping to take the guards by surprise. It all went smoothly and in less than three minutes he was untying the bonds of his astonished brother.

Chetton looked pale and unkempt but there was no sign of any major injury, just a faded bruise across his temple.

"God, Chris, but it is good to see you." Chetton grabbed him in a bear hug. "How did you find me and what the hell took you so long?"

"The telling can wait till we are out of here and on our way back to Isobel."

He helped his brother to stand just as Jean finished tying up a scruffy young man and shoved a rag in his mouth. An older man, having hardly put up a fight, was already seated in a chair with his hands tied behind his back.

"Isobel. She is here with you?"

"No, I am not that fool hardy. I would never bring her into possible danger. But she is here in Rouen, a short ride away."

"Thank God. And how is she?"

"Well, let us just say that she will be better when she sees you."

He glanced around the room and then at the tied up men.

"There were only these two, there is nobody else?"

"No."

"I am surprised the pair could hold you, brother; are you losing your touch?"

Chetton frowned at him as he felt the yellow bruise on his head. "I was under a slight disadvantage at the beginning. Now I am looking forward to getting some answers, and I don't much care what I have to do to get them."

He cast a black look at the young man, who hunched down and looked at the floor.

"So you do not know what this is all about either, why you were taken?"

"No, but I am about to find out."

Lord Chetton strode across the room and yanked the younger man's prone form up into a sitting position. Without any warning he picked up a jug from the table and dumped the contents over the surprised man's head.

"I figured I owe you at least that much, Jonny boy. Whatever else happens will depend on what you have to say to me."

Lord Chetton removed the gag from Jonny's mouth and tossed it on the floor, wiping his hand on his trousers.

"Who hired you?"

Chris could smell the fear emanating from the rough young man, who shook the water off and tried to bluster with a shouted, "Buggar off, mate." Before he could register it his brother had grabbed the scoundrel by the throat.

"Pass me the stiletto you carry, Jean, will you? I have a need to see some blood running down it."

A cool draft blew in from the shattered doorway, but it was not that which caused a chill to creep down Chris's back. He had never been on the receiving end of his brother's true wrath. He almost pitied the hapless man in front of him. Almost. Jean tossed the blade in Chetton's direction and it was neatly caught in midair and thrust beneath Jonny's left eye.

"Care to try again, lad? Or are you really as witless as I think?"

"The Guv paid me to come here with Shep. That's all I know."

"And who is the Guv when he is at home, then? I require a name."

Jonny stared back at him with stubborn eyes.

"Well?"

Chetton increased the pressure of the blade until a delicate drop of blood appeared but did not run down from the tiny cut.

"Don't, don't hurt me, sir. I don't know no more than that."

Jean knelt down beside Jonny's chair and glared at him.

"Want me to 'ave a go at him. It don't look as though it would take me long to find out what you want to know." Jean unhooked a long curved knife from his belt and laid it across Jonny's lap.

There was a noise from behind them. Shep was jostling in the chair he was tied to and muffled sounds came from his bound mouth. Chetton went over to him and undid the gag.

"He's telling the truth. He probably don't know any more'n I do, which ain't much."

Chris could tell by the way Chetton looked at the older man that there was no undue antagonism between them. This was confirmed when Chetton poured the man a glass of beer.

"All right then, Shep, but you still have some explaining to do. Where were you when this Guv hired you, for a start?"

"I was at home, in Surrey, in England."

"Do you know his name?"

"You had better shut yer mouth, old man, or you'll be a done for," shouted Jonny from across the room. Jean gave him a clout across the back of the head to silence him.

Shep paid the outbreak no mind. "No, but he talks plummy, like you do, sir."

Chris suppressed a smile as Chetton loosened the ties at Shep's hands.

"Did he find you or were you looking for work?"

"I done some bad things in my life, sir, no doubt about it. But I ain't done nothing like this afore. The man found me. Like I done told you, it's personal. He's got something on someone I cares about."

"Yes, so you said. Is he threatening you about your daughter?"

The old man swallowed hard and nodded his head.

"It's me Mandy. She's but seventeen, and a good girl. She works up at the abbey. The blasted Guv said she stole a pair of silver candlesticks from the chapel there and he was going to set the law on her. He said he found them under her bed and it was proof she were a thief, but I tell you she's a good girl and would never steal nuffin, 'specially from Thrushgrange. Them Sisters been good to her. She were set up, like, though I don't know why."

Something dark and dangerous flickered across Chetton's face as his back went rigid.

"So you were hired in England, and then came to France, like I guessed earlier?"

"Not directly."

"What do you mean?"

"We stopped off in Guernsey for a few days and then set sail for France."

"Guernsey, you have been to Guernsey?" Chris said, unable to hide his surprise.

"Aye. It was there that the Guv got the idea to come to France and grab you, sir, though I didn't know who you was at the time."

The room became very quiet, the silence broken only by Jonny's intermittent snivelling. Chetton's voice dropped even lower. "Do you know why he wanted me?"

Shep's hand shook badly as he took a gulp of his beer.

"It ain't you he really wants, m'lord. It's the little miss. The one that was up at the abbey until a few months ago. My Mandy used to do for her. She liked her, and said she were a true lady and kind despite what happened to her."

Chetton squeezed his eyes shut for a few seconds.

"But who is he speaking of?" Chris asked. "What lady in what abbey?"

Chetton turned to his brother and reached out a hand, a look of desperation on his face, then his arm dropped by his side as all the energy drained from him.

"Isobel. Isobel was at Thrushgrange Abbey. She was ill several years ago and sent there to recover after her husband died. Her uncle stands to gain control of her estate."

Chris struck the table with force. "Good God! And she is left unprotected in the city. Whatever have I done?"

Jean surged upwards and laid a hand on his shoulder. "I also thought the girl should stay away. *Mon Dieu*, what a *catastrofe*."

"That's right," said Shep, "the Guv's related to her. He said she was sick, and didn't know what she was doing. She'd run away and was under the influence of a blackguard."

Shep looked hard at Chetton. "It was you, m'lord? You took the little lady off from the abbey? I don't believe it."

"No, do not believe it, Shep." He gave a bitter laugh. "I am like you and have done some questionable things in my life, but I would never do anything so low as that. I met the lady by chance on our way to Guernsey. Alexander Radford is your Guv, is he not? He is the lady's uncle and wants to keep her locked up so he can control her estate and assets. I have been trying to protect her from the villain."

His failure to safeguard Isobel would cut at his brother deeply, Chris knew. Always the realist, his brother ground out the question.

"Do you know where Radford is right now?"

"Not exactly. He was going to head to Caen, and then said he got a better idea."

Shep started to reach for his beer cup, but Chetton stayed his hand. "And then, Shep, what did he say?"

The old man flinched but he looked Chetton square in the eye.

"He told me he would bait the hook here with you, sir, in Rouen. You would make it much easier to get the prize he really wanted."

Chetton heard both Chris and Jean swear at the same time but his mind was already on other things. He began planning what they would need for an immediate departure. He wracked his brain for anyone trusted he could send immediately to watch over Isobel, and concluded it would be faster to ride there themselves than to try and send a message ahead.

Chetton threw an arm around Chris and Jean and drew them in. "You did the best you could under the circumstances, gentlemen, have no regrets. Let us just go to her as quickly as we can."

They started towards the battered doorway when Shep spoke.

"Can I go with you? Radford's a bastard and has used me too, I'd say. I want to help you find him and the little miss what was so kind to my Mandy. Will you let me go with you, sir?"

Chetton nodded and they were away.

CHAPTER THIRTY-TWO

Isobel stared at the dregs of cold tea in the cheap cup. She wished she believed in the black art of reading leaves. At best it would give her an inkling of how events were unfolding with the rescue. At worst it would provide her with a small diversion. The night seemed to be passing so slowly that she could not be certain the oily candle was diminishing over time. Its rate of burn was not measured in minutes or hours but by the unruly beat of her heart.

Morpheus, god of sleep, must have visited her unannounced. Something stirred her back to consciousness. The fickle candle had now gone out and darkness clothed the small, sparsely furnished room. Her arm was numb where her head had rested upon it, yet she had no energy to move. Its dull ache served to center her mind and anchor her in the present, away from the fitful dreams that clawed at her. She was content in this state until the sound of another presence rippled in the murky predawn air beside her. With a scream of surprise she sprang out of the chair and slammed into a large body. Hands grabbed her and a lamp was struck with light. Terror spun through her mind, too deep for imagination.

"Well, girl, you've led us on a merry chase."

She struggled to get free of the man who held her from behind. Her Uncle Alex was standing in front of her but her foggy mind hardly believed he was real.

"That is not a proper greeting after so long, cousin, come here."

Her cousin Maxwell turned her in his grasp and planted a wet unwelcome kiss on her resisting mouth.

"Leave her be for now, son, though I know you have always wanted her."

Isobel's stomach turned at the thought. She glared at her uncle and said, " So you have found me."

Alex's lip curled up in a way that Isobel remembered all too well. "Yes, your fleeing Thrushgrange Abbey has caused me considerable aggravation, not to mention time and money, I grant you. But I have my way in the end, as you see."

Her uncle took a measured look around the room. "Really, my dear, how many men have you passed yourself around to, only the Chetton brothers? They seem to have deserted you."

Panic surged through Isobel but she would not give her sneering uncle the satisfaction of letting it show. How long could he have known about Chetton and Chris, and was he aware of tonight's events? Maxwell pulled a chair up beside her and sat close enough that she could smell the stale whisky on his breath. Her stomach heaved at the remembrance of her father's weakness and the bleakness of her life came full circle.

"How did you manage to trap someone like them? Did you play the innocent victim or the femme fatale? I cannot imagine the noble Earl of Chetton sullying himself with you. Maybe he just wanted the Widow Barnestowe to warm his bed. Oh yes, I am up to all of your tricks, you little wanton."

Isobel let the insult wash over her. It was not the time to let her uncle's twisted view of things further distress her.

"Never mind, I am not at all interested in your sordid history, Isobel. Here is what is going to happen now. You have ten minutes to pack and then we are leaving. We are going back to England, where, tragically, you will be found to be insane."

She would not endure another word and lunged at her uncle with nails drawn. He casually batted her aside and she fell hard, landing on her side. Maxwell was upon her in an instant and straddled her prone form. Uncle Alex bent over her and grabbed her chin in a fierce grip.

"Listen here, my wayward little niece, try anything like that again and I will let Maxwell have his fondest wish with you." Her uncle curled his lips in disgust. "Although, I do not know why he would stoop so low."

If her throat hadn't been so dry, she would have spit at him.

"What does it matter to you where I go, when I am no longer associated with you? You have won, I have left England."

"Believe me when I tell you I would just as happily sell you to a brothel here in France for all the bother you have caused me. Unfortunately, you *do* need to be associated with the family as you are linked with the entailment of the estate. I had your father sign the management over to me in one of his weak moments, the only proviso being that you are looked after. The idiot showed some paternal feelings at the end, or possibly he just wanted to make matters more difficult for me. No matter, by law you need to be seen to be taken care of, either that, or a death certificate will do."

A malicious smile spread across his face, then he continued.

"Yes. I have thought about it. But England will not accept a death certificate from France without an investigation and a lot of questions being asked. So, despite the annoyance you have caused me, I am prepared to make you an offer. You see, there are two directions this may go, Isobel. You can come willingly, enter the asylum I have chosen, and play your part. Then perhaps in a few years I will let you out and you can retire from the world in a small cottage somewhere."

He pinched her chin again.

"Or, you can come unwillingly. There are many ways to subdue women. Perhaps you will go to Bedlam Hospital or some such private institution. We shall see, but be assured it will be a much stricter facility than the abbey, and you shall never be heard from again."

He stood and brushed a hint of dust from his trouser leg, then glanced at his pocket watch.

"Your ten minutes begin now. I would advise you not to waste them. Anything not packed and ready to go will be left behind. Let her up, Max, but make sure she does not try anything stupid. I will see to the coach and return soon."

Max released her to stand, but as soon as his father exited the room, he grabbed her again and pushed her up against the wall. Isobel kept her face cast downward so she wouldn't have to look at him. He leaned in aggressively.

"Just so you know, dear cousin, I don't care what it takes to get you back to England. Either way you will be available to me. The old man will not be alive forever and I am next in line for the inheritance. I will make sure I have special access to you whenever I want."

Even though she knew Maxwell was enjoying her discomfort, Isobel could not but close her eyes in revulsion.

"I will make you tremble all right, my dear, more than those Chetton brothers ever could." He stood back and pushed her away from him. "Now hurry up and pack before I have to discipline you."

Isobel stumbled across the room to the small alcove that held her portmanteau. Tucked deep inside it was her only thread of hope.

※

Chetton kept his mental demons at bay as best he could on the wild ride towards the far side of Rouen. Chris and Jean rode shoulder to shoulder with him, Shep and the other men just behind. There were no wasted words, they spoke only when necessary. He understood the decision to leave Isobel alone weighed heavily on Chris and Jean. He faulted neither of them for it. All of his will and stamina were directed at making speed towards the inn Jean had described. He refrained from letting himself think of Isobel directly. The image was too painful. It might distract him or make him falter and cause precious moments to be lost.

He relished the ache in his shoulders caused from gripping the reins so tightly during their headlong flight. The pain was a tangible thing that directed his concentration away from the despair that threatened to swamp him, but memories of the tragic night from his past invaded his thoughts. The rational part of his mind acknowledged that it had been long ago, with a different woman, and under very different circumstances. He prayed that this conclusion would differ.

He strengthened his resolve.

There are moments in life, thought Isobel, when one simply has courage or one does not. She had cause to know this in great particularity. She had let fate dictate to her once before, and was still enduring the consequences of that decision. The odds against success no longer mattered to her. She would act.

Isobel threw a few clothes into the portmanteau for good measure. She heard Maxwell approach her from behind.

"Hurry up Isobel, father will be . . ."

Isobel turned and without hesitation thrust her sewing scissors into Maxwell's face.

"Aaahhh." Maxwell's high-pitched scream terrified her, as did seeing the small, finely crafted scissors protruding from his cheek. She pushed past her screaming cousin and headed for the door, pulled it open, and ran with full force into Alex. He grabbed onto her to prevent them both from losing balance and took one look at his bleeding son.

"Bitch!" He hit her soundly across the face. She reeled from the vicious blow and caught her temple on the wooden arm of the settee as she fell. Oblivion greeted her before she hit the floor.

CHAPTER THIRTY-THREE

The riders had hardly slowed their pace upon entering the old streets of Rouen. Only the confines of narrowed roadways and slick cobblestones forced caution. Jean crossed himself and thanked God that the area they were headed to was fast approaching. He clung to hope and prayed that events would somehow coalesce into a miracle. They needed one.

They leapt from their horses and entered the inn at a run.

"Second door on the left, upstairs, room six," reminded Chris as they crossed the public rooms. Chetton was in the lead and only slowed his gait when he crested the stairs and heard cursing from down the hall. The cursing was in English. It was male and loud and foul.

"On three we go in, quick and quiet."

Chetton steadied his breathing. Then he mouthed the words, "One, two, three, now!" and powered through the door with his shoulders and then stopped abruptly. There was a man with a bandaged face crouched down behind Isobel's portmanteau, but it was the man standing with Isobel's limp form held carelessly in his arms that halted Chetton in his tracks. She had a livid bruise across her cheek and obvious swelling on her forehead. The bastards would pay heavily for both.

Isobel lay still and unresponsive. Chetton moved toward her.

There was murder in his heart. He let it show in his eyes to the startled man who held her.

"I take it this is what you want," the man said. He hitched Isobel up higher in his arms.

She moaned softly and Chris took a step towards them, but the rapid flick of Chetton's wrist signalled his brother to stop.

"It is no use, Chetton, you cannot have her. I am her legal guardian and she is returning with us to England tonight."

"Where you will continue to take such solicitous care of her, no doubt," he said, indicating Isobel's head.

"Yes. Well, she shouldn't have been unruly. Women need to be taught their place. From the stories circulating in the London clubs about your various liaisons, you must know the way of it, Chetton."

"Bastard," breathed Chris. But Chetton again stayed his younger brother's agitation with a shake of his head.

"Do you know about the little wanton, or has she blinded you to her past? My niece looks all innocence and goodness, but is not. She could fool any man weak enough to let himself become besotted with her."

He understood Isobel's uncle was trying to goad him. Knowing it did not lessen his desire to pound the man. He continued to keep still.

"You have no response to that I see, Chetton. It is of little consequence to me. She is my ward and has been ill, not in her right mind. I have the papers to prove it."

"They prove nothing but that you are a conniving bastard," said Chris.

"To the contrary, sir, my documents are sound according to our fine English law. As I am sure you are aware, the immediate care of someone without mentis competes reverts to their male relatives. She is my brother's child after all."

"Isobel is as sane as anyone I have ever met. How can you

claim otherwise?" Chetton took in Alex's cold eyes, thin lips, the arrogant tilt of his chin, and could not remember ever wanting to thrash a man so intensely. But Alex had Isobel for the moment and it was necessary to understand all of the legal cards that the man was holding.

"Father, we have to leave now," said Maxwell, holding his bandaged face. With Jean standing over him Isobel's cousin had not yet attempted to rise from his position on the floor.

"For God sakes, Maxwell, stand up like a man!" said Alex with disgust. "My craven son is quite right though, Chetton, we do have pressing travel arrangements. Another time I would be happy to oblige and show you the medical reports and testimonies documenting my niece's sad decline into dementia. You will just have to take my word for it at the moment."

"That won't do, I am afraid," Chetton said with quiet resolve.

Alex carelessly shifted Isobel again in his arms. He looked a fit man for his age, quite different from his thin, whey-faced son.

"It is not bloody up to you," Alex said. "It would not look good for the Earl of Chetton to interfere. Think of your position and diplomatic status and all of those who depend upon you. Even great lords can fall out of favour."

Chris stepped forward and said, "Are you really trying to threaten my brother, you disgusting vermin?"

Chris's family loyalty was currently misplaced, thought Chetton. It was not prudent to antagonize Alex while he clutched Isobel in her helpless state.

"You cannot be that enamoured of her already, Chetton. From what I hear she would hardly fit into your stable of voluptuous fillies anyway. She does not have the spirit of those you usually like to mount, by all accounts."

"Pray, continue to dig your grave further," said Chris.

Alex drew his hand along the side of Isobel's pale cheek. "I could offer you some new suggestions on the matter, Chetton. We are men of the world, after all."

Chetton's chest tightened. Somehow he refrained from lunging for Radford's throat.

"Forget about my niece. She is not your concern, after all. I will trade her for the names of a couple of pliant but discreet females, if you like. That should satisfy a man like you. Well, as you seem to have so little to say for yourself, we will be going. Perhaps I was wrong and you care not for the little baggage, or you tire of her already. It will be simpler this way."

Chetton started to let the man pass and hazarded a significant look at his brother. The moment Radford approached the door Chetton delivered a well aimed blow to the side of his head. Radford promptly released Isobel but Chris caught her before she landed on the floor. This allowed Chetton the opportunity to direct the full fury of his emotions towards Radford. He had to admit that the older man at least put up a semblance of protecting himself and landed a hit or two, which was a much better showing than his snivelling son ventured with Jean. He had seldom enjoyed delivering a sound beating to anyone so much as at the present moment. It was only his concern for Isobel that stopped him from continuing.

He directed Shep, who had charged in to the room at the commotion, to deliver the Radford duo into the care of Jean's hired men and they were ushered out of the building. Chris had put a wet cloth on Isobel's forehead, after laying her on the bed. Chetton knelt beside her, bone weary and heart sick, and lifted one of her chilled hands into his. She was very pale and her breathing was shallow. It was disconcerting to witness the rapid movement of her eyes beneath closed lids.

Jean picked up a small blue medicine bottle and swore. "*Mon Dieu*, the bastards, they drugged her."

Chetton grabbed the near empty laudanum bottle and dropped

his head. "We have to get a doctor, have her examined." He tried to swallow.

Chris put a hand on Chetton's shoulder and gave it a gentle squeeze. "Take it easy, brother, she will survive. "

He looked up to see complete conviction in Chris's face.

CHAPTER THIRTY-FOUR

It was a cruel blow to Chetton to have to watch Isobel suffer under the effects of the laudanum. Despite the doctor's prediction of ultimate recovery Chetton would not leave the hotel, terrified of returning to find the lifeless form of yet another loved one. He slept but fitfully.

Chris often kept the vigil with him in the well appointed hotel suite that they had engaged. Chetton knew the measure of his younger brother's concern by his uncharacteristic silence. He vowed that when this was over he would make a point of thanking Chris for his unfailing support and quiet strength, but was unable now to direct his concentration away from the slight form being attended to in the next room.

He was occasionally allowed bedside visits by the respected doctor and cautious nurse. When he could resist it no longer he gently took the small hand into his to stroke, trying to will the untapped reserve of his strength into her.

The only other time he had dared to challenge the heavens he had been denied his wish. In a fit of mad grief he had held a tiny chilled body and had begged God to take the life from him and bestow it upon his son. He needed to stay strong for Isobel and would not let himself diverge from positive thoughts into the type of despair which that other loss had led him.

Such grief was a killing frost to the soul. It blocked out the civility of empathy and shared pain. It crashed through all barriers of restraint and bordered on the obscene. Not because of the purity of deeply held emotion, but because it extinguished hope. Grief like that was self-consuming, a cancerous growth that advanced inexorably towards a crippling, isolated end.

What he sought was a new beginning. With Isobel. He could acknowledge now his love for her unencumbered by contorted worries of her duplicity. During long hours of the silent bedside watch, he had managed to dispel reservations about the rightness of the liaison, about the fitness of himself as a partner for Isobel. His reluctance to claim Isobel was embedded in years of remorse and self-reproach. He had been young and naïve when he fell under his wife's power. He was neither of those things any longer.

In hindsight he recognized the faint-hearted choices he had made with women over the years. He had deliberately sought out shallow partners who were too self-absorbed to miss the fact that he had no true affection for them. He had not wanted to open up any part of himself to them.

Yet he knew on a fundamental level that life was made for challenges, for testing one's mettle against all of the possible good and ills that existed. Nothing was guaranteed. Not love nor happiness, nor, thank goodness, loss and pain. Risk was inherent in what it meant to be human and to be alive. He wanted to confront all of these possibilities with Isobel if she would but allow him the opportunity to do so. He made himself believe the future was there waiting for them.

※

A soft summer rain pattered on the window as dusk fell the next evening. Chetton was staring at the flame of the oil lamp as it twinkled against the brass fittings, his exhausted mind blank of coherent thought from several nights' worth of lost sleep. The nurse who was tending to Isobel had allowed him a quick visit as she went to have her dinner. The gentle rustle of blankets forced his gaze towards the bed where he beheld two green-grey orbs quietly observing him. A tenuous smile curved under them.

He swore softly and grabbed her thin hand.

"Chetton, you are here. I thought I might be dreaming."

"No, angel, I am real enough."

He turned to offer her some water. Her hand stopped moving half way to accepting the glass.

"And, my uncle?"

He strove to keep the anger out of his voice. "He decided to extend his visit to the continent. I believe he and your cousin have gone on to Italy."

Isobel struggled to sit up. "But he wanted to take me."

He gently settled her back onto the pillow and laid a hand along her cheek. "Shush now, everything is fine and as it should be. There is not the least need for you to worry."

She was weak as a kitten and hadn't the strength to dispute his words. A single tear escaped and made its way down the slope of her cheek much like the meandering raindrops on the window. But this small, golden drop of moisture was warm, born of emotion and powerful for all its solitude. He felt it slide under his finger and meld with his own skin.

Remnants of the strong drug claimed her once more and she was pulled towards sleep and away from him.

༄

The next time Isobel surfaced from the bonds of oblivion she was more fully herself. Chris was sprawled on a chair beside the bed.

She looked at him and he smiled across at her.

"You are not so lucky this time, Isobel, it is only me here to see to you. Chetton made me promise to make you drink lots of water, as per the doctor's orders, to not tire you out, and not to upset you. The list went on and on."

Isobel's eyelids started to flutter closed again.

"Now, Isobel, you will be getting me into dreadful trouble if you do not drink a little of this spa water. I shall have to fess up to Chetton that I failed to follow the doctor's orders for you and then all hell will break loose. My brother can be an ogre, really."

At the continued sound of his voice Isobel rallied a little. She blinked and looked at him. "Yes, why is that?"

"Why is he an ogre? I do not rightly know, just the chance of an ill wind at his birth I suppose."

Isobel shook her head against the pillow. "No, you preposterous man, why do people always seem to have to tell him the truth? What is it about him that impels us to do that?"

"Well, I am glad you are including yourself in this. It is rather awkward to admit as a grown man that my big brother makes me tell the truth. I do not understand it either. I suppose it has something to do with the force of his nature, his seeming insight into the heart of what really matters. And then there is always the fearful pounding he will deliver if I am caught out in a lie."

Isobel smiled drowsily at this bit of foolishness.

Chris supported her back as she took a few sips of the water. When she was settled back down, she asked, "So where is Chetton gone, then?"

He squeezed her hand. "Well, it is the first time he has left the hotel since you regained consciousness. All he said was that he and Jean had a few loose ends they wanted to tie up."

Chetton, Jean, and Shep had each taken a turn at questioning Alex Radford and his son, and all had come away with different pieces of the puzzle. It was difficult to decide which of them was the most angered and disgusted with the pair.

Chris met up with his brother for a drink after Isobel had fallen back to sleep and the nurse resumed her supervision. Chetton explained to him that Radford had been shadowing Isobel for much longer than anyone had anticipated. He had known of Isobel's flight from Thrushgrange Abbey almost immediately and made the connection that Emma must have been a party to it in some way. She had been tricked into divulging Isobel's destination by the simple expedient of circulating a tale about Radford's own imminent demise. Maxwell applied to Emma's kind nature to tell him where Isobel was in order that she have the opportunity to attend her uncle's death bed. Maxwell, the deceitful little coward, had stressed the fact that his father was desperate to make amends for previous misunderstandings and wanted to die with a clear conscience.

"So, armed with the location of L'Ancresse cottage, they went to Guernsey to collect her," said Chetton. "Maxwell used his hired men to scout around and they discovered her frequent presence at La Rocquette. He says he was surprised by his niece's connection, and his plans were momentarily stymied, it being impossible then to grab Isobel, as he bluntly put it, because her absence would so readily be noticed. He knew of my diplomatic status and then he hit on the idea of creating a diversion with the hint of a foreign association. And so the fire was set in the stables and Duke was killed in order to force me to spend more time overseas."

Chris noted that his brother's substantial hands had slowly knotted into fists. "But how would that help Radford's cause?" Chris asked.

"My absence was supposed to increase his access to Isobel, and facilitate her removal from the island. He was thwarted when Isobel set off in haste after receiving the warning letter from Emma, who, clever lady, soon realized that she had been duped by his immanent death story."

Chetton took an appreciative swallow of his wine and reached for a piece of Camembert. Chris turned the tray around and said, "Leave the soft cheese and try a bit of this Mimolette. The younger ones taste like a good Parmesan, but an aged piece like this has an intriguing nutty flavour that will do justice to your Burgundy."

Chetton threw Chris a look of mild exasperation, but did as he was bid. "Hmm, talking about nutty, brother! Anyway, I got to Isobel first in France, but with the help of his thugs, Radford picked up our trail. He again thought it necessary to wait until Isobel was isolated to snatch her. It would not do for anyone to know of his intended treatment of her. And so, for a little while, he bided his time."

"Well," said Chris, "Isobel told me that she had stayed inside the Grand Hotel in Place Royale as if she were sequestered there. At least that offered little opportunity for Radford to put his plans into action in Caen." He grinned at Chetton. "It must have thrown him into a tizzy when I arrived. He was back to his original dilemma. That is when he must have decided to change tactics and use you as bait to lure me away from Isobel."

"Yes, the rogue had the audacity to boast about being so close to success, but a sharp rap across his head brought him down a peg or two. What he had not counted on was Isobel's plucky nature in stabbing her cousin, or of us piecing together his plans so soon when you freed me. We have Shep's willing confession to thank for that."

Chetton clapped Chris on the back. "I confess, brother, it feels like fair justice to use the triple threat of physical force, the law, and my own resources to ensure Radford never contacts Isobel again. After I put a word in the ear of a few bureaucrats, he will find his access back into England closely monitored. Maxwell's snivelling weakness can only be ignored. He is beneath contempt and no satisfaction can be gained by pursuing him."

CHAPTER THIRTY-FIVE

Isobel was sitting up in bed when Chetton entered the room late the following evening. He could detect the strain her body had undergone by her pallor and the darkness around her eyes. He must be gentle. It was not the time to discuss the full extent of her uncle's sins.

"I am glad you are awake. How are you feeling?"

"I remain a little shaky, I suppose. But I am generally better, thank you."

"Have you been out of bed at all? Tried to walk about a little?"

"Not yet, though the physician recommended it. I thought perhaps tomorrow."

He sat on the chair across the room. He did not trust himself to be close to her and not try to hold her in his arms. She was still fragile and the time was not right.

"Chetton, I do not know what to say. I am sorry all of this misfortune came to you because of me."

He started to shake his head in negation.

Isobel lifted her hand to stop him. "No, let me continue, please," she said.

He let her proceed because he knew she needed to say such things, not because he needed or wanted to have them said.

"Of course there is no way in which to adequately apologize for all of the strife. I am so very ashamed that my uncle and cousin were behind the turmoil you have had lately. Your delicate work being upset and you being taken hostage." Here her voice wobbled and she sought a handkerchief and refreshed her face.

Chetton moved to open the shutters to allow the fresh night air into the room. "I believe I will have a word with Chris about his choice of topics of conversation."

"No, do not say that. I made him tell me."

"You made him?" Chetton raised his eyebrows.

"Well, I could not seem to stop weeping, it must have been the effect of that horrid drug. And Chris could not bear it and so he told me what I wanted to know, what I needed to understand."

"There is not the least need to fret yourself into a pucker about all that now, Isobel. You must only rest and get your strength back. Let us change the subject. Look, I have a mere trifle here to divert you."

Chetton approached the bed. He reached into his pocket and withdrew a small worn box, which he then placed on the bed next to Isobel. She just stared at the little container until Chetton took it back, opened it up to reveal a tiny diamond brooch in the shape of an arrow. He set the box on the bed beside her.

"I would like you to have this token, Isobel. It originally belonged to Mother. She won it at an archery house party as a young girl and gave it to me years ago, as rather a jest, really, when I bested her one day."

Isobel began fidgeting with the lace on the cuff of her nightgown. Her eyes were cast down towards the intricate ivory threads. He watched her slender fingers and remembered how sweet it had been to feel them clasped in his hand.

"You should not be offering me the brooch."

She moved suddenly to pick up the jeweller's box as if she might return it to him. This was not what he wanted.

"Will you not accept a gift from me? After all, I kept this." He put the bronze donkey effigy beside the box. "Fair is fair, after all."

She shook her head. "It is much more than a simple gift."

"I must not have explained things very well, then." He had meant it as a modest gesture. Why was she making this so difficult?

"But, it was your mother's."

"And now I wish it to be yours, Isobel. It is a trifle only." He stood up and started to pace the room.

"I cannot accept it, it would not be right."

"Why ever not? I think you are being too exacting in your level of propriety in this matter."

The small box was cupped in her hand. She was now holding it against her heart as though it was precious to her, even as she was trying to come up with reasons why she should not keep it. He frowned at the contrary wench. He took the box out of her hands, removed the sparkling arrow, and deftly pinned it to the neck of her nightgown.

"There," he said, with what he hoped was great finality.

The back of his hand had come into contact with the soft skin of her throat. Her eyes fluttered closed for a moment as she thanked him. He willed his hand not to linger more than was necessary. When Isobel began to trace the pattern of the brooch with her fingertips in a circle, he knew it was time to resume his perch across the room.

"Chris explained about where you were being kept prisoner here. Was it awful for you?"

"Mostly because I knew you and he would worry when you found out. Other than that, it was not so bad, really. Old Shep tried to take care of me."

"Shep asked to come and see me for a few moments. Did you know? He was so upset about his forced part in all this. I knew his daughter at the abbey, she is a sweet, simple girl." Isobel sighed deeply and rubbed her forehead.

"What is it, have you the headache?"

"No. It just stuck me again how many people's lives have been damaged by my wayward family."

"You must not concern yourself with thoughts in that direction."

"Yet it is impossible for me to refrain from doing so. Let me innumerate." she said ticking off her fingers. "It is not my fault, how was I to know, I cannot be responsible for. I understand all the reasons for avoiding guilt, Chetton. It does not change what happened, both to the people I care about and to those I did not even know existed at the time."

"No. It does not."

Such a simple thing to say and yet it was only recently that he had come to believe it. The shadow of his former self recognized the familiar path of vicarious complicity, guilt by association. It provided a haven of sorts in which to bury oneself. But he wanted more for himself and more for Isobel.

He retraced his steps towards the bed and stood looking down at her.

He could see she was hesitant to give him more details and his rage at Radford for his treatment of her had no decent bounds. Chetton had felt the cold malice of death in his heart and had wanted to mete it out to the man. The malevolence beat there still. He would not, in the end, murder Isobel's only remaining family. It was not in him to do it, whether through weakness or compassion he could not have said. All he knew was that he desired a forward looking relationship with Isobel, not one that began with his vengeance upon her relatives, vile as they were.

"Isobel, I know we have had a rather curious relationship. We have been together under unusual circumstances and yet I believe we have drawn closer because of them."

He paused, but there was no engagement from her. He tried to reach for her hand but she squirmed farther away as though she could not bear his touch. It wounded him unmercifully.

"Isobel. I thought, that is, I had hoped that . . ."

"No. Do not speak the words. Pray, do not continue."

"You are not well. I should not have spoken so tonight. My timing is appalling."

She threw a momentary glance his way. Her eyes were large and over bright. "I desire you leave. Please. Immediately."

He straightened his spine though he had lost all feeling in his body. "Lady, I assure you. You have made your wishes abundantly clear."

He pondered over Isobel's behaviour. He could not immediately fathom why she would not even speak to him, and this aloofness, so unlike her true nature, had taken hold. Something fundamental was amiss, something beyond the delicate condition of her health.

Chetton regarded her calmly as though there was no immediate need to depart. After a moment he gracefully extended a hand in her direction.

"What I mean, my dear, all I ask, is that before I leave you tell me why you will not let me continue my suit when it is patently clear that you have affection for me. And it must be some reasoning I can fathom, even if it should be difficult to accept."

A further slice of silence ensued as they continued to look at each other.

"Come, Isobel, I can see there is something always holding you back, something you are guarding. Your uncle spoke of some troubles. Can you not trust me enough to reveal what is truly on your mind?

☙

The strain of subterfuge was too great for Isobel to bear any longer. She had glimpsed the depth and subtlety of Chetton's spirit. The open generosity of his nature called to her to be truthful and it was a lure she could not resist. Perhaps it was the promise of his inherent strength, a glimpse of his implacable resolve, that allowed her to speak the next words.

"I am not a widow."

"I beg your pardon, surely I misheard you?"

"I believe, my Lord Chetton, you heard me correctly."

"The captain, he still lives?" Chetton became absolutely still.

She could tell by the look on his face that she had wounded him. "No, not exactly."

"I see."

Of course she knew he didn't, couldn't. "Let me be clear, there never was a captain. It was all a falsehood. I was not married. To anyone. Ever. It was all a complete ruse, a fabrication."

Isobel felt quite naked after her revelation. But she knew this was only the beginning.

She must continue.

"Will you tell me why you felt it necessary to employ the deception? This duplicity was not just towards me, after all, but involved my family and friends as well?" Chetton asked, his body rigid.

Isobel accepted the essential fairness of this expectation. But how can such things be shared, spoken about, she wondered. There are no words, only the stretch of existence, the beat of the heart as memory unfolds. So familiar, and yet so loathsome.

She felt the full penetration of Chetton's attention. His restless strength was now reigned in. He was determined to listen. She blinked, tried to swallow, took a breath, and still he waited, tense and implacable.

"Isobel." It was half statement, half question. She must take it as her beginning.

"I want to tell you, to try to explain." She saw the bronze skin tightening on his jaw.

He moved towards her, cursed, she knew, by his own innate kindness and the need to take some of the burden from her. Strong of body, comprised of such a complexity of honour and responsibility. He sat on the side of the bed and drew her into the sheltering enclosure of his arms. She felt a slight tremor pass through him. It was ruthlessly stopped by his implacable will.

"Isobel," he said again, this time like a talisman to save them both.

He held her closely, head bent towards hers, ready to receive what she would reveal. He seemed to know the telling was crucial to her. To be listened to like this was a blessing, a gift. She would take the balm, she would tell him, even if it would only expunge a tiny portion of the past. Of the future she had no thought.

Another, yes, just one more moment while she drew a breath in his arms. She tried to shift position to see his face, his enigmatic eyes, to see the reaction her story would have on him. He tightened his powerful arms, she couldn't move. Perhaps he knew better than she that she must speak without looking at him, or would flounder in the sea of old misery. It was necessary to begin.

"Almost two years ago I was driving home in my phaeton. I was hurrying because it was almost dark. One of the wheels hit a rock and I heard the crack of the axle. I managed to calm my horse and stop without further mishap but I was still a good distance from home. I was deciding what I should do, when I heard people approach. The two men were unknown to me; they looked like vagabonds. When they saw me they dropped their bundles, and gave chase."

Isobel reached for the cup of water, and Chetton passed it to her. She swallowed quickly to help relieve her dry throat, because the words had to keep coming now. There was power in words, and here and now, truth was paramount. To be shared with this strong, watchful man, even if only for tonight. Even if the telling of the truth, the spending of the words had no purchase on the face of tomorrow.

So she continued to talk about the events of that night in a solemn monotone. She spoke about how the men had dragged her into the bushes and pushed her to the ground. She told about how the first man had used his knife to slice open her dress, about how they held her down while each took his turn. No detail of the attack was left out. Not the stink of their whisky-fuelled breaths nor the savagery of their assault.

Isobel told Chetton everything she could remember about the night that had changed her life so mercilessly and of the time that followed. She exposed the determination of her Uncle Alex to have her remain in seclusion at Thrushgrange Abbey and hide her shame for the sake of the family. She revealed her attempt to devote her energies to the rhythm of life in the abbey, of how she tried to make the best of what her life had become, to submit her will and wishes to a higher power. She acknowledged that she had wanted so much for the gentle cycle of work, study, and prayer to be enough for her. But it was not.

Her secret withdrawal from the abbey was explained. She disclosed the necessity of using her ruse as a captain's widow with the random name of Barnestowe to facilitate her travels and to conceal them from her uncle. Her fabrication about the nature of her intimate relationship with her invented husband was revealed as a roundabout of explaining her reticence to be close. All this was shared in fits and starts during that long night.

She spoke not one word about how she felt or what it meant to her personally, either at the time, or now, after almost two years.

CHAPTER THIRTY-SIX

Chetton watched Isobel take another hurried swallow of water, the way her throat, so delicate, moved to force the liquid down. He saw the shadow play across the contours of her cheek and deepen the complexity in the green-grey of her eyes. She had quieted her movements from the frantic nervous stirrings of earlier. She was circling, mobilizing her strength and her often hidden but formidable will, to confront the picture she now painted of the past. It was a struggle for her. He could feel the elemental nature of her distress, deep-seated as it was. That he could not lighten her burden beat at him with each breath. He must have shifted slightly because Isobel's eyes sought his for a brief moment, then moved on and settled again, somewhere apart from him, mired in despair.

She talked and he listened. It took all of his control to just sit there and listen. All of the power of his will was needed not to show any emotion, not to ask any questions, not to crush her to his heart. Not to smash something. In a life too full of desperate moments, it was one of the hardest things he had ever had to do.

When the candles had long since gutted out and the room was devoid of even the echoes of speech, he rose quickly, almost violently, and strode to the window, gripping the sill. His restless vigorous body could be still no longer. His gaze stole out to the darkened yard. There was a gap in the trees that allowed the moonlight to course unchecked over the ground. A twitch of movement gave away the location of some small night creature. Clouds glided in front of the moon, deepening the dark. How many cold bleak nights had he spent in foreign locations, ready to either incite swift violence, or keep covert a silent mission? So many of the nights of his life spent alone, or with unfulfilling company.

The silence was palpable, and as it lengthened took on a surreal aspect of timelessness. Isobel's breath, almost suspended, whispered out of her. Chetton heard the catch in her throat. It drove him to turn abruptly towards her. He was at a loss to decipher her movement, her mood. Isobel seemed now to lack the energy even to sit up, and slowly eased her head and shoulders back against the pillow for support. She laid back in a boneless pose of tranquility, which was belied by the unnatural squeeze of her closed eyelids, the strain apparent across her forehead.

He had to again resist the temptation to go to her, gather her in his arms and hold her against him. Yet this was not finished for Isobel. He knew instinctively that she had bared only a part of herself to him.

As he thought of her pain filled words from earlier, his vision blurred with a relentless anger and the need for retribution. But a clouded mind and revenge filled heart were not what she required of him now. He searched for the calm center of himself. Willed away the despair, and sought the core of stability, which had seen him through countless battles and dramas. For her.

The face she must see, the composure he must radiate would, he hoped, allow her to continue. To search through the quagmire of revolving emotions which kept returning her to that unforgiving place that held her captive. The chance to clear and cleanse herself of her painful history was what he desired above all things to give her.

☙

Isobel turned towards Chetton. She ruthlessly brushed the tearstains from her face. It was time to continue. There would be no going back from this, no possible recovery. Once she divulged her faint-hearted actions Chetton would see her for the incomplete person she was. She lacked the moral fibre of conviction and he would turn away from her. She nearly lost courage when she saw the concern etched along the clean, strong lines of his face. But she could not dismiss the fact that Chetton deserved better than she. If this could be her only gift to him, that of awakening him to the reality of her nature, then so be it.

"I want to tell you what really happened that night. What I did, and what I did not do. You see, the next morning when I awoke," she sighed at the memory, "I did not know myself. I did not want to know myself because, because you see, it brought everything back. So I drew a line, not of forgetfulness, that was not possible, but a line of defence, a barrier in my mind. I thought if I could corral the horror, the hurt of that night into a corner, I could somehow contain it. It was not possible to believe I could accept or conquer, not then, only that I might be able to contain those events for a brief moment of respite against the swamping nature of regret. My regret."

Chetton stirred as if he didn't understand.

"And of my cowardice." Her voice was starting to rise. "Yes, cowardice. I had let this occur."

"No!" Chetton spat the word and shook his head. "No," he said again more softly and yet the vehemence of his negation was stronger for the forced calmness. "Do not even try."

Isobel pressed her lips together.

She had known this would be his reaction, his insistence that she had been ensnared, unable to help herself. And, she acknowledged again, as she had learned to do, that she had been trapped not only by those horrible men, but by the more soul destroying idea that she had made the choice herself. She had let them ruin her and thus lost a precious part of herself forever. And even if she could not have entertained the possibility of any other option at the time, it was still a pact with the devil. And the devil, history told, always got his due.

"You believe me blameless, a victim, someone who was caught and then forced. You will believe as you do, despite me, I know. You will think the best of me, the worst of them, and a great part of that is true. I was the one hurt, after all. But what you do not, perhaps cannot, understand, is the unrelenting nature of my complicity—and, perhaps more importantly, the consequences to me of that choice. Chetton, I have never told this to anyone before. Not even Emma. I could not."

She could see the concentration in his face. If she could only make him understand.

"I thought when the men grabbed me and threatened me that this bargain made in hell had some degree, however little, of integrity. It was a step towards helping myself, saving something of myself from a larger wrong, a stronger danger. And if I could not hope that it held a thread of valour, my submission, it might have a kernel of choice that I could grasp onto. And if I could have choice, of even such as this, my spirit could not be broken. But I deluded myself. I was wrong. For when it began, I so quickly lost myself in the revulsion and pain that my fear held all the sway. I had agreed, really, to let them take me without a fight and because of my terror, I had given them a free hand."

She took a shallow breath. "I should have fought them no matter the consequences."

Her fingers were clasped tightly together, and she glanced down at them for a moment. Then she quickly undid the front buttons of her nightgown, pulled the material back to her shoulder to expose the upper part of her right breast. Just below where her corset would sit there was a nasty two-inch-long scar angling downward.

"This is their memento." Isobel ran her finger lightly over the old wound. She saw Chetton clench his fists. "I traded my honour for them to stop." Then she raised her head to look Chetton squarely in the eyes.

"This is the person I truly am. I deserted all of my principles in a moment of fear." She paused and touched the tip of her tongue briefly to the middle of her upper lip and then said firmly, "Now you know why I cannot marry you."

☙

It was impossible for Chetton to remain in one place while taking in this grim assessment. His restless nature got the upper hand and he paced in front of the hearth, his hands still fisted tight with repressed outrage. In his peripheral vision he could see Isobel quickly close the buttons of her nightgown. The weight of her shame was palpable.

"Isobel!" He was unable to contain himself any longer. "Do you really believe your resistance, on any front, would have made a difference? Your fate was sealed. Surely you must know that?"

He had asked the question rhetorically, but could see from her reaction that Isobel did not understand it as such. Her uncertainty caused the bitterness that burned at her heart to flare through her eyes.

"Doing something under duress is not tantamount to acceptance or willing compliance. People do not always have unencumbered choices in life, Isobel. There are times when free will is an illusion."

She stilled in her reverie, seemingly lost to the pattern of the dying flames, then whispered, "But surely to a man such as you honour is an absolute. It cannot be corrupted or bartered."

"It is a word like any other, and can be manipulated to mean many things. To some, honour denotes only glory and reputation; to others it is a sign of respect to family or country. The value of honour comes from what it relates to, the idea upon which it is based. As an ideal it is dangerous if taken out of context or if it is rooted in an unsound premise."

"I do not understand. Honour or the lack of it seems absolute to me."

"That is because for women honour has been narrowed down to mean primarily one thing. We both know what that is. It is synonymous with chastity or virginity. If that is taken, then a woman is seen as being dishonoured. But in your case, what was the option? Disfigurement or death. You took the rational, life preserving choice. Do not fault yourself for that."

He could see Isobel was blinded by her perceived cowardly behaviour. In a voice ringing with regret she said, "I should have tried to stop them. It is supposed to be a fate worse . . ."

He spoke sharply now, his ill hidden wrath volcanic in its intensity. "I have seen death, Isobel, much of it. There is no honour in accepting an unnecessary death. It is too final, I assure you."

He needed to reign in his anger and use all of his persuasiveness to reach Isobel. She was lost in the bleakness of self-recriminations. How well he knew the desolation which that path led one towards. He wished to release her from her cloak of despondency.

"Listen to me, my dear. Honour is an empty dream if it leads only to death for death's sake. If you could only see yourself and your actions as I do, Isobel. Absolutely none of this is your fault or blame. Please try to understand the other side of the equation, how your actions should be considered as pure bravery."

Isobel had closed her eyes and began to shake her head. Such a stubborn, misguided soul was the woman he loved!

"Has no one ever told you that bravery or honour is not about how you feel, Isobel. It is about what you do, or refrain from doing, despite not feeling courageous. It doesn't matter in the least that you were scared at the time. That is a rational feeling considering the danger you were in. I tell you from the bottom of my heart that soldiers in battle are absolutely terrified, whether they admit it or not. They have been trained and instilled with a sense of duty which helps to override those fears, but they are there, believe me."

He wanted to touch her, to have a physical bond with her right now. She seemed so forlorn it was tearing at him, but it had to be her choice. He reached out his hand towards her and she looked at it, and then at his face. Uncertainty swirled around her like a cloud and made her hesitate. He unwittingly spread his fingers.

The gesture beseeched her to respond to him and, thankfully, she did not ignore it. The merge of hands connected the empty space between them, as his words had sought to do. It was a beginning. Perhaps it would be enough for the present.

CHAPTER THIRTY-SEVEN

After a fitful night Isobel relinquished all hopes for sleep and arranged her pillows to sit up in bed. Her morning hot chocolate would be at least an hour away, she guessed, as the room was still gloomy before full light. The morning held no solution to her dilemma. Although she could now admit that Chetton cared for her, it mattered not. In fact, it complicated her position. She had schooled herself for the separation she knew must come. After her complete confession last night it was now paramount to distance herself from him.

Her association with him had been a debacle from the start. No amount of good intentions could change the facts. Quite apart from the malicious intentions of her uncle and cousin, which alone was more than enough to require her to keep her distance, she was also a woman with an encumbered past.

In truth, his declaration itself was not the question, although it had taken her completely by surprise. She believed she would have stayed with him without such. To be with him was enough. There may have been a little space of time they could have found to be together before she would have had to cut the ties. Dallying overlong would not have been correct. Her admissions dashed even that hope, since she could not now stay with him under any terms.

Despite acknowledging this ominous fact, Isobel's heart was

soothed by the way in which Chetton had received and reacted to her confession. To begin with, she had not revolted him, as a part of her had dreaded might be the case. It was not really that she was grateful to him for this, it was more that his acceptance of her spoke of a determination to acknowledge the very worst that life handed out, and then to actively choose to move onwards from it. She recognized that despite his own sad history he had the strength and vitality to be able to realign his life towards useful purpose and enjoyment. Their conversation while visiting Le Dehus and how affected she had been by the Guardian of the Tomb suddenly came back to her. She remembered how Chetton had spoken about the expansive and accepting nature of people and the fleeting span of one's existence. She was astounded to acknowledge that she was glad that she had confided in him, whatever this might mean for her future.

Though she hated to contemplate it, she knew she could not return to Guernsey and the gentle confines of L'Ancresse Cottage. Its proximity to the La Rocquette would be impossible to bear. She would go to England and stay with Emma until she could work out what she wanted to do. Chris had mentioned something about Alex relinquishing control of the unentailed portion of the estate to her, due to Chetton's influence. This was good news as it was the major part of her family inheritance.

She picked up the small jewellery box from the bedside table. Her fingers returned unconsciously to frame the shape of the diamond brooch Chetton had given her. She might just let herself keep it after all. It would be both the beginning and the end of his gifts to her. The shape of the little arrow seemed always to be pointing in one dire direction, away from him. She barely registered the prick of the pin from the back of the brooch as it pierced her finger. A single drop of blood welled up. She drew her finger into her mouth to capture it. Just one drop and yet she felt as if her life's blood had drained from her. Such was the pain in her heart.

Chris came by after lunch. It was the first time she had been able to sit up properly to eat a meal. He arrived just as she was returning to the comfortable settee after walking slowly around the room. While it felt good to stretch her legs in movement, the other half of the enjoyment came from regaining a small sense of control over her life. Being ambulatory meant she could begin to put plans in order and move towards her future.

"Good to see you up and about, but you should have waited for my arm to steady you." Chris smiled at her. It was a pro forma smile at best, and didn't touch his eyes. He scanned the remains of the lunch tray disapprovingly. "I have just finished a meal, but I can see you have hardly touched yours."

Such strict adherence to polite conversation was suddenly unbearably annoying. The compelling safety of it rankled her.

"You might as well just come out and say it, Chris."

He turned to look at her. "I am sorry?"

"Yes, I imagine you are. For your brother's sake at least."

"We are going from bad to worse, Isobel. Now I am confused. Has Chetton made a misstep? It is so unlike him. Do tell?" It was evident his curiosity was piqued and he was truly interested. She felt flustered by her assumption that Chris knew at least the basics of last night's exchange between Chetton and herself.

She lifted the weight of her hair off her neck in agitation.

"He has not spoken to you then?"

"No, I have not seen the man. He was up and gone before first light."

Isobel shivered with this news.

"He left a brief note about some diplomatic concern he had to see to. I am a bit cross with him, to tell the truth. He left abruptly and took Shep with him to help the old man on his journey back to England. I would have offered to do that for him had I known of his desire." Chris kicked the leg of the bed soundly. "Head strong idiot."

Well, apparently she had gotten what she wished for, though it didn't feel at all gratifying. At least she would be spared the need to try and formulate a farewell to Chetton. That daunting task was removed. She could not believe she had hurt him too badly, but supposed the hasty departure was to spare them both embarrassment. It allowed him to save face and a modicum of dignity, so important to a proud man. The condition of her own shattered heart was another matter altogether.

"What was it that happened between you then, if I may be so bold as to inquire?"

Chris was watching her closely. She had to say something.

"It was just a misunderstanding, it is of no consequence now." She picked up the fork and began to push the remains of the chicken a la bretonne slowly around her plate. "Did he mention how long he would be detained?"

"No, Isobel, there was not a word about that. I doubt it will be too long a period though. From the state of his room when I looked in he had not taken much with him."

It was like a chess game, thought Isobel. She would have to figure out her next few moves in advance if she wanted a clear path to escape. She would rest and gain her strength for a little longer and then head out surreptitiously, just as Chetton had done. Leaving unannounced. It was something she was getting quite good at.

❧

The next few days flew by. Although she tired rather easily and continued to have an intermittent headache, Isobel managed to quietly make arrangements for her departure. She was hampered by Chris's attentiveness. Hating to lie outright, she became adept at giving vague answers, or smiling encouragement without the commitment of words. Then one day Chris deserted her too, explaining that he must return to Guernsey and inform his mother in person of the events with Chetton now that the danger was over, as he had not wanted to worry her unduly during the actual ordeal. She felt a little bereft at his abrupt leave-taking, as she felt him to be a friend. But it did open up a window of opportunity for her departure and thus simplified matters greatly. She would leave by private coach two days hence and sail to Southampton the following week.

There had only been one moment of indecision. Isobel ran into Jean when carrying a bundle of luggage tags to her room. The Frenchman had been discreet and not spoken to her directly when she was recovering, but as she began to venture into the hotel's common rooms she had often seen him from a distance. He always smiled or raised his hand and she felt sure Chetton had asked him to stay on her behalf until she recuperated. Caught with the labels in plain sight, she had sought to distract Jean with a question about the hotel's upcoming musical evening of entertainment.

The man was not to be put off so easily. He took her hands between his with the tags openly visible.

"*Cherie*, did you know I once had a great love? She was an angel of a woman. Beautiful, passionate, with a fiery temper. And she was a superb cook." He sighed. "*Mon Dieu*, but I worshipped that woman."

Taken by surprise, she could do nothing but listen to Jean as he continued.

"But I was a much younger man then, and not nearly so clever as I have obviously become."

Isobel smiled as she was supposed to do.

"I loved her, but couldn't believe she could love me back. I was not rich then and I have never been a handsome fellow."

Isobel shook her head in denial. Jean's mismatched eyes held hers sharply and he frowned for a moment. "Do not pity me, *chérie*, I know what I am." He squeezed her hands to gentle the reprimand. "So, I said nothing to the woman about how I felt. I expected her to know I loved her, to understand."

He closed his eyes for a brief moment. "And, *ma petite*, I didn't want to gamble with my feelings. I was a coward, *non*? *Mais*, of course it wasn't enough for the lady, though I didn't see it at the time. And so she left me and I didn't even see it coming."

He released Isobel's hands carefully and somehow managed to take the luggage tags from her. He patted them into a neat pile and handed them back to her.

"Ah, *l'amour*. Love is a delicate thing, *chérie*. Who knows what the other needs? We have to have faith, and trust to the feelings of our heart. *Mais*, as I learned long ago, we also have to believe in ourselves, and take a chance, *oui*? A chance that love is strong enough."

She couldn't utter a word and knew not where to look.

Jean patted her on the back, said he would see her at the musical fete that evening, and left her standing in the hallway.

Later that day there was a quiet knock on Isobel's door. She had been reading a book and must have dozed off for a few seconds. Supposing it to be someone from the housekeeping staff, she didn't open her tired eyes, but called out, "Enter."

A young maid came in. "A letter for you, madame."

Isobel took the correspondence and tipped the maid a sou. Seeing that the thick letter was from Emma, she quickly broke the seal and opened it.

> *My dear girl,*
>
> *I must begin with a heart-felt apology. I am so sorry I betrayed your whereabouts to Alex. Maxwell*

really had me believing the old viper was on his deathbed and wanted reconciliation with you. I started asking a few questions round the village, and when I learned of his deceit I wrote straight away and was nearly demented that you get the letter in time. But the damage had been done. Really, I cannot forgive myself.

Lady Chetton wrote me a long letter, with her son's permission, explaining things. I know little about how you met Lord Chetton, but I want to know how you feel about him. Do not concern yourself about what others think or feel, what is it that you desire? What are your intentions?

She sighed and answered out loud, "I hardly know myself, Emma," then turned the page over. Isobel poured more tea from the recently delivered tea service. Unaccountably she had no desire to taste any of the prettily arranged assortment of biscuits and chocolates which accompanied the tea. She played with arranging and rearranging the embroidered linen napkin on her knee.

Isobel lay reclined for a long while upon the chase longue, letting the cool breeze blow over her as she contemplated Emma's query. She wondered if she was indeed intentionally pushing away a chance of being happy.

She hated that she had let her life fall into a state of passivity while she tried to heal. The precious coin of time and energy could have, should have, been spent on other things. It was such selfish waste, she realized. Life was writ large on an immense canvas and she had narrowed it down to the limited confines of her own hurt and feelings of worthlessness for much too long. She was guilty of restricting the measure of her world to encompass only her own misery, far past the point when it had been necessary or helpful to do so. Such complicity was not productive. It went against life and the elemental forces of rebirth, healing, and creation.

She had lived for too long in the isolation of her own mind. If she could but learn from this. If she could marshal the courage, energy, and inclination to put her life on a new path, perhaps there would be some recompense for it all to have happened. She was not gifted with sight of the future. But surely there were lessons here to be gained from the past, from a reconstruction of her reality.

She tried to envision herself escaping from the constricting circular path that turned always inwards upon itself, and to see instead the wider vista of a future not blocked by despair.

Perhaps this was what Chetton had attempted to convey to her?

CHAPTER THIRTY-EIGHT

The next evening, Isobel decided to have dinner in the dining room downstairs. A light meal in an open area appealed to her and would also help to fill some of the long hours before she could retire.

She dressed carefully in a becoming peach silk and lace bell-shaped creation that had caught her eye in the dressmaker's shop beside the hotel. The arrow broach was hidden beneath the wide double collar of her dress. Flirting with the charade of having someone to dine with gave Isobel the excuse to ask the hotel's maid to dress her hair *à la grecque* with ringlets spiralling down the side of her cheeks. It was a novelty to be pampered and fussed over.

Her appetite had not fully returned. She lingered over choices on the menu until the maître d' bustled towards her, worried that nothing was to her liking. She finally settled on the dishes and was just starting on the second course, poached veal with a delicate saffron sauce, when a disturbance outside came to her attention. She cast a glance out the open window. A commotion had been caused by a reckless man on horseback who had not been able to control his mount and overturned a cart of vegetables. The farmer was vocal in the extreme over the loss of his cash crop, while the arrogant rider seemed disinterested in the whole affair. She watched the animated exchange with amusement. The farmer began hurling pieces of ruined vegetables at the careless man with great determination.

"Good evening, Isobel."

She was so engrossed in the spectacle outside that it took a moment for the voice to register. Then a hot frisson of shock needled down her spine. She daren't turn to look or she would be undone.

"May I join you, if you have no objection?"

Chetton slid into the seat facing her. She felt the table shake slightly as he adjusted his chair. It was not possible to remove her eyes from the window, but she was acutely aware of Chetton's calm regard in her peripheral vision. She caught a breath of the aromatic male fragrance, so unique to him, and gradually swivelled her eyes towards him.

༒

Chetton had seen Isobel as he passed the open doorway of the dining room on his way upstairs. He had been loath to leave her so soon after she shared her tragic episode with him but his obligations to duty were deeply ingrained and he had to attempt to conclude his discussions with Finance Minister Laurent. Chetton was relieved that no one in the British Embassy in Paris had disturbed his office in his absence and the vital papers condemning Villiers and Mercier were still there. After he offered Laurent an abject apology for his unexplained delay, the finance minister was only too happy to receive the information and documents to pressure the dishonest Villiers and Mercier to do his bidding and attempt to dissuade or at least slow down the king.

During most of his trip, Shep had been with him. Chetton had not had much time alone to think. The old man was full of stories and comments about the "Frenchies" and their funny ways until the moment he had handed him the necessary funds for his passage back to England. But after Chetton's diplomatic concerns were dealt with and he was on his return to Isobel, thoughts of her consumed him. He found he could not dwell too much on the details of her horrendous attack, as the black rage it created was not helpful to him or her. Rape was one of the ugliest of crimes. And like the response from Isobel's uncle, the woman was often blamed and shamed for the foul incident. As a man of power he hated it when power was misused, especially against women or children. While he did not want to ignore or minimize the pain and horror of the tragic event for her, he wanted to aid Isobel in being able to move beyond her past and to know she was desirable and worthy.

The foolish, foolish woman did not see, not for one moment, what was so patently obvious. She held herself to a standard that was unattainable in this danger fraught life. Even as he saw that this caused Isobel inner harm, he accepted the strength that drove her to this precipice. Her exacting nature, the surety of her conscience was the measure of her integrity. And while he could despair at the result of her self-deprecation, he could not fault the underlying strength which bred it.

His mind's eye had a fair knack for detail, but nothing compared to the reality of having the warm beautiful woman before him once again. She had not requested that he leave her table. This small token of peace between them pleased him enormously.

They sat, simply looking at each other.

Little by little the reality of the busy dining room—the clink of china, the glitter of crystal, the murmur of conversations, and the smell of delectable food—returned them to full awareness of their surroundings.

Chetton smiled. Isobel shook her head.

"My lady, you are looking well. I am gratified to see a little bloom is back in your cheeks."

Isobel dropped her eyes to the table. "I am leaving soon."

This was not the way forward he desired. "Are you indeed?"

"Yes. I am returning to England for an indeterminate period. I shall leave in the morning." She wet her lips. "At least it will be under my own steam, so to say."

She spoke brightly. Perhaps over brightly, he thought. He did not believe her show of light heartedness but continued with the charade. "Well, you seem to have distanced yourself from the events enough to find humour in them. I suppose that is a good thing."

He fiddled with the wine decanter and took a perfunctory sniff of the contents, setting the crystal down carefully.

"I will go to Emma until things are settled and then perhaps to London for the season. We shall have much to do and see there. I expect to be busy."

Chetton abruptly leaned across the table. "Do you think to run from me again, Isobel? Why have you the need to do so?" His intensity surprised him, as if tightly leashed emotions would slip the bounds of his stringent self-control.

Isobel placed her napkin on the table and carefully smoothed out the wrinkles before speaking. "Let us part as friends, Chetton, and not bring up matters which will only serve to unsettle us."

He would have none of it and shook his head. "Perhaps it was I who should have kidnapped you." Christ, what an odd statement to make, he thought, rattled at his unaccustomed tactlessness.

Isobel's cheeks coloured and she glanced out the window again.

"Forgive me for that indiscretion, Isobel, do. If I have not lost all credibility in your eyes, may I suggest you finish your dinner? Indeed, I feel I should prevail upon you to do so for your recovery."

In answer Isobel arranged the silver knife and fork across her plate and slowly pushed the sparsely touched meal away. Apparently her fickle appetite had deserted her completely with his arrival. Marvellous!

He chuckled at her blatant act of rebellion then stood and bowed slightly. "I see I have failed with that suggestion, but will you accept an invitation to join me later in the salon for a farewell evening?"

He was both pleased and relieved when Isobel consented to his offer. After retiring to her own rooms for a little, she met him in the private sitting room attached to his suite. It was a handsome, well-appointed space. Someone who was gifted in such things had lavished great care on the draperies and soft furnishings. Subtle burgundy walls met rich brocade draperies. It was a place of near enchantment that evening with carefully placed candles, and festooned with the dazzling variety of fresh flowers he had ordered. Even the soft evening breeze wafting in through the balcony doors added to the soothing mood he wanted to create.

Chetton handed Isobel a glass of champagne. She accepted it with a quizzical look.

He said, "Well, if this is not exactly a celebration, there are always other reasons to drink champagne. It is, after all, practically the national drink of France, it is alive with bubbles, and, besides, I know you adore it."

He knew she couldn't argue with any of this, particularly the last point. He smiled when she raised her glass to him and took a sip.

"Please make yourself comfortable, Isobel. Will you take a seat?"

She selected a chintz wing chair near the window.

"I know that you do not wish to bring up certain delicate matters between us, but I do feel it necessary to talk with you once more, now that you have regained some strength and are feeling more the thing. Then I promise you, on my honour, I will not mention another word on the subject."

Chetton took two long swallows of the beverage in quick succession, then put his champagne glass down on the mantle.

"You know, Isobel, people go through many periods in their lives. Change is inevitable and we must accept it whether we want to or not. Hopefully we can learn from, from . . ."

Chetton surprised himself by suddenly kneeling at her feet. "Christ, I sound as if I am making a speech, when the truth of what I want to say is simple. I love you, Isobel. I adore you, in fact. I do not think there exists anything within the bounds of decency or without that I would not do for you. I want to marry you and spend what portion of time we are allotted together." He clasped her hand in his. "Isobel, will you do me the exquisite honour of becoming my wife?"

His face was on the same level as hers. His eyes beseeched her to agree and accept him.

ලා

I should not drink anymore, Isobel thought, not if I want to keep even the semblance of control over my emotions. Yet the fine etched crystal floated to her mouth and the sparkling amber liquid slid down her waiting throat. This was an argument she thought she had won previously. She must prevail for Chetton's benefit, although her own resolution to do so was sadly diminished. She slowly withdrew her hand and stated her reply. "Chetton, I have spoken before on this matter, and declined your suit. I am sorry."

There. The words were unequivocal.

Her heart was not.

Chetton now understood everything about her, and yet still wanted to plan a life together. How could this be? Was it from mere pity? No, that was not the reason and was, she now felt, a very unfair assessment of both of them. Had she failed to recognize or appreciate the true meaning of something else fundamental, then?

ලා

Lord Chetton hesitated for a moment then rose and sat down

facing her. He put his hands on his knees and leaned towards her.

"Are you truly sorry? I sometimes wonder. However, can I ask forbearance from you? Will you delay your final decision for a little longer, please? I want you to understand everything that is in my heart before you decide."

Isobel looked down as she began to smooth out the folds of her skirt. Then she answered faintly, "I suppose that is only fair."

"First and foremost, my darling, I do not accept the harsh verdict you have imposed on yourself for your past. I am humbled by your courage and frustrated that you allow yourself no mercy for what you see as an inadequacy. Especially so, because your kind-hearted nature is so forgiving to others. Isobel, my dear, I want you to emphatically understand that whatever you decide about my offer, you should be proud of your ability to survive and I hope only the best for you as you reclaim the adventure of living your life."

Isobel closed her eyes for a moment and did not speak. Finally, she gave him a small smile and said, "Thank you, Chetton, that means more to me than you can possibly know. You are very kind and I am trying, very hard, really, to accept myself and expand my dreams."

"I am glad we have common ground on that issue." Chetton stood and cleared his throat.

"Isobel, forgive me, for this huge change of direction, but I know you will remember when I explained about Maddie and my son to you."

She looked at him askance. "Your tragic loss is not something I am likely to forget, I assure you."

"Yes, my loss." Chetton reached for his glass and finished the contents. "Please remember what I am about to tell you is only to explain, if that is possible, how I reacted to that situation over time, how I came to be the man I am now."

He could see that Isobel was searching his face intently as he refilled both of their glasses, but she said nothing. He settled back into his chair and let the memories claim him.

"Sometime during that hellish night Dr. Hoskins approached me again. 'I'm loath to give you this, son, after all your sorrow tonight,' he said.

"He held out a letter to me. When I made no move to take it, the doctor placed it in my hands and said, 'They were your family and you have a right to read whatever it says. I'm truly sorry for your troubles, Chetton, my dear boy.'

"It took a few moments for me to decide to open the letter. It was addressed in Maddie's handwriting and I imagined it was some sort of an explanation or apology, if such terms have any meaning, for her actions."

Isobel shook her head in apparent incredulity and put her hand over her mouth.

"Yes. I wonder sometimes how the pattern of my life would have differed if I had simply destroyed the letter before reading it. But I had no notion of the added pain and humiliation I would have by breaking the seal and revealing the twisted contents. I can remember it completely; it read like this."

Chetton closed his eyes and in a monotone recited the words that had been burned into his memory.

"*Chetton,*

"*You will understand to what lengths my distress has taken me that I cannot even bear to use the term 'dear' when writing this farewell to you. And it is a final farewell. I am leaving you and going to meet my true love, the man I should have been with in life, and now can only be with in death. I will take my son with me so he, too, can be with his real father, the three of us bound together for all eternity.*

"*Please try not to think too badly of me. I have suffered as you cannot imagine. And do not place the blame on yourself; you were always kind to me.*

"I am sorry you could not be the husband I wanted.
"Maddie Colton

"I could hardly force air into my lungs by the time I finished reading the letter. I could not make sense of the name she had used to sign it with. If she rejected my name in her distress then why had she not just used her maiden name of Perrault instead? It was not till much later when I caught sight of the tear stained piece of newspaper by her pillow that I began to understand. It was the obituary of a young man from London who had been travelling in India and had died there recently of malaria. The man's name was Samuel Colton."

Chetton could see the alarm spread across Isobel's face and the tender pity in her eyes. It wasn't sympathy he wanted, it was for her to understand his actions and how they had unwittingly led to his faith in the essential goodness of women being shaken.

"Maddie's note and the story of Colton's death helped to explain a great deal of her distance and bizarre actions during our marriage, but it didn't help with the guilt I felt for not having guessed more of the truth. I had armed myself with a view of the world that I thought would be to everyone's benefit. But I had missed so many vital clues along the way, Isobel, so many."

"But, surely you do not blame yourself?"

"All I can see now is my own colossal arrogance, which is hard enough to accept, but what is worse is that my blinkered optimism led to two deaths. That Maddie took her own life was somehow understandable, in her crazed sense of reality, but that she took Sammy with her . . ."

He could not continue and rose to pace the room.

"It is unimaginable."

Chetton could not quite finish what he wanted to say. Even at the end, in her letter, Maddie had not accepted him as Samuel's father, and that thought still bothered him. Perhaps it was her vicious way of repaying him for her own sorrow, but it was devastating.

"What happened then?"

He struggled to regain his train of thought and answer Isobel's whispered question.

"As is the way with most privileged families, the whole matter was smoothed over. The deaths were explained as having been caused by a sudden bout of a deadly influenza that was running rampant that year."

He could not keep the bitterness out of his voice.

"You know, all the pity and condolences I received as the young bereaved father and husband only darkened my despair and culpability. The shame and regret were my burden; there was no penance I could conceive of to lessen their weight."

"Did you not tell anyone about the letter?"

"No, I only showed the letter to Chris, but that was much later and under great duress. My family worried about me for a long time. About two years after the deaths Chris finally brought everything to a head."

Chetton smiled in spite of himself.

"What do you mean?"

"My clever brother filled me with brandy and then provoked me into a fight. It was only when he mashed my face into the wall that I understood how much my health had suffered. Chris had never been able to best me."

He saw Isobel roll her eyes at the masculine bravado, but he had to wait a moment before he continued. Action always helped to center him and he took his time closing the balcony doors and arranging the heavy drapery over them.

"After I showed him the note, he held me sobbing like a babe in his arms. I did not realize how much I needed his understanding until that moment. We have never mentioned that night again."

CHAPTER THIRTY-NINE

When Chetton turned back into the room, Isobel was regarding him. She set her champagne glass on the table. "Now I understand why he is so protective of you."

"He is, much too protective, really. We had always been close, but after the tragedy, well, even more so."

"It must have forged a deeper bond between you."

"I worry sometimes that it has clouded Chris's view of women, as much as it has mine."

"I am not certain I understand your meaning?"

Chetton gestured helplessly.

He saw the look of apprehension on Isobel's face. He had revealed to her all of the sordid details of his past and perhaps she could not accept them. Or him. Why the hell had he ever spoken about his traitorous wife? There was only one reason. He wanted, he needed, truth between them. He had not had it with Maddie. And he would not consider a life with Isobel without it.

"Do not be alarmed, there are no more catastrophes, as such. This is more about my life since then, and the disservice I have done, not only to you."

Isobel shook her head. "I have been guilty of the same when trying to deal with my own history. I have a noted tendency to accept unhappy memories as if they were an unholy penance, one that I deserve to suffer. I do not now believe that should be true for either of us."

"Well, I am very glad to hear that, Isobel. Beyond your caring nature and your concern about how my responsibilities affected me, you appreciated the sadness and loss. Whatever happens between us, your sensitivity to my pain has been a balm to me that I will never forget. And no woman I have been with has ever cared enough to bother to inquire about my thoughts." Chetton shook his head.

A rosy blush spread slowly across Isobel's cheeks and her hand played with the concealed arrow broach at her neck. "But you spoke of disservice?"

"Yes, at least that, if not outright harm. I can see you do not understand, but let me ask you this, Isobel, why do you think it was that I suggested we pretend to be married when I first found you in France?"

Isobel shrugged her shoulders. "Well, I assumed it was to protect me from Captain Pictou, and to make it more difficult for my uncle's men to track and follow me. That is what you said."

"Yes, that is what I said. And you believed me. But it was not the truth. Or at least not the whole truth."

Christ! This was more difficult than he had imagined it would be, harder in a way than it had just been to tell her of his past, because this related directly to his trust in her. And that had been sadly lacking.

"You know about my disastrous marriage, not only the sad end of it but the deceit which with it began. It changed me in ways that are hard to describe."

"Well, naturally it would."

He shoved a hand through his hair. "Yes, but my darker moments have led me to make some very foul choices in my life. What I am referring to is that they broke my faith in the essential goodness of women. I do not quite know how else to put it. I began to distrust all women, not my mother, naturally, but all women I was interested in. I wanted to possess them, take pleasure in them, but not invest any of myself in them."

Isobel looked away from him. She must recognize the loathsome unprincipled thing he had become and yet he had to carry on. "I looked for women, and many were attractive young widows, like the image you presented when I first met you."

Isobel dropped her gaze to the clenched hands in her lap and said, "You do not need to tell me about the other women in your life. I certainly do not want to hear about them."

He had better try and make a quick end to this. "No, you misunderstand. Isobel, look at me please. This is not a confession of past liaisons. If that were the case, then I would never intrude upon your delicacy to mention them unless you asked in particular, and then I know I could rely on your generous nature to forgive and forget the actions of a lonely man. No, this is about you understanding that I came to believe that most women were false, even deceptive by nature, and could not be trusted. And it was often reinforced by the very women I chose as partners." He took a deep breath and blew it out slowly. "That is why I was suspicious of you."

"Suspicious. You were suspicious of me? Whatever for?"

"There seemed to be many little reasons, most of which were absurd and some of which are beneath me to now bring up."

Isobel nodded her head. "But of course you were suspicious. You had every right to be. And you were correct. I was lying to you, in fact, to everyone. I am sorry. It is so easy to forget one's own culpability in matters. Did you realize that I was running from something?"

"Not at first. It went much deeper than that. And it goes back to the question I asked you earlier. Why did I suggest a sham marriage?"

The pink stain deepened across Isobel's cheeks and she closed her eyes. "Surely it was not just to, oh, how very awkward this is!"

Lord Chetton almost smiled at the irony of their ridiculous situation, but too much was at stake.

"No, my dear I assure you. I am not yet quite such a blackguard; I have not cut the bonds to all sense of honour. As tempting as you were and are to me, no, it was not to take such advantage of you. I was led to believe through a set of circumstances which are no longer important that you might be an emissary sent out to disrupt my diplomatic mission."

"Me? Do you mean you thought me to be a spy?"

"Yes. I know it sounds ludicrous now but I had been warned that a woman, an agent provocateur of sorts, was set on discrediting my name and political objectives." Chetton held his hands out in supplication. "And I began to believe that that person was you."

☙

While Isobel was surprised at Chetton's candour, she struggled to make sense out of what had just transpired. It had been a very odd exchange of confidences. She was reeling from the enormity of his strange charge. It was only the look of absolute seriousness on his face that prevented her from lapsing into giggles at the absurdity of it all.

"And you thought this femme fatale was me? Really, how infamous of you, Chetton!"

"I thought it might be you. And there were so many coincidences, which only added to the theory. You had recently come to Guernsey, you were reticent to say from where, or who you were connected to. You were in close proximity to La Rocquette and ended up staying there for a time."

She nodded her head in agreement. It was possible to see merit in some of his suspicions.

"I have a few burning questions, if you would not mind answering them, Isobel. But I want you to understand that you are under no obligation to even listen to them. I trust you completely. It would just satisfy my curiosity if I understood things better."

She smiled at him, a little nervous, but ready to answer what she could. Now that she comprehended his amatory history with other women, and how he had taken pains that their relationship be so different she felt very special and valued by him. The feathery lightness of her heart lifted her entire spirit and made her feel secure and brave.

"Go ahead. You can ask me anything you want."

"Thank you, you are good."

Chetton leaned over and took both of her hands in his large ones. She delighted in the warmth and strength of them. He cocked his head slightly in question, but was still very intent.

"Isobel, what in the world were you doing in my study at La Rocquette very early one morning when you were looking after Teddy?"

Oh, dear, she had no idea what he was talking about.

Chetton noticed her hesitation. "Apparently you took something from there, wrapped in a shawl?"

Then it occurred to her what he was describing. The ridiculousness of the situation, the tension of their previous conversation, the expansive nature of releasing her deeply held emotion, and the champagne she had drunk all combined to catapult Isobel into a fit of hilarity. She burst out laughing right in front of Chetton's confused face.

She wrenched her hand out of his and tried to cover her mouth in an attempt to regain some degree of control, but the insidious, relief-induced mirth would not leave her. Added to this now was the look of startled surprise on Chetton's face.

"I am obviously missing something here. Would you care to let me in on the joke?"

But his dry tone, the very pitch of his voice sent her into another round of giggles. She grabbed her sides and attempted to catch her breath.

"If you only knew. It is so silly," she said, wiping her eyes.

Chetton cleared his throat and was trying to be patient. She knew it was hard for him to be so in such a situation.

"Really, I am not laughing at you."

"How very reassuring."

She settled herself down. "The reason I was in your study that morning is that I was keeping a promise. I did take something with me. But it was not yours and it was not mine."

She rose, stepped towards him, and put her hand gently on his arm.

"Dr. Hoskins had to clean Teddy's wound that morning and it had hurt him, poor boy. I promised him I would do something to cheer him up for being so brave. Teddy asked me to get him a sack of sweets that he had hidden in a cabinet in your study. He knew he should not have put them there and worried about someone finding them. He swore me to secrecy. I agreed because he was so solemn and sweet about it and I thought he deserved a treat. You had already offered me the use of any of your books, so I did not feel I had to ask permission to go into your study. I never dreamed anyone saw me."

Chetton just stared at her. He didn't speak at all, and then the beginning of a smile lifted the corner of his mouth. "My God! Of all the damned . . . of all the ridiculous . . . that is what you took? Teddy's bag of horehound?"

"Yes, it was horehound. How ever did you know?"

Chetton barked out a short laugh. "Because I gave it to the little beggar! Christ! If you knew what I thought it was you took from there, you would not believe me."

"What did you think I took? Go on, tell me."

"First, like Teddy, I will have to swear you to secrecy on this." Chetton smiled down at her and planted a quick kiss on her forehead. "I had been given a French seal of authority. It doesn't matter now by whom or for what purpose. The fact is that it had gone missing with a few papers, and you had been seen and, well, two and two made five in this case."

Her smile faded and was replaced with a look of concern. "A French seal? To imprint documents? Like the Great Seal of England?"

Chetton looked at her oddly. "Well, yes the very same kind."

"Oh, dear! And it is still missing?"

"I assume it is. Look here, Isobel, what could you possibly know of such a thing?"

She put a hand on her forehead and shook her head. "I think I have a good idea where it might be."

"What do you say?"

"If I tell you, you must promise not to punish the culprit."

Chetton's brown eyes darkened. "*If* you tell me?"

She was ready to concede this small point in the hope that she could use it to bargain in favour of the about-to-be-accused.

"Fine then, sir. *When* I tell you. Please remember to be merciful."

Chetton's face looked grim and she was under no illusion that he would compromise a diplomatic concern in any way. She could see he was trying to speak calmly.

"This affects a matter of state, not to mention my reputation. Do not try to plead for leniency with me! Now, tell me, who is guilty?"

"I am."

"WHAT?"

"I am sorry, but I am at least partially to blame."

Chetton closed his eyes as if in deep pain. Without opening them, he said, "Explain yourself, please."

She knew she was trying his patience sorely but she could not control a little giggle, part nerves and part amusement.

His eyes shot open and he said, rather loudly, Isobel thought, "You think this is amusing?" He gave her a little shake. "Do you also like to bait bears?"

She had to put him out of his misery. She crooked her finger at him, wanting him to lean down closer to her. He tightened his jaw but did as she indicated so she could whisper in his ear.

"I am afraid to say that I think our little sweet tooth filched it."

Chetton's head jerked up. "What, Teddy?"

Isobel pulled him down so she could continue, thinking it best that what she was about to reveal be told in a soft low voice.

"I have seen the seal you described in the nursery playroom. It was partially hidden and I didn't get a close look at it. I must say it is rather small and does not look to be very official. Anyway, when I asked Teddy about it, he said he had borrowed it from you, with some papers. I assumed it was out dated or broken and just something for the child to play with so I gave it no more thought."

Chetton wrapped his arms around her and pulled her against his body in a tight embrace. She revelled in his muscled power and the heady male scent of him. He whispered something quietly in her hair.

"Pardon?"

"I said, hell's bells. It seems you two conspirators are working together again!" He backed her up against the wall so she couldn't escape him. "And this time you will take your punishment immediately," he said as he feathered kisses across her cheek. "My God, woman, I have been waiting a long time for this moment, this moment right now."

He moved his mouth over hers fully and built the pressure until Isobel's lips parted. His tongue swept the inside of her mouth and she rocked in his arms, the movement totally enchanting.

A few minutes later they pulled apart, both breathless.

"Have I answered all of your inquiries, my lord?"

"I am not sure I am brave enough to attempt another one."

"Go on then, I will be brave enough for both of us."

"Then answer me this, if you will. Who gave you the note in the teashop and what was it about?"

She hit him lightly on his chest. "You knew about that?"

He growled at her and winked at the same time.

"Yes, well, Chetton, it was something that I neglected to tell you about, that is true. And it was rather important at the time, so you are probably not going to be very happy with me."

"Then, my lady, you will just have to take more punishment, won't you," he said as he moved to reclaim her mouth.

"Idiot man, do be serious."

"Impossible when I have you at my mercy like this." He began to plant kisses along on her neck.

"No, I must tell you. I want you to understand everything. Will you stop trying to kiss me and listen?"

"No to the first and yes to the second."

She laughed as she leaned away and sandwiched his face between her palms.

"You need to pay attention to me."

"But that is my wish too, love. I want to pay a very great amount of attention to you." He gently secured her hands between them and leaned in towards her. His weight, full and heavy and delicious, pushed against her. It was full of resolve. Isobel surrendered to his kisses, even as they became more demanding. They mirrored her own desire.

Sometime later they pulled apart.

"Now, what were you going to tell me about the note and the man who gave it to you? Start with the man."

"I didn't know him."

"Good. But then why did you accept the note?"

"If you saw what happened you know I did not really accept

it, it was dropped on my table. It was a threat against you; that is why I tried to leave the hotel, do you recall? Now I know the whole charade must have been arranged by my Uncle Alex."

"I see. But you opened it. I just want to make sure that my future wife is not going to be in the habit of paying attention to the notes every appreciative man may throw her way."

He gave her another long slow kiss.

Isobel rested her head against Chetton's broad chest and sighed, "Am I really going to be your wife?"

He straightened up and looked serious for a moment.

"Only you have the answer to that question, Isobel. But since you are not running away from me again, I rather think the answer should be yes, don't you?"

Then the devil sparked in his dark eyes and he continued his assault on her lips, ratcheting up the passion further.

When they finally halted for a moment of breath, Isobel looked up into Chetton's smiling face. Her mind filled with myriad images of him from the first moment they had met. There was no more pretence; she could no longer delude herself into believing her passion was transient or unworthy. She wanted him on an elemental level that was wonderfully staggering. It was liberating to finally give reign to her true feelings. For once she would take an offensive position.

She leaned into Chetton, grasped his neck, and pulled him down for a long deep kiss. She had a moment of great satisfaction to note that she had truly shocked him before he responded and lifted her off her feet to continue the kiss. There was nothing but the feel and smell and heat of him. All that she wanted.

When he finally set her down several intense minutes later, he did not speak.

"You do truly love me, don't you?"

He groaned aloud in frustration. "You are a little slow, my love, to have just figured that out now, but yes, I. Do. Love. You. Isobel." He punctuated the words with little kisses on her forehead and then drew her again into the circle of his arms and the heat of his mouth.

Then he stopped and he set her aside. "But, what about you?"

"I think I have always loved you." There was a pause that transcended time. She took his hand between hers and set it above her heart. "The thing is, now I want you too, and I do not believe I will ever let you go, my dear Guernsey Diplomat," she finished with great simplicity.

It was all that mattered.

CHAPTER FORTY

The time passed quickly through the height of summer. Chetton's control over the French officials held some sway but by now no one seriously believed they could alter the future of King Charles's path. His desire to give power back to the Catholic clergy and the looming French conflict with Algeria were the new concerns. Still, London was pleased with his endeavours and was not so gently hinting that Lord Chetton should take a higher profile with wider diplomatic concerns. He had not given a definitive answer for the moment, pleased as he was with the turn of his life and the future he wanted to enjoy with Isobel.

※

The sun shone brightly as Norris had predicted it would. The last days of summer were gone, but a pleasant warmth remained in the early days of autumn.

Emma had come to L'Ancresse almost immediately after Isobel and Chetton's return to Guernsey. The dear friends delighted in their reunion and spent many hours exchanging confidences. Isobel gave herself over entirely to Emma and Lady Chetton's organization and ministrations about the wedding planning. Emma herself dressed and arranged Isobel's hair on the wedding day. Lady Chetton's last duty was to add the bride's only piece of jewellery and pin the tiny diamond arrow brooch over Isobel's heart.

A few hours later Teddy performed the role of ring bearer with unusual solemnity. Jean had conducted Isobel down the aisle and, as surrogate family, had given her, blushing and beautiful, to his friend of many years. Jean had spared no expense in procuring immaculate attire for the important event. He had even deigned to ask the advice of Chris about the most fashionable way of tying his new cravat to best suit the occasion. It bespoke his deep sense of happiness for Chetton and of his acceptance and appreciation of Isobel.

His official wedding gift to the couple was a superb pair of matched greys from a stable of Arabian bloodlines. To Isobel he had quietly given a delicate figure carved from pink coral.

"See here where the lady sits," said Jean as he unclasped the outer walls of the cylindrical statue and gently drew back the curved doors. "She is lovely, *non*? Just like you, *ma petite*. *Oui*. A tiny Madonna for you." He kissed Isobel on the cheek. "You and the lady, gentle spirits, but great strength. Be happy, *chérie*. You have made my friend so."

After the ceremony, Chris sat beside his mother and took her hand. "Are you content, Mother?"

"Yes, for Chetton, I am very pleased. And for Isobel too, she is a fine match for your brother and I think they will do well together."

"That is not really what I meant."

"I know, son," she said and covered his hand with hers. "I must be getting old and sentimental, I cannot help but feel the spirit of your father here today. It rather saddens me, but is a comfort too."

"Well, that is to be expected, I suppose. After all, your eldest son married the woman he truly loves today. You cannot improve upon that for sentimental."

She regarded him keenly. "And what of my younger son, then? How long will you make me wait to see you happy, Chris?"

He was no longer looking at his mother. "Oh, I am quite all

right, do not worry on my account," he answered absently. "Mother, who is that lovely creature in blue with the extraordinary hair?"

The guests had enjoyed the wedding breakfast and were now being entertained with music and song. For the present, the newlywed couple was nowhere to be seen.

※

Chetton guided his wife carefully by one hand and kept the other firmly placed over her eyes. "We are almost there," he whispered in her ear. The new Duchess of Chetton gave his hand a squeeze and suppressed an undignified giggle.

"Now, meet Le Gran'mere du Chimquiere,' he said as he removed his hand.

"Really Chetton! You have *not* brought me to a cemetery on our wedding day!" Isobel looked around her in disbelief.

"Now do not be getting angry, wife, it is only a churchyard," said Chetton laughing. He pointed her in the direction of the old church in St. Martins' parish. "Look at the gate, my dear love, beside the entrance, and see where Gran'mere sits."

Isobel took in the sight of an ancient stone carving. Though its edges were softened by time it was clearly the form of a female. They walked slowly over to the prehistoric statue.

"She is a very old gran'mere, possibly from around 2000 BC." Chetton placed a coin in Isobel's hand. "Put it there, on her head. Good."

The golden coin reflected sunlight towards them. Chetton turned Isobel to face him.

"I wanted you to see Gran'mere today, my darling, because she is thought to bring good luck to newlyweds." He gave her a long and ardent kiss. "And also fertility," he added with a wicked gleam in his eyes.

"Pagan," she whispered before returning his kiss.

ACKNOWLEDGEMENTS

This story would never have come into being without the positive attitude and practical support of my husband, Allan, and an endless can-do belief in me from our son, Josh. My sister Bev's patience and sense of humour, along with the encouragement of my lifelong friend Barb, the gentle editing wisdom of Barb Howard, and the calm advice of poet/writer/friend, Anne Sorbie, all sustained me over time. I thank each of them for the gifts of their unique and generous natures.

    I would also like to acknowledge the friends that I made while living in Guernsey. Though we may be scattered around the world, certain memories and faces never leave me.

ABOUT THE AUTHOR

Sandy L. C. Bezanson is a lifelong fan of historical romances. She has lived in several places in Europe where her "old soul" thrived on art, architecture, and antiques. When not writing, she loves to have a camera, paintbrush or cooking utensil in her hand. Long walks and talks with friends are best finished with a cup of tea . . . or a glass of wine. She always treasures visits from her busy son. Sandy lives with her husband, and loves their view of the foothills of the Rocky Mountains.

Printed in the USA
CPSIA information can be obtained
at www.ICGtesting.com
LVHW040223020724
784445LV00028B/130